Myrlyn's Gate

Dan Ehl

Credits

Cover Artist: Designs by Ms G
Editor: Christine Young

Printed in the United States of America

Dedication

To my grandchildren: Amira, Shay and Stephen

Chapter One

There was only suffering and darkness. Garin sluggishly rose from the soundless depths of a torpid, black sea. The closer he came to the surface, the more intense the agony stabbed through his eyes and deep into his skull. He struggled in vain against the current, but the tolling of a faraway bell called him, impelling his ascension.

Garin opened his eyes. He couldn't think. There was nothing--no memory, no emotions--just the overwhelming pain--and the bell.

~ * ~

Drestin placed his hand on the chest of the piebald and felt for a grating feeling that might signify pleurisy or pericarditis. He stepped back to look up into a pair of watery, bloodshot eyes.

"It has shortness of breath and an overall rundown appearance. I'm guessing lung flukes," Drestin told the cluster of older men following him through the hangar and down the long row of stalls. "The farmer who owns him should run ducks across the field to get rid of the snails that are carriers of immature flukes.

"I'd want him under observation for several days to make sure it is not tumors of the lungs, but I would start him immediately on a mild tea of ragwort and sulfa. If it is not lung flukes, the tea will not hurt him, though it would kill most mammals."

Drestin knew he was sweating profusely and hoped the examiners weren't noticing the expanding dark spots around the armpits of his cotton jerkin.

One surly-looking old man hobbled slowly to the front of the black and white dragon then turned to the young apprentice. "How do yah know it is not tuberculosis?"

Drestin smiled. "That also would become evident over the course of a few days observation, but that I doubt. The drake is not exhibiting a fever, coughing blood, nor oozing a vitreous humor from the nostrils. Farmers about here are also familiar with tuberculosis. They know it is incurable and that the dragon would have to be destroyed. If the farmer suspected it was tuberculosis, I am sure he would have fed it foxglove, a wild plant that would mask the symptoms long enough to sell it to some trader who would not discover the problem until he had traveled a couple days hence."

"That is illegal," the questioner snorted.

"Yes, it is, and very shameful behavior," admitted Drestin, who couldn't help but wonder if the rotund, obnoxious little man wasn't suffering from some form of dwarfism. If he had a dragon with a similar large wart growing above the eye as the guildmeister wore, he'd treat it with a red-hot poker. He decided now was not the time to volunteer such an opinion. "But most farmers around here can hardly afford the financial loss of dead dragon."

A sour look crossed the face of the guildmeister. It took all of Drestin's will power to firmly clamp his jaw shut and not reply with one of several impudent thoughts crossing his mind. His childhood had been marked with a number of beatings at the hands of large bullies not amused by his idea of wit. A score of cuffs to the head from his master almost taught him the wisdom of leaving certain thoughts unspoken.

The guildmeisters walked a dozen paces away to circle and begin their final review. Drestin looked nervously about the large dragon hangar and spotted his own master, Keldlief, silhouetted in the main doorway.

Was the dun dragon suffering from a vitamin B deficiency as he diagnosed? There was fish on its breath and some fish contain enzymes capable of breaking down the vitamin. Drestin knew the partial paralysis could also be caused by encephalitis, but for some reason he felt that was not the case. The apprentice had come to trust his hunches, no matter how such reasoning enraged Keldlief.

Drestin sighed. Right or wrong, he knew, it was all over now. The guild dragonmasters were currently reviewing his declaration of "crazy chick disease" for the spasming draglet, as well as reviewing his other diagnoses of descaling scabies, black dung fever, tongue worms, foot rot and a fractured femur.

The dragon Drestin said was suffering from lung flukes lowered its head and sniffed at the young man. He reached out and gently rapped the weary animal behind the single horn growing from its forehead. It was an older drake, Drestin guessing its age at sixty or seventy years by the wear of its teeth. Farm dragons had their wings clipped as soon as they hatched, and two ragged scars could still be faintly seen on its back. It measured nearly twelve feet from nose to tail.

Drestin might complain to his friends about having to work with such pedestrian animals, but he secretly loved the plodding beasts, even if they weren't the sleek dragons he'd see flying over his village.

The judges were returning. Drestin could detect no clues in their walk or facial expressions as to their decision. He tried to maintain an outwardly calm composure.

"Apprentice Drestin, you appear to know your dragon maladies," spoke the tallest of the five men. He was gaunt and gray and resembled an old dragon. "As to a few of your unique remedies, only time will tell. One of us will return three days hence to see if this drake be cured with your ragwort tea. At that time a final decision will be reached."

The apprentice bowed to his superiors and maintained a taunt smile as they trooped out the door past Keldlief. The anti-climatic finish left Drestin feeling numb. It was highly unusual not to be told the outcome at the end of the two-day grilling every dragon apprentice must pass to become a member of the guild and practice his or her trade. What did it mean? Was he going to flunk and become a lowly stable hand?

"Well?" Keldlief's growl jerked him back to his surroundings.

"Ah, one of them is to return to see if my prognosis for this dragon is correct."

Keldlief turned and eyed the sickly creature. "It is tuberculosis, ain't it?"

"I think it is lung flukes. I recommended ragwort tea and sulfur."

"Lung flukes? Ragwort?" his master snapped irritably. "What the hell ever gives you these ideas? You and your weeds. No wonder they did not pass you, making some idiotic remark like that. Did not I tell you to prescribe chilled elephant blood for at least one of the animals? That way they will know you are aware of modern practices beyond this stench-filled valley."

"The herbs work. I tried them after watching Old Sally collecting plants in the woods. Besides, where would we get chilled elephant blood?"

"That is not the point. They are going to wonder what kind of dragonmaster I am with such an imbecile for an apprentice. Get back to the stables and clean out those stalls. You might as well get accustomed to it since it looks like that is what you will be doing from now on. Hell, lung flukes..."

Drestin watched him march away in disgust. Keldlief appeared upset, but Drestin believed the old man was secretly pleased that his apprentice might not have the chance to climb the guild ladder higher than himself. Keldlief made no bones of his bitterness at still being in charge of a third-rate dragon dealership in a backwater farming village.

After ordering a stable hand to see that the dragon received the proper medication, Drestin plodded down the worn brick streets to his master's place of business. Faded red and blue pennants flapped listlessly in front of a crumbling stone barn and a small courtyard filled mostly with weeds.

Stretched across the gate was a banner reading, "Excellent Draft Dragons Just In From Hesthren--Clean, Treated Against Flare Grubs and Thread Worms--Bred for Dependability. We Accept Trade-Ins, No Reasonable Proposal Spurned. Ask About Our Leasing Program."

Pasted on the wall was a poster, "Coach Dragon, Only Used On Grog's Day To Take Widow To Temple. Would Make Good Family Dragon."

He paused to grab a scoop shovel at the doorway before ducking his head and entering the murky interior. The odor hit him immediately and watered his eyes. Drestin waited until he had adjusted to the dimness then began filling a large wheelbarrow.

Drestin grumbled as he lifted a shovel load of dragon droppings, though he would hesitate to call them droppings. The dragon apprentice sourly mused they were more like bombardments. They were the size of muskmelons until trampled into a mush by the large creatures. The smell was the meanest part of cleaning the stables. The odor lingered long after numerous scrubbings, having permeated his clothes and hair. Drestin could detect the odor on his leather belt or wool hat for days after the chore.

An apprentice in his or her sixth year of training was not usually commanded to clean a stable, but Keldlief appeared amused he could order his apprentice to complete the chore. The manure was then taken by "honey wagon" to some farmer's field as a rich source of nitrogen.

Drestin paused to give his aching back a respite and mused about how long it would take to get the stink off before he could go out on the town. It was to have been a double celebration--in observance of his eighteenth birthday and graduation. The evening was not becoming as festive as he had earlier planned.

"Need any help?" Standing in the doorway was a figure in a wool cowl, tight cotton trousers and suede boots--the all-gray uniform of an upper level magician's apprentice.

"Sure, roll up your sleeves and grab a shovel," Drestin laughed.

The other set an old pair of boots down, bent at the waist and grabbing the hood in both hands, began sliding out of his robe. Who appeared was a young man similar in age and build to Drestin. He was also wearing old and much-mended canvas work clothes. Both young men were lean and stood almost eighteen hands in height--tall, but not exceedingly so. But where Drestin was light in hair and complexion, his friend's aspect was that of dark brown eyes and waves of unruly hair that fell to his shoulders in black ringlets.

"Elfred, I was only joking," Drestin protested when his friend grabbed a scoop.

"You do not want to be here all night when we will have two young ladies waiting for us at the Boar's Breath Inn. Besides, I could use a little exercise."

"Now there will be two of us with dragon reek. We will probably get thrown out of the inn if the women do not disavow us first."

"Not to worry," Elfred grinned as he slung a shovel full of the dragon sludge into the wheelbarrow. "I purposely picked a destenching spell before I left Manfred's lair. We will be smelling prettier than a rose garden."

"I thought magic was not to be used for such mundane purposes? Will not your precious guild be upset?"

"I think it can be excused for one's coming of age. Besides, removing the odor of dragon dung is not a simple chore but a task that can challenge the greatest of mages."

Drestin's spirits were lifting with the arrival of his childhood friend. Though both had been selected for different professions at the orphanage, they remained close despite what most considered a great difference in station. Good dragonmasters were looked upon with respect, but they were still basically hired help, while magicians wielded great powers and often became very wealthy.

"How are your studies coming?" he asked, eager to hear of Elfred's latest adventures with his notoriously eccentric master.

"We will know when I go in front of the board next week, though I hear Jayleb is taking five to one odds against me."

"That little ass. He is just jealous he was apprenticed to a soap maker. Has Manfred been of any help?"

"Sure. He will answer any question I have or tell me where to find the solution. No one can deny that he has a magnificent library. But most of his time is spent drinking or delving into some supposed danger from the north. He mumbles about prophecies and quests--I think he believes he is to be part of it. I just wish he would not make me waste time walking through the woods with him when I should be studying."

"Does he still make you go swimming?"

"Yes. He says the mind cannot work without a healthy body and there is more to learn than what is in a bunch of musty old books. 'Do you want to wind up like those finicky, sallow old bags of bones at Iceholm?'" The apprentice perfectly mimicked his master's gravelly voice. "'Life is more than just holing up in some dreary tower studying the mumblings of pompous frauds who died centuries ago.'"

Drestin couldn't help but laugh at his friend's excellent parody of the old wizard.

"He says I have plenty of time to both study and play since most apprentices are kept busy doing half of the work for lazy magicians," Elfred added then grabbed the handles of the wheelbarrow and began pushing it to the door.

The several dragons Keldlief had on hand silently watched from their stalls as the magician's apprentice passed in front of them. Drestin shook his head at the sorry lot of beasts before noticing that stall number five was completely closed. It had been empty earlier in the day. He walked to the stall and found a large, brass padlock keeping the upper and bottom halves of the door locked.

"What is the matter?" Elfred asked when he returned to find his friend frowning in front of the stall.

"I am trying to figure out why Keldlief would lock the door. The stall was empty this morning. This has happened several times before, and he always tells me to mind my own business when I ask."

Drestin placed his ear to the door and could hear an animal shuffling impatiently behind the wood panel.

"There is a dragon in there, but why would Keldlief lock the door? It is pretty warm not to leave the top half open."

"Who knows what that rapscallion would do? Let us take a peek inside."

"I do not know if--" was all Drestin could say before the apprentice magician waved his hands and muttered a few foreign words.

The lock sprang open and dropped to the floor. Drestin drew in a deep breath and reached for the top handle. The door flew out, smacking the dragon apprentice in the head and sending him reeling. Drestin clamped a hand to his forehead and prepared to unleash a heated curse at the animal before the words were choked off by his surprise.

Looking out the door was the head of a young dragon, but not some work beast doomed to spend its life pulling wagons or dragging plows. It was a pure black male with a gold stripe running down its back--and the drake had wings!

Both young men stood silently in astonishment. The dragon's polished scales gleamed in the faint light and its wings brushed the sides of the narrow stall, even though they remained folded against the body. The amazement was natural considering that it was a high offense to possess a winged dragon. Only members of the Trinton militia, royal guards, or couriers were allowed to ride them.

"Holy dragon dung," Drestin finally gasped. "Keldlief has finally done it. Selling a dragon with tuberculosis is one thing, but having a flyer is something else."

"How did he do that?"

"Foxglove," Drestin answered absent-mindedly as he viewed the magnificent beast before him. "Where could it possibly have come from?"

"From Iceholm. I have heard rumors that some have been disappearing from the royal stables. It is probably on its way to be sold to some tribe of hill rebels. They would pay a pretty silver to own one of these."

Voices outside spurred the two into action. Drestin slammed the door and Elfred retrieved the padlock. Both grabbed shovels and were busily scooping dragon droppings when Keldlief entered the building with two tall blond men in their late thirties to early forties. They bore the weathered look of the King's Wardsmen who patrolled the wild boundary realms of mountains and forests. But having heard strange accents when the three were still outside, Drestin knew they were not in the King's employment.

"You can go now," the dragonmaster barked.

Drestin normally would have been eager to escape the dragon lot, but the mysterious strangers and dragon ensnared his curiosity.

"What is the matter, are you deaf?" Keldlief snapped.

Elfred grabbed his friend by the tunic and began tugging. The dragonmaster grumpily watched as the two made their way out the door.

Drestin shook himself from Elfred's grasp. "What is going on?"

"We are better off not knowing," cautioned the apprentice magician. "Forget you ever saw that dragon or it might be you swinging next to Keldlief when the constables come looking for dragon thieves. Let us go clean up and celebrate your birthday with two charming maidens."

They walked to Mage Manfred's dwelling on the banks of a small creek bordering an edge of the village. It was a modest dwelling for a magician, though the three-story stone structure was one of the largest private homes in the village of Ramshire. Elfred had a small room on the bottom floor with its own entrance. True to his promise, the mage-to-be cast a spell and the vile odor of dragon dung disappeared in the whoosh of a magical gust of wind. They donned the only good change of garments they owned and headed across the cobbled streets to the Boar's Breath Inn.

Chapter Two

The bell would not stop sounding.

Garin was afraid to move. The slightest motion pounded spikes through his eyes. Fingertips lightly brushed across a forehead and came away wet with a dank sweat. Garin's arms shook as he pushed himself into a sitting position. He forced his eyes open but could only make out the dimmest light through an open doorway. From that direction also came the sound of the bell.

~ * ~

Vlad was mumbling heatedly as he climbed down the narrow stone steps leading to the dungeon.

"That crazy old bastard, I will have him on the rack," he cursed the Bulgavian royal torturer. He wouldn't, though. The young king had once ordered such a punishment and still felt a burning shame at the memory.

Not that the old man wouldn't deserve it. It was the second prisoner this year who Gregor had attempted to sneak off with. Vlad had been headed to the bath to meet his favorite serving maid when alerted by a groom that the old torturer was seen slinking away with an imprisoned poacher. Gregor was still chafing under the King's decree banning the torture of prisoners, errant servants, or just the occasional travelers who once were considered fair game by Vlad's infamous ancestors.

10

Vlad knew the first Dragol began the brutal tradition while defending his country against a flood of Bercassians. Chronicles from that time tell of thousands of captured invaders staked outside the castle walls, their piteous screams growing fainter each day as they slowly died of thirst and loss of blood.

He was also the first military leader to successfully train and use dragons in warfare, though initially only for reconnaissance. The ancient Bulgavian word for the magical winged beasts was Dragol and it became the title of the royal Bulgavian family.

Vladimir Dragol II continued Bulgavia's defense and the last wave of the Bercassian ocean beat itself in vain against the rocks of Castle Dragol. Then came the Mogyals. The Bercassians had been driven westward by clans of Mogyal horsemen from distant drought-stricken plains. While many neighboring kingdoms were trampled beneath the hooves of the small steppe ponies, Dragol halted their advance at his eastern border and the murderous Mogyal hordes poured around Bulgavia like water parting at the bow of a swift corsair.

Carrying on the tradition of his father, Dragol II astounded even the vicious Mogyals with his perverse cruelties. It is said a son of one the great khans arrived at Castle Dragol as an emissary. He was making a peace overture to divert a war that would most likely destroy Bulgavia but also seriously weaken this major Mogyal clan. Vladimir refused to allow Mogyals within the walls of his fortress and held the audience upon the bone-littered plains before the castle. When the young Mogyal refused to kneel before the king, Dragol had his soldiers force the proud prince to the ground and spikes were driven through the back of his knees and into the earth.

The outraged Mogyal khan rushed his forces across the border when news arrived of his son's plight. Dragol and his army were waiting among the steep crags and treacherous abysses that made up the heavily timbered and mountainous region. Above their heads flew the first Bulgavian dragon scouts who closely followed the invaders' route.

The steppe-dwelling Mogyals were unfamiliar with such rugged terrain. Their war tactics depended upon swift surprise attacks on open plains. They were easily slaughtered in the narrow valleys and twisting overpasses. From there Dragol led his men to attack the nearly defenseless Mogyal women and children camped at the foot of the mountains. The resulting carnage shocked even Dragol's war-hardened neighbors who certainly had no love for the invaders.

A celebration feast was held in Bulgavia with Mogyal prisoners as the entertainment. All the children perished, and the few surviving women were kept as slaves. Traces of their high cheekbones, dark eyes, and black hair could still be seen in some of the castle servants and peasants.

Vlad stopped briefly under the glaring countenance of a long-dead Dragol staring down upon him from an oil portrait. He couldn't remember which Vladimir he was observing. The Dragols in the numerous paintings scattered about the castle seemed interchangeable with their dark, good looks--a handsomeness ruined by the same cruel and demented eyes duplicated generation after generation.

The castle was also full of depictions of great-great-aunts and distant cousins. They bore the looks of frightened hares forced to live under a kennel of starved hounds. Vlad had no idea who many of them were and wished his family had thought to write their names on the back of the portraits.

He shuddered under what seemed like a sinister scrutiny by the painting. Vlad felt no affinity for this distant forefather nor any of the other malignant patriarchs perched in rows down gloomy halls like vultures above a dying stag. Vlad decided that tomorrow the paintings would all come down.

In vogue among neighboring kingdoms was the use of satiny fabrics instead of canvas for paintings. He decided he would have someone attend the next itinerant artists' fair and purchase a number of velvet nudes. Their display would show he was not only a royal patron of the arts, but trendy in a jaunty and contemporary way. Being an autocrat didn't mean one couldn't have good taste.

~ * ~

Peace did not return to Bulgavia with the passage of the Mogyals. King Dragol died following a late-night orgy, some say poisoned by his own son.

Vladimir Dragol III was only fifteen when he climbed to the throne. Raised in a dysfunctional royal family, he was abused by his father and spent his free time playing in the castle torture chambers. His playmates were captured Mogyal children or unwanted orphans who sooner or later found themselves tied, chained, or nailed down for the young Dragol's sadistic pleasures.

He never lost his tastes for such depraved entertainment, and eventually the Bulgavian king declared war on a neighboring principality. His excuse was to rid the country of Mogyals who had supplanted the original rulers, but his dungeon soon filled with prisoners of both races. Dragol was able to maintain this reign of terror with the aid of an inherited magical talent--he was able to detect the most subtle lie.

Vlad hesitated at the massive oak door leading down into the labyrinth of tunnels worming their way through the solid bedrock on which the castle was built. He didn't like descending into this section of the castle, all too aware of the grisly ordeals that had taken place beneath his feet.

A cold, dank flow of air rushed up from the darkness when he heaved open the door, it smelling of fungus and decay. Countless dehumidifying spells had proved no match for the sweaty, stone walls.

A whispering chorus of toads stopped when Vlad's torch sent a flickering light down the crude steps. He was reminded of a childhood poem of which he could only recall the last few lines.

Beneath the webs of glutted spiders,
the heap of flies grow steep and wider,
while nervous rats grow old and bitter,
from missing mates and devoured litters.
And small black toads with pale blue eyes,
keen in the dark with mournful cries,
and dream of meals that once had been,
the times they dined on human skin.

He shuddered, knowing cellar toads with their tiny pointed teeth were notorious scavengers, and it was all too likely the poem had some basis in reality.

Vlad paused to wonder if the souls of his evil ancestors might be inhabiting the cellar toads.

The Dragols maintained their tradition of conquest for three centuries until they ruled a country many times the area of the original Bulgavia. Some areas were virtually uninhabited because war was not always a viable option for the rulers' cruel sports. This left the wretched peasants as the only available fodder for beastly rituals practiced in the castle vaults. Even some of the queens joined the grim diversions. Dragol VI humored Queen Baetrene and slaughtered a horde of innocent servant girls because she believed bathing in milk and the blood of virgins would keep her young.

King Vladimir Dragol XI would have continued the gruesome customs if he had not been so sickly. He wasted his health at a very early age and died at twenty-three, but not before carrying on a murderous plunder of nearby lands and siring Vladimir Dragol XII. The queen was a princess from one of the conquered realms. The Dragols had nearly annihilated her entire line, and she held a steadfast hatred of the Bulgavian family. Queen Annaraine once considered killing herself while pregnant to prevent the birth of another Dragol, but with the premature death of the king, she vowed to break the line of monsters with her own son.

Vlad was shown all the love and kindness Annaraine could give. She isolated him from the royal advisers who were themselves monsters and protected her son from the other cruel realities of Castle Dragol life. At night she would stare intently into the sleeping child's face and search for traces of the Dragol ruthlessness. Vlad had the features of his father, but she believed they were devoid of the family sickness.

~ * ~

Vlad paused in his descent. Had he heard a faint, echoing scream? He held his breath and listened. All he could hear were the toads, which took up their whispering murmurs once he had passed and they were returned to darkness. Above his head, stuck to the wall with plunger-like toes, was one of the toads. It looked down upon him with unblinking, solemn blues eyes while flashing a grin of sharp little needles--much like the portraits of his ancestors.

The king had not donned footwear in his haste and the clammy steps were distracting. He stood on one leg like a crane and warmed the sole of a foot on the calf of his other leg. Damn that crazy Gregor, he fumed. Why did torturers always have to be so difficult?

And for the first time, Vlad stopped to think about what an odd toad rhyme that was for a young child to learn. He looked about the slime-covered granite walls and wondered if anyone else also thought they had had a strange childhood. He shook his head--probably not.

~ * ~

The mother queen was too successful in her mothering. Jealous staff and senior advisors saw their powers slipping through their fingers. They reached their prominent posts by pandering to the warped tastes of the previous kings and were not happy to see their future ruler lacking in these traits. Annaraine died when Vlad was 17 years old, poisoned by a royal counselor. He might have escaped undetected, but the murderer failed to realize the young king had inherited the family ability to detect lies, a gift that skipped appearances in his father and grandfather.

At first it seemed Vlad had slipped into the evil ways of his ancestors after discovering his mother's killer. A blinding rage swept through him, and he ordered the counselor tortured and nailed to a courtyard tree. Vlad spent that first day crying alone in his room and refusing to let anyone enter. He emerged when it was time for the sentence's completion.

The counselor was a broken man and had to be carried through the yard. Patches of hair were missing from his scalp and burns and bruises covered every portion of visible skin. An eye was gone and a leg dangled uselessly. The anger fled as fast as it had possessed Vlad. It was replaced by shame. Knowing his mother would have been horrified to witness this scene, he ordered the guards to take their prisoner to the infirmary for care until well enough for exile.

The next day Vlad entered the main hall of the castle and walked down the long line of the king's men-at-arms. On the massive stonewalls were hundreds of weapons, shields, banners and other war trophies from the numerous campaigns the Dragols had successfully waged. Though one year short of the legal age to become monarch, Vlad climbed the seven steps and seated himself on the intimidating throne that had seated eleven Vladimir Dragols before him. No one objected since Bulgavia's history was crowded with juvenile Dragols every bit as villainous as their elders.

They were mistaken if they believed Dragol XII would follow in the footsteps of his ancestors. Vlad called for the men and women administrating the castle and country. He grilled the leaders of the military and the officers of the castle guards. He interrogated those in charge of the courts, tax collections, and supply purchases. For the next two weeks his liege lords were called from near and far dukedoms and villages. No lie or half-truth escaped his notice. Vlad took note of loyalties, as well as appetites too similar to those of his own forefathers. Those appearing overly anxious for a palace coup were immediately discharged. Others, once realizing the legendary power of the Dragols was back, fled before they were made to face the king.

The next five years were spent finding suitable replacements--not an easy task in a country that had survived two centuries of such brutal treatment. It was a constant struggle, but Vlad believed he was finally seeing a change. The castle servants laughed while they worked. Peasants in the field no longer cowed when his retinue passed. Parents could again let their children sing and play in the parks without fear of them being snatched away to the castle.

Gregor the Torturer was an unhappy holdover. He'd never been replaced because there was no longer a need for the post. Since Gregor was old and slightly crazy, Vlad let the long-time servant remain in the lower chambers of the castle under orders not to ply his trade. The torturer was falling into senility and occasionally imagined he was back in the days when the castle was seldom quiet of moans and screams. Such was the case tonight.

Vlad finally reached the bottom of the stairs and found himself in the middle of a stone burrow. A string of stout doors with small, barred windows disappeared in both directions beyond the light of his torch. Gregor and his victim could be in any of the cells, though Vlad believed they were occupying a large cavern used exclusively for torture.

There! He heard a scream. Vlad began running, again cursing the old torturer and the rubble beneath his bare feet.

The distant light of his destination became visible after several turns of a snaking hallway, more a shaft through the bedrock than a corridor. Vlad was huffing when he reached the doorway and stopped to catch his breath. The light from the few torches was not strong enough to reach the darkest recesses of the large chamber. They did send loathsome shadows dancing across the wall where Gregor was busily pumping the bellows of a small forge. He was heating several rods of iron and their tips were beginning to glow cherry red. Hanging in the shadows and chained to a wall was the pale, unclothed figure of a woman.

Vlad stopped in mid-step as the prisoner became more visible. She was the most beautiful woman he'd ever seen. She appeared to be Vlad's age or just a few years younger. The image of her ivory body against the black, slime-encrusted wall was burned into his mind. She radiated a pale light like the moon. Her hair hung down in a veil of gold and only half succeeded in covering her full breasts. It was if Gregor had somehow captured the Goddess Aurora.

The torturer turned from his fire with a length of iron that glowed ruby red at the tip. He waved it in front of her beautiful face and Vlad could see she had deep blue eyes.

"You should not have kicked me like that, my little bird," Gregor groaned.

"It was my ill luck that you had nothing to injure between your legs," the young woman hissed, unbowed by the threat. The torture master jumped when Vlad's hand fell upon his shoulder to spin him around.

"Have not I warned you about this?" Vlad said in his firmest, deepest voice. "Leave and we will speak of this tomorrow."

Vlad wanted to say more to the old man, but the woman was too much in his thoughts. He waved Gregor away and turned back to the captive. She paled visibly when the torch lit his face and she saw the narrow face, long thin nose and piercing eyes of the Dragols. Just one glimpse of his countenance accomplished what a burning piece of metal couldn't do. Terror shone in her eyes.

He could have spoken soothing words or mouthed apologies. He didn't. Vlad knew they would be of little use. The few times travelers lingered at Castle Dragol had shown Vlad the deeply ingrained fear, hate, and distrust outsiders still harbored for his family.

The woman flinched as he reached above her head to unclasp the manacles. Her toes dangled several inches off the floor and Vlad's eyes were on the same level as the prisoner's. Though she bravely struggled to return his stare, Vlad thought she retained the frightened eyes of a trapped rabbit. Several seconds passed before Vlad realized he had paused in his manipulations of the shackles and that his heart was pounding rapidly.

He took a deep breath and placed one arm tightly around the woman's waist before releasing her wrists. Prisoners are unable to stand on their own after such treatment. Her hands fell like dead weights, and he swung his other arm under her knees. Vlad carried her into the corridor and began retracing his steps. No longer carrying a torch, it was difficult seeing by the lights of the infrequent torches set in the walls.

"I am sorry you have been so abused. I will find you comfortable quarters for tonight where you can rest and eat."

Vlad knew speaking was futile and he wasn't surprised when she answered. "Why? So I will be stronger for more abuses?"

He smiled and she paled even more.

"You do not cower at a hot poker and yet my smile daunts you?"

"It could only burn my flesh, a Dragol can eat my soul."

It was late and most of the servants were in bed. They reached his chambers unseen. He carried her across the large room and laid her on the bed. She immediately pulled a light cover about her. It was a chilly night and Vlad threw several more logs into the fireplace then began to ignite several lamps scattered about the room. He turned to view the woman in the brighter light and found her even more comely. He was also in for a second shock, and his gasp made his frightened guest clutch the cover even tighter.

"You are on a quest," he blurted.

The strange glow he had attributed to the dungeon torches still radiated from her face. Three years ago a knight stopped at Castle Dragol. Vlad had been pleased when the guest had shown no fear of his host, but the young king had been even more impressed by a soft glow that surrounded the traveler. Vlad spoke little of it since no one else could see the aura.

A year later an exceptionally brave, though not exceptionally talented, bard made a stop at the castle. He sang of the knight's exploits and how he had freed the Lady Duor from a clutch of mountain trolls and prevented a bloody war. The lengthy ballad even contained several lines mentioning the hero's stop at Castle Dragol. Vlad knew the brief stay in the infamous hold was included to show the knight's bravery, yet he was oddly pleased with just being involved in a ballad that did not portray the Dragols as terrible fiends. He also envied the knight and for several months daydreamed about being the central figure of a ballad instead of just a footnote.

And now he was gazing at a second person displaying this inner light.

"You are on a quest," he repeated, this time sounding more sure of himself.

"I am lost. I was traveling with my father, a grain merchant, and became separated from the caravan. I will see that my family rewards you if you let me go."

"You are lying," Vlad shouted in his excitement, and cursed his clumsiness when she drew away in fright. "But I understand. You are on a quest and fear the Dragols. It is only natural. I promise you, the Dragol family is no longer villainous. You are safe and I will do all that I can to aid your venture. Do you need a dragon, an armed escort, supplies...?"

"I need only my traveling garb and gear returned and to be on my way."

"I would be honored to personally see you safely across Bulgavia."

"I said I need only the personal property I arrived with and my freedom," she interrupted even more curtly.

Vlad tightly clenched his jaws and drew himself up stiffly. It was no use. The curse of almost a dozen generations of Dragols clung to him like a stench that could not be washed away. He forced himself not to react when his abrupt change in posture startled her.

Vlad said in the coldest voice he could muster, "As you wish. I will see that all your belongings are returned and you may leave in the morning. You may sleep here tonight, and I will find other quarters."

He was preparing to turn for a haughty exit when his door flew open and a breathless, buxom chamber maid flew into the room.

"Where have you been? I have been waiting in the bath pool for an hour. I think I have been bad today and need a spanking."

She stopped her prattle when she saw the strange woman. "Oh, excuse me, my lord. I did not know you had company."

"Ah, Remona. Would you see that the property taken from the woman arrested for poaching is returned to her by morning. And for now I would like you to see if there is something suitable for her to wear from my mother's room."

The servant curtsied and quickly backed out the door. The guest turned and eyed Vlad after a drawn out silence. "Spanking?"

"Ah, well, ah, you can't let the staff become completely undisciplined," he uncomfortably replied.

The silence continued and this time it was the young woman who closely examined her captor/host. Vlad found himself awkwardly shifting his stance and nervously ran a hand through his hair. The woman released a long sigh and seemed to dwindle in size, as if finally allowing herself to show her fatigue.

"If you grew fangs and flew across the room, I do not think that would have surprised me as much as seeing a Dragol blush."

Vlad wanted to make a witty reply but found himself totally lost for words. He felt another blush coming and he made a quick bow and turned as if to leave.

"Wait."

Her request surprised Vlad and he forced himself to turn back slowly.

"I am on a quest. It involves an ancient threat from the north," She seemed to force herself to speak. "I must find the son of the exiled Darmond of G'Hnad. This lord is rumored to have fled to Bulgavia twenty years ago with an infant son."

"Your quest is to find Darmond's son?" Vlad asked in a disappointed voice.

"No, but I need him to fulfill an ancient family prophecy to counter a great peril. I can say no more. Can you help me?"

Vlad was crushed. He thought he had been winning over the mysterious woman--maybe to the point where he could take part in the adventure. Instead, she wanted his distant cousin, Render, who Vlad had last seen, and detested, during his coronation.

"Yes, that will be all too easy."

The chambermaid created less of a scene on her second entrance. She was carrying an armful of dresses and her expression made no secret of her surprise at his request.

"Remona. See that a dragon courier is dispatched to retrieve Render, son of Darmond of G'Hnad. I would like him to appear before me by morning."

The maid was growing more puzzled over the odd turn of events, but she remained quiet before the beautiful stranger in the king's bed. He motioned that she could leave.

"Could you please tell me the part this subject of mine plays in your drama and what the prophecy refers to?"

"I do not think that would be wise. If you truly wish me well, then I ask that you let me speak to this Render and that you let us leave in peace."

Vlad winched at the use of "us."

"Could I know your name, my lady?"

The woman paused then answered "Velcene."

He smiled sadly and did not refute her lie. Watching his face, she remembered whom she was speaking with.

"I do not think I should."

"As you wish. I will see you tomorrow morning."

He was almost out the door when she again asked him to wait.

"It is Lady Rorianne."

Vlad's smile wasn't quite as sad when he shut the door behind him. He turned and walked down the corridor leading to his mother's room. It was also cool, but he left the fireplace unlit and laid fully dressed across the top of the covers. Vlad hadn't slept in the room since he was eight years old and fled to his mother's bed after a bad dream. He stared at the ceiling and remembered her singing him to sleep with a song about a cat that could leap to the moon from a juniper tree. He hummed a bit of the song before falling asleep.

Chapter Three

Vlad stopped in front of the door to his chambers with his hair still wet from the bath. He debated letting it dry before seeing Rorianne, but his impatience won out. The servants had been ordered to take water to her room since he knew many foreigners felt uncomfortable bathing with others. He stared at the carvings of vines and flowers flowing across the thick oak door. He smiled and touched a humming bird frozen in flight above a trumpet-like bloom. He once sat for hours in the garden watching the tiny birds flashing in the sun like jewels as they darted about in their search for nectar.

After shifting his scabbard to a jauntier angle and smoothing a wrinkle in his fresh tunic, Vlad took a deep breath and rapped on the door.

"Who is it?"

Vlad was in a quandary with that question. Queen Annaraine raised her son insulated from most of the royal court proceedings. Fearing the overbearing and vainglory nature of the Dragol blood, she strived to teach her son modesty. His selected playmates were second and third cousins and even children of the servants. Today they held trusted positions and still called him Vlad when they spoke in private, even the servants. This informality was unheard of in surrounding kingdoms.

So, while at official gatherings he might be "His Royal Highness, King Vladimir Dragol, Supreme Ruler of Sylvquin, Lord of the Western Mountains, Protector of Anjeiv, Master of the Red Plains and Emperor of the Bulgavian

Empire," he felt more comfortable as just plain Vlad. There was still a formality he had to observe when visiting with foreigners--all depending upon their rank and birth. That was why he was confused on how to answer his mysterious guest. Just who was Lady Rorianne? A princess, countess, a commoner, or even a thief?

"It is Vlad." He decided that a king could call himself or others whatever he wanted.

The door cracked and a blue eye appeared. "Yes, Your Highness?"

"May I come in?"

"No."

"No?"

"No." Vlad studied the lone blue eye in surprise.

"No?"

"No."

"But I am the king. You have to let me in."

"Would you force your way into a woman's room?"

"It is my chamber."

"But I am a guest and have its use."

The rapport he thought they were developing last night had obviously evaporated in the morning light. She was like the others, he surmised, unable to see a person through the thick veil of assumptions and reputation.

"As you will," he answered in his frostiest voice. This time no clumsy chambermaid arrived to break the ice. "Render should be arriving at the eyrie. I will send him to your room as soon as he arrives."

The blue eye stayed at the door and watched the brooding figure disappear around a corner.

The long walk to the eerie gave him time to stew over the maiden's behavior. Why would she need that worthless Render to fulfill a prophecy? That pimply-assed ne'r-do-well was as useless as teats on a boar. His father, Darmond, had been a distant cousin of Vlad's mother. Queen Annaraine offered Darmond sanctuary after he fled his native country over a dispute with his own king. Rumor was that it involved an undisclosed amount of funds missing from the royal treasury.

The way to the dragon hangars took him out a door exiting onto a long catwalk made of wood. The narrow bridge was constructed so that it could be easily collapsed during a siege. It connected the main structure in which the king lived to the massive stonewall circling the entire hilltop. Within the wall was a small city made up of stone structures housing government officials and soldiers.

Surrounding the fortress outside the walls was Ghasda, the capitol of Bulgavia. The city had grown with the castle. Five hundred years ago the hold was a crude circle of upright logs crowning the very top of the hill and surrounded by a squalid village of shacks and tents.

Ghasda became a bustling commercial center for the area by the time of the first Dragol. The following invasions by the Bercassians and Mogyal hordes forced the fortress to expand until by Dragol V's reign, it covered the area now occupied by Castle Dragol. With the spread of the Bulgavian Empire, the castle walls swelled thicker and higher and the number of buildings grew within and without.

War spoils fattened Ghasda, and the city grew in proportion to the amount of blood spilled in battle. The city now circled the base of the small mountain and flowed across a valley right up to the shore of a lake.

Vlad paused on the rampart and gazed across the hazy valley to the distant body of water. The streets ran outwards from the castle like the spokes of a wheel, with avenues connecting the streets. They flowed arrow-straight through the dips and hills. More than one visitor remarked quietly about the city's resemblance to a large spider web--with Castle Dragol at the center.

An area bordering the lake was currently under renovation and Vlad purposely ordered the streets to twist and wind with the shoreline. He also ordered saplings brought from the surrounding forests and planted along the streets and open areas. Several ancient prisons were torn down and replaced with parks. Residents were slowly adapting and many were putting flower boxes in their windows or painting the wood and stucco buildings something other than black or grey. Prosperous for several centuries, Ghasda was only now looking habitable.

Though there were still several bitter factions of deposed government and military officials, they had been unsuccessful in attempts to drag the upstart from the throne. The people adored their boy king from the first day when he emptied the prisons and instigated numerous reforms to improve their lives. The merchant class was also supportive of the king. Freer borders meant more trade among their neighbors and greater profits. It also helped that it was impossible to fool the king, despite his young age.

Assassination was feared most by the king's aides and that concern lessened each year. Still, his counselors never failed to voice their displeasure when he left the castle walls without an escort. Sometimes he did it just to hear them fuss--such as now.

He descended a spiraling stone stairwell running down the inside of the fortress walls to the main courtyard. A small gate used only by soldiers and couriers was located at the bottom. Vlad saluted several guards who snapped to attention as he passed. The passage was more like a burrow and its large ceiling stones could be dropped in case of attack.

Another narrow bridge led to a nearby hill circled by a smaller wall. At its flattened peak were several long, stone buildings and an open yard. This was where the dragons were sheltered. More guards kicked their heels and smacked their foreheads with the back of their right hands. Vlad's return salute was more of a wave.

A dragon was being unharnessed and watered by a flight crew. It was a beautiful blue drake that sat calmly as several men fussed about it. Nearby were the courier and his passenger. The civilian stood stiffly and unmoving with his arms crossed. Every line of his tense body said "dullard" and "dolt," thought Vlad, who had never liked his distant cousin and now had even more reason for the aversion.

Still, he was a guest. "Good morning, cousin. I hope you had a pleasant flight."

"No flight is pleasant," Render snapped back, almost crossing the line of civility expected when addressing the King.

The courier frowned disapprovingly at his recent passenger, saluted his king and excused himself.

"I am sorry if you were indisposed," Vlad said, purposely ignoring the rudeness. "I have a mysterious guest who said she must meet you. I believe her to be on a quest, and she seems to think you are destined to be part of it."

"Who is this woman? Why should she want me? I want nothing of some foolish quest."

"She calls herself Lady Rorianne. I have no knowledge of where she is from or what this quest involves--only that she said it concerns an ancient threat now appearing in the north. She is very tight lipped."

He looked to his cousin and was surprised to find Render turning pale.

"Are you all right? Do you feel ill?"

"It is nothing, just the flight. No, I mean it is the thought of such a quest. I find it not to my tastes."

Vlad pretended not to notice the slip and they continued their passage to the castle. The king puzzled over Render's answer as they entered the shaft through the wall. Render had not been telling the truth when blaming his pallidness on the trip. The distant cousin quickly realized that the statement could be easily detected as a lie and changed his story. Vlad was used to dealing with people who knew of his talent and tried to circumvent it with half-truths or evasion. Render hadn't paled until after the menace was mentioned.

"Are you aware of a prophecy dealing with an ancient evil to the North?"

"Ah, there are many prophecies. I discount most of them. If one was to worry about every prediction of doom, who could sleep at night?"

Render was speaking the truth, though he skirted the question.

"Does a certain revelation worry you?" he pressed.

"Many could be cause for concern."

"Such as one dealing with a threat in the North?"

"Sire. Your queries seem to say you believe I am hiding something. Is this an official inquiry? If so, I believe you have given the right of counsel to all Bulgavians. I would like one if this is the case."

"Do not be an ass," Vlad snapped as they crossed the catwalk to the castle. "I want to know why the mention of some prophecy made you ashen. Tell me what you know of it."

For a brief moment Vlad believed Render would go for his sword. The visitor's shoulders tensed and he faltered in mid-step as his right hand wavered over the hilt. The distant cousin remembered whom he would be drawing a blade against. Though mild mannered, Vlad bore a blade like his berserker ancestors when pushed into a corner. At age sixteen the king bested the finest swordsman in Bulgavia, no mean feat in a country still valuing courage and sword prowess above art or literature. Along with his looks and ability to detect falsehoods, Vlad inherited the uncanny swiftness and strength that terrified generations of Dragol enemies.

Render again displayed a quickness in thought. "Forgive me, Sire, if I sound elusive. I will know more of the matter after discussing it with this mysterious lady. Then I am sure I will be able to discuss it with some intelligence."

They continued their walk and Vlad's reflections were lured away by another observation. Render carried no glow. He did not have an inner light like Lady Rorianne. What could this mean? He reached his chambers still perplexed.

Lady Rorianne opened the door on the first knock and motioned Render to enter. She made to shut the door as Vlad followed.

"I would speak with Lord Render alone," she said with a commanding voice that told Vlad she was more than just a merchant's daughter.

"Then I would speak with you alone before you hold this audience."

"No."

Lady Rorianne again moved to shut the door. Vlad stuck his boot in the crack and looked directly into the young woman's eyes.

"I speak in all earnestness, Lady Rorianne," he whispered fiercely so that only she could hear. "Beware of this Render. I know him well and there is something wrong. You are in danger."

His sudden vehemence unnerved her and she fought to not show her fright. "I believe I have only you to fear, Vladimir Dragol."

The king pulled back and the door slammed in his face. Vlad felt the blood rise to his cheeks as a red anger gripped his body and sight. It was no figure of speech when it was said the Dragols could be blinded by rage. But for this Dragol, the fury didn't stay long nor was a great battle needed to fend it off. The passion slowly drained from the king, leaving behind a pale and shaking young man. It was this ability that separated Vladimir Dragol XII from his ancestors who never forgot a real or imagined slight.

Vlad looked up and down the corridor, hoping no one had observed the fleeting spell. The hallway was usually empty as this floor of the north wing was traditionally reserved for royal family members--which now meant one lone king. He stood bewildered as to what to do next.

He knew she was in danger. A foreboding filled the air so thick that he could hardly breath. A cold panic clutched at his heart. Hardly aware of what he was doing, Vlad unsheathed his sword and stood back from the door. He held the curved saber carried by the kings of Bulgavia since Dragol II took it from a dying Mogyal khan. Forged in the distant East, the magical sword had an edge that never dulled. The hilt was adorned with unrecognizable red and black gems. Down the length of the blade ran a twisting viper and unintelligible script yet to be deciphered by any scholar.

Vlad drew the blade back above his right shoulder like a woodsman preparing to hurl his axe into the heart of an oak. He waited--for what he didn't know--until he heard a muffled scream and the ring of sword blades. He slashed down and shattered the door into kindling, sending splinters flying. One shard grazed the king's face. He didn't notice the slight cut as he shouldered his way through the tattered remnants of the door and instinctively ducked a blade that whistled over his head.

Vlad continued his fall, rolled and came to his feet four-blade lengths away from his attacker. He spun and prepared to parry another blow, only to find himself facing a determined Lady Rorianne advancing behind a formidable blur of sword blade.

"Lady Rorianne, put down your sword. I am your friend."

"Would I have a viper for a companion?"

Vlad retreated several steps and almost tripped over Render's body. A familiar knife was lodged in the dead man's chest. The weapon had hung upon the wall beside the fireplace. Render's sword was now in the hands of the distressed woman.

"Everyone in this country is cursed. Lord Render tried to murder me before I could even explain my quest and the prophecy."

"I tried to warn you. Please, put down your blade. I do not want to hurt you."

"It does not matter. The prophecy can no longer be fulfilled," she cried bitterly. "Darmond's son was the last of the line of the Rohnelds. He was to have found the jewel. If I have failed in this, at least let me be remembered as having rid the world of the last Dragol."

Vlad took several more steps backwards, straightened from his defensive posture and placed the tip of his saber against the floor.

"I will not fight you, Lady Rorianne. I am not your enemy."

She paused, surprised and confused by his action. It took only a few seconds for her to regain her composure and she continued her advance.

"And not only will you be ridding the world of the last Dragol, but of the last of the Rohneld bloodline."

Rorianne again hesitated. "What kind of trickery is this?"

"Why do you think Darmond and his child were given sanctuary? They were distant cousins to my mother, but all the same, the only relatives she knew who still lived. Her grandmother was a Rohneld, just as was Darmond's mother."

"You lie."

"Do I? Inspect the blade that now protrudes from my cousin. It and a twin on the wall belonged to my mother. They were of the few remnants she managed to bring from her pillaged home. They belonged to her mother's family and their name is engraved on the blade. I am sure Render would find it very ironic."

"I do not believe you. It is a trick."

Vlad continued his retreat across the room. "It is no trick, examine the knife."

Keeping her eyes on Vlad, Rorianne knelt and took hold of the hilt. She withdrew the blade and wiped it on the dead man's tunic. She carefully took several steps back before looking at the red-smeared weapon. Almost invisible, seven very small letters spelled out "Rohneld."

The knife and sword dropped from her hands and the young maid would have joined them on the floor if Vlad had not sprinted to catch her. He carried Rorianne across the room and laid her carefully on the bed.

"Can I get you something to drink?" Vlad asked in concern as he looked down into her beleaguered face. "Would you like some wine or water?"

She returned his gaze and didn't answer. He pulled a cover over her as a number of castle guards came rushing through the door. He waved them away after telling the captain that all was secure and he would speak to him of it later.

"Lady Rorianne, I meant what I said--I would be your friend."

After a great length of silence, she answered, "This prophecy has damned me."

Rorianne shut her eyes. Vlad knew she was still aware of him, using the fainting as a way to avoid speech. It was then he noticed a blood smear near her hairline.

"Are you injured?" Vlad asked and brushed back her hair. There was no sign of a wound. Another drop appeared on her cheek before he realized that it was his own blood.

She grabbed his wrist as he tried to wipe the blood from her face and glared back at him like a trapped animal. The strength of her grip surprised him. He studied her anger and found that that it no longer could hurt him. Instead it raised an anger of his own.

"Why you should be chosen to fulfill a quest is beyond my understanding. I have offered you nothing but kindness, and yet you insist upon judging me by my ancestors. Do you believe all of yours were so pure? I would not begrudge you a certain amount of wariness, a bit of suspicion until you came to know me better, but this hatred and fear is blinding you. You are not worthy for even a minor task."

"You have no right to judge me," cried the woman. "My father did not murder your parents. My name is Princess Rorianne Cevonte of Thurbia."

Vlad released Rorianne's wrist and stood.

"I do not care. I am tired of visitors looking at me as if I were a monster. Maybe you think your name should mean something to me, but it does not. I am rather removed from court gossip since we are seldom visited by our royal neighbors.

"I expect you will tell me that my father is responsible for the death of your parents. I am sorry they are dead as I am sorry for anyone orphaned just as I was. But I did not kill your parents and I refuse blame. Believe me or not when I say that if my father or grandfather were alive today, I would gladly lift a sword against them.

"Listen closely, for I will make this offer only once. I see a glow upon you that I believe means you have been chosen to accomplish something great. I do not know of your prophecy, but you say it needs one of the Rohneld bloodline. As I am the last in a direct line of Dragols, I am also the last known descendent of the Rohnelds. Tell me of this quest, and I will give you what aid I can. If you will not, then leave when you desire."

The Lady Rorianne continued glaring at the Bulgavian king. He waited through a minute of silence before turning to the door.

"Wait."

He looked back. He could see a struggle going on within the woman.

"I will accept your help, but it calls for you to leave Bulgavia."

Vlad had known that such a quest would most likely demand travel outside his kingdom, but actually hearing it from Rorianne's lips stirred a chill in his soul. Leaving Bulgavia without an army meant that he would be traveling through lands where every man's hand would be turned against him. It was a death sentence if his identity became known. But if he were successful, it could also mean a partial erasing of past evils from the name of Dragol.

"So be it."

Rorianne was surprised by the king's acceptance, also mindful of his danger.

"I know that certain forces are aware of my journey, and I fear they are closing in on me. Somehow they reached Render ahead of me. We must leave immediately. The quest cannot start until others have joined us. We must find them next."

Vlad sat on the edge of his bed. "Now, please, tell me of this prophecy and what evil comes from the North."

Chapter Four

The damn bell. It prodded Garin to his feet, though a wave of dizziness and nausea nearly forced him back down. He stopped in the doorway and pressed his head against the cool wood. There were grubs, he decided, eating their way out of his brain like ghouls digging through graveyard soil. He wanted to sit on the floor, but the bell wouldn't let him.

~ * ~

Drestin liked the smoke-filled inn, though he seldom had the coins to order even a stein of weak ale. Inn keeper Keldlief was not noted for his magnanimity. It had taken the dragon apprentice several months to save up for this night. They picked a seat not far from the fireplace and ordered two ales while they waited for Freta and Annabeth to arrive.

The inn was not yet busy with the evening crowd. Several old men sat in a corner, smoking their long-stemmed clay pipes. Three traders noisily hacked at a pile of sheep ribs and wiped their greasy fingers on rags supplied by the kitchen. Another pair of strangers sat quietly by themselves and nursed large mugs. Drestin guessed them to be young caravan guards by the well made, yet plain cut of their clothes. The smaller one wore his hood up, though the inn was warm. His face remained shadowed. The other's black hair fell to his shoulder, much like Elfred's, and he had the well-muscled arms of someone who vigilantly practiced his sword skills. A curved sheath hung at his side.

"What if they do not show?" worried Drestin. "We will look pretty stupid waiting here all night."

"Relax. They will be here. Sip your ale and enjoy the evening. Tomorrow you will be a legal adult. Why would not they want to eat with two handsome fellows on their way to becoming respected men in their professions?"

"Maybe--or in several days I could find myself a stable hand forever scooping dragon turds."

"You worry too much. Here they are now."

The two had learned their manners well at the orphanage before being apprenticed at the age of twelve. Drestin and Elfred stood as the two sisters weaved among the empty tables. Freta was the older at seventeen. She was almost as tall as the apprentices and had a milky complexion that spoke of indoor labor. She worked for a seamstress.

Annabeth was sixteen and shorter, but just as slim. Her ruddier hue was from working for the inn where she took care of the garden and chickens. The portly man behind the oak bar grinned and winked, sending Annabeth's face a deeper rose color. Her good nature had made her a favorite of the innkeeper, a Pallin D'Cannor, who looked upon her as a daughter.

Drestin knew any misbehavior on his part with Annabeth would result in the wrath of the stout innkeeper, something no sane man wanted.

"Have you been waiting long?" asked Freta, flashing a warm smile at Elfred.

"It seemed like an eternity," he answered with exaggerated rakishness. "But time drags whenever you are not with me."

Both young maids laughed. Freta shook her head. "I did not think magicians were so polished. I thought of them as stodgy, tiresome old grumps. Will you become like that after you end your apprenticeship?"

"Not if Manfred can help it. He even ordered me to take Drestin out tonight and gave me a pocket full of coins."

"You must be bribed to spend an evening with my sister and me?" Freta asked as if slighted.

Elfred's answer was never heard. The main door slammed inwards as if by a battering ram. Seven black-garbed Lancene Rovers swaggered into the inn, and a chill seemed to descend upon the suddenly crowded room. Conversations ceased. The three traders looked nervously down at their plates of lamb.

A chair clattered to the floor as a Rover kicked it from his path. They arrogantly crossed the room and picked their seats not far from the apprentices' table.

"Where is service? Are we to be insulted by sluggards too lazy to wait on Rovers?" roared one the men.

They looked irritably about the room until spotting Pallin. The innkeeper was frowning fiercely from behind the bar. It was not easy for the man to hold his tongue, but none dared to anger Rovers, especially seven of them. They haled from a larger kingdom to the north. Most Trinton citizens feared that someday the warriors of Lancene would come boiling across the border to add the small country to its latest territorial spoils. As it was, bands of the Lancene soldiers crossed Trinton at will by right of a humiliating treaty.

And of all the Lancene warriors, none were more feared or hated than the Rovers. They were reputed to have been trained for war from infancy and carried dark spells of empowerment that guaranteed them berths in the deepest recesses of Hades when they finally fell in battle. Their cruel treatment of prisoners was legendary and only surpassed by the Dragol monarchs to the south.

"And is not this just darling," drawled a Rover with a particularly nasty scar running diagonally across his face. "The children are out for tea. How cute."

The man's lecherous looks at the two young women were devoid of any of the paternalistic feelings he expressed. Drestin's blood started to heat.

"Would you like to play a game with me?" one of the foreign soldiers leaned over and spoke in a low, oily voice to Annabeth.

The other Rovers were amused by their cohort's actions and grinned widely, showing broken and yellowed teeth. The rest of the patrons were nervously looking every way but toward the Rovers. Only one seemed not affected by the unfolding drama. One of the caravan guards remained comfortably slumped in his chair.

Annabeth's face turned a deep red as Drestin's paled. He tightly gripped his mug and forced himself to take a long slow sip.

"We are taking a room in this pig sty," the Rover continued. "I believe we will want entertainment for the night and you girlies would do just fine. That is unless your little friends object."

Drestin turned to the Rover. He felt a boot toe painfully kick him in the shins before he could open his mouth.

"By your leave, sirs," Elfred quickly spoke before his friend could recover. "We can only say that being members of your country's military, you would not want to do anything that would violate the agreements between Lancene and Trinton. This includes respecting the citizens and laws of each other's land. "

"Whoa, we have a little diplomat with us," the Rover roared with laughter, "but we always respect our neighbors--as long as they respect us. And it would be very disrespectful of these two girlies if they showed us not the hospitality of this village."

Drestin slid his legs to the side to avoid another kick. "We are a hospitable folk and we would like to provide you with suitable entertainment. But for one with such disfigurements and most probably suffering from a number of diseases, I'm afraid we could only offer you the company of an old she-dragon. Even then I fear the dragon would refuse since we are prone to geld animals as ugly as yourself."

The Lancene warrior cocked his head and inspected Drestin through narrowed eyes as a bird of prey would examine its next meal. The look sent a cold draft stirring in Drestin's soul, and he fought to keep from shivering.

The Rover did not take his eyes from the apprentice as he nonchalantly reached out and took a fist full of Annabeth's black hair. He pulled her effortlessly across the gap between the two tables and as a lover might nibble affectionately on the ear of his betrothed, placed his lips against the side of the young girl's face. Annabeth stared helplessly at Drestin as she was pulled to the Rover, then screamed as he pushed her away, a thin stream of blood running down her cheek.

Drestin's reaction was without thought. The pewter mug he still tightly clenched was slammed against the side of the Rover's face, snapping the man's head back and sending him crashing to the floor. The other six jumped to their feet and drew their swords with looks of pleasure sweeping across their battered features. They were obviously pleased with the young apprentice's foolhardy move.

"For that you will die very painfully," growled the Rover as he climbed back to his feet. He rubbed where the mug had caught him, a slight swelling already occurring.

"Stand back," ordered Elfred in a surprisingly masterful voice. "I am a powerful mage and you face an uglier death than the one you have planned for my friend if you do not leave at once."

Drestin pulled the two women out of the way and gratefully let Elfred face the warriors.

"A pup claiming to be a wizard," scoffed a Rover who appeared to be the leader. "We will see what kind of magic stands up to our iron."

The Rover pulled his blade back for a swing and Elfred unleashed a heat spell meant to turn the blade into a molten mass of metal. Whatever cursed charms the Rovers wore, one of the enchantments deflected the apprentice magician's spell. It sparkled briefly about the Rover like thousands of gleaming gnats before fading moments later. The black-garbed warrior grinned evilly and swung. It would have decapitated the stunned apprentice if the Rover's sword wasn't in turn deflected, not by a spell, but by the curved saber of a caravan guard.

The Rover grunted in surprise and waited too long for his parry. The other's blade whipped lightly across his neck and sent a gush of blood spraying across the floor. The youths' surprise defender kicked over the table and lunged forward, catching another Rover off guard. They were not used to someone using the tip of the blade, wielding their own swords only to slash and hack.

The second of the strangers had by now pulled his blade free and the two kicked tables and chairs clear until they stood back-to-back in the center of the room.

The Lancene warriors quickly circled their challengers while watching for an unguarded opening. The soldiers did not seem impressed with the duo. Not only were the Rovers taller and heavier, the five assumed with an unshakable arrogance that any one of them could defeat three normal warriors, let alone five against two. They considered the death of their comrades an amazing fluke and were now belittling their prey with insults.

"Elfred," Drestin urgently called to his friend, "do something."

The apprentice magician took a deep breath and stepped back. The spells protecting the Rovers had taken him by surprise. He guessed that they had many others to ward off further magical assaults. Though he wanted to reply to Drestin's plea, the abruptness of the events left him almost in shock. What good were an apprentice's meager spells against such formidable magic?

A Rover dashed in and after a brief blur of blades ringing loudly in the inn, retreated with a slash across one cheek. He appeared dumbfounded that such a thing could happen. A callous taunt by a comrade sent him back into the fray and the black-haired swordsman almost effortlessly sent him stumbling to his knees, from there to fall motionless onto his face. This outraged the remaining four. The Rovers threw themselves at the pair in one mad rush. The two withstood the charge and held the Rovers at bay with astounding swordsmanship. Yet it was obvious they would ultimately be overwhelmed by the superior force.

Drestin picked up a chair and threw it at a Rover. The Lancene warrior easily dodged it and fixed his gaze upon the dragon apprentice.

"You will not die as easily as my comrades," the Rover promised before returning to the attack on the swordsmen.

"The spell is not everything," Elfred could suddenly hear his master saying. "You can memorize a thousand spells and they will do you a rabbit's ass of good if you do not know how to use them. When you are faced by an impregnable wall, do not knock your head against it--go around or over it."

The strangers were doing an unbelievable job of warding off the blows from their opponents. The Rovers were looking upon the two with growing caution, especially the curved saber as it wove a blurred net of steel between its owner and the Lancenian thugs. Still, it was only a matter of time before they wore the two down. It appeared the smaller one was already beginning to tire and two of the Rovers were closing in on him.

Elfred took a second deep breath and uttered the same fire spell, only this time aiming it at the feet of the Rovers. The wood planking burst into flames. The warriors grinned unscathed from within the separate fiery blazes. The jeering turned to looks of surprise when the flooring gave way and they plummeted into the basement below. Elfred uttered another spell--that of water--and the flames were quickly drenched.

Dristan rushed to one of the openings and peered into the darkness below. He could barely make out the four crumpled forms. The fall was at least 12 feet to a rough stone floor and only one of the warriors seemed to be moving.

"Excuse me," the taller stranger said as he pushed the dragon apprentice to the side. "An unpleasant task must be finished."

He dropped to set with his legs over the side of a hole rimmed with charred wood, then pushed himself forward and dropped to the basement below. Drestin preferred not to observe what next followed and returned to his friends.

Annabeth was lightly sobbing and had her head buried in her older sister's shoulder. Pallin was nervously patting her back, his face as white as the handkerchief Elfred was firmly pressing against the girl's ear.

Drestin stood paralyzed for a minute as he took in the scene. He asked with a choking voice, "Are you all right?"

She didn't speak, only shaking her head yes. He looked helplessly at his friend.

"She will be fine," Elfred assured him.

"It is my fault. The Rover would not have harmed Annabeth if I had held my tongue," Drestin lamented. He was vainly fighting off tears.

"They most likely would have continued with their sport until no honorable man could have remained quiet," said the dark-haired stranger. He had soundlessly reappeared from the basement.

"We owe you gratitude," Drestin spoke and held out his hand, hoping the other would not notice how it shook. "My name is Drestin, dragon apprentice, and this is Annabeth, Freta, and my good friend, Elfred, apprentice magician."

"My name is Elvon, and this is my comrade, Drant," he replied, studying both of the young men before taking their offered hands. His friend just nodded from beneath his cowl. "I believe it is we who owe you, especially the adept."

Drestin didn't understand the meaning behind the words and studied the men closer. He hadn't paid a great amount of attention to the stranger when he first arrived. There was still not much to observe about the hooded, quiet one. He was lean and dressed in the baggy, canvas trousers used by caravan guards during bad weather. A brown wool cape and cowl hid his features, keeping the face and even the color of his hair a mystery. Several brief glimpses caught during the sword fight spoke of a face belonging to a very young man.

The second fellow drew more attention. A solid figure with unusual boots that went to the knees, the man named Elvon looked to be in his early twenties. Also garbed in a cape, Elvon wore the hood down. He had the face of a young man, yet it carried some weight or burden that gave an impression of age. His gray eyes were now friendly enough, but their coldness during battle made even the Rovers hesitate several times.

Elvon was returning the inspection with a judging gaze of his own. He nodded his head as if the apprentices had passed some personal grading.

"We must clean up this stink if ill consequences are not to follow," Elvon declared as he turned to the innkeeper. "Their deaths could bring down the wrath of other Rovers. We must dispose of the corpses and release their mounts and hope they fly to join their wild kin in the mountains.

"And none must speak of this," he ordered in a louder voice as he faced the three traders then turned to the old men in the corner. "It does not matter that you did not take part in these proceedings. Being here is enough to earn you unpleasant deaths."

The traders paled, their fearful expressions enough of an answer.

"Take the maids home and return. You have embroiled yourself in more than just a tavern brawl," spoke Elvon to the apprentices.

Drestin opened his mouth to voice opposition to the sudden, brusque orders from the stranger. He looked at the four still smoking holes in the floor and back to the swordsman's commanding gaze. He could feel a subtle charge in the air and realized he was in the presence of a very uncommon caravan guard.

"Help me take the girls home," Elfred said. "Annabeth needs rest."

Drestin wanted to argue, but he was still bewildered by the crazy turn of events. He meekly followed the three out into the warm summer evening.

Chapter Five

Garin cursed the bell, yet it continued its call.

~ * ~

"I find it hard to believe these boys are the ones told of in the prophecy," Rorianne said as she sank wearily onto the foot of the small bed. She pulled the hood down and gold tresses spilled across her shoulders. "Are you sure it is not the old wizard and dragonmaster that we want? These two seem so young."

Vlad laughed. "Are you so much older? Even if I could not see the aura about the two, I would choose them over their masters. The wizard is too contentious and the dragonmaster a thief and rogue. No, they are the two who will follow us through the world gate for the Stone of Myrlyn."

Rorianne remained somber. "You would have them join us, even though the prophecy reveals that one or more of the questmates are to die before this venture is concluded?

Vlad's smile tightened and he stared intently at the Thurbian princess until she turned to look out a window into the dark.

"What I would have is not part of this venture," Vlad said softly. "As you have said, this saga was foretold long before we were born. I would place those two beyond hurt, but the prophecy says they are needed to defeat this evil. There will be no safe haven for them or any others if we are not successful. Besides, there are few better ways to perish than in a just cause."

"You speak like a soldier," Rorianne said as she turned back to face her traveling partner, "but those boys may prefer to die in bed as weary old men, or at least in their home village."

"It is you who are launching this quest," Vlad said in puzzlement. "Are you doubting the prophecy? Tell me now, for I fear any faltering or wavering on your part could prove fatal for us all."

"No," she sighed. "But suddenly this quest seems too real. It has always been just the 'family legend,' something nursemaids told among other bed stories. It would someday come to pass, but never in my lifetime. Even then it was to be a prince of the Cevonte blood, never a princess.

"And now I find myself leading this quest and asking two youths to partake in a venture that may mean their deaths. How would I feel if this came to pass?"

The two fell into a brooding silence, Rorianne pondering her new burdens and Vlad noting that the princess displayed no anguish over his own participation and possible death.

~ * ~

"This is madness," Drestin gave his opinion for the seventh or eighth time as they headed back to the Boar's Breath. "I say we cajole a bottle of wine from Manfred and hole up in your room until those two leave the village. Why do we want to mix in such matters?"

"You seem to easily forget your vow of gratitude to Elvon," Elfred reminded his friend. "Do you not feel some debt remains to be paid for their intervention?"

"Yes, of course," Drestin grudgingly admitted. "Though Elvon did say he also owed us, however that was reckoned."

"You have not figured that out yet?" asked the apprentice magician.

"What do you mean?"

"Those Rovers were obviously after our new friends. When was the last time warriors of Lancene bothered to stop in Ramshire? They use Trinton as a shortcut to locales of more importance, but our humble village is not on those routes. Despite his plain garb, this Elvon is someone of importance. It would be extraordinary happenstance that they should all stop at the Boar's Breath on the same evening."

Drestin stopped dead in the middle of the quite cobblestone alley. "Is not that more the reason to seek cover for the night? These events do not seem like something two apprentices should mix in."

"But we will soon be masters in our own professions, and a foe of the Rovers is not someone to turn away."

"You said it, 'soon.' We are not yet masters. Even then we will be novice masters and under the guidance of elders in our guilds."

It was too late for further arguing. They had reached the door of the Boar's Breath and Elfred impetuously pushed his way into the inn. The two were greeted by a sober crowd of evening patrons. Though they might have no knowledge of what transpired earlier in the hostel, the group seemed to be aware that some event of great import had occurred. The patrons were nervous and acted unnaturally constrained.

Drestin noticed that boards had been hastily nailed across the holes in the floor. Pallin greeted them when they reached the bar.

"Annabeth?"

"She will be all right," Drestin answered tersely, making sure no one could overhear. "It was just a nip, though we had a lot of explaining to do to her father. Try telling of a giant dog leaping from the shadows to take a bite of your daughter's earlobe. Where are the two?"

"In the room above the kitchen," Pallin nodded his head toward the stairs. "Be careful. They are not evil men, but danger dogs their heels as sure as those Rovers are dead."

"Did you hear that? 'Danger dogs their heels.' Even Pallin is nervous and he fought for five years in the Ghoul War," Drestin protested as they climbed the stairs.

"He's an old worry mom," Elfred replied flippantly, but paused as if having second thoughts when he came to the mysterious swordsmen's room.

"Well? What are you waiting for, Sir Brave and Almost-A-Master?"

Elfred raised his fist to knock. The door opened before his knuckles touched wood. Both apprentices were taken by surprise, and Drestin took several involuntary steps backwards before catching himself.

The warrior looked up and down the hall and motioned the young men into the room. The mysterious swordsman returned to his bed where he had laid out another suit of clothes. It was a day of surprises for Drestin. The garb was that of a Bulgavian Dragoon flight uniform. At the head of the bed was the black leather jacket with a wool lining and rows of shiny steel studs. On the right shoulder was the Dragoon emblem, that of a dragon flying across a swollen, blood-red sun. Next to it were a black, light canvas tunic and trousers and a leather cap with earflaps and goggles. To the side was a pair of black leather chaps. Drestin's eyes were drawn to the knee-high boots at the foot of the bed. Now he knew why the footwear had seemed so strangely familiar when first seen on Elvon.

Elfred also took in the wardrobe and looked to his friend in astonishment then turned to the swordsman. "You are a Dragoon?"

"Not much of one," the Bulgavian warrior said after a short and bitter laugh. "It is hard to be a Dragoon when you have not a dragon."

He noticed the two's puzzled looks and continued. "My dragon was attacked last night, I am not sure by who or what. We were crossing the peaks that lie south of this valley when it happened. I could not see because it was so dark, but my mount must have seen or heard it coming. He screamed loudly and swerved. We would have been thrown off if we had not been buckled to the harness.

"It happened so quickly I was not even aware the dragon had been struck until later. He shuddered and tucked his wings. We dropped a few thousand feet in seconds. He was a good mount and opened his wings just in time. The landing was still a boneshaker. We started a small fire so I could examine him, but he was dead by the time I had made a torch. Half his abdomen had been torn open."

Both apprentices were unnerved. They were standing in the presence of a legendary Bulgavian Dragoon--the dragon soldiers who had repulsed waves of Eastern Steppe dwellers, easily conquered neighboring lands, and once even crushed a Lancene army sent to conquer Trinton. Bulgavia cared nothing for its smaller neighbor's independence, but it did not want it ruled by the larger country to the north. The Dragol lords preferred that Trinton remain as a buffer strip between the two empires.

Elfred closely studied the soldier's face but could see no sign of the mythical evil those in the service of a Dragol were reputed to possess.

"I have heard the young Dragol sets a different course for Bulgavia," Elfred said hesitantly, not wishing to offend the swordsman.

The swordsman laughed at the apprentice's caution. "Yes, he would seek to gain his country's prosperity through trade rather than war. He does not worship the death gods as did his fathers."

"That is good to hear," admitted Drestin.

Drestin realized the Dragoon's cohort was not present. He swiveled and saw the other swordsman sitting in the shadowed corner of the room.

"Why did you not take one of the Rover's dragons?" asked Elfred.

"They are trained to accept no other riders and are useless to anyone but a Rover. Even then, the brutality in which they are trained makes them half crazed, so they occasionally turn on their own masters."

"Is your friend also a Dragoon?" Drestin asked.

"No, I am not," the stranger said with what the apprentices first thought was the voice of a boy. The swordsman walked into the circle of lamplight and drew back the hood.

Both apprentices' eyes widened at the surprise at the sight of a woman.

"My name is Princess Rorianne Cevonte. My brother is King Grantor of Thurbia," she said as if reciting from a tome. "I am on a quest to prevent the king and mages of Lancene from finding the Stone of Myrlyn. A prophecy warns of great evil for the whole world if the jewel falls into the hands of Lancene King Vasper and his dark conjurers. King Vladimir Dragol has joined the quest as foretold in the Chronicles of Myrlyn, just as it is foretold that you will also accompany us."

Elfred and Drestin turned in unison to stare at the King of Bulgavia and Drestin's knees felt as if they were about to buckle. He stumbled back two steps and grabbed a table for support, shaking the lamp and sending shadows wiggling on the wall. Before him was the king that countless numbers of children had been warned about for centuries--"If you are bad, King Dragol will get you."

"Holy dragon dung," was all he could say.

~ * ~

"I still think we are crazy," admonished Drestin when they returned to Elfred's room. "I say we send the king on his way. After all, we helped him shake those maniacal Rovers and now we are getting him a winged dragon, an almost impossible task in Ramshire. What more can he expect of us?"

Elfred stared down at the floor and frowned. He pushed a piece of foolscap around with the tip of his boot and drummed his fingers on a knee pulled up to his chin.

"But Princess Rorianne said there was a danger from Lancene," objected Elfred.

Drestin sighed and rolled his eyes. "When is not there a danger from somebody? Are not we orphans because our fathers answered the King's call in fighting his evil cousin, Drownlen the Usurper? And where did it get them or us? I am just saying that this time next week we might both be guild members. Are we going to throw that all away because some royal berserker says he needs the help of a couple provincial apprentices for some mysterious venture?"

"I feel power around him. Why, I do not know, but I believe him. I know it is like saying you trust the devil, but we cannot ignore the real threat of Lancene. Manfred has spoken of a great evil coming out of the north."

"Fine, now you are also listening to the mushroom-induced, hallucinogenic ramblings of an alcoholic wizard," Drestin protested.

Elfred stood and hit his friend in the chest with the flat of his palm. A surprised Drestin caught himself before he fell over a mangy stuffed boar Elfred had picked up in a junk shop. The dragon apprentice appeared angry as

Drestin straightened. He advanced on his friend with clenched fists. Drestin paused and several emotions waged their struggle across his face. A sheepish look won out, and Drestin ran his fingers self-consciously through his hair and took a deep breath.

"I am sorry, Elfred, I really am. You know I did not mean any disrespect toward your master. I know you disdain ill remarks about Manfred. I guess I am afraid."

Admitting to being afraid was something neither of the young apprentices would reveal to anyone but each other. Drestin's acknowledgement was enough repentance for his friend. Elfred flashed a crooked smile that Drestin took as a sign of forgiveness and both turned their thoughts back to the current happenings.

They were interrupted by Elfred's pet wyvern, Ralp. It looked like a miniature white and brown, pudgy dragon, putting on so much weight it could hardly make it through the small entrance cut into the base of the door. It had pushed up the flap covering the hole and peered in at them as if debating the wisdom of joining such felonious company. Ralp's hunger won out. It squeezed through the entrance and romped across the floor to begin lapping at sour goat's milk.

"You truly believe Princess Rorianne is on an important errand?" Drestin asked. "And not just one of those fanciful quests bored knights and royalty like to amuse themselves with?"

"Does King Dragol look like someone to be sent on a fool's errand? We are talking about a monarch more feared than the king of Lancene, not some idiot like our Prince Rindoll."

Drestin walked to the window and looked out into the dark streets of the village. Only a few windows were still lit at this late hour.

"If that is how it stands," Drestin finally spoke, "I know for sure I am not going. I have listened enough to old epics to know that most heroes eventually wind up dead. They may have minstrels singing of their feats, but they still meet very uncomfortable ends in far locales. And with the princess saying the prophecy speaks of the death or deaths of some of the questmates, you can count me out."

The door to Elfred's room was flung open before he could counter Drestin's comments. King Dragol stood in the hallway. Though Vladimir Dragol appeared almost likable, the apprentices couldn't help but let centuries of fear intimidate them. King Dragol shrugged as he repositioned a pack slung over one shoulder.

"Well?" he spoke to the two apprentices, eying them impatiently. "Are we ready to view this mysterious winged dragon?"

Drestin looked to his friend then back to the royal swordsman.

"Ah, do you think we should pack a lunch?"

~ * ~

"It is a good looking mount," admitted Vlad as he critically studied the young beast. "It appears someone is pilfering dragons from your king's stables."

Drestin couldn't take his eyes off the beautiful animal. A dragon's wings contain the magic that enables the massive creature to fly. The magic must do more than just lift the heavy body, reasoned the dragon apprentice, since none of the farm dragons gleamed this metallically. The stripe down its back ran like a vein of gold through highly polished obsidian. Its head reached more than twice the height of the humans, and Elfred stepped back nervously as it stretched its leathery wings.

"Are you sure you really need Elfred and I?" asked Drestin as he helped Vlad harness the dragon. "What help can two apprentices from an outback village be?"

"That you will have to ask Lady Rorianne. She has read the entire Chronicles of Myrlyn, not I."

"The epic poem describes an immense battle that occurred over five hundred years ago," she took over, "in which the Giants of Sothic were defeated with the aid of a gem called from another world by Myrlyn, a master sorcerer, who was also my ancestor. The gem could boil the seas and level mountains. Worse, it could suck the souls from men and turn them into automatons. Mountains were leveled and forests turned to ashes when the battle was finally finished. In grief over what he had brought about in order to defeat the giants, Myrlyn cast the stone back through a world portal located in Lancene. Since then it has been known as Myrlyn's Gate.

"But Myrlyn also had a gift of prophecy and foretold when a mighty and evil nation would attempt to find the jewel. He listed signs that would reveal when this would occur. Many of these harbingers have already transpired: the earthquake in Reghen, the three-year drought, the Red Elf plague and the violent death of the head priest of Vrgten. He said the enemy could be stopped by a warrior of his own descent, as well with the help of an offspring of a Rohneld--and a dragonmaster and wizard from the village of St. Luopes. I searched the archives of many temples and libraries before I found a map old enough that showed this settlement. It is now known as Ramshire, your own village. We four and possibly one or more in addition--it is too vague for certainty--are to travel through the world gate and find the gem. It appears we will return with two more questmates to destroy the gem with the Lights of the Pillars That Hold Up the Sky."

Elfred tried not to look worried as he furtively gazed at the Bulgavian king. It did not go unnoticed by Lady Rorianne.

"Yes, I too worried about including a Dragol in this quest. But he is the only known surviving member of the Rohneld bloodline. The prophecy says that it is such as he who will be able to recognize the jewel. And," she added skeptically, "he tells me the Dragols are no longer blood-thirsty beasts."

Both apprentices tensed at these words and nervously eyed the Bulgavian.

"Swords and stones can break my bones..." smiled Vlad.

"But we are not a dragonmaster and wizard, that would be Keldlief and Manfred," blurted Drestin. "You have the wrong two."

"I might think so if it were not for the nature of your masters, as well as a gift of King Dragol's--he says he can see emanations about people who are chosen for quests. King Dragol knew I was on a quest before I told him, and he says both of you are aglow."

"If we are to be among strangers," the king interrupted, "I would prefer to be called Vlad rather than by a royal title--in private as well as in public--so that it will be second nature. 'Like father, like son,' seems to be a universal belief. A slip of the tongue could cause an onerous scene."

"What are we to do?" inquired Elfred. "What can the likes of Drestin and I offer?"

"The chronicles do not explain everything, but we are now four, and I believe it is time we leave. Somehow Vasper of Lancene is aware something is about," Rorianne said. "I have no notion if our downing was a random blow in the dark for Vasper or if he has singled us out. We should leave immediately so as not to become a sitting target for further strikes."

There appeared to be no use in arguing, especially when a king of Bulgavia was involved. Drestin dragged the remaining tangle of leather, light chain, canvas and thick silk cords from the back of the stall. There was no longer any doubt the beast was from the royal stables. The red leather straps studded with silver medallions marked the harness as belonging to the king's air cavalry. The dragon lord and dragon apprentice began harnessing the animal as Elfred and Rorianne watched. The mount shuffled impatiently. It was ready to stretch its wings and fly after its cramped confinement.

The black canvas covered the dragon's back from its front shoulders through the gap between the wings and to its rear haunches. An arrangement of straps toward the back was for luggage. Attached to the harness were silk cords that hooked to the belts of riders as a safety measure. There were enough cords to secure seven riders.

There was a marked lack of enthusiasm as the apprentices tugged and pulled at the straps to secure their bundles of clothing and gear. Drestin carried two extra packs containing the instruments of his crafts. One was a long and cylindrical canvas bag, the other smaller and made of black griffin leather.

"Do not worry," Vlad spoke in an understanding voice as he watched Drestin and Elfred. "Your guild memberships are assured for these services you perform. I will see to that."

While Vlad checked outside before the large sliding doors were pushed aside, Drestin paused in his work and said to his friend, "Maybe this is not going to be so bad after all. It is not as if my passing the exam is a sure thing. We ride with the k..., I mean Vlad (both were having a hard time calling the Bulgavia monarch by such an informal title) for a while, get the gem, take a leisurely journey back, and become masters of our trade."

Elfred laughed bitterly. "And what if the k... Vlad does not live through this to come to our aid? Or worse, if we do not?"

"You dance to a different tune fast enough. Just a minute ago you were ready for adventure."

"That is before I discovered the king was contemplating a venture into Lancene. There they have no interdictions against delving into the darker mysteries. The very land stinks of evil. An apprentice such as I would be but an amusing diversion from their disgusting labors."

"Do not underestimate yourself, Apprentice Elfred," said Vlad. He again surprised the two with his silent tread. "I grew up around court sorcerers and am familiar with their incantations. The emanations from your fire spell felt as strong as any I have experienced. You also showed resourcefulness when overcoming the Rovers' defenses."

"I did not overcome their defenses," Elfred said bitterly. "They were too strong for my magic. I had to resort to trickery."

Vlad laughed and slapped the apprentice on the back. "Then let us hope you have more trickery left. I doubt full adepts could have mastered the Rovers without scurrying to their books. They often value obscure and intricate spells over speed."

There was no escaping the king's wishes. They led the dragon through the door and stopped in the center of the weed-filled courtyard. The dragon automatically turned into the light breeze and eagerly stretched its wings. Vlad helped Rorianne and the apprentices onto the mount and secured them to the harness. Elfred found sitting on the ridge of the dragon's back was not as uncomfortable as he feared.

Drestin forgot his earlier recriminations. He was on a winged dragon! Many rural dragonmasters went their entire life without actually riding an unclipped animal.

The great shimmering beast flexed its legs and raised its wings. With one vigorous down stroke, the dragon leaped into the air. Elfred tightly gripped a strap in front of him and clenched his teeth. It seemed impossible that something so large could take to the air with such small wings. He was certain it would fall back to the earth with a mighty crash--but it didn't. The magic was true and the beast ascended into the night sky.

Drestin had never experienced such pure joy as the ground and buildings dwindled beneath him. The feeling surged through his chest like a jolt of lightning. He felt lightheaded and twisted to look over his shoulder at Elfred, who was staring intently to the ground. Drestin followed his gaze and saw three small figures far below. The rounder of the trio appeared to be jumping and waving a fist. It was Keldlief with the two hill men. They hadn't left a second too soon.

Vlad steered the mount so the moon hung to their left and they were pointed to Lancene. A cool wind teased their hair and watered Drestin's eyes. He now saw the need for the goggles.

"We will rest the dragon at daybreak. If you are able, it would be..." the Ranger spoke between the whooshing of the wings' downbeat. ".... to your advantage to get some sleep."

Drestin snorted. How could anyone sleep riding high above the earth on the back of a sleek war dragon? He pulled his cloak tighter about him because of the chillness of the higher air and returned to gazing about. He wished it were dawn so he could see the villages and farms spread below like the toys of a child.

But after no more than an hour, the rhythmic beat of the dragon's wings lulled him to sleep. The black dragon and its four passengers continued through the night sky. Drestin was hoping that as seen from the ground, only the mysterious blinking of the stars betrayed their passing.

Elfred was more sensitive to magic than his traveling companions and could faintly see the power discharging in waves around the dragon's wings. It shimmered like the northern lights in a rainbow of colors. Elfred first amused himself by letting the aura flow through his fingers and then channeled the energy into strange patterns with just his mind. He had never tried such a thing and soon his head felt like a seldom used muscle protesting after a heavy workout.

Elfred was startled when the wings skipped a beat and the dragon slid sideways before regaining its pace. Something had spooked it and Vlad drew his saber. That something was now buzzing excitedly around the head of the dragon--it was Ralp, seemingly elated about meeting a big dragon that could actually fly. Elfred called the wyvern and it settled easily on his lap. The apprentice magician was surprised at how glad he was to see his little pet. Soon the monotonous cadence of the wings lulled both Ralp and his master to sleep.

Vlad was an experienced aviator and had been taught a warrior must take advantage of sleep whenever possible, yet he remained awake longer than his passengers. He went over and over what little Rorianne had told him about the venture, trying to think of what all could go wrong. He wished the woman trusted him enough to tell him more of the quest. She rode behind him and Vlad imagined the young woman placing her arms around his waist and leaning her head on his shoulder.

Vlad landed the dragon in the clearing on a wooded hill as the morning sun first showed itself. There were plenty of groans as the riders stretched their stiff limbs in the chilly air. Drestin made a small fire and heated a pot of water for tea. Elfred retrieved several packages of waxed paper and opened to them to reveal coarse black bread and cheeses. One by one the members of the party disappeared to make their toilets.

Elfred's curiosity led him to several mounds halfway down the hill. High above his head circled Ralp. The scattered remains of stone foundations crowned the knolls like jagged, broken teeth. He kicked at loose chunks of rock and found nothing of interest. A twig snapped, and he looked up to see Lady Rorianne picking her way through the rubble.

"I wonder if these are the remains of the war you spoke of," Elfred said when Rorianne remained silent.

"I doubt it. Our world is littered with such bones, some older and others as fresh as the scars living men bear."

"How did you get involved in this, Princess Rorianne?" Elfred asked, hoping he would not offend the princess, yet driven by curiosity.

"You should call me only Rorianne. Vlad is right, we would not want strangers to know of our real ranks or mission. As for my role, it was foretold, though nothing was mentioned that the warrior of Myrlyn's line would be a woman. Maybe it was to have been my brother, but he was injured when my parents were killed. I often would listen to my father singing the Chronicles of Myrlyn to my brother. We would act out the saga, and my brother would always play the hero.

"He now walks with a limp and one arm is useless. But a hero needs more than a good arm. My brother is broken in more than body. After that, I dreamed of fulfilling the prophecy, though everyone laughed at me. My uncles only let their orphaned niece practice with the sword to keep me out from under their feet. Vlad, with his talk of unseen glows, is the first man to take me seriously."

"You speak to him very coldly for a traveling companion."

Rorianne examined a weed growing from between two stones and reached down to slowly wrap it around her finger. "His father killed my parents."

She spoke so matter-of-factly that at first it did not register with Elfred. He jerked his gaze from the weed and stared at the woman in surprise, at loss for words.

"Bulgavian warriors swooped down upon a Thurbian caravan. My parents and brother were returning from the Duke of Sapheneau's wedding. I do not know if they were aware my parents were in the train or only that it looked ripe with spoils, but they left most dead and the survivors believing the others more lucky."

"Then the former King Dragol did not actually take part in the attack?"

"They were his father's men," she snapped furiously.

"I do not mean to offend my lady, but Drestin and I bear you no ill will, yet our fathers were killed by Thurbian mercenaries in the pay of Drownlen the Usurper."

Elfred braced himself. He couldn't believe he was arguing with someone of royal blood, let alone defending a Dragol. She straightened, pulling the weed from between the stones and sending bits of dirt flying. He thought she was going to strike him, and he tensed his muscles for the blow. It seemed to Elfred that the morning had suddenly turned unnaturally quiet. They stared at each other for a dozen heartbeats until a deep breath escaped the woman's lips and she slowly relaxed.

"We must not fight among ourselves," she said and turned to face the camp. "If you grew up hating someone then discovered that person did not exist, it would not make it any easier forgetting that hate."

Vlad pretended to be busy feeding and watering the dragon as he watched the pair returning. He struggled against being captivated by her easy walk and the graceful way she performed the most common chores. She approached the dragon and opened one of her pouches. Withdrawing a piece of parchment, she kneeled and unfolded it on the grass.

"This is where we go," she said, pointing to a spot marked along a small river in the south of Lancene. "A temple was here half a millennium ago. The Chronicles of Myrlyn seem purposely vague on the portal's location, though I finally deduced it after a lengthy search through family archives.

"I doubt even King Vasper yet knows the exact location, though I am sure he is close to the discovery. This is where a weak spot in the wall exists between worlds, waiting to be found with the right magic."

"This is true? Such things are not myths?" wondered Drestin. "I thought those were only stories told to children before bed."

"There are other worlds and portals for those who know ways to find them."

"And you can do this?"

"I cannot," she said softly then turned to look at Elfred. "That is why we brought the master magician."

Elfred didn't think his nerves could take too many more shocks in one morning. "What? I have no knowledge of doors to other worlds. Such arcane laws are studied only by elder wizards in the courts of kings. I doubt Manfred would even know of such things."

"But you have the light within you," Vlad reminded him. "Therefore you will be able to perform this task."

Elfred wished he were just half as confident as Vlad sounded.

"We have other obstacles facing us before young Elfred is called upon," Vlad continued. "Though Bulgavian warriors no longer fly war sorties, we occasionally send flights to probe the defenses of possible enemies. King Vasper keeps close watch on his borders, and it will be difficult to enter his domain without being detected. We will have to do this at night, which means it will be difficult finding this temple ruin."

"That should not be difficult," said Rorianne. "The Chronicles speak of the mage perceiving a glow about the gate not visible to others."

"Even night flights will be dangerous with Vasper certainly alerted to our coming. I am sure he knows the prophecy as well as Rorianne and will be moving to block us," said the Bulgavian king. "He will have doubled the number of patrol dragons along the border and probably will also be employing magic for the detection of intruders."

Vlad suggested they wait where they were and continue after sunset. Though Rorianne was anxious to continue, she recognized the wisdom of avoiding travel during the day and so, grudgingly agreed.

Chapter Six

No matter how Garin cursed the bell, it would not stop its hellish ringing as he trudged down the long, narrow hall.

~ * ~

Elfred and Drestin had found a dragon's back was not the most restful place to nap. They gladly kicked together mounds of leaves beneath a giant ash tree and threw their capes over the makeshift mattresses. Drestin stared up at the traces of blue sky through the rich greens of the foliage and wondered what Keldlief was doing at that moment. The miserable dragonmaster would hardly be able to report his apprentice as a runaway without incriminating himself in a much worse offense. Drestin looked over at Elfred and saw that his friend was already asleep. A small black ant was walking across Elfred's forehead. The apprentice magician frowned and brushed at the ant.

"Elfred."

"Hmm?"

"You asleep?"

"No longer."

"What do you think is going to happen?'

Elfred opened one eye. "Worried?"

"Some."

"Do not be. We are now official champions fulfilling a prophecy."

"Wonderful, heroes on a venture in which some are to die. Maybe you or I play the heroes whose part is to end halfway through the ballad."

"I was hoping you would not have remembered that. We best pray those who are yet to join the quest are cowardly knaves and they will play the black role."

Drestin looked back at the blue sky and dwelled on that thought for several minutes. He was going to continue the discussion until he turned and saw Elfred had drifted back to sleep. Though Drestin felt weary and sore, sleep didn't seem very probable. He sat up and pulled on his boots, deciding a walk might calm his nerves.

~ * ~

Vlad led the dragon deeper into the woods where the thicker canopy would hide the beast from the air. The drake dug a shallow basin in the rich, black soil of the forest floor and gratefully curled into a ball. It looked at the human for several seconds before closing its eyes. Vlad was impressed with the dragon's personality. Many young males were stubborn and overly aggressive. It lifted its head for just a second when Ralp came fluttering out of the trees to land next to its larger cousin. The wyvern hopped around the dragon like a puppy playing with its mother before it also settled down for a rest next to the drake's head.

Vlad felt grubby. He'd accompanied the Bulgavian Dragoons on numerous field practices and minded none of the hardships except one--the lack of a daily bath. He'd seen a creek before landing and decided to search for it among the numerous small hills. He had slipped out of his flying leathers and into the clothing he had worn when first meeting the two apprentices.

The lumpy area as seen from the air reminded him of the skin of a plucked goose. It took only 10 minutes to locate the stream twisting through the small hills. He followed the creek until finding a bend where it was more than knee deep.

Vlad waded out to chest-high water and dunked his head. The creek was cold and he sputtered after pulling his head back out of the water. Fighting shivers while he soaped his hair, the bath now hardly seemed worth it, though he knew he'd feel better once dry and in clean clothes.

"May I join you?"

The king of Dragol spun and grabbed for a sword that wasn't there. He relaxed only slightly when he saw that it was Rorianne. He mused that it was difficult to decide if he needed his blade when she was near.

"I asked if I could join you."

"If you would," he replied hesitantly.

The Princess Rorianne looked up and down the bank for a spot that wasn't too weedy or muddy. She picked her way carefully to a half-submerged rock leaning against the bank. Stepping onto the stone, she began pulling off a boot. She looked up before removing the second.

"Will I bother you? I have heard that Bulgavians have public bathhouses where everyone bathes--men, women and children. I believe I remember a certain chamber maid asking for your presence."

"Yes, we bathe together. I was not aware Thurbians followed similar customs."

"We do not. But I have yet to get the past week's road-dust off, and I feel safer in this strange land with another person--and it might as well be with someone for whom the sight will not be new."

"I did not think you would worry greatly after seeing your sword-work at the inn."

Rorianne paused as she was about to remove her tunic. "Is it proper to watch a lady disrobe at your bath houses?"

He reluctantly turned his back but continued talking. "I have been trying to plan how to sneak undetected into Lancene. Does the prophecy convey such lore?"

"No, but I am not surprised. Dragons were not yet tamed when Myrlyn wrote of this quest."

"That would not matter if he could read the future."

"You may be right. May I borrow your soap?"

Vlad slowly turned to find her standing within arm's reach, which entered his mind when he saw her so close. She was already shivering from the cold water that reached almost to her chin, though her breasts were still clearly visible in the crystal clear stream. Rorianne held out her hand and he laid the small cake of soap in her palm. He tried switching his thoughts to other matters as she rubbed the suds into her hair.

The princess bobbed up and down several times to rinse. Her hair fell to spread outwards across the water like a fallen blossom. He watched several droplets trickle down a cheek. Her beauty made Vlad ache, and he wanted to be angry that she would tease him so. Rorianne read the change in his expression.

"I am sorry I spoke as I have. I can know in my mind that you are not to blame for my parents' deaths. I can even believe you are a good person. Though my heart still rages and I do not know if it can ever find peace, I promise to treat you from here onward as an ally. I believe I can even trust you."

Vlad was eager to hear and believe the words, but he couldn't help feeling cautious. "Why this sudden turnabout?"

"The apprentice magician revealed something of import to me. And there were your servants and aides--until now I denied what I saw in Castle Dragol. You are not feared there as one would expect of the Dragol of legend."

Rorianne shivered and hugged her shoulders. "I must leave this water before I turn blue."

Vlad was also fighting back the cold, and would have continued to do so as long as Rorianne remained beside him. He knew the moment would be over once they left the creek, and he sadly watched her wade back to shore.

~ * ~

Vlad was luckier than he knew--Drestin's walk took him away from the swimming hole. The dragon apprentice was enjoying the commonness of the scenery. The land was rolling and covered by tall red and green grasses and scattered groves of trees and shrubs. There were no magic jewels to find, no Rovers to fight, no wrongs to right--just a light breeze in his hair, a warm sun on his cheek and the music of songbirds. He rounded a bend of the deer path and almost tripped over a little man dressed in dirty green and brown rags. Both men were equally startled and grabbed for the knives at their belts.

They cautiously lowered their blades after measuring each other for several heartbeats and deciding there was no immediate threat. It was then Drestin noticed a sorry looking dwarf dragon lying in the grass. A saddle lay next to the beast.

"Mornin'," the stranger mumbled.

"Morning."

They stood uncomfortably, neither knowing what to say to a newcomer met in the middle of nowhere.

"Dragon sick. Waitin' for friends."

"What is wrong with it?"

"Do not know."

"May I look? I am a dragon apprentice," Drestin said as he looked over the man's head while trying to get a better look at the creature.

"You?" He eyed the youth suspiciously.

Drestin pulled out his apprentice medallion. It hung under his shirt on a leather cord. The bronze showed that he was near graduation. A look of relief swept across the man's face and suddenly he seemed full of energy, almost dancing around Drestin.

"Never thought I meet this kinda luck the way the week's goin'. Is anything you can do for my Bittie? She buckled here an hour ago. Before she be shiny as silver."

He stepped aside and Drestin slowly approached the dragon so as not to spook her. He needn't have bothered. Her eyes were glazed and she made no indication she was aware of Drestin's approach. The apprentice first checked the major indicators--the smell of her breath, ear lobe pulse, wetness of the nostrils, coloring under the nails, body heat, coating of the tongue, and gloss of the scales.

She didn't look good--Drestin guessed some type of poisoning by the quick onset, something affecting the central nervous system. Her lungs were clear, yet breathing was labored and her heart was beating erratically. The apprentice asked for help and the two forced her mouth open. He picked a piece of chewed vegetation from her teeth for examination, rubbing it between his fingers and sniffing at it. It was only clover.

The little man looked on as Drestin began an inch-by-inch examination of the animal's body and was asked to help when Drestin rolled the dragon over. He found it near the mouth--a very tiny thorn-like stinger was pulled from an unprotected spot by the lips.

"From a hagwasp," Drestin noted sternly. "As a rule a dragon does not react so severely to such a sting unless it is sick or misused. I do not believe this animal has been fed or rested adequately for some time."

The dragon's owner looked to his feet in guilt and wrung an old hat nervously in his hands.

"Tis true enough, but we been hurried."

"Hurried?"

The little man looked even more anxious and gazed about as if to see if they were being spied upon. He licked his lips and shuffled his feet, several times looking as if he was about to speak. He finally looked at the dragon and asked, "Will my Bitte be all right?"

Drestin had a vial of waterchoke syrup that would counter the toxic venom of the sting, but it was back at camp. It was his turn to be apprehensive. What would the others say if he brought back a stranger? Could this insignificant bit of a man be a spy for King Vasper?

"Please," begged the stranger, seeing the debate going on in the apprentice's face. "Help my Bitte. I can pay you when the rest catch up. The boss can reward you in copper."

"Others?" Now Drestin was worried. He was a fool for walking this far from camp.

"Yes, but do not worry. We are no thieves, just poor folks trying do make a livin'."

A light came on in Drestin's head.

"You are smugglers!"

Several times Keldlief had sold pack animals to questionable looking strangers who appeared to know the dragonmaster. He once saw two such customers leaving the stables. Elfred told him they were smugglers, those outcasts and brigands who skulk about the Lancene border to dodge the outrageous tariffs imposed by royal custom agents. It was possible to make a great deal of money in such ventures--or wind up drawn and quartered in the square of some fly-infested border garrison. It was too dangerous for most except the greedy, maniacal, or desperate. And this ragged, meager scrap of a human was looking desperate.

"I have an elixir in my medicine pack. Wait here and I will get it."

When he noticed the stranger looking wary, he added, "Do not worry, you are safe with me. I have no love for the Lancene. Be patient and I will save your dragon."

Drestin's legs were beginning to ache by the time he reached the wooded summit. Elfred was still sleeping and Rorianne and Vlad were talking under a nearby tree. The two watched as Drestin searched through the pack he'd left by his cape. Vlad stood and strode over to his traveling companion.

"What occurs that you rush so?"

Drestin looked up sheepishly, not knowing what to say. "There is need of my skill."

Vlad immediately came alert and studied the direction in which the apprentice had appeared.

"Who and where?"

"He is harmless. A little man with a sick dragon. I think he acts as a scout for a band of smugglers, though by the looks of him, they do not appear to be very successful."

"Smugglers? They practice a dangerous sport in these parts."

"I know. I am sorry I have let my presence be known, but there is an ill dragon, and I must answer such a call. It will not take long, I promise."

Drestin pulled several long slender tubes from the canvas bag and screwed them together. One end was slightly flared. He then removed a small vial from the black leather case and stood.

Wait, I will go with you," Vlad told the apprentice then turned to Rorianne. "We will return shortly, and maybe with an answer to our dilemma."

Drestin explained how he met the man and the appearance of the dragon as they walked down the hill.

"Did he tell you how many were in his party?"

"No, we did not speak much. He has a funny way of talking. I have never heard such an accent."

The little man was keeping guard from a nearby tree when the pair arrived. He looked with suspicion at Vlad.

"It is all right, he is a friend," Drestin said.

"He has the looks of a borderman or king's bounty hunter."

"I am neither," laughed Vlad, "just someone as you who desires to enter Lancene undetected. My name is Vlad and this is my traveling companion, Drestin. I do not believe we have had the pleasure of meeting before."

The dragon's owner didn't look convinced, but he grudgingly climbed down from the tree and walked to his mount.

"Me name is Babbe. Did you get somethin' for my Bitte?"

"We will try this. It should work unless your mount is too ill."

Drestin had Vlad and Babbe lift the dragon's head and open its mouth. It was an elderly thing by the looks of the worn yellow teeth--the apprentice guessed at least 80 years old. He slid the tube deep into the dragon's throat. Pulling the cork from a small bottle with his teeth, Drestin tipped the vial and poured a trickle of thick syrup into his end of the tube. This was followed by a bit of water. After corking and returning the container to the pocket of his jerkin, he put his lips to the tube and blew in a couple deep breathes.

"That is all we can do now. We should know if it works within an hour. From now on, Master Babbe, I suggest you rest and feed your mount better than you have."

"You bet on it, dragonmaster. She be treated as a princess."

"I am not a dragonmaster, yet, but thanks to you anyway."

"Have you come this way often?" asked Vlad.

"Often enough."

"When will the rest of your party arrive?"

It was obvious Babbe did not trust this tall, lean stranger who had the bearing of a soldier or border patrolman. He rose to check his dragon as an excuse not to talk with Vlad. Drestin smiled and shrugged his shoulders. The minutes trickled by and the apprentice regularly knelt by the dragon to check its signs. The little man watched on with a permanent look of gloom.

"Is she better?" he'd ask each time.

Vlad walked to the edge of the dozen trees they were under and gazed at the scattered hills and thickets. Everything appeared peaceful. It sounded too peaceful, which was what alerted him. The birds were silent. He placed his right hand on the hilt of his sword and kneeled so as to be partially concealed by the tall grasses. He stood and quietly made his way back to the others.

Drestin jumped when Vlad laid his hand softly upon his shoulder. He would never get used to the silent tread of his traveling companion.

"Someone is coming. Be ready to make a hasty departure if they are unwelcomed guests."

"It is probably me mates," Babbe said after overhearing Vlad's warning. He put two grubby fingers to his mouth and blew the shrill call of a mothhawk. A similar call answered. It was easy to see that the little man was greatly relieved. Sitting with the two strangers and his sick dragon had worn his nerves thin.

Several minutes later a party of seven dwarf dragons and four smugglers took shelter under the cover of the trees. Babbe ran to greet them and immediately began prattling about what had occurred. The leader, a sullen man with a face etched deep with wrinkles, glared at the two strangers with little welcome in his eyes. Besides him were two young men about Drestin's age and a girl barely seventeen or eighteen.

"What are yah doin' in these parts?" the leader wanted to know.

"We are travelers like yourself. My friend happened to run into your traveling mate and his unfortunate dragon. Though only an apprentice, he is still sworn to offer aid when needed."

Just then Bitte weakly lifted her head and whined. An ecstatic Babbe went running and cradled her head in his arms.

"Her eyes be cleared," he shouted. "She's gettin' better. Oh, thank you, dragonmaster, you saved me Bitte."

The leader looked a bit less suspicious and reexamined the two.

"Travelers, eh? The only travelers in this god-forsaken land be smugglers or thieves. Which be you?"

"Neither," Vlad replied warmly, as if chatting with his best friends. "We have personal business in Lancene, and we would like to enter with as little fanfare as possible. Until now we have been debating the best way to do this, but I think our fortuitous meeting could prove good luck for both our parties. We will pay you in silver if you lead us safely across the border."

"And just how many be in yah party?"

"Four, and a dragon."

"I see but two."

"The others are resting nearby."

"What's to keep us from just takin' yah silver, now?" the leader smiled evilly, showing teeth just as worn and yellowed as Bitte's.

Babbe watched on in consternation. "Gerrene, yah canna harm them after they have aided me Bitte as they have."

"Do not worry, Babbe. Your friends would not think of harming us," Vlad spoke as warmly as before, but his smile had chilled.

He was also resting a hand on the hilt of his sword in a very meaningful way. The head smuggler's expression also changed. The cocky look was gone from his face. There was something about the stranger's cold gray eyes that sent a chill through the smuggler.

"Only jesting, me mate. I's always ready to make an extra coin. Me name's Gerrene and dese are me two sons, Heften and Lefter. The girl's Lefter's intended. She's a bashful one so yah should leave her alone. We would not wanna to scare her."

Drestin and Vlad nodded their heads in greeting, but the two youths just stared back coldly at the strangers. The brothers were large and swollen like overstuffed sausages. Drestin would have diagnosed glandular problems if they'd been dragons. They also dressed very differently from the other two smugglers.

While Babbe's drab garb bordered upon rags and Gerren's jade cape and kilt were a subdued pattern of swirls that spoke of a River Bergandt origin, their attires still easily fused with the surrounding scape of swollen, velvet-leafed grandma's hedge or the dry and brittle stems of midget wort. From thirty feet they effortlessly faded into the weeds and bushes of the savanna.

But Heften and Lefter were dressed in impractical fabrics and brazen colors that could have only harmonized with the painted lips and dyed hair of temple prostitutes. If spotted by a border patrol, the brothers would stick out like peacocks on a haymow.

The girl kept her face lowered, looking up at the two for only a second. She was slim and had long brown hair, with a face much more intelligent looking than her groom-to-be. The apprentice dragonmaster thought he detected a look of desperation in her brief glance and took an immediate dislike to Gerrene and his brood. Drestin didn't notice the brief puzzled look Vlad gave the girl.

The smuggler agreed to wait in the copse while the two returned to fetch the rest of their party.

~ * ~

"You are touched," Rorianne said when she heard Vlad's new plan. "Why should we plod through this wilderness when we can travel far above it in one night?"

"That is the point. King Vasper must certainly know that the characters picked to play in this drama are on their way and riding a winged dragon. He would not expect these heroes to be slinking in with a pack of wretched smugglers. And, we are not that far from the border. We can reach deep inside within two days. Then we can take to the air."

Rorianne finally agreed that his reasoning made sense. Vlad and Drestin rearranged the harness and luggage, covering the dragon's wings so they appeared to be extra cargo. The smugglers were still waiting for them and the dragon apprentice was happy to see Bitte was now on her feet. Ralp circled the sick dragon several times before returning to perch on Elfred's shoulder.

Gerrene and his sons rudely stared at Rorianne as she entered their camp. Her return look was enough to make the two young men pale and suddenly go off to check their pack animals. Gerrene missed the glacial glance, now too busy looking at the new dragon more than twice the size of his own.

"Ah, she's a beauty, she is. I'd like to 'ave one as this, but she be too big," he said sadly. "She'dah be seen too easy by the bordermen."

After eating a brief meal, the trip began with one of the young smugglers in the lead. They wove onto and off different deer trails in a seemingly random pattern, though Vlad noticed it took them through numerous groves of trees and heavy thickets as if to take advantage of every bit over cover from the sky. The land became increasingly rugged and the paths more challenging.

Several times large orange and blue lizards darted from clumps of grass to go skittering off on hind legs. The caravan often cut through a dark purple grass and the stomping sent clouds of a mint perfume drifting in the wind. Elfred stopped to admire occasional flowers that dotted the valley. They stood at least ten feet in height and bore giant blooms with red petals and blue centers.

Drestin worried about their dragon. It was probably unused to traveling far on foot, though the drake appeared to have no problem maintaining the party's steady pace. He walked beside the dragon and occasionally it would turn its head and seem to smile at the human with the grin of a friendly dog, tongue hanging out and all.

"The girl likes you."

"What?" Drestin asked, startled by the sudden appearance of Elfred.

"I said the girl likes you."

"Get out of here."

"I am not jesting. I have seen her taking quick looks in your direction."

"So, why should that be worth notice? All women are attracted to dragonmasters. They know we are a masterful lot, yet sensitive to a woman's needs and desires."

"Maybe she just likes the smell of the dragon manure on your boots."

Drestin stopped and raised a boot then the other--they were both clean. He looked at his grinning friend and punched him in the arm.

The forest cover had increased to the point where their being spotted from the air was now next to impossible. That appeared to make Gerrene a happier smuggler. Lefter, unfortunately, was not. The girl drifted back during the walk and fell into step besides Drestin. Thinking of what Elfred had said, he greeted her cautiously. She remained silent and glanced up shyly from behind a veil of fine, dirty hair that almost covered her face.

They marched so for a half hour until the brothers changed as point man and Lefter fell back. A look of malice flashed across the young smuggler's face when he saw the girl walking besides the dragon apprentice and he ambled back to the pair in an exaggerated swagger.

"So, that be the garb of an apprentice dragonmaster," sneered Lefter at Drestin's faded khaki tunic, while resplendent in his own garish outfit of vermilion and mauve. "I be sure the color was chosen to blend in with manure stains."

Drestin glanced sideways, a bland expression on his face. "So, that is the garb of a thug. I'm sure the colors were chosen to blend in with the fine webbing of veins embellishing your wine-sotted, bulbous nose."

Lefter's eyes narrowed and his lips thinned. Drestin felt Elfred's elbow jab him in the side, a silent warning to his cohort to watch his perilous tendency to speak before reflection.

"So, yah think yah's a real court jester?"

"I'm not the one dressed in a..." he began to answer when cut off by another sharp poke to the ribs.

The dragonmaster apprentice tightly clamped his teeth shut to hold back further outbursts. Drestin could feel his jaw muscles cramping. Lefter observed his discomfort and interpreted the silence as cowardice. Like all bullies, he took that as provocation for more ridicule.

"I canna see where yah might be jealous of us smugglers," Lefter continued while apishly strutting. "We cut quite the romantic figures."

"Most likely with a knife thrust from behind," Drestin mumbled, then winced and shot his friend an irritated look while furtively rubbing his side.

"Wadya say?"

"He said, 'What an exciting life you must find,'" Elfred quickly inserted into the exchange.

Lefter eyed the pair with suspicion. Drestin tried wearing a meek, harmless look and coyly batted his eyes at the smuggler. "I wager you are a veritable damsel maggot."

"Ouch," Drestin ruefully cried and turned to his friend in feigned innocence. "What did I say? I stated only that our esteemed smuggler must be a damsel magnet. How could that be amiss?"

"Hey, what's a magnet?" growled Lefter, "That sounds not good."

"It is very good," Elfred said, leaning out so he could look around his friend at the smuggler.

"Yes, it means the wenches are attracted to you as maggots to carrion," added Drestin helpfully and all too clearly.

"Yah? That's right?" Lefter slowly answered after a pause as if contemplating the image.

Elfred grimaced and made as if to punch his friend for the fourth time.

The smuggler scratched his chin and smiled. He flicked his thumb at the girl who was now staring morosely at the ground as they walked. "Yah, I am a damsel magnet. I am stuck with her 'cause me father says it's time tah settle down and sire some whelps tah carry on the family name."

Drestin looked at the miserable figure of the girl, vainly attempted to hold back a caustic retort and finally dropped back out of Elfred's elbow range. "And what would that family name be--Imbecile, Cretin, or Pinhead? It must be quite the disappointment not to follow the family tradition of marrying your sister."

"What did yah say?" snapped Lefter.

"He wanted to know if your surname was Umbilical, Crouton or Pinnate," Elfred again jumped in. "Those are very common names where we are from."

"And just where be you from?" the young smuggler asked, still eying Drestin with suspicion.

"The Amnesian Islands," replied Drestin before his friend could intercede.

"Amnesian Islands? I never heard of that land. Where be it?"

Drestin scratched his head in bewilderment, looked at the smuggler and guilelessly replied, "I forget."

Lefter wasn't sure how, but he feared the apprentices were playing him for the fool. His eyes narrowed and he clenched his fist.

Elfred tensed and Drestin braced himself for retribution when a shadow fell across the four, followed by the head of the largest traveling companion--the dragon. The gleam in its eye was no longer that of a playful puppy. It went eyeball-to-eyeball with Lefter and released a long, low hiss like steam escaping from the broken whistle of a giant teapot. It was the sound of a very pissed-off dragon. The smuggler was only used to meek pack dragons, and he rapidly backpedaled in alarm. He eyed the creature with new respect when he reached what he felt was a safe distance away.

"Searene, come here," he barked.

She hunched even more and returned to the side of her intended. Lefter gave Drestin a last hateful look and dragged the girl away.

Drestin looked up at the dragon and rapped his knuckles on its long neck. "Thanks, I owe you one."

"Drestin, you blockhead," Elfred whispered when they were far enough away. "Why anger such a simpleton? It is if we were back at the orphanage and I find you baiting the bullies."

"I could not help it," Drestin sheepishly defended himself. "I cannot believe there are such villainous numbskulls in this world. Did you see how he treats the poor maiden?"

Elfred shook his head. "Riling him will make it no better for the girl, and could even cause her more grief. You cannot fight all the brutes in the world."

Drestin worried about Searene for the rest of that day's walk. His anger towards Lefter grew to where he almost wished the dragon had not interceded.

When they finally made camp, Drestin searched the leather harness of the dragon until he found a small, brass plate bearing the dragon's name-- Shadow Lightning.

"That is a mouthful. I hope you do not mind if I call you Shadow."

The dragon gently butted its head against Drestin. He rapped his knuckles on its forehead, a gesture of affection much like scratching behind a dog's ear.

They made their camp under the overhang of a towering cliff. Plants grew out of the pockmarks along its face and vines hung down to hide the hollow behind a green curtain. Vlad told the smugglers the animal snored loudly at night and took Shadow to a nearby grove of trees. He removed the coverings and the dragon gratefully stretched its wings.

That night Drestin had a difficult time falling asleep. The image of the girl's sad face appeared whenever he shut his eyes. With Annabeth waiting for him, the apprentice wasn't interested in the girl for any reason except he hated seeing her doomed to such a miserable life.

The group was up at the first hint of sun and Drestin walked through the dew-drenched grass to see how Shadow spent the night. He was getting ready to untie the dragon and lead it to a nearby creek for a drink when a voice shouted behind him.

"A flyin' dragon. I knew there was somethin' odd about it. Wait till me father 'ears of this. He won't want yah with us. That's bother there," Lefter predicted with a sneer. "There's probably evenah bounty on yah heads."

"Ah, wings? What are you talking about? What wings?" sputtered Drestin.

"What am I talkin' about? Yah know damn well what I'm talkin' about. Yah got a flyin' dragon."

"Are you amok? How could..." Drestin continued as he turned to look at Shadow, then threw his hands up in mock astonishment. "Great Gods, the dragon has grown wings! Amazing, I've heard of such regeneration, but have never witnessed it. This will be worth a paper in the 'Journal of Modern Dragon Management.'"

Lefter cocked his head and glanced back and forth between the dragon's wings and Drestin's face.

"Yah, can't tell me the dragon's wings just grew overnight."

"Yes, I can."

"No, yah can't."

"Yes, I can."

"No, yah can't."

"It is not that I do not enjoy this insightful discourse, Master Lefter," said Drestin, crossing his arms, "but I am the dragonmaster apprentice and I say the wings sprouted by spontaneous regeneration, much as the docked tails of a swine sometimes grow back."

"Pig tails don't grow back."

"How can you say that," cried Drestin, sweeping a hand back to take in Shadow, "when you've just seen the miraculous regrowth of a dragon's wings? After this, does not the simple germination of a swine's tail seem commonplace?"

"Ah, maybe," the smuggler admitted, by now thoroughly confused. "But I still must tell me father of this."

Drestin watched the retreating figure leave the shelter of the trees. He had seriously considered sucker cuffing the dolt from behind, but it would have only been a temporary solution.

A movement in the sky caught Drestin's attention. He shouted a warning to Lefter, but the smuggler ignored Drestin's pleas in his haste to tattle on the new travel mates. Drestin rushed to the edge of the trees and watched the young smuggler tromping a path through the tall grass. He was almost to the cliff when six shadows glided across the meadow. Lefter was lost from sight after a half dozen Rovers landed around him.

Chapter Seven

The rest of the group watched from their hidden nook as the Lancene soldiers dismounted and roughly grabbed Lefter.

"Maybe they think he be alone," Gerrene hoarsely whispered, obviously more worried about his own hide than what was about to occur to his son.

Though it was too far to hear what was being said, they watched as Lefter turned and pointed to the cliff hideaway. His father cursed and ran to pick up his rusty sword. Heften had already retrieved his blade and Babbe was holding a small axe in trembling hands.

"I guess this means we are in Lancene territory," Elfred said to no one in particular.

He was desperately trying to think of a spell that might help. The grass was far too dew-wet to burn. He turned to see Vlad and Rorianne not waiting for the enemy to come to them. They had left the shelter with swords drawn. He noticed Vlad had thrown on his black leather Dragoon jacket. The Rovers weren't expecting to find anything but a small band of smugglers. They gaped at Vlad.

"So, we have a mighty Bulgavian Dragoon. Have they fallen to smuggling now that they have a woman king?" said the leader, trying to sound jaunty, but obviously startled by the sudden appearance of the ancient rival.

They expected the stranger to stop when he reached the edge of their circle and were caught by surprise when Vlad's fast pace did not slow until he was in their midst--no one man ever willingly fought a group of Rovers. Vlad decided there was no purpose in talking to the Lancene soldiers unless he meant to surrender, which he didn't. Following close on his heels was Rorianne.

The Lancene dragons might have aided their riders if a young apprentice mounted on a black drake had not come soaring out from a woodland to skim above their heads, the beast screaming a challenge that could not be ignored. The battle dragons bounded upward to the curses of their riders. The distraction allowed Vlad to cut down one of the Rovers before the others returned their attention to the battle at hand.

Little Babbe was running to help with his axe waving wildly in the air. Ralp entered the fray and dived at the Rovers while chattering madly. Gerrene and his remaining son were nowhere to be seen. Lefter tried running from the battle and was cleaved in the back.

It was a day of surprises for the Rovers. One, overconfident because he was fighting a woman, took a blade through the stomach. She regained Vlad's side as the four remaining Rovers circled them, almost a replay of the fight at the inn.

Elfred hurled a fire spell at the Rovers just to see if they were also warded against such attacks. They were--the spell sparkled harmlessly about them. He would wonder later what gave him the inspiration. Elfred muttered a much stronger degree of the spell that had cleaned Drestin and him of the dragon stable stench--except in reverse. The wizards of Lancene had cast protective spells against numerous types of attack, but none had apparently thought of dragon dung reek.

A horrible, vile odor permeated the Rovers' clothing so potently that Vlad and Rorianne were forced to back away. The Lancene soldiers' eyes began running with tears and one vomited noisily. They pulled themselves together and tried continuing the attack, but were too overwhelmed by the horrible fumes. Rorianne and Vlad forced themselves back into to fight, expending all their energy in one fierce fusillade of swirling blades. The engagement was soon ended.

Elfred cleared the air with a wave of his hands and Vlad and Rorianne stumbled away to sink thankfully to their knees, breathing in great gasps of fresh air.

"Thank you, wizard, one more time you have saved us," Vlad finally found the breath to say. "You are already proving a bane to the mightiest wizards of Lancene."

Elfred was attempting to think of something humble to say, though he was basking in the praise, when he noticed the fallen figure of Babbe. He rushed to the little man's side. A big knot, as if he had been kicked, was on the side of his head. The apprentice magician was relieved to see he was still breathing.

"As small as he is, this Babbe has more courage than the others of his party put together," Rorianne said as she kneeled and felt his neck for a pulse. She then peeled an eyelid back. "I believe he will be all right, though he will have a bad headache when he awakes."

"Drestin," Elfred blurted, only now remembering his friend luring off the Rovers' mounts. "I hope he can elude those dragons."

Vlad looked up to the clear sky. "His dragon is young and well rested. He has a good chance. But if they are caught, the savage Lancene dragons will tear them to shreds."

The Bulgavian king was sorry even as he spoke, seeing the dragon apprentice's friend pale. "But do not worry. The young drake is fleeing for his life, a very strong inducement when it comes to flying fast."

Vlad asked Elfred to carry the small smuggler back to the camp as he began dragging the bodies of the Rovers to concealment. He laid Babbe on a blanket by the now-dead fire and covered him. Gerrene and Heften were long gone, having escaped with their dragons through a gully when the fighting began. They were most likely miles away by now. Elfred was startled by movement to the back of the overhang. Appearing from the shadows was the girl.

"Is Lefter dead?" she asked.

Elfred was surprised by her sudden lack of accent. He didn't know what to say. Even though the young smuggler treated her badly, he had no idea if she cared for him. He decided to be to the point.

"Yes. I am sorry. He was killed by a Rover."

"Good." There was now heat in her voice. "I can only wish he had died more painfully and slower."

This girl is hard, Elfred thought, then she burst into tears. The crying caught him off guard. He awkwardly put his arm around her and patted her on the back. Searene buried her head in his shoulder and sobbed. As the crying receded, she pulled away and looked up into Elfred's face and asked between sniffs, "Is the dragon apprentice safe?"

"Ah, we do not know yet. He led the Rover dragons away on a chase. We hope he is unhurt and shall return soon."

The girl straightened and rubbed her eyes with a dirty hand. She looked down at a spot washed clean by a tear. "I must bathe. I have gone unwashed since sold as a bride to Gerrene's son."

She silently went through her pack and pulled out a simple, ivory-colored cotton dress then disappeared through the wall of vines as Vlad and Rorianne entered. They seated themselves next to Elfred.

"We will wait here one day then we must set off."

Elfred began to protest Vlad's statement but was silenced when the Bulgavian gently took his arm.

"I know you two are very close. I am sorry the pair of you were drawn away from your homes, but it was predetermined by forces we can only guess of. Drestin will be back before morning if he manages to escape. We can only assume the worst if they have not returned by then. To wait longer will endanger the quest."

Elfred didn't reply, only shaking his head silently in agreement and half-heartedly. He began starting a fire for breakfast.

"If he doesn't return," said Rorianne later when a small kettle began to boil, "we will have to continue on foot. We must convince Babbe to lead us the rest of the way."

"That will not be necessary," the girl said as she returned from her bath in the creek. Searene was nearly unrecognizable, no longer slinking with her face downcast. Her hair was shiny and untangled, her skin clean and several shades lighter. The dirt and air of dejection had been a disguise that hid a strong, attractive, and intelligent face.

"I can lead you wherever you want to go. I was born in Lancene and know all of the large cities and most of the smaller ones. My father was a minor official, and I often traveled with him before he fell from favor."

Vlad looked thoughtfully at the girl and said, "We are on a quest that is at odds with King Vasper. Does it trouble you to help us?"

"No, I despise the King of Lancene. His officials ruined my father."

"Rorianne. Would you bring us the map to see if this girl can help us?"

"Is this a wise thing to do? If King Vasper or his henchmen discover our..."

"You forget, Rorianne," Vlad interrupted, "that I can detect falsehoods. We can trust this girl. The sooner we begin heading in the right direction, the sooner we arrive at our destination.

"And besides," he said almost as an afterthought, "she has the glow."

"What?" the princess said in surprise. "And you did not tell me until now?"

"It seemed better to wait in silence until her part became apparent."

"My name is Searene," the girl informed the three as Rorianne grudgingly retrieved the map.

They soon had it spread across the rock floor of the shelter. Rorianne pointed to a smudge on the parchment made to look like an accidental stain. It was located near foothills on the opposite side of the small chain of mountains they were about to cross.

"This is the city of Gvenheim," Searene said as she examined the map, "and here is the River Rugg. That means this mark is in the Silver Forest. It is forbidden to enter these woods. Even the Rovers shy from entering it when pursuing outlaws or escaped slaves."

The girl purposefully scrutinized her three new traveling companions. "Do you plan to travel there?"

"We must," answered Rorianne. "We search for a gate to another world."

"Because of Myrlyn?"

Rorianne's eyes opened wide in astonishment. "You know of this?"

"Every child has been told of Myrlyn's battle and how he defeated the giants. Our legends say the gate is hidden in the Silver Woods."

Rorianne folded like a deflating bladder. "If this is common knowledge, then King Vasper is already to the site."

"What good will it do him if he cannot detect it," Vlad reminded her. He kneeled and placed an arm around her sagging shoulders. "We are in Lancene and still free. We have a guide who can lead us. The prophecy is still working."

"Except for my friend," Elfred said with bitterness. "He was right when he said heroes often meet uncomfortable deaths in far locales."

"I do not believe he is dead," Vlad firmly told the young apprentice magician. "There is rhyme behind these happenings, I know it. We must not give up hope so easily."

Rorianne shook herself free, though not as if she were repulsed by the King of Bulgavia's embrace. "Your words are sound, I yield too easily. We will wait here through the day and night, then resume our quest. I cannot surrender to flagging spirits."

It wasn't long until Babbe woke with a throbbing headache. They asked if he would accompany them on the journey, but the little man reluctantly refused, saying he would have to catch up with the father and son to regain his Bitte.

"Dey're cowards, dey are. I'll get me Bitte and set off by meself. Maybe even git honest work. I is too old fur dis kinda of rough business."

The members of the camp found different chores to keep them busy as the day progressed. Vlad and Rorianne practiced swordplay. Elfred watched them for a while before climbing the bluff where he gazed at the sky for signs of a dragon. Searene joined him later. She didn't speak and also watched the skies.

The group gathered when the sun was at its highest point and snacked on bread, cheese and dried beef. Elfred found a spotted berry patch, and they wandered through it, collecting dessert.

"You and the dragon apprentice are very close," Searene spoke in half question, half stated fact.

Elfred had heard the girl coming and hoped she would continue her silence of the morning. He reluctantly answered.

"We were orphans together. We had nothing but each other's friendship. Drestin is more than my brother, and I fear I have led him to his death."

"You cannot blame yourself for his following of the Chronicles," she said softly. "His part was written before we were born. I now see how happenstances have drawn me here. I believed the gods had forgotten me until now."

"They could have continued to overlook my friend," Elfred replied in bitterness. "Drestin never wanted to be a hero, just to be a handler of his beloved dragons and to marry his sweetheart."

"I do not think your friend has fallen. His task in the Chronicles remains unfinished."

"The thought of being a heroine never occurred to me," she continued, "but I welcome it gladly over that of being a kitchen slave or chattel to such as Lefter."

"Even if it means your death?"

"I was dead. Now I have the chance to live, and if only for the time of the quest, it still be a better fate."

The girl's heart made Elfred feel is if his protests were the whinings of a coward. He remained silent and turned his face back to the sky.

~ * ~

The fire that night was kept small for fear a glimmer of the flames would warn unfriendly eyes. Rorianne and Vlad slept with their boots and swords close at hand. Elfred volunteered to take the first watch. He picked a tree not far from the cliff where the grass was waist high. The crown of the tree was snapped off as if from a fierce storm.

Elfred climbed to the top and sat on the highest limb. He was startled when Ralp appeared from nowhere to settle next to him. He reached out and drummed his fingers across the small beast's head, and it hissed in pleasure.

The apprentice magician leaned back and gazed about at the night sky and its familiar constellations. There was the hunter carrying a buck. Further over was the dragon and the sight of that constellation almost made him cry. Elfred reminded himself he was almost a full-fledged wizard and rubbed his eyes. In his self-absorption he failed to notice a swath of stars blinking one after another. The sudden explosion of a dragon's wings snapping open after a sustained dive almost sent Elfred plunging from his perch.

"Who-o-oo-ou-ou-ou-i-ou-e-e-e," a cry shattered the valley, silencing the crickets and sending an owl flapping irritably away. He heard a "whoosh" pass directly over his head.

Elfred watched a chunk of blackness sink into the moonlit meadow. He almost hurled a stink spell at his prankster friend, but instead rapidly made his way to the ground and ran to embrace Drestin, who was just climbing down from his own perch.

After a sound hug, Elfred stood back and punched the dragon apprentice in the arm. "That is for scaring the hell out of me."

The noise had drawn the others from their sleeping mats. Drestin was surprised to receive a hug from each of them, including Searene.

They all began rapidly asking questions until Vlad shouted for silence.

"The dragonmaster may tell us his adventures once we get the drake properly bedded for the night. Drestin is probably hungry. Someone heat the remaining stew while we remove the harness and tend the dragon."

Shadow was soon tied under the trees and Drestin sat within the small circle of traveling companions. Vlad told of the fight and Elfred's smell spell reversal. Drestin recounted how he let the drake have his head once the chase began and of a freezing climb into rarefied air before a violent plunge that made his heart climb into his throat. The pursuit lasted for most of the day. Twice the other dragons almost forced them to the ground.

They were saved by the mountains. A tiring Shadow, weighed down with a human, strained to reach the monstrous sweeps of granite ahead of his pursuers. The mountains were unusual formations, massive square columns of rock rising to unimaginable heights. Lightning and thunder constantly laid siege to the shadowed depths with swords of flames. Shadow reached the pillars first and banked sharply to soar among the immense columns in an attempt to lose their pursuers. It was a perilous task because of the unpredictable winds beating at them, trying to throw dragon and rider against the walls of stone or pull them to the lower depths where the lightning sizzled and crackled.

The gales also buffeted the Rover dragons. One that nearly caught up to them in its reckless haste was seized by the winds and smashed against rock. Broken, it fell, spinning to disappear into the frightening abyss.

A powerful draft lifted Drestin and Shadow to a pillar summit, and the dragon frantically tucked its wings to land roughly in the middle of the table top. Shadow clawed to keep a grip in the fierce gales and pulled himself into a fissure. Twice, bolts of lightning struck not far from them, splintering stone and sending grit into their narrow haven. There the two waited out most of the day until they were sure the other dragons were gone.

Elfred went back to his watch in a better state of mind. Once he walked to the nearby grove to give the stalwart dragon a fond rap on the scales. Dragons, especially ones this big, usually made him nervous. But he felt nothing but affection as he looked up into Shadow's large, brown eyes.

The night progressed smoothly with Rorianne then Vlad keeping watch. They broke camp at the first sign of dawn and continued their march on foot. Drestin was surprised at Searene's accompaniment and how the others seemed to accept her addition with no questions.

Searene again fell in besides Drestin, only this time she held her head up and looked the dragon apprentice in the eyes as she began her questioning. Only after several hours was he able to ask of her life. Searene told of her father being beheaded for a theft she believed was carried out by his superior. She was forced to become a scullery maid, only her refusal to bed the cook resulted in a beating. She fled to the beggars' quarters and was rounded up one night by a sweep of the city guards. From there she was sold in slavery to the smuggler's son only a week ago.

By mid-afternoon the group reached the cloud-covered foothills of the mountains they needed to cross. It was decided to rest and attempt crossing by air after dark. The weary apprentices welcomed the news and removed their boots to soak their blistered feet in a small stream.

Shadow seemed just as glad to end travel by land as the foot-sore humans climbed onto his back that evening. At Vlad's command, Shadow eagerly thrust his wings down in a mighty heave and lunged into the air. The Bulgavian king admitted to himself that he was also glad to be back in the air.

Not all his reasons had to do with weary feet or a rush to complete the quest. Rorianne sat behind him and occasionally she touched his shoulder as she leaned forward to speak.

The mountains on the map were the same odd, massive columns Drestin had described. Shadow occasionally turned into a spiraling climb when he needed to quickly reach a higher altitude for clearance and to keep above the lightning. It was an amazing sight. The sliver of a moon and stars were enough to dimly set the pale rocks aglow against the black sky.

Beneath them was a performance that not even the most talented conjurer could recreate--the continuous thunder and lightning like that of giant smithies sending out storms of sparks as they beat steel blades meant for gods.

Through it all continued the relentless beating of the dragon's wings. Though Shadow now carried five people, he still seemed to easily cross the highest peaks of the mountain chain and begin the downward flight. It was the strength of the creature's magic as much as it was the bone and muscle of the wings. The air grew warmer as they continued the descent. Elfred wished he had been able to view the strange formations during the day, though he was ready to forego the experience if it meant having to be pursued by murderous dragons.

He watched Searene lean forward to speak with Rorianne and point into the night-cloaked horizon. Elfred guessed she was giving directions to the Silver Forest. The Lancene girl said the woods were so named because of the trees. The undersides of the leaves were grayish-white and would flash silver during a wind.

Shadow shifted course a few degrees and Elfred could see Vlad leaning to the side as if looking for a landmark. The apprentice magician craned his neck but could just make out a river or creek far below. It gleamed faintly in the moonlight like a silver thread in the blackest of velvet.

Elfred was rudely jerked from his admiration of the night by what felt like Shadow slamming into the mountainside. The dragon had thrown its head back, braked with a powerful down stroke and dropped with closed wings. It was a classic evasive maneuver and only Vlad immediately recognized the dragon's tactic. The others gripped the harness tightly in terror at the unexpected plunge. Ralp squawked as he was thrown from his perch. The sharp crack of the wings slamming open was heard by Shadow's passengers as only a muffled report. Their ears had yet to adapt to the thicker air of the lower altitude, and their shouting sounded as if it were heard through wads of cotton.

"Rovers," came the cry from the front and each of the humans realized they were now in flight from the terrible Lancene warriors.

A message was passed back with Drestin turning to yell to his friend, "We will be flying over the Silver Forest in ten minutes. You must begin looking for the glow of Myrlyn's Gate."

It was a strange chase. The dragons were the only ones capable of seeing each other in the night sky, their dodging and turnings unexplainable to the night-blind humans. Shadow skimmed treetops in an effort to lose his followers, weaving and dodging among the foothills. The young dragon seemed to know he'd lose any race in the open sky carrying five passengers.

"Now," came a shout back to Elfred. He frantically began looking about the lightless terrain for any sign of a mysterious, glowing passage into another world. Twice Shadow made jarring changes in direction to escape his unseen pursuers. The third time was nearly too late, the massive dark body of another dragon almost clipping the humans from their seats as it hurtled overhead.

"We have passed the forest," Drestin relayed a message minutes later and the dragon sharply banked to make another pass over the woods.

Elfred felt his stomach clenching and he clamped his jaw shut to keep his teeth from clattering. Everyone was depending upon him, yet he could not see the gate. Elfred also knew that any second the Rovers might descend on their dragon, killing everyone and ending the quest--all because of his failure. Maybe Manfred was the wizard that should have come, the apprentice worried, as he continued to anxiously search for a sign.

The strain was preventing him from breathing. Elfred was panicking and felt his chest muscles constricting. He leaned his head back and forced himself to take a deep breath then let it out in one explosive discharge when he saw a ring of light high above them. No wonder he hadn't spotted it, Elfred thought in almost hysterical relief, he had been looking in the wrong direction.

"It is there, it is there," Elfred screamed as he pounded on Drestin's back. The dragon apprentice looked over his shoulder to see Elfred pointing wildly into the night sky. He leaned forward and repeated the message and hand signal to Searene. The message was passed on, and suddenly the dragon shot almost straight up, using all its reserve energy to reach their goal as quickly as possible.

The sudden shift to a higher altitude caught the other dragons by surprise and Shadow was able to quickly climb without having to dodge attacks. Vlad waited for another call as to the direction to send the dragon while mentally kicking himself for the foolish way he had seated everyone. It wasn't until they were over the mountain and looking for the gate that Vlad realized he should have placed Elfred right behind himself. He knew it was because he had been thinking too much of Rorianne. The Bulgavian king prayed his stupidity would not bring disaster to the quest.

Rorianne tapped Vlad on the shoulder and pointed to their right. He translated the command into knee movements and Shadow instantly veered.

The ring of light was actually moving in an attempt to escape the dragon. Elfred now realized why no one had been heard of accidentally traveling through the gate. The glimmering locus suddenly dropped. and he was about to relay another command when Shadow violently lurched. The dragon had been clipped and was tumbling out of control.

Chapter Eight

Garin wanted nothing more then to return to the peace and silence of darkness. He knew the room he was about to enter contained the bell and that once entered, he would be forced to confront it. Taking a deep breath, he stepped across the threshold.

~ * ~

Shadow overcame what was probably searing agony in his torn wing to pull himself out of the dive, though he wasn't able to do much more than begin a semi-controlled glide to the ground. Besides the pain, the dragon seemed dazed from a blinding light that exploded in front of him moments after the attack. He glided awkwardly to an abrupt landing.

Drestin was the first to dismount, forcing his bruised and battered body to slide to the ground and stumble to Shadow's injured wing. He kneeled and began his examination in the growing morning light, running his fingers along the strong, yet light, hollow bones of the wings. The apprentice was working fast to complete the inspection before the dragon regained consciousness.

He sat back and sighed. No bones were broken or major ligaments torn. The right wing had a slash about the length of his arm that would have to be sewn. The dragon wouldn't be flying for at least a week and even then not more than for a few hours at a time. Shadow's wound would take about three weeks to completely heal.

Drestin stood and began circling the animal to check for other injuries as the rest of the riders dismounted. He kneeled at the front of the dragon and looked for head injuries. Shadow opened his eyes and weakly licked Drestin's hands.

"How is he?" asked Vlad.

"I am not sure yet. We will have to wait until he can stand. He might have broken something when landing. The tear will heal, but it will take weeks."

"Weeks," Rorianne cried. "We need to enter that gate soon or Vasper will beat us to the jewel."

Elfred leaned back and squinted his eyes. The horizon was turning from a dark blue to deep scarlet. He could no longer see the gate.

Vlad gazed about and frowned. They had landed outside the Silver Forest in what appeared to be a meadow surrounded by common oak and maple trees. There was now enough light to see a barn at the far end of the clearing.

"We have landed on a farmstead. See if the dragon is able to walk. Maybe we can hide him in that barn before a patrol of Rovers spots us," Vlad said to Drestin.

The dragon rose shakily to his feet and painfully tucked in the injured wing. Vlad watched the sky nervously as Shadow slowly limped towards the shelter, surrounded by his human companions who could only offer verbal comfort.

A strange gate latch had to be worked before the group entered a yard next to the barn. Drestin led his patient through a large, sliding door and into a room with a rock floor. The building was filled with the smell of the hay and straw stored in the loft above their heads.

Shadow sank to the ground and closed his eyes.

Rorianne turned to Vlad and asked, "Now what?"

~ * ~

Garin hesitated, dazed by the fierce headache. It was time to silence the bell. He didn't feel strong enough for the deed, but there was no other choice. He reached out and picked up the receiver.

"What?"

"Mr. Garin Hemphill?"

"Yeah."

"Good morning. I'm calling about our new triple-paned aluminum storm windows now on sale..."

Garin had predicted the night before that it was going to be an ugly morning, the kind that made dying in one's sleep an attractive option. The suspicion first reared its ugly head at two a.m. when a blurry-eyed Garin first noticed the army of dead beer cans littering the war zone of the kitchen floor. A few of the casualties had even made it to the living room before giving up the spirit.

Luck was certainly not on Garin's side. He had hoped to sleep through the morning and most of his hangover.

"I don't need new windows. The ones I have are perfectly good."

"But sir, you haven't seen our deluxe, triple-paned, easy access windows guaranteed for the life of you or your house, whichever goes first. What's your heating bill?"

"What?"

"Your heating bill. Our windows can slash your heating bills in half."

Garin stretched the phone line and slumped into a kitchen chair. He winced at the bright morning light streaming in through the rippled glass of the old windows.

"My heating bill is fine. I don't need new windows."

"What color is your house?"

"What?"

"What color is your house? We also have a full line of enamel coated window frames that can be matched to any house color."

Garin guessed the telephone call must be some kind of penance. What other reason could there be for this torture?

"And?"

"And what?"

"What color is your house?"

"Chartreuse."

"What?"

"Chartreuse."

'You're putting me on. Your house is yellowish-green?"

Garin rubbed his eyes and wondered if the cord would reach all the way to the medicine cabinet where the aspirins were located.

"Yes, chartreuse. Do you have some kind of problem with that?"

"No, it's just that we don't get many chartreuse houses. Did you pick that color?"

"What?"

"Did you pick that color?"

"As a matter of fact, no. My mother picked it fifteen years ago. Of course it's getting a bit faded, but it is still recognizable as..."

"As...?"

"Shit."

"Shit?"

"Shit. I just saw something fly by my window."

"An aluminum window?"

"No, a tiny dragon."

"What?"

"A dragon."

"Now, is your window an ..."

"I just saw a tiny dragon fly toward the barn."

"Listen, if you don't want to buy new windows, why don't you just say so?"

"I have said so."

"You want to buy new windows?"

"No, I don't want to buy new windows. The ones I have are good enough."

"But sir, you haven't seen our deluxe, triple-paned easy access window guaranteed for the life of you or your house, whichever comes first. What's your heating bill?"

"What?"

"Your heating bill. Our windows can slash your heating bills in half."

Garin staggered across the kitchen and hung up the phone. There was some guilt involved. He'd read a recent Associated Press story about the psychological problems experienced by telemarketers. Continual rejection, much of it very rudely worded, resulted in severe trauma. The suicide rate for telephone salespeople, the story claimed, was almost as high as for people who consistently listened to country music.

He didn't bother putting on a shirt or shoes, wearing only his jeans as he rushed out the door. He was numb to the gravel under his feet as he picked his way across the rocky and weedy farmyard. He climbed the fence of the empty cattle yard, walked past the wooden feed bunks and stopped at the barn door. This was going to be as bad as answering the phone, he worried, and stepped inside.

It was worse than answering the phone. Five people were sleeping in a pile of straw thrown down from the mow. Four looked as if they were dressed for a Robin Hood movie. The fifth was clad in the leathers of a biker, but instead of a big Harley, sprawled across most of the concrete floor was an immense black dragon.

Garin only had so much stamina and it gave out when a small wyvern darted into view and stopped only inches from his nose. They stared at each other eyeball-to-eyeball before Garin's legs buckled and he collapsed to the floor.

~ * ~

"Does he have the plague?" wondered Searene as they kneeled around the fallen stranger.

"I think not," Drestin answered dryly after peeling back an eyelid and sniffing Garin's breath. "It appears this farmer is recovering from a bad case of alcohol poisoning. I would guess it to be an ale from the smell."

"His dress is strange," observed Rorianne. "Look at this odd device on his pants."

Garin blinked several times, made a feeble attempt to rise and yelped when he saw an unknown woman working at his zipper. He slapped her hand away and climbed shakily to his feet.

"Who, ah, what the hell is going on?"

The others also stood and Vlad touched the hilt of his sword meaningfully. "We mean no harm, but do not try and sound an alarm or we will be forced to have you bound and gagged."

Shadow was intently studying the new human. He remained prone, but his long neck brought his head directly over Vlad's shoulder.

"What is that?"

Vlad turned and looked around the room. "What?"

"What? What the hell do you think? That, that lizard."

"Dragons are not lizards," Drestin replied, sorely offended. "Dragons are warm blooded and more closely related to fowls."

"What? Are you trying to tell me this is a big chicken?"

Vlad eyed the stranger closely. "You have never seen a dragon?"

"No, and I don't think I'm seeing one now. This is crazy. I'm going back to bed and you'll all be gone when I wake."

"What country are we in?" Vlad demanded as he grabbed Garin by the arm.

He tried jerking free, but the King of Bulgavia's grip was like steel.

"What country are we in?"

"Give me a break. My head's killing me."

"What country are we in? Is this Lancene?" Vlad firmly persisted.

"No, this is Iowa. Now let me go to bed."

Vlad continued, closely scrutinizing the stranger before releasing him and turning to Rorianne.

"I believe we do not have to worry about pursuit by Rovers, Princess Rorianne. By the grace of the gods, it appears we have passed through Myrlyn's Gate."

Garin leaned back against the wall and watched expressions of amazement cross the faces of his odd visitors.

"How is that possible?" Rorianne asked, looking about her in new interest.

"We were right above the gate before Shadow was attacked," supplied Elfred. "By luck, we must have fallen through it into this world."

Rorianne was elated. "We have only to find Myrlyn's Stone and return home."

"It will not be that simple. Shadow needs time to mend," Drestin reminded the rest of the party. "And how do we find this stone?"

"The prophecy of Myrlyn says the heir of Rohneld will recognize the jewel," Rorianne replied.

Despite his pounding headache, Garin found himself reluctantly drawn into the conversation. "Gate, this world, prophecy, Stone of Merlin? What in the hell are you people talking about?"

Garin would have thought he'd stumbled onto escaped lunatics if wasn't for the dragon. As it was, his own voice carried a slight trace of hysteria. Vlad detected the tone and spoke to the citizen of this new world in a voice meant to be soothing.

"As I said, we mean you no harm. We have entered your world to find a dangerous weapon that it will not fall into the hands of an evil monarch and his loathsome mages. Our coming was foretold by an ancient wizard, Myrlyn, the same who hid the jewel in your world five hundred years ago."

"Merlin?"

"Yes, you have heard of him?"

"We have legends, really just fairy tales, of a magician called Merlin."

"The fairies know of Myrlyn?" Rorianne asked excitedly. "Where do they live, we must speak with them."

Garin eyed the woman as if he feared she was playing an elaborate joke. "There are no such things as fairies, just as there are no such things as wizards, magic, dragons, or...."

He paused on the last words and tried not looking at the large head watching him over the others' shoulders.

"Strange," Elfred said almost to himself. "A world where there are no wizards, dragons or fairies. This must be a very backward land."

"If there are no dragons or fairies," Rorianne asked suspiciously, "how do you know of them?"

"They're myths, children's stories. I can't take this any longer. My head is ready to burst. I gotta go get an aspirin."

"Aspirin?"

"Yeah, medicine for my headache."

Garin turned and headed for the door. The others made no move to stop him. They followed him outside and across the farmyard.

"By the way, my name is Garin." Politeness was so instilled into Garin that he now felt himself feeling guilty over not being cordial to dream characters. The others, in turn, introduced themselves.

He motioned them to enter his house and made a beeline for the medicine cabinet. Drestin watched with interest as Garin poured a glass of water and downed three of the white pills. Searene, who had been remaining in the background, touched the faucet and looked questioningly at Garin.

"Don't tell me you don't have running water?"

"We have it in streams or wells."

"Listen, I have to get a few more hours of sleep or I'm going to die. Make yourself at home. There's plenty of food in the refrigerator and cupboard."

Garin motioned to the refrigerator and received puzzled looks. He opened the door to reveal the food. Rorianne ran her fingers across sliced corned beef wrapped in plastic.

"You say you have no magic, yet there is an invisible cover over this meat, and it is very cold."

Garin just shook his head. He was too ill to be sucked into explaining the science behind heat pumps to figments of alcohol dementia.

Elfred bent over to closely examine a miniature toaster stuck to the door. "What is this?"

"Ah, a refrigerator magnet."

Looking with puzzlement between a small stove and the bigger version across the kitchen, the apprentice magician asked, "Are these familiars for larger machines that their magic may work?"

"No, they're just...ah," Garin began replying while rubbing his aching head and looking at his mother's numerous magnets plastered across the front of the refrigerator. Some were advertising local businesses and others were just tiny replicas of everything from grocery carts and Coca Cola bottles to fruits, vegetables and appliances. Most gripped family snapshots or clippings from the Bear River Community Press.

"They're, ah, our highest form of art. I'm a collector," he answered as he headed for the bedroom. Garin stopped at the kitchen door, sighed to himself and paused just long enough at the stove to demonstrate turning on a gas burner. He ignored the further gasps of surprise.

Drestin was starving and he wasn't about to turn down an offer of food. He retrieved the corned beef and began hunting in the refrigerator and cupboards for further sustenance. He pulled out plates and glasses and laid them on the table. Drestin couldn't identify much of what he saw, but he recognized bread, cheese, butter and eggs. A meal began taking shape.

"Look at this," said Searene, shaking a can of beans next to her ear. "These metal containers have pictures of food on them. Do you think they are of what is inside?"

"The artisans who accomplished these works should not be squandering their talents on such trivial tasks. I have never seen paintings appear so real. These are works of art," said Vlad, examining a can of Campbell's Soup.

"Let us see if these likenesses speak of the contents." Elfred pulled a knife from his belt and cut through the can. "They are beans and appear to be cooked."

Drestin followed suit, slicing off the top of another can.

"These look like tomatoes. I thought they were poisonous."

"Um, this is very good," Searene said after opening a third metal container. "I have never tasted anything so wonderful."

Vlad held the can up and examined at the label. "The letters are very simplistic, but similar to our own writing. It says 'Spam.' It must be a delicacy."

The questers continued to explore the kitchen as they ate.

Elfred returned to the magnets and read haltingly from a slip of paper under the replica of an Allis Chalmers tractor, "Check oil in Dodge, pick up jacket at cleaners, pay electric bill, dentist at 2 p.m. Monday."

"I would believe this to be the incantation that cools this box," Elfred began, then opened the door and poked at frozen fish sticks and ice cubes. "but I detect no signs of chill spells within this chest."

The others were just as mystified and mused over their own thoughts of this strange world.

~ * ~

Garin opened his eyes and reluctantly lifted his head. He was relieved to find the worst of the headache gone, leaving only a dull ache in its wake. He stared out the bedroom window and tried guessing the time. It looked like at least noon. From sitting, to sliding his feet off the edge of the bed then standing, each move had to be almost choreographed. He felt like he had the agility and reflexes of a twenty year-old dog. His recovery began speeding up once he made it into the bathroom.

A shower and clean clothes made him feel much better. Garin finished buttoning his shirt and headed for the kitchen. It wasn't until he spotted Elfred and Searene doing dishes at the sink that his earlier period of wakefulness came back to him.

Okay, there is a logical explanation for this, Garin thought while struggling to retain his composure. I must have met them earlier, and still half drunk and half asleep, I incorporated them into a silly dream about dragons and wizards. Garin was feeling pretty pleased with himself until the dreadful howling of an enraged cat tore at his eardrums.

The galloping of little feet could be heard coming down the stairs, across the living room floor and into the kitchen. Garin's old tomcat came sliding around the corner. It hit the outside door at a dead run and sent it flying open. He had only a couple more seconds to watch the cat before it disappeared behind the woodshed.

"I wonder what...?" was as far as he got before a miniature dragon zipped through the kitchen at eye level. It hit the door and punched a hole through the screen.

"Damn it, Ralp, cease chasing that cat." Elfred looked apologetically at his host. "He will not hurt the animal, he but likes to chase them."

Garin quickly made his way to the table and collapsed into a chair. His world was again unraveling, only this time he didn't have a massive amount of pain to distract him from the outlandish happenings. He could see the others of the troupe through the window. They were standing around the larger dragon as if discussing its health.

Searene picked up the last dish and crossed the kitchen to sit next to Garin.

He watched her drying the plate and said, "I have a dishwasher."

"Oh? We have not met anyone else. Your servant must not be home."

Garin sighed and shook his head. "I'm going nuts. This can't be happening."

Searene gazed at Garin in worry. The thin, pale man looked as if he were about to faint again. She reached out and touched his arm.

"Do not your eyes tell us that we are here? Cannot you hear us? Do you fear you are under an illusionary spell?"

Vlad entered the conversation and looked sternly at Garin.

"You protest too much, Master Garin. We are here and it is as we have spoken. We are on a quest from another world in search of Myrlyn's Stone. We ask that we can stay here at your holdings until we have completed our task and the dragon is healed. We will pay for our stay."

Vlad rolled three gold coins across the table and they wobbled to a stop in front of Garin. He picked one up and examined it in amazement. It was a beautiful coin with a dragon on one side. Turning it over, Garin saw the likeness of a man with a profile very similar to that of the visitor who had just tossed the coins.

"It is my grandfather," Vlad explained after observing his host's look.

An unacceptable notion flittered about the edge of his thoughts, and he tried shooing it away. It wouldn't leave. Garin held the heavy coin up higher and rubbed it between his fingers, feeling the raised lettering and the reliefs of the face and dragon. He looked across at Searene and noticed what a pretty young woman she was. He liked the way a stray strand of hair fell across her cheek.

The outlandish notion continued its nagging. He rose and walked to the door to stare through the screen at the mythical scene unfolding in the graveled driveway.

Bam. He staggered back and grunted, partly in surprise and partly from the remnant hangover protesting the sudden movement. Hanging on the screen door like a farm cat wanting to be let in, was the tiny dragon about the size of a small dog.

"Damn it Ralp, behave," Vlad complained.

Garin forced himself to press his face almost against the screen to closely examine the wyvern. It looked back at him with the expression of a mischievous pup. If the creature held perfectly still, it could have been an amazing piece of artwork--the creation of a talented, but demented jeweler. The eyes were gems and the tiny luminous scales looked like enameled pieces of metal or maybe porcelain. Only when Ralph opened his mouth did he take on the aspect of a living creature. He had the common pink, wet mouth of a cat or dog.

The feeling continued growing stronger, a strange churning in the gut and that rose to tighten his chest in a buzzing grip--the crazy belief this was all real. Garin reached out and hesitantly, with a trembling finger, touched one small claw hooked through the metal mesh. It felt cool and smooth. He was forced to take a deep breath and retreated to his chair where he took another deep breath.

"You're real, all of you, aren't you?"

Garin felt a surge of excitement and his dark mood abruptly lifted. He slid the coins back across the table.

"There's no need for paying," he protested, knowing his parents would've had a fit at the thought of charging guests for a visit. "You're right, I'm protesting too much. I'll blame it on the hangover."

"Have you tried hair of a dog?" Searene asked helpfully.

"No, I don't think I'll be able to look another beer in the face for a while."

"No. I mean hair of a dog. It works for the bite of mad dogs and over imbibing."

"Ah, no, I haven't, but I'm feeling much better now."

"We can use your help, Master Garin."

"You don't have to call me master. We usually just call everyone by their first name."

"Then what do you call your noblemen?"

"We don't have any royalty, unless you consider movie stars and doctors. We have a form of government called a democracy. That's when we all get together and pick our governing officials for a set amount of time."

It was now the Vlad's turn to look incredulous. "And this works? The commoners are intelligent enough to chose wise rulers?"

"Not all the time," admitted Garin. "Case in point was George W."

The Bulgavian king pushed aside these strange musings and returned to his original line of thought. "We need your help since you are familiar with this land. Have you ever heard of this Myrlyn Stone? It was left here five hundred years ago."

"That would have been before Europeans settled this area."

"Europeans?"

"Yeah, people with our color of skin. My ancestors came from another continent in the east. To me, you dress like Europeans did hundreds of years ago. Another people controlled this entire land then, but they've mostly moved west and south. Though there is a Mesquakie settlement about one hundred miles from here."

Garin could see he was just confusing Vlad.

"And you know nothing of a jewel of power?"

"That sounds like magic, and I've told you, there is no magic here. I've never heard of a jewel of power."

Instead of the wonder of these strange visitors wearing off, Garin found himself continually growing more excited. He stood and walked to the door where he could better see the others. It was a marvelous sight. The black dragon was like a highly-waxed limo, its thousands of ebony scales gleaming under the noon sun. Every movement sent waves of sparks shimmering across its flank.

"I'd keep that dragon in the barn most of the day. If word ever leaked out about him, you'd have more reporters crawling around here than flies on a cow pie."

"Reporters?" Vlad asked

"Yeah, people whose job it is to tell everyone the latest news."

"They sound like our village criers. It is true that we do not wish to bring attention to ourselves. The king of Lancene may find a way through the gate any time and we would not want our whereabouts known."

Garin was hardly listening. He eyes were riveted to the dragon. "I can't believe it, a real dragon. This is crazy. And you say it flies. Would it let me pet it?"

"It is not a dog," answered Vlad. "It would not feel such pats through its scales. But it does like attention from humans and loves to be rapped behind the ear. Come, you shall meet Shadow."

The sun was very bright. It threatened to send a repeat performance of the hangover straight through Garin's eyeballs and deep into his brain. He shaded his eyes and tried to ignore the pain, which wasn't that difficult since he was about to meet a dragon.

"Drestin," Vlad said, "will you introduce Shadow to our host?"

"Certainly, come over here."

Garin kept a wide berth as he walked behind the dragon as if it were a cow that might kick. He went to the front of the dragon and stood next to the apprentice. He tried not to flinch as Shadow stretched his neck and sniffed at the newcomer. Garin tentatively reached out and touched the single horn growing from the dragon's forehead. It was smooth and polished like an ivory piano key. He ran his fingers down the horn and across the scales. They felt like glass.

Remembering what Vlad said, he made a fist and lightly rapped along side Shadow's head. Garin was surprised when the dragon made a face like a grinning dog, though its tongue alone had the size of a miniature poodle.

Vlad walked to Rorianne's side and recounted his conversation about the jewel with Garin. She didn't know whether to be distressed or not. It seemed like such a formidable task, and yet they had made it through the gate against great odds. If only the chronicles would have said more about the part of the quest taking place this side of the gate.

"It is a strange world, and also familiar," she said. "Look at the sky or the grass and trees. They seem very ordinary. Yet there is a feeling I cannot put into words, a sense of difference."

Searene joined Garin and Drestin and looked up at the dragon's face. Shadow cocked his head and returned the girl's gaze.

"I, too, have never seen a flying dragon this close until meeting Shadow," she said.

"Dragons are rare in your world?"

"No. There are many dragons, but most have their wings clipped at birth. It is the law in all the nations to so abuse the creatures. Only the military and royalty are allowed winged dragons. The rulers fear the thought of commoners having the freedom that flight would give them."

It was easy for Garin to detect the bitterness in her words.

"It seems like a crime to mutilate such beautiful creatures," he agreed.

Drestin drifted over to Elfred while the other two continued their admiration of Shadow. Though still in pain from his injuries, the dragon seemed to enjoy the attention.

"Looks like you are about to have your woman stolen away," Elfred whispered loudly to Drestin. "You better get back there."

The dragon apprentice smiled. "Good, Annabeth would not have understood my need for two girlfriends."

"Oh, so you do consider yourself and Annabeth as a duo?"

Drestin ignored the bait and walked over to Vlad and Rorianne.

"We should put Shadow back into the barn. I have done all I can do. The stitches will hold until his wing is healed, but he needs a great deal of rest."

"That sounds sensible," Rorianne replied to Drestin. "And Vlad tells me it would be best to keep the dragon from the sight of others in this world. Take him back to the barn and we will all meet to discuss our future plans."

~ * ~

"I thought finding and crossing the gate safely would be the biggest challenge," said Vlad as he paced the kitchen floor, "but it appears locating the jewel will be the greatest task."

The others were seated around a massive oak table mounted on legs ending in imposing lion paws. The table was built to feed a large farm family as well as hired hands. Such a crew hadn't been served around it for more than fifty years, long before Garin was born. It originally belonged to his great-grandmother who had eight children. Garin was an only child of his generation.

"There must be some legend, some trace of Myrlyn's travel here," Rorianne insisted. "Is not there a wise man of the local village who knows of such things?"

Garin snorted. "We're talking about Bear River, Iowa. I doubt there's a wise man for a hundred miles. I got out of this berg years ago, but here I am, dragged back all the same."

"You are not happy here?" asked Searene.

"No, I'm not. I went away to college and hoped to never return other than to visit my parents on holidays. I graduated a year ago and now work for a large corporation in public relations..." Garin paused, seeing his guests had no idea of what he was talking about. "Anyway, I can't think of anyone who could be described as a wise man in Bear River, unless it would be Lorenzo Spasm."

"Lorenzo Spasm?"

"I'm just kidding. He's a local character who hangs around with my uncle. There are all sorts of stories floating around about him. My aunt swears he was a student of Timothy Leary's, a CIA operative in Tibet disguised as a monk, a member of Hell's Angels, helped in the development of the theory for the stealth aircraft and is an expert on everything from anthropology to quantum physics. All I know is that he lives in a big house way back in the woods and that he spends every afternoon in a bar."

The others were still looking puzzled.

"I'm saying he has a reputation for being some kind of genius, though I'm guessing he's more of an idiot savant. He'd have to be to come back and waste his life around here."

Garin paused when he noticed Rorianne's strange expression. "What is the matter?"

"The Chronicles, they mention a Lorenzo. It is a vague passage, and I thought it referred to a city or country. It is a strange name," Rorianne said. "We must go visit this man. Do you know him?"

"I've met him a couple times. Like I said, my uncle hangs around with him. They have a couple beers together almost every afternoon when Uncle Al gets off work."

"Does something worry you?" Vlad asked.

"I was just trying to figure out how I'd explain this to Lorenzo. He'll think I'm nuts."

"We will show him Shadow," Drestin said with a smile. "It appears to have worked with you."

"Okay, I'll give him a call."

Garin stood and crossed the kitchen to an old dial phone that hung on the wall. The others' puzzled looks magnified.

"This is a telephone. I can talk to people great distances away on it."

"And it is not magic?" asked Elfred.

"No, it is science. I'll try and explain it later."

Garin didn't know why he felt so stupid standing in front of a skeptical audience of five while holding a piece of plastic to his ear. They were watching him so intently that he nervously turned and faced the wall. A year-old calendar hung next to the phone. On it, in his mother's precise handwriting, were a half dozen phone numbers written in pencil, his number included. Seeing it caused an unexpected watering of his eyes. He was grateful to hear Lorenzo answer the phone.

"Lorenzo? This is Garin Hemphill, Al Chives' nephew. I don't know if you remember me.... Good. Ah, listen, something very strange has happened and I'm hoping you might stop out at the family farm. How strange? Well, about as strange as it gets, believe me."

Garin was nervously twirling the phone cord and pacing at the end of it like a dog on its chain.

"No, nothing like that. What? No ghosts." Garin covered the phone and whispered loudly, "See, I told you he was a nut. Wanted to know if I'd seen ghosts."

"And have you?" whispered back Searene, looking nervously about the room. "I saw two last year."

Shaking his head, Garin put the receiver back to his ear.

"No, it's not a UFO. What? Well, it's hard to tell you over the phone. I don't think you'd believe me. No, really, you'll have to see it to believe it.... OK, you asked for it. I have five people from another world who crossed over on the back of a thirty foot black dragon and are searching for a magical stone tossed here five hundred years ago by a wizard named Merlin."

Garin tensed, waiting for Lorenzo to hang up. Instead, Garin's eyes opened wider and he said, "Sure, I guess I could come there. An hour is fine. Thank you."

He hung up the phone and slid down onto on a small stool.

"Will this Spasm come?" asked Rorianne.

"He wanted us to meet him at the bar in an hour."

"What did he say when you told him of us?"

Looking dazed and confused, Garin quoted Lorenzo's simple reply, "Not again!?"

Chapter Nine

The day was turning into a roller coaster for Garin--from a late night, drunken self-pity fest to near-death pain upon awakening then from total denial of his visitors to now eagerly taking part in a preposterous "quest." Garin felt good, really good. He hadn't felt this good since before being notified of his parents' deaths in an auto accident six weeks ago. Those memories began surfacing, but he strongly pushed them away. He refused to let himself fall into that trap.

The sky was incredibly blue and a few scattered clouds glided by lazily. He hung his elbow out the window while his hair whipped in the wind. He looked over and smiled at Rorianne and Searene. He found it funny that they were excited about driving down a gravel road in an old pickup after sailing through the skies on a dragon. He checked his mirror to see how the others were handling it. Drestin caught his glance and waved. The three in the back of the truck were grinning widely at the experience. The mood was contagious. Even Rorianne seemed to be lightening up.

Garin had forgotten some of the good experiences of growing up in rural Iowa. He remembered driving this pickup in high school. He and his friends spent Sunday afternoons traveling the back roads with the radio blaring. Every few minutes someone from the back would climb onto the running board and into the passenger side of the cab while the driver slid out the other door. The rider in the middle would then scoot behind the wheel and take over driving. This circulation would go on all afternoon.

Kicked-up rock was pinging on the underside of the truck, and the dust swirled behind them, leaving a slightly gritty taste in his mouth. It was a great day, Garin thought, as he admired the vibrant green of the knee-high corn. A shadow flittered across the road and he looked up expecting to see a hawk or turkey vulture.

Garin hadn't meant to slam on the brakes that hard. The two women threw out their hands to catch themselves on the dash and the men in back went tumbling. The rear began to slide and the pickup came to rest sideways in the middle of the road. Vlad was already out of the truck with his knife drawn. Garin had talked him into leaving the sword at home, but no amount of arguing would convince him the knife should also stay.

"What had happened? Are we under attack?"

Garin climbed to the ground and coughed a couple times because of the dust cloud.

"No, everything is fine. It's just that it caught me by surprise."

"It?"

"It. That thing." Garin was pointing to the sky. Circling above them was the wyvern, Ralp. "We can't let anyone see that thing or the whole countryside will be in an uproar."

"Ralp, get down here," shouted Elfred. "I mean it, come here now."

Ralp reluctantly obeyed and drifted down in a lazy spiral to land with a thud on the truck's hood. The mini-dragon nonchalantly began licking himself. Garin had been told that wyverns and dragons produced a wax in their saliva for polishing their scales.

"Ralp, I told you to stay with Shadow," Elfred snapped. "Now get back there."

The wyvern gave no hint of hearing his master. The apprentice magician reached across the hood and gave a good jerk to Ralp's tail which sent the creature whirling around and chirping madly. Garin could still hardly believe he was really seeing a little brown and white dragon rather than some fantastic puppet. Ralp was peeved and glared back in outrage at the indignity.

"Do not give me that look," commanded his master. "Now get back to Shadow or I will lock you in a box."

The plump wyvern gave one last incensed rebuke that sounded like the angry chatter of a squirrel then launched himself into the sky and back toward the farm.

"He could really screw up some bird watcher's day," noted Garin as they climbed back into the truck.

The rest of the trip was uneventful. Garin couldn't help glancing occasionally at Searene. He had never seen such a beautiful face. Rorianne was also attractive, but he found her too intimidating. Searene was still wearing her white cotton dress while Rorianne wore a pair of Garin's jeans. The princess had been wearing pants as part of her disguise, but she told Garin women didn't normally wear them in her world. She was surprised and delighted to find that women commonly wore them in Garin's country.

"It is so hard to sword fight in a dress," she commented with a straight face. Garin didn't know if she was kidding--and he didn't want to find out.

The two apprentices were also wearing some of Garin's blue jeans along with their own shirts and light jackets. They were both close to Garin's build and height. Vlad refused to wear anything but his black, light canvas shirt and pants. He was also wearing his black leather jacket and chaps.

Only the apprentices appeared overly impressed with Bear River as they climbed from the truck and headed across the street to the New Yorker Lounge and Supper Club. They'd all given Garin brief backgrounds about themselves. Garin guessed the castles and capital cities the king and princess lived in were much bigger than his hometown. Searene had also spent much of her life visiting many cities in Lancene. Drestin and Elfred were the only two of the group who grew up in a small village.

They stopped outside the door and Vlad slowly read the name of the bar on a sign hanging above their heads.

"It's not really a supper club," Garin warned. "I think it is somebody's idea of a joke."

"I do not know what a supper club is, but as long as they have ale, I will be satisfied," remarked Drestin.

Garin opened the door and led the way inside. He paused for several seconds to let his eyes adjust to the smoky, dimly lit bar. He was glad he had thought to explain cigarettes to others before leaving for town. Garin spotted Lorenzo sitting by himself in a corner. He had to admit there was a presence about the man, something immediately noticeable when first meeting Lorenzo. If Garin had to describe him, he would say Lorenzo had the air of a Jesuit priest who had seen God face-to-face and decided to become a gunrunner. Then again, he thought, maybe it was all the supposed LSD and magic mushrooms he'd taken in his fabled youth.

Lorenzo stood when the group reached his table. Rorianne and Searene were both surprised when he also shook their hands--such greetings were not extended to women in their own world.

Garin saw that even Vlad was staring oddly at the man.

"I see you made Vlad and Rorianne leave their swords at home," Lorenzo said after they sat.

"How did you know?" Garin asked in surprise.

"The same way I know Drestin is quite often around dragons, Searene is used to long trips, Elfred is a magician, Rorianne is a member of a royal family and originated this quest and Vlad is a prince or a king. Also, all five of you are orphans and recently killed several people."

"Magic," Elfred said with certainty. "He has used a farseeing spell, though I cannot detect any sign of it."

Lorenzo smiled. "Just simple deductions. Drestin's boots are deteriorating in the same way a farmer's boots begin to rot from the uric acid in cow or hog manure. You did mention they flew here on a dragon, so I took a lucky guess that he was responsible for the dragon's care.

"It's hardly worth mentioning that Searene's shoes are made for walking and climbing. The leather does not appear that old, yet the shoes show the scuffs and wear of excessive use.

"The smell of sulfur and a tincture of copper still lingers lightly about Elfred, as well as that of several other odors I can't identify. There are various chemical stains on his shirt and fingernails. In our world, these would be the signs of a chemist. Since Garin mentioned there was magic in your world, I guessed that he was either a magician or dabbled in alchemy.

"Rorianne carries herself in a way that suggests she is used to having others obey her. She could be the daughter of a rich merchant or trader, but she also wears a ring with a royal crest.

"Rorianne and Vlad were visibly wary when they entered the bar and both made unconscious gestures with their right hands, as if wanting to rest them on the pummel of a sword that would normally hang from their left hips. At first Vlad was a puzzle to me. He moved like a trained soldier, yet also like someone used to giving orders. He is too young to normally be a high-ranking officer in the military--unless he is also a ranking member of a royal family. It would not be unusual for a king or prince to have military training."

"How did you know we were all orphans, recently killed several people and that Rorianne originated the quest?" demanded Vlad.

Lorenzo leaned back in his chair and smiled. "Sherlock Holmes once said, 'I believe I will not tell you more of this at the moment, sir. You know a conjurer gets no credit once he has explained his trick, and if I give away too much, you will certainly think me the ordinary fellow.'"

Garin had been impressed by Lorenzo's statements, but he now saw how obvious the observations were. He wasn't going to be taken in by this lunatic, no matter what his aunt and uncle thought of him. There was one thing about the man that puzzled him.

"You don't seem very surprised by all of this," Garin noted. "Are you accustomed to people visiting from other worlds?"

He'd meant it to be sarcastic, but Lorenzo didn't notice or chose to ignore the younger man's tone of voice.

"Strange things happen. Now tell me," Lorenzo said turning to Rorianne, "what you are doing here and why?"

"We are on a quest. Five hundred years ago a great magician named Myrlyn battled the sun giants..."

Rorianne told of the Chronicles of Myrlyn and how she gathered the others for the quest. A waitress took an order for a couple pitchers of beer while Rorianne related the recent events. Her audience leaned back in their chairs to relax. Garin could tell Drestin was struggling not to show amazement when the jukebox began playing.

A half hour passed before she finished the tale. There was a moment of silence, and Lorenzo stared at a wall lost in thought before finally speaking.

"Have you ever heard of the Inner Macedonian Revolutionary Society, Ibn Saud's Wahabis, the Knights of Templar or Dorga, the fish-headed god of death?"

The five stared back in puzzlement.

"It was just a thought."

"What does that have to do with this problem? Can you help them or not?" Garin asked.

Lorenzo looked intently at his friend's nephew. "I'm sorry about the auto accident and your parents' deaths. I heard you were taking it pretty hard. They were nice people."

The mention of his parents caught Garin by surprise.

"I also hear you're pretty upset about having to stick around while the estate is settled. Been holing up at the farm drinking a lot. Bear River must seem pretty mundane."

Garin fought back an angry response. He didn't want to appear surly in front of his guests.

"I'm getting by."

Lorenzo turned to the others. "This does present a problem. Our people are relatively new to this land. Before us, this area was sparsely populated by a race that had numerous languages and cultures. This state, Iowa, is a territory within a larger nation. Its name comes from a native word meaning beautiful land."

Lorenzo was falling into his lecture mode, a delivery his close friends were all only too familiar with.

"The first few humans arrived in Iowa about 12,000 years ago, though since then numerous groups have lived here..."

Lorenzo continued for about ten minutes. Garin glanced at the others, expecting them to look bored with the recital. They all appeared to be intently listening to the mini-history lesson.

"The Oneota first appear about 1,000 years ago. Within three hundred years it appears they drove out the Great Oasis people, along with others who had arrived in Iowa, including the Mill Creek and the Glenwood peoples."

"For God's sake, Lorenzo," interrupted Garin. "These names and dates mean nothing to them. Get to the point."

Instead of agreeing with Garin, the others looked aghast and Elfred said, "Garin, I beg of you, do not interrupt a teacher when he speaks."

Garin shook his head and hunched down in his chair. Give me a break, he thought.

Lorenzo ignored the outburst and continued.

"The Oneota were the only people to last into Iowa's modern history. They became known as the Ioway and were related to the Oto tribes. They extended into states to the east. About three hundred years ago the first written record of contact between the Ioways and people of European descent, or Whites, who Garin and I number among, was made in Wisconsin. The European culture continued to press westward and about one hundred seventy years ago the Ioways were forced to Missouri, a state to the south of Iowa. They were later moved to an area to the west on the border of two states called Nebraska and Kansas."

Lorenzo had drawn a rough map of the Midwestern states on the table with a finger dipped in beer. The members of the quest almost touched heads as they leaned forward to watch him pointing out the migration routes.

"Also about three hundred years ago two other tribes moved into Iowa, the Sac and the Mesquaki, also known as the Fox. War between the Whites and Sac and Mesquaki broke out about the same time the Ioways were moved out of Iowa. The native tribes lost and were forced to leave the state about one hundred sixty years ago. The Mesquaki were persistent. Many hid out and others slowly slipped back from the reservations in Kansas. The White governing body of Iowa passed a law one hundred fifty years ago allowing them to stay. The tribe bought 3,200 acres about one hundred miles from here and they remain there to this day."

Rorianne looked up from the beer map. "But according to your tale, these Mesquaki were not here when Myrlyn hid the jewel."

"Correct."

"Does this mean we must travel here," she asked, pointing to an area on the tabletop, "to find the people who once lived here?"

"Yes, except there is one problem. From what I know, this forced move and resettlement with other tribes has all but wiped out their language, arts and religion. The Europeans basically destroyed their entire culture. I doubt any memory or tale of such an event would still exist"

"From what he knows," Garin scoffed in a low voice to Vlad. "I wouldn't be surprised if he made the whole thing up."

Vlad sighed and looked at his new friend. "You forget I have the gift of truth seeking. He speaks only honest words. And besides, he also has the glow."

"Doesn't Myrlyn's prophecy mention anything about how the jewel was hidden?" Lorenzo asked Rorianne.

"The Chronicles only say that Myrlyn sent the jewel through the gate to keep it out of the hands of those who would abuse its powers."

"And what better place to send it than a world where magic is unknown," Spasm noted.

"The Chronicles also prophesize that the King of the Black Lake, with the help of dark powers, will seek out the jewel for a conquest of unbelievable horror and evil. Such a war, it says, 'will leave both the people and the earth barren, each inhabited only by charred souls and corpses.'

"This can only be averted by a group seeking to reach the jewel first, and destroying it by magic with 'sky fire' in the Mountain of Pillars. I have sought some meaning to this in many libraries and ancient tomes, yet it still escapes me.

"Some members of this quest are specifically described and told where they could be found, others are spoken of in only the vaguest terms."

Lorenzo seemed lost in thought as he twisted strips of a paper napkin into string.

"You say dragons were not yet domesticated during Myrlyn's time. This means he either levitated or somehow hurled the stone through to my world. I suggest we make a search of the area immediately below the gate where it might have landed. How is the gem described?"

"There is no description. It is only written that the magician will be able to identify it."

"Perhaps it will glow like the gate." Elfred volunteered.

Vlad noticed Lorenzo still seemed distracted. "Is there something else that worries you?"

"More like puzzlement. There are several things about your world and your entry into ours that raise questions in my mind, but nothing we have to worry about right now. The day's a wasting. I say we begin our search."

Lorenzo pushed his chair from the table and stood. The others followed suit. The door opened as they reached the front of the tavern and in walked four men and three women, all obviously bikers in their leather jackets, engineer boots and bandannas. One had an "ABATE" patch on his right arm. The men silently eyed Rorianne and Searene as they headed to the bar. The tallest of the group stopped and took a second look at Vlad.

"Hey dude, where's your bike? I didn't see any parked outside."

The biker was the same height as the Bulgavian, though about twenty years older and fifty pounds heavier. If it weren't for the age difference, potbelly, and graying hair, the two could have been brothers. Both wore their hair long and were dressed in black leather jackets, chaps and boots.

Vlad answered him with a puzzled look, "Bike?"

"Yeah, whatcha riding?"

"A dragon."

"Dragon?" Now it was the other's turn to look puzzled. "I hope you don't mean a Jap bike. What's its name?"

"Shadow."

"Shadow? A Honda Shadow? Hell, you shouldn't be wearing those leathers if you're riding a Honda."

The tone of the conversation was taking an ugly turn. The other three men sitting at the bar spun on their stools and watched with interest. To Drestin, the scene was beginning to resemble the run in at the Boar's Breath Inn. Garin was tensing, fearing the worst.

Lorenzo stepped between the two. "Excuse my friend, he doesn't speak English that well, being from Bulgavia. He wouldn't think of riding a rice burner. Shadow is just the nickname he's given his Fat Boy."

The biker stepped back and eyed the newcomer with suspicion.

"And who the hell do you think you are?"

"My name is Lorenzo Spasm," he answered, holding out a hand.

The other's eyes opened wide and he backed up another step. The tavern took on an uncommon silence and the bartender nervously edged towards the phone.

"Did you say Lorenzo Spasm?"

"Do I stutter?"

Garin felt a lump settling in his stomach and Rorianne ached to have her sword.

"God damn," the biker roared and stepped forward to put Lorenzo in a bear hug. "Spasm, you son of a bitch. I haven't seen you since ninety-nine in Frisco. You probably don't remember me. I'm Happy Bear."

Happy Bear turned to his companions. "This here is Lorenzo Spasm. He rode with the Angels out of L.A. Craziest partier I ever saw. He's still a legend on the West Coast. Spasm's even sat in with the Dead."

The others jumped from their stools and were soon shaking hands and pounding Lorenzo on the back. Garin stood in silent amazement as the members of the quest were introduced to Roxanne, Michelle, Hairy Moe, Wart and Steve.

The seven Harley riders were heading cross-country to New York when Bear's engine blew early that morning. They were stranded in Bear River for at least two days until parts arrived. Lorenzo promised to meet them that night at the bar for a few drinks.

"The Dead, did he mean the Grateful Dead, the rock band?" Garin asked as they walked to the pickup.

"Yeah, Jerry and I used to hang out. It's no big deal," Lorenzo modestly answered. "We met when I used to fill in as a drummer for a Moby Grape reunion."

"Moby Gape?"

Lorenzo sighed. "You are young, aren't you?"

The topic ended when they came to the pickup. Lorenzo jumped the tailgate with Drestin. Joining them were the two women.

"Tell me about Fat Boys and rice burners," Garin heard Vlad asking Lorenzo as he climbed in behind the wheel.

The truck retraced its route for several miles of blacktop then turned onto the gravel road Garin guessed to be closest to the gate. He passed two pickups and a tractor coming from the opposite direction, both times returning their minimalist farmer waves--straightening the two fingers of his left hand from the steering wheel.

Elfred kept his eyes glued to the sky. Garin pulled off the road two miles north of his farmhouse. On the left side of the road was a cornfield with a wooded, rolling pasture to the right.

"This is about where the gate should be, according to your directions."

The apprentice magician climbed out of the truck, shaded his eyes and searched the skies. He frowned.

"It see no trace of it. I would not think it would move far from its position."

"Try driving another half mile," suggested Lorenzo.

"What will a half mile help?" asked Garin in exasperation.

"If the gate only opens in one direction," Lorenzo patiently explained, "it would only be visible from one side, and that would be the side facing the farm.

Elfred jumped back in the truck and they continued slowly down the road. A couple minutes later Garin put on the brakes when his passenger began shouting excitedly.

"There, I see it. It is over there."

Elfred was pointing to a spot high above their heads and to the right. Everyone craned their heads to view only blue sky.

"I think Old Man Moeller owns that land," said Lorenzo. "I'll run up to the house and see if he's home. It's a couple months late for mushroom hunting, and he'll probably wonder what the commotion is about. Why don't the rest of you spread out and see what you can find."

Garin reluctantly slid out from behind the wheel of the pickup. He didn't know why he found taking suggestions from Lorenzo so irritating. Maybe it was because he'd already formed an image of Lorenzo as a kook and Garin hated being proved wrong. Or maybe he was just jealous that Lorenzo seemed to have taken over. Garin was not normally that petty, and the irrational feelings bothered him.

Lorenzo noticed Garin's hesitation.

"You're his neighbor. Maybe it would be better if you spoke to Moeller. You could take Searene with you. It might be easier with a pretty young woman."

Garin was going to protest, but Lorenzo was already halfway across the ditch and catching up to the others climbing the fence. Searene smiled. Garin shook his head and slid back behind the wheel.

The limestone farmhouse was just up the road, set back at the end of a long lane and surrounded by ancient oaks. It was built in the late 1800s and still had the gingerbread trimming around the porch and windows. The house was in need of new shingles, but it and the yard were neatly kept.

Moeller, probably now in his middle 90s, had always been an old man to Garin, ancient even when he was still a kid. He remembered occasional visits here with his father. The farmer was a bachelor and always seemed eager to talk.

"It seems very peaceful here," remarked Searene as they drove down the lane. "Your king must be very pleasant."

Garin smiled but didn't feel like going into another long explanation dealing with government.

"It is peaceful," he admitted, "too damn peaceful. Nothing ever happens here. You might as well be dead."

"I have seen people die when things are not peaceful. The people of this land are very lucky."

He didn't know how to answer that, especially after hearing her story.

"You seem very bitter. Maybe you will think differently after traveling to our world."

He looked over in surprise. "Your world! What makes you think I will be going to your world?"

"The Chronicles. Rorianne said they speak of others from this world returning to guard and destroy the jewel. I heard Vlad telling her that you, as well as your friend, carry the fire that signifies a member of this quest."

The shock didn't have time to settle in. Old Man Moeller was hanging a row of identical bib overalls and blue work shirts out to dry. The farmer waved at the familiar pickup and began walking toward Garin and Searene.

"Good afternoon, young man. I haven't seen you since your parents' funeral. Was wondering if you'd come for a visit."

"Hello, Mr. Moeller. How are you today? This is a friend of mine, Searene."

The old man grinned at the girl and gave the young man what he thought was a sly wink. Garin suddenly realized he didn't know what to say. Whatever excuse Lorenzo had concocted for having a half dozen people traipsing across the farmer's land, he had failed to it pass on to Garin.

"Ah, Mr. Moeller, Searene and some of her friends are from out of state and they've never really seen what Iowa countryside looks like. They saw your timber from the road and wanted to walk through it. I thought I better tell you so you'd know what was going on."

"That's fine. Don't mind people hiking or fishing, just those darn hunters from the city. They're almost always shooting a cow or hog. Tell your friends to look for the remains of a log cabin by the windmill, that's where my great-grandfather built the first house in 1849. Not much of it left now. My grandfather moved to higher ground 'cause the creek kept flooding."

"Your family was the first to settle this farm?"

"Sure was. I remember my grandfather telling how they had to cut the trees with handsaws and cleared the fields of stumps with teams of horses. Almost wish the fields were back in walnut and oak. They're worth more now than corn."

"Were there still Native Americans about?"

"You mean Indians? Sure was, though my grandfather said there were only a few left when he was a kid. Said they didn't know about knocking on doors, would just look in a window to see if anyone was home. Used to scare the heck out of my great-grandmother."

Garin kicked at an acorn and wondered how he'd broach the subject of the jewel.

"One of my friends is a geologist. Do you know of any interesting rock formations around here? Something out of the ordinary?"

"Well, let me think." The farmer cocked his head and scratched at his white-stubbled chin. "There are a lot of fossils down by that old quarry. Watch out, it's filled with water and pretty deep. Got some nice bullheads in it, though. And every now and then geodes turn up in the creek. Of course you won't find anything as interesting at that big piece of quartz my grandfather found when he pulled up a tree stump. It was tangled in the roots, green like a Mason jar and as half as big as my arm."

"Green quartz?" Garin tried not letting his excitement show. "Do you still have it?"

"Heck no," laughed the old farmer. "You young people don't know anything. My cousin wrote a story all about it for the Bear River Centennial Book. No, my grandfather gave it away years ago."

"Gave it away? To whom?"

"Why, to the Dickeyville Grotto. It's still the prettiest stone there, almost glows."

It was all Garin could do to keep from running back to the pickup. An almost impossible job--to track down a jewel tossed into this world five hundred years ago--and he did it. Garin politely refused an invitation in for lemonade and forced himself to walk slowly to the driver's side of the truck.

"I can't believe it," Garin screamed as he headed back to the gravel road. "The jewel is in the Dickeyville Grotto."

"Rorianne will be very excited," said Searene. "I think she was believing her quest almost impossible."

"And I did it. That'll show Lorenzo."

"Yes, it was fortunate that he thought of visiting the old man."

Garin frowned at the comment.

"Why do you dislike this Lorenzo?"

"I don't dislike him."

Searene shook her head. "No, I see your impatience with him, even disrespect."

"I don't know," Garin sighed. "I guess it's because he stuck around here. Life seems so dead here, so pointless. You have to be stupid or crazy to live in Bear River."

"And yet your parents choose to live here?"

"They didn't have a choice. They were born here and had to run the farm."

"But you born here and still had a choice?"

"Yes I did," Garin snapped. "And I made that choice. I left."

There was silence in the truck as they followed their way back to where the others had crossed the fence. He pulled the pickup to the side of the road and turned off the engine.

"I'm sorry I yelled at you," Garin apologized. He stared out the window and watched a cow and calf grazing in the shade of a large cottonwood, lazily brushing at the flies with their tails. "There's been a hang-up in my parents' will, and I've been trying to straighten it out. Staying here this long is really getting on my nerves."

Searene smiled in understanding. At least Garin took it to be understanding, though he was just glad she wasn't pressing the issue. They climbed the fence and crossed the narrow pasture to the trees on the side of the hill. Hidden in the shadows were outcroppings of rugged limestone covered with a plush carpet of haircap and broom mosses. Small, twisted cedar trees, ferns and wild flowers grew from the pockmarks, turning each projection of rock into a Japanese garden.

"There is a small world here," said Searene as she picked a snail from the moss. "This is a pretty land."

Garin was only half listening, searching the surroundings for any sign of the others' passings. The day was turning hot, and he could feel a trickle of sweat rolling down from his armpit.

"I wonder where the rest have gone."

"That way," she replied, not looking up as she examined the blooms of a blue phlox.

"That way? How do you know?"

Searene patiently turned from the plants and took his hand. "I will show you."

He didn't like the way she spoke to him, like Lorenzo had, as if they were humoring a small child. Garin also wanted to object to her leading him like he was a toddler, but found he liked the feel of her smaller hand in his.

119

"See these weeds, how they have been stepped on?"

"Maybe the cows did it"

"Cows do not wear shoes." She was pointing to a footprint.

"What, cows don't wear shoes in your world?"

She looked at him suspiciously then smiled. "No, only silken bonnets."

They both laughed and Garin found himself relaxing. Several times she asked the name of a flower or tree and Garin had to admit ignorance. He could tell she thought his lack of knowledge about the land he grew up on very strange.

The timber was alive with the sound of birds. They flittered above their heads, stopping to scold the humans when they passed too close to their nests. A number of bushes and trees were flowering and their sweet scent mixed pleasantly with the wet smell of the rich, black dirt of the timber floor.

"If I hadn't heard the whereabouts of Myrlyn's Jewel from the old man," said Searene, "I would have believed they found the stone."

"Why do you say that?"

"They split into different directions but returned to follow someone on this path. I believe the lead person to be Lorenzo, and he found something the rest wanted to see."

The pronouncement put Garin back into a gloomy mood. What if the green quartz was really just that, and Lorenzo had found the real Jewel of Myrlyn? They crossed the ridge and the two could hear the faint sound of voices. Several minutes later they came to a clearing and stood on the high side of the quarry the old farmer had warned them about. The other side was almost level with the water.

Garin looked down to see the party splashing and swimming in the water. He shook his head at their lack of dedication to the search and turned to follow a small path leading around the quarry. It wove through the numerous trees and large chunks of rock. It was only after he and Searene reached the other side that he realized the others were swimming naked. The clothes were left in piles on the bare rock as if the people in them had dissolved.

"Come on in," yelled Lorenzo, who was lazily dog paddling across the water. "Reminds me of the time I skinny-dipped with Jenifer Aniston at a Burning Man festival."

Searene put her hand to her mouth and giggled at the sight of the wavering blurs of the apprentices' pale bodies against the quarry's deep, dark waters.

"It's a common practice in Bulgavia, and only the unsophisticated find it amusing," huffed Drestin as he turned his back to her.

The girl looked questioningly at Garin then turned to scurry behind a bush. It seemed to take only several seconds before Serene came running out, a white flash that disappeared in a large splash of water. She came up laughing and sputtering. The brief glance was enough to tell him that whatever her age, Searene had the body of a woman.

Garin was hot and the water looked inviting, but he wasn't used to swimming naked with friends, let alone virtual strangers. He had also been imagining the looks on the others' faces when he told of finding the gem's whereabouts. That image did not include his awed audience splashing around buck-naked. He glanced quickly at Searene then forced himself to turn away.

"I'll meet you at the truck when you're ready to hear my news."

Garin was sticky with sweat by the time he was halfway back to the road. More than once he regretted his hasty decision as he wiped his sleeve across his forehead and remembered Searene's run to the quarry. He cursed himself, and he cursed Lorenzo for taking the time to goof around in the quarry when there were such important tasks to accomplish.

"Garin. Garin, please wait."

He turned to see Rorianne running breathlessly to catch up with him, her wet hair flying and clothes in disarray.

"Is it true? Did you find the stone? Searene says you know where Myrlyn's Stone is. Do you?"

Rorianne had taken hold of Garin's shoulders and in her fervor was almost shaking him off his feet. She hadn't stopped to completely button her shirt and with any other woman as beautiful as Rorianne, Garin would have been aroused by the sight of her breasts slipping in and out of view. The running had reddened her cheeks and her gray eyes were wide and bright. But the warrior woman appeared nearly crazed and her steel grip held him too firmly. He knew she was only excited about the possible discovery of the stone's whereabouts, yet her enthusiasm was frightening.

"Please, Rorianne." Garin managed to twist out of her embrace and step back. "I think I might know where it is. The old man who owns this land said his grandfather found a large, green quartz crystal buried beneath a tree. I've never heard of anything like it, so I'm guessing it's the jewel."

"And he has it?" She reached to grab him again, but Garin quickly jumped out of reach.

"No. He says it was donated to a grotto years ago. I know where it's located, only about an hour and a half's drive from here."

"This is called Indian ginger, because the first American people used its root as a spice. The bloom remains hidden under the large, velvety leaf and close to ground. It's fragrance smells like rotted meat because it uses scavenger bugs to pollinate it." Lorenzo was coming into view, giving Searene and the others a tour of the woodland plants as they followed the path. "This is blood wart and was once used for whooping cough. Now fleabane can be made into a tea for rheumatism and the wild onion for bee stings.

"About a ten miles from here is a wetlands where sundews grow. They are an acid bog plant that have sticky hairs on them to ensnare insects, which they digest to supplement their nitrogen intake. My favorites are parasitical plants. The bastard toadflax is a partial root parasite, so it still has green leaves and makes most of its own food. Now the dodders and cancer-roots are completely parasitical and have lost their color.

"Indian pipes will bloom later in the summer and have glistening white stems and leaves. They get their food from a mycorrhizal fungus, that in turn gets its food from the roots of trees."

"We call them widow's bouquet," Drestin said. "Pigs get sick when they eat them."

"Vlad, Garin may have found Myrlyn's Stone. He said it is not far from here."

She rushed back to the young king and seized him in a fierce bear hug. Garin was surprised not to see Vlad grimacing. He even appeared pleased by her rough attention. Rorianne suddenly released the other member of the quest and stepped back. She looked confused. At last noticing her state of dress, she turned her back to the rest and fixed her buttons.

122

"Searene told us of Old Man Moeller's comments. Good going, Garin," Lorenzo said as he gave a light punch to the other's arm. "It's Friday, which means the place will be pretty crowded tomorrow. The best time to go will be about 3 a.m. Sunday when things are quieter.

"Why not go tonight?" Rorianne asked impatiently.

"I want to case the place first. You just don't walk into a grotto and swipe a stone from out of the wall."

"Case the place? Swipe a stone?" Garin repeated the phrases nervously. "Just what are you planning?"

"What else?" answered Lorenzo. "We're going to steal the Stone of Myrlyn from the Dickeyville Grotto. You didn't think we'd just walk in and ask for it?"

"What about the police?"

"Do you think they keep an around-the-clock watch on a small town church grotto? Don't worry, it will be a piece of cake. You'll do fine."

"I'll do fine?"

"Sure. We can't send in the others. They wouldn't know what to say if they were stopped. Come on, let's get back to the truck. I'm getting hungry."

Garin watched as the others passed him one at a time.

Searene was last in line and she took Garin's hand. "Come. You are now part of the quest. This has all been foretold."

Garin felt slightly embarrassed holding hands with the girl, though the others didn't seem to notice. The walk back to the truck was almost enjoyable. The dark cloud that had hung over Rorianne was gone. Up ahead the two apprentices joked as they walked and Lorenzo and Vlad were deep into a discussion.

Garin dropped Lorenzo off in Bear River so he could pick up his car, a 1947 cream and tan Plymouth sedan. Back at the house, Garin showered and changed into clean clothes. He felt much better as he began dinner. Searene followed him around the kitchen, asking questions about the appliances and food. Drestin tended to the dragon, Rorianne paced nervously about the house, and Lorenzo and Vlad continued their talk. Garin peeled potatoes and watched Elfred through the window over the sink. The apprentice magician was playing fetch with Ralp. The tiny dragon was retrieving a Frisbee like a dog, only catching it about 20 feet in the air.

Lorenzo announced after dinner that he and Vlad were going to make a reconnaissance of the grotto.

"You better take my car," Garin suggested. "Yours is way too conspicuous."

"Let us return to the inn," Drestin suggested to Elfred. "This will be one of the few chances we have to relax over an ale before we go back to our country. What do you say, Garin?"

"Vlad and I could meet you there. Please tell Happy Bear, Roxanne, Michelle, Hairy Joe, Wart and Steve I was held up by a pressing engagement," said Lorenzo.

Garin looked to the two women.

"We are planning to get some rest," Rorianne answered. "But you men do whatever kind of drunken mischief you think is diverting."

~ * ~

Things were spirited at the New Yorker Lounge and Supper Club as they looked through the open door. A haze of smoke hung over the long, narrow tavern and the jukebox was blasting out an old Doors' tune. The three pool tables were busy, little islands of light to the rear of the dimly-lit bar. They slid into a booth and relaxed as they sipped their beer.

"Where's Spasm?"

Garin looked up to see Happy Bear grinning drunkenly and holding a cue stick.

"He said he'd be here later. Had to do some business first."

"Good. There's somebody here looking for you dudes. I said you'd be here tonight."

"Looking for Lorenzo?"

"All of you. He said he's an old buddy of yours."

Garin craned his neck and looked to the back of the bar. It was too dark to make out any familiar faces through the smoky haze.

"All of us?"

"Yeah, I've never heard of the club he rides with, but they must be bad dudes. He keeps opening his beer bottles by biting off the tops."

"Do you remember what he said the name of his, ah, club is?" Elfred asked hesitantly.

"Yeah, the Rovers."

Suddenly, looming over Happy Bear was a giant dressed in black leather. A pair of goggles like Vlad's hung around his neck.

"Hey, here he is. Look at this," Happy Bear pointed to an empty scabbard hanging from the Rover's thick leather belt. "Can you believe it? He came in wearing a sword. Hilda made him check it in at the bar."

Garin looked at the two apprentices who were both sitting with their mouths open.

Happy Bear glanced at the three then to the hulking figure.

"Hey, ain't he a friend of yours?"

"Out of my way, little man," the Rover said as he shoved the biker to the side and leaned to place ham-sized fists on the table. He grinned evilly at the trio. "You will come with me."

"Shit," was all Garin could think to say. He wrinkled his nose and pulled his head away. The Rover had very bad breath.

"I thought you said you were a friend of these guys?"

The Rover again shoved Happy Bear to the side, this time with more force. The biker fell back into a table and sent it tumbling to the sound of breaking glass.

"I can kill one of you now to show that I will not suffer any delay or antics..."

The Rover's speech was cut short by the sound of a cue stick breaking across the back of his head. Happy Bear was pissed. Wart, Hairy Joe and Steve were running to aid their buddy. The Rover stood and shook his head then turned to face his attacker. Drestin leaped from his seat and swung his beer mug, bringing it down with all his force against the giant's head. Garin scooted out of the booth and far enough away not to be under the Rover when he toppled.

But he didn't fall. The Rover shook his head and picked up a chair. Happy Bear stood in awe, looking down at his broken cue stick then back to the now beer-drenched giant.

"Holy fuck," the biker gasped, still so astonished that he barely had time to duck the thrown chair.

Hairy Joe flew through the air and hit the Rover in the back of the knees, expecting the man to fold. He didn't. The giant seemed to barely notice as he almost absentmindedly kicked the fallen biker to the side, backhanded Wart and grabbed Steve by the scruff of his neck, sending him crashing into a line of now empty bar stools.

He turned and faced Garin. "Who has the Jewel of Myrlyn?"

"Hey, what the hell?" screamed a voice by the door.

Something skimmed the top of Garin's head to slam into the Rover. It was Ralp, irate as hell. The wyvern sunk his claws into the Rover's face and angrily chattered as it bit wildly. The giant screamed and began staggering about the bar. Tables and chairs went crashing and the floor was slick with spilled beer and nasty bits of broken glass. He finally tore the small dragon away and Ralp twisted from his grip before the man could take revenge.

The bar was pure chaos. Patrons were stampeding out the front and back exits. A brawl was one thing, but a giant bat from hell was something else. The Rover angrily kicked the fallen furniture out of his way and drew a long knife out of his jacket. Blood was running down his face.

"Elfred, do something," yelled Drestin.

The apprentice magician had his palms pressed together near his mouth. There was a look of concentration on his face. He brought his hands out in a wide arc and mumbled of a string of foreign-sounding words. From back of the bar the cigarette haze thickened into an impenetrable fog. Garin grabbed his two new friends and pulled them to the front door as a wall of smoke advanced. They stumbled after him, watching over their shoulders as the gray cloud rolled across the tavern, swallowing the Rover and the other patrons who hadn't managed to escape.

Garin looked wildly about for the truck. The smoke was now pouring into the street and showed no sign of thinning. Ralp came flying out and circled above their heads, still clucking angrily. The bar refugees gathered in front of the tavern took off running with the reappearance of the small dragon.

"Let's get out of here." Garin was trying to herd the apprentices to the car.

"We cannot," protested Elfred. "That is most likely the Rover who attacked us. He must have also fallen through the gate. We cannot let him return to his dragon, or he will be even more dangerous. Now is the time to stop him."

"Are you crazy? That guy's worse than the Terminator. Let the police worry about him. They should be arriving any time now."

The smoke continued to flow down the street and was climbing to their waists like rising floodwaters.

"You can turn off the smoke now," Garin said as he looked about the fog-flooded street.

"I cannot, the spell is no longer in my control. I have never heard of this happening. It must have something to do with this world."

They heard the siren only moments before the squad car came skidding around the corner and screeched to a halt. Two cops popped out with their revolvers drawn. They looked about in bewilderment. One yelped and ducked as Ralp flew over his head. He swore and fired wildly into the air until the other cop grabbed his arm and screamed for him to stop. The fog continued to thicken, and the squad car's headlights gleamed eerily through the smoke.

Ralp stepped up his screeching. He had spotted the Rover staggering from the bar and come in low for another attack. The wyvern zipped past the giant, raking him with his needle talons. The Rover collapsed.

"Quick, we must get him," ordered Elfred who was already wading through the smoke to where the Rover disappeared.

Garin shook his head but followed anyway. Drestin found him first. He tripped over the body and his head disappeared into the fog. When the dragon apprentice reappeared, he shouted his discovery. The three took deep breaths as if they were going under water and kneeled. They felt blindly for handholds and began dragging the fallen body to the truck. Not only was he big, he was heavy. It was a struggle to shove him into the back of the truck.

The fog was now over their heads and the streetlights appeared like moons behind cloud cover. The headlights couldn't penetrate any deeper into the smoke than three or four feet. Garin hunched tensely over the steering wheel for the first two blocks until the fog began fading.

"I think it has stopped," said Elfred. "It should now begin to dissipate."

"I hope it sticks around long enough to keep the cops off our tail until we get out of town," Garin answered.

"I believe I understood what you said and I agree," Drestin answered.

Garin pulled the truck to the side of the gravel road once he was a mile off the pavement. He reached across to open the glove compartment and pull out a flashlight. The two otherworlders were impressed by its light beam as they followed Garin to the back of the pickup.

"He must be out cold," Garin said. "It was a pretty rough ride and I could see him bouncing all over the place in my mirror."

Drestin asked for the flashlight and examined the Rover, peeling back his eyes and feeling his neck.

"He is more than dazed, he is dead. Those many blows to the head must have finally slain him."

"What, dead? He's dead?" A wave of nausea swept over Garin, and he stumbled to the ditch to throw up. It left him cold and shaking. Hearing Drestin pronounce the man dead was like a kick to the stomach.

"Come, friend, do not suffer over the likes of him, he who has probably killed many innocent people in his life. He would have gladly had us face the same fate." Drestin bent over Garin and tried comforting him with a firm hand on the shoulder. Elfred joined him and the two apprentices helped Garin to his feet.

He sat several minutes behind the steering wheel before feeling steady enough to continue the drive home. Drestin brought out Rorianne and Searene and they helped Garin into the house. He felt humiliated being this weak in front of the warrior woman, though she appeared very sympathetic.

"You will be fine," Rorianne assured him as she firmly pushed him into a living room chair. "The first time is always this way. To lightly take a man's life is an ill sign."

Outside, Elfred and Drestin debated how to best rid themselves of the body. The apprentice magician wanted to try a conflagration spell, but he was afraid of a fire so close to the farm buildings. By Garin's flashlight, they dragged the body far into the pasture. There he spoke words of power and was almost crisped by the sudden explosion of heat, a giant fireball hurtling up into the night sky. The far trees and farm buildings were brightly lit by the blaze. Only ashes and a large circle of scorched grass remained five minutes later.

Elfred was half dazed by the intensity of his supposedly minor spell.

Garin finally felt good enough to put on a pot of coffee. The others hesitantly tried the offered steaming cups. Rorianne immediately liked the new drink. Garin told the others that it often took a while to develop a taste for the bitter brew. They gathered around the television, and Garin flicked through the channels before finding the movie, "The Seventh Voyage of Sinbad." He had a hard time explaining that it was just fantasy to people in his world.

He switched over to a news channel.

"I know that man," cried Searene, pointing at former Vice President Dick Cheney. "He was a eunuch guard at the slave market."

The news was ending as Lorenzo and Vlad drove down the lane. The group went to the kitchen to meet the two when they came through the door.

"What the hell happened in town?" Lorenzo asked as he kicked off his boots. "The New Yorker is closed for the night and everyone's talking about an attack of demons and giants."

Garin let the apprentices explain while he leaned against the counter, not really wanting to hear a recounting of the evening.

"Of course you know this means Hilda will probably bar you," Lorenzo said with a smile to Garin. "She hates fights."

"The Rover is dead? Are you certain?" Vlad asked Elfred.

"I will take you to the spot if you would like to see the ashes," he offered.

"That will not be necessary. You have done well."

"Well? Well?" Garin interjected. "We flooded half the town in smoke, smashed a bar and terrorized the local populace. We'll be lucky if the National Guard doesn't circle the house before morning and start blasting us with mortars.

"Wait, don't tell me," Garin said while holding his hands up to Lorenzo. "You were special forces in Afghanistan and a small skirmish like that would be a nostalgic trip down memory lane."

"It's all right, Garin," Lorenzo assured him. "From what I could tell, it was so confusing, no one can figure out what happened. The two officers who arrived first were initially talking about a ten-foot dragon, but now they seem to think it was just the smoke affecting them. No one has connected it to you. By tomorrow, everyone will chalk it up to mass hysteria and a fight between two biker gangs."

"We have something else to worry about," warned Drestin. "This world seems to be affecting Elfred's magic, magnifying it beyond his control. What if it gets worse?"

"Our young apprentice magician will have to refrain from using his spells while we are here," said Vlad.

"But you forget," replied Drestin in a worried voice. "Dragons fly by magic. Ralp flew with an amazing speed tonight. If we stay too long, can Shadow even take us home?"

The room was silent as the members of the quest considered the somber thought.

"Damn, that is not all there is to worry about," Garin said as he pushed himself away from the counter. "What about the Rover's dragon? Didn't you tell me they were vicious animals? It's out there somewhere, and what's going to happen when it gets hungry?"

Chapter Ten

Garin found he was glad his childhood home was a rambling, five-bedroom farmhouse. The two women were sharing a room, as were Drestin and Elfred. Vlad and Lorenzo each had a separate room.

The yard light lit up the lane and the fronts of several farm buildings. He remembered his father installing it after several neighbors reported gas being stolen. Garin could see the faded red bulk gas tank from his bedroom window, set eight feet above the ground for easy access to the tractors. He idly wondered if there was fuel still in it.

Weeds were growing around a windmill that hadn't been used since the 1930s. The sight was enough to bring on another guilt attack. His father would have never allowed the farmstead to become so overgrown.

Garin turned and glanced about his room. Except for the dust, it hadn't changed since the day he left for college. He once kidded his mother that she had turned it into a shrine. On the wall above his bed was a poster from the old movie version of "King Kong." Several high school wrestling trophies were lined up on the top shelf of the bookcase. He knew he'd even find his letter jacket if he searched deep enough into the closet.

Garin looked out the window again. Drestin was returning from the barn after making sure Shadow was secure for the night, much like his dad did after checking the livestock each evening. Drestin glanced up and waved when he saw the silhouette in the window. Garin waved back.

He decided he should go to bed. Tomorrow had the makings of a long day. There was the hunt for the other dragon, as well as the night raid on the Dickeyville grotto. It was impossible for him to even imagine what might happen after that. Looking at the bed, he decided it was impossible to sleep this early and headed downstairs to see if Searene was still awake.

"...Though some turtles bury themselves headfirst in the mud at the bottom of the pond," Lorenzo was saying to Searene as Garin entered the kitchen. "They hibernate through the winter by extending part of their intestines out their anal openings. The intestines will absorb oxygen from the water, so they actually breathe through their butts."

Garin shook his head at Lorenzo's latest natural history lesson. The two were sitting at the table. He caught Searene's eye. She smiled and held up a finger as if to say, "Just a moment."

Garin was about to head through the dining room and into the living room where he heard other voices when Elfred motioned for him. The apprentices were perched on the kitchen counter.

"Vlad and Rorianne are alone," Elfred said, as if that was enough explanation why Garin shouldn't seek them out.

"Oh?"

Elfred and Drestin traded looks and broke into foolish grins.

"His Royal Highness, King Vladimir Dragol, Supreme Ruler of Sylvquin, Lord of the Western Mountains, Protector of Anjeiv, Master of the Red Plains and Emperor of the Bulgavian Empire," began Drestin, "is courting Princess Rorianne Cevonte of Thurbia. Only neither would admit that it is happening. For the King of Bulgavia, this is a quest as difficult as finding Myrlyn's Stone."

"Probably just as dangerous," Garin added, causing the other two to laugh and nod in agreement. "So how are we to find this dragon tomorrow? It must be deep in the woods not to have been noticed yet."

"We're going to rely on Ralp," answered Elfred. "He has a good nose and should be able to locate it. The mount cannot be too distant from here if the Rover was in your village."

"And?"

"And?"

"And what do we do with it once it's found? According to Vlad, it doesn't sound like it's apt to let itself be staked out in the back yard."

Elfred appeared uneasy and delayed answering. Garin glanced to see Drestin examining his boots, his posture suddenly slumping.

"Ah, the dragon does present a problem."

"It will have to be killed," Drestin interrupted. He took a deep breath and stood. "Lorenzo said he has a weapon that will kill the dragon."

Elfred looked flustered but explained, "It is not an easy subject for Drestin, who has been trained to care for the animals, not destroy them."

Now it was Garin's turn to feel unsettled. "I'm, ah, sorry, Drestin. I guess I didn't ..."

He was saved by Searene. She took him by the arm and pulled him across the kitchen and out the door. They stopped on the porch and Searene pushed him onto the porch swing. She sat next to him and looked up at the chains.

"This is a strange bench."

"It's a swing. Here, let me show you."

He straightened his legs and set the swing in motion. Though the yard light barely penetrated a wall of vines into the shadows of the porch, it was enough for Garin to see Searene smile. She pulled her legs up and wrapped her arms around her knees. He expected Searene to say something, but she just turned her head to look at him, resting a cheek on her knees.

Garin tried chiding himself for reacting like a school kid. His heart was racing, and he was afraid to say something for fear his dry throat would only be able to make croaking noises. Why should he suddenly feel so awkward? It was hard not to think about the trim body under the dress. In fact, it was impossible. He couldn't put the picture out of his mind of Searene racing from the bush to the quarry.

"What do you think so far of my world?" Garin asked to break the silence and erase Searene's image from his mind.

"I find it very pleasant," she answered. "It seems so peaceful. As a child, I delighted in the small adventures while accompanying my father on his

133

business. But I have grown tired of the wandering and weary of the misfortunes that of late have plagued me. This gentle world seems like a haven."

"It can be boring," Garin repeated from the afternoon conversation.

"I envy the apprentices their lifelong friendship," continued Searene. "I wish to lead a life where I can have real friends and not just brief travelmates. I envy you, who has only to walk the streets of your village and see cousins and other blood family--to belong and not be just a caller. I would not find that boring."

Garin couldn't think of an answer and watched the cat hunting something in the darkness of the farmyard.

"What were you thinking before you asked me that question?" Searene asked.

"Ah, I was thinking of that old cat and a dog we once had named Chumly. They were great friends. We usually only had mutts, but Chumly was a Lhasa Apso that a friend gave my mother. Their hair tangles easily and needs constant cutting. One day mom took Chumly in for a professional grooming and he came home trimmed, perfumed and with a bow in his hair. The cat took one smell and look at him and high-tailed it to the barn. Didn't even recognize his old buddy. It was days before the cat would have anything to do with the dog."

"That is what you were thinking?"

"Sure."

"No, you were not."

"I wasn't?"

"No." She leaned forward and pressed her lips against his.

Garin saw it coming and was prepared to pull away, to explain that it probably wasn't a good idea. He instead found himself wrapping his arms around the young woman. She slid over and turned to sit on his lap. The move didn't interrupt the kiss. He ran his hands down her waist to her hips and Searene moved against him.

Garin broke way long enough to ask, "Have you ever seen a hay mow?"

~*~

Elfred and Drestin had watched the screen door slam shut behind Garin and Searene.

"It appears what they say about spring is correct," noted Elfred. "Maybe our host will have a brighter outlook come morning."

"I do not believe all is as well with the king and princess," Drestin said as he cocked an ear to catch the muffled voices coming from the living room.

Rorianne's voice had risen in pitch and the tone was not that of a happy lover. Whatever her declaration, it was followed by her footsteps loudly climbing the stairs.

"Oh well, they shall both need their sleep for tomorrow's duties," Elfred philosophically observed.

~ * ~

Garin felt a weight on his chest and he sleepily opened his eyes to stare in surprise at a mini-dragon looking him closely in the face. Ralp was curled like a cat, his chin resting on the end of his tail. Garin hoped this meant the wyvern was in a peaceful mood after witnessing its savage battle with the Rover.

A minute passed with both quietly observing each other. He tentatively raised his hand and touched the dragon's scaled neck. It felt and looked like a china plate. Ralp blinked once but otherwise seemed not to mind the attention. Remembering what Drestin has said about petting dragons, he lightly flicked it behind the ear with his fingernail. The brown and white wyvern stuck his tongue out and began panting like a dog.

Garin heard a noise at the door. His mother's tabby walked in and began meowing loudly, a sure sign its food dish was empty. He was too slow in his grab for Ralp. The wyvern was already across the bed with its little wings spread. It made a half leap, half glide across the floor and landed with a thud directly in front of the cat. All hell broke loose.

The cat arched its back and howled loudly, spitting and lashing out with its claws while backing rapidly to the door. Ralp was hopping up and down and chattering madly. Up from the sheets popped Searene. She was looking around in sleepy surprise and brushed a stray wisp of hay from her hair.

"Ralp, damn your soul," Elfred yelled from down the hall.

The bedroom door flew the rest of the way open. The cat lunged between Elfred's legs and disappeared into the hall. Ralp tried continuing the chase, but his leap threw him into the apprentice magician's arms. Elfred stumbled back a few steps then secured his hold on the struggling pet.

"I am very sorry for Ralp's intrusion," Elfred apologized.

Garin self-consciously pulled the sheet around him and looked to Searene. He was relieved to see she was also now covered.

"Ah, that's all right," he stammered.

Elfred, still holding the squirming wyvern, managed to shut the door behind him.

Garin felt dazed. "Hi," was the only thing he could think to say to Searene.

"Morning, Garin. I believe it must be time to rise."

"Yeah, I, ah, guess so."

Searene slipped her legs over the edge of the bed and stood, then walked to a chair where her dress was draped. It was the first time Garin had gotten a good look at the girl. Her hair spilled down a lean, muscular body. She also had what people around Bear River would call a farmer's tan--an ivory white torso except for her brown arms and face. He quickly climbed out of bed and pulled on a pair of jeans.

"I feel I need a bath," she declared suddenly and turned to look at Garin. "Will your tub hold two?"

He paused as if contemplating his bathtub's dimensions. "If it doesn't, I have a shower."

An hour later the members of the quest were gathered around the kitchen table eating and planning the dragon hunt.

"I have a launcher and a few small armor-piercing rockets lying around that should take care of the problem," Lorenzo was saying as he sipped his coffee.

Garin almost voiced his skepticism then decided to keep his mouth shut. With everything else that had happened since he woke yesterday morning, Lorenzo having an illegal anti-tank weapon would probably be the most mundane aspect.

Lorenzo caught the brief look on Garin's face and explained, "You can still pick the things up a dime a dozen in Libya."

Elfred looked at Garin and Searene then smiled. "I've already sent Ralp to search out the dragon. It shouldn't be that difficult since dragons and wyverns can detect each other's magic."

Drestin hunched in his chair, looking glum.

Vlad spoke, "I promised Drestin we would first give him leave to coax the Rover's mount into letting us take it peacefully. Lorenzo will use his weapon if this plan fails."

The apprentices volunteered to clean the breakfast dishes, and Garin followed Lorenzo outside.

"I shouldn't be more than an hour," Lorenzo said from behind the steering wheel after rolling down his window. "Don't let anyone leave until I return."

Garin watched the car until it disappeared. It was another beautiful June day. A light breeze played with his hair and made the windmill creak as its rusty blades slowly spun. It was hard to imagine he had felt bored to death only two days ago.

This whole adventure was going way too fast, he decided. You just don't wake up to meet a bunch of people and a dragon from another world and immediately join their hunt for a magic jewel. Then there was the bar room brawl, the magic smoke, the body and last, but not least, going to bed with a woman he'd only known for a day.

He might actually find himself sucked into journeying to another world if he kept this up. No, Garin decided, he was going to be firm and call a halt to this madness. He would start with refusing to go on this crazy dragon hunt.

Garin felt much better after making the self-declaration. He was distracted from his thoughts by the raucous cawing of some far away crow. Only it wasn't a crow, it was Ralp. He was still a dot skimming above distant trees, though swiftly growing in size and chattering furiously. Seconds later Garin saw a second dot. It was also increasing in size and promised to grow much larger. It was the Rover's dragon in hot pursuit of Ralp.

"Ah, Vlad, Elfred," he hoarsely yelled. "Rorianne, Drestin, anyone."

Maybe it was the boost in magical power from the new world, but the two animals were coming towards him like bullets. Ralp had obviously spotted Garin and was speeding to him for protection. Garin frantically looked around and decided the woodshed was a whole lot closer than the house. He sprinted across the lane and dove through the doorway. Pressing himself against the wall, he hoped the two dragons would forget about him. They didn't.

A madly squawking Ralp came rocketing into the shed, not braking in time to prevent himself from crashing into an old refrigerator. The wyvern flapped about then launched himself into Garin's arms.

"No, get out of here. Go for help, run away, just get out of here."

Garin squeezed the little dragon's beak shut to cut off its noisy yelps and held his breath. The sudden silence was almost a shock. Only the windmill was still making a creaking noise, and he prayed the dragon had continued on with its flight. He counted a dozen loud heartbeats and began leaning to look out a small window when the roof exploded. Pieces of it rained down and he threw his hands up for protection. It was impossible to see because of the small pieces of flying debris. His ears were ringing.

Garin crawled to a corner and forced himself to look up, blinking and rubbing his eyes because of the dust. There was only blue sky. Ralp twisted loose and launched himself into the air. He could hear the others yelling something from the house. Suddenly a shadow fell across Garin and an extremely large set of teeth was descending toward him. He shrieked and rolled across the floor and out the door as the remaining walls of the shed collapsed under the dragon.

Garin was running towards a clump of trees before he even realized he had regained his feet. It was a tight squeeze between two close growing maples. He spun and peered at the dragon from behind the V of the massive old trunks. Ralp was circling overhead and still chattering ferociously. The wyvern spotted Garin and made another beeline for the human.

"No, you god damned idiot, stay away."

Ralp glided through the tree limbs to again land in Garin's arms, who threw him back towards the dragon.

"Be still, dragon. Lay down." Drestin was crossing the yard with his arms spread. "Hear me. Stop. I am now your master. You will obey me."

The dragon apprentice was pale and his arms were trembling, but he continued his advance. The beast stopped and craned its neck over its shoulder to peer down at the puny human. Garin now had the time to examine the animal that had almost made him brunch. It was bigger than Shadow, with many of its yellow and blue scales nicked and scratched.

"There, that is right. We are your friends. Calm down."

The rest of the group looked anxiously from the house. Vlad stepped off the porch and tightly gripped his saber. Drestin flinched when the dragon snorted and spun to fully face the audacious human. Its tail scattered gravel and knocked over a riding lawn mower.

"Down, lay down. Now, lay down."

The dragon cocked its head to scrutinize Drestin with one eye then actually began lowering its neck. Drestin smiled weakly and motioned it to continue. Its head was just about to touch the ground when the beast changed its mind, rearing onto its back legs and spreading its wings. The sound of a train derailment roared from its throat and its massive thigh muscles tensed for a leap. Drestin stumbled back and Vlad ran to his side. Elfred began frantically shouting a spell.

The dragon pushed itself forward and in midair was slammed sideways. No one had noticed Shadow hurtling from the barn. The dragons rolled across the earth towards Garin's temporary haven. This time he was too shocked to move and the trees in front of him shuddered under the impact.

Elfred's incantation was left uncompleted. It was impossible to use the fire spell without also risking Shadow. He watched helplessly with the others as the beasts struggled before them. The windows in the house rattled each time one was slammed to the ground.

Garin shook off the shock and retreated to a metal machine shed. In the building was a large combine used to harvest corn. The small cab was perched high on the front. For an instant Garin thought he might be able to use it against the rogue dragon. But as large as it was, he realized, it was not built like some heavy piece of earth moving equipment. Either of the dragons could turn it into scrap metal in seconds, as they had just trashed the windmill.

Male dragons in the wild will often fight for a female, but rarely are the fights to the death. Their scales protect them from all but the most ferocious attacks. Only their wings are vulnerable and some instinctive code of honor keeps them from targeting this weak spot. Usually the loser retreats with all but his pride intact. This isn't always the case with domesticated dragons, and it certainly wasn't true for the Rover's mount. The old battle-scarred drake was purposely trying to tear at Shadow's wings. At the moment they had both pulled apart to catch their breaths and each take stock of their adversary's condition.

"Dragon down, dragon down," a voice thundered.

The large dragon froze then turned its head to gaze at the advance of a new human dressed in black leather. Garin gasped. It was the dead Rover whose corpse he had helped lift into the back of his pickup. The giant shouted the order again in his harsh command voice. The dragon reluctantly lowered itself to a position used for mounting, though keeping a wary eye on the other dragon. Drestin ran to Shadow and prodded him away from the drake.

Turning to point into the sky, the Rover shouted, "Attack." He was pointing at another dragon flying two or three miles away. It was just big enough to be visible. The beast lowered its head then launched himself skywards. The Rover was temporarily forgotten as everyone watched the old male flying eagerly to its next challenger. It grew closer and closer to the other dragon until they merged into one dot then suddenly disappeared from sight.

Vlad looked away from the startling scene to warily confront the newcomer, only now he faced a beaming Elfred.

"An illusionary spell," the king said with approval. "But what happened to the dragon?"

"I made the invisible gate appear as a visible dragon."

Rorianne rushed passed Vlad to grab the startled magician's apprentice in a congratulatory embrace that lifted his feet several inches off the ground.

Garin was thankful it was someone else receiving the hug. Soon the others were surrounding Elfred, pounding him on the back in relief and gratitude.

Garin wiped the sweat from his face and wearily walked to the smashed shed. His body ached from being slammed around. Nothing remained of the small building but splinters. He contemplated how close his body had come to joining the pulverized wood.

"A favorite shed?"

Garin didn't turn to answer. "A family heirloom. You're late."

"It certainly looks like it. I turned back when I saw the monster skimming treetops. That should certainly give the neighbors something to talk about."

Lorenzo and Garin walked back to the laughing and shouting mob. Garin could tell by their jubilance he had not been the only one scared witless. As if by some wordless command, the members of the quest abruptly shifted their attention to Shadow. They circled the dragon and showered him with praise. Garin didn't know how intelligent the creatures were, but it was obvious Shadow understood their tone of voices and seemed to beam from the attention. Drestin pointed out the one sour note.

"He has damaged his wing even more. This will take more than a couple days to heal. He has a shattered bone and torn tendons. He will not be able to fly for at least a month."

Rorianne took it the hardest, but after almost being smashed by the wrathful dragon, even the warrior princess didn't appear completely down and out. Drestin led the limping Shadow back to the barn, and the others retreated to the house to collapse in the living room.

"I thought I would loose my bowels when I saw that dragon stomping on the small paddock in which Garin sought shelter," Elfred admitted.

"What about when it almost landed on Drestin?" Vlad joined in. "I believed there was no hope for the lad."

The group continued trading impressions of the brief battle then went on to discuss the other close escapes they had survived since beginning the venture. The more Garin listened to the chilling stories, the more he knew he did not want to join the quest, especially after a discussion between Vlad and

Drestin revealed the prophecy spoke of one or more of the adventurers biting the dirt before it was all over.

He slipped quietly from the room and went outdoors. Garin stood idly in the farmyard before finding himself entering the barn. Shadow was slurping from a cattle trough and stopped when the human entered. He turned his head to Garin and waited as if expecting some learned discourse.

Garin smiled at the great beast. He was no longer afraid of the dragon, though still leery of getting too close. He didn't want to get stepped on or accidentally slapped by its tail.

"Thanks a lot, buddy. You saved our lives."

Shadow lowered his head to human level, and Garin reached out and thumped him behind the ear. He wondered what his father would have thought of such exotic livestock inhabiting the barn. He sat on a bale of straw, and the two quietly examined each other. Garin found the silence of the barn more comforting than the boisterous house.

His attention was attracted to the massive oak beams overhead that supported the haymow. The barn was built by his great-grandfather in the 1880s. The beams were held in place by wooden pegs. Probably by similar methods used in the world of Rorianne and the others, he thought. On the wall were dust-covered pieces of equipment and tools. Most were obsolete, and he had seen their likes hanging in fancy restaurants for atmosphere.

He stood and pulled a hay bale hook from the wall. It had a wooden handle and ended in a hook similar to the one worn by Peter Pan's archrival, the good captain.

This simple tool was used to lift bales of hay every summer by my father and grandfather, Garin mused, thinking of the sweat the wooden handle had absorbed over the years. He grasped it as they would have and tears unexpectedly came to his eyes. Garin hadn't broken his quiet aloofness at the funeral, but he now found himself silently crying uncontrollably. He wished more than anything he could walk outside and see his father working on the tractor or his mother hanging out the laundry.

He took a deep breath and sat back on the straw bale. His bout of nostalgia made him think of his old high school buddies. He hadn't even looked them up since he had returned. Thinking of them, Garin realized they'd been the last real friends he'd had. Grades had meant more in college than relationships, and there was too much competition within his office for such trivial things. It was funny, but the people in the house were probably the closest he'd come to making friends in the past six years--and here he was ready to let them go out of his life.

"Heavy thoughts?"

Lorenzo was standing in the door. For once Garin didn't feel antagonized by his presence.

"Yeah, pretty heavy."

"Want to be alone?"

"No, that's all right. I've done my quota for the day."

"Pretty strange stuff happening. Wait until you tell your friends back in Chicago what you did for summer vacation."

Garin laughed. "Yeah, and they think farm life is boring."

Lorenzo eased himself on the bale and looked at the hay hook. Garin held it up for inspection. "I was wondering what restaurant this would wind up in."

"I prefer forks, myself."

"Sissy."

"It works for me."

"Lorenzo, how do you explain all of this?"

"I don't. When you get to be my age, you just realize some things don't have answers."

"There's got to be a rational explanation. Haven't mathematicians theorized about other dimensions?"

"Sure, but I doubt any of those scientists included flying dragons and magical spells. How would you explain our questers speaking modern English, a form only several hundred years old?"

"I never thought of that."

"Don't think about it too much or you'll just twist your brains in knots. The best thing is just to take it as it comes."

"You speak as a man with experience."

"I've seen some weird things in my life."

"Stranger than this?"

"Much."

Garin looked at his new friend with a little skepticism. "Mind if I call in Vlad, the human lie detector?"

"Be my guest, but it will only confuse you more. It does me."

"So, you're going on this adventure?"

"Wouldn't miss it for the world."

"Even though the prophecy says not all of us will come out of it alive?"

Lorenzo shrugged. "Some people jump out of planes for excitement knowing they could be killed if the chute doesn't open correctly. Others pursue multiple sex partners without protection knowing they could get AIDS.

"And some people lose themselves in large cities where they can get killed in traffic or mugged by a wino," Lorenzo continued, looking pointedly at Garin. "And when it's over, what have they accomplished? Did it give their life any more meaning? Did they leave a mark on another person or the world?"

"Do you have to risk your life on a quest to have meaning?"

"Certainly not. You think the people who built this farm led a boring life. And yet, I bet when a hard day of work was over, they'd sit on that porch and feel that they'd accomplished something."

Garin scratched meaningless patterns with the hay hook in the dust coating the cement floor. "I'm getting to feel very close to these people. I think it might be worse than dying to lose one of them."

"That's only human, like World War II pilots becoming terrified to make new friends for fear the others won't make it back from the next sortie. But if what they say is true, you're needed on this quest, and staying here won't help them. You'd just live the rest of your life wondering what happened."

Neither of them spoke until Lorenzo added with a grin, "And maybe there is a special one among the group that you are worried about?"

Garin couldn't help but smile, which made him feel better. He laid down the hook and stood. "Just a few minutes ago I was ready to call it quits, but suddenly I've changed my mind. I must be going crazy."

"Join the crowd. But just between you and me," Lorenzo stepped closer to Garin and said in a conspiratory whisper, "there are always ways to circumvent fate. Destiny is bullshit."

"Yeah? I'll try not to blurt that secret out, though Vlad said we all live a prophecy of birth and death. Or do you think the marvelous Lorenzo Spasm can also escape that?"

"They say survival is the slowest form of suicide, but I do happen to have a friend involved in secret government research dealing with genetic..."

Their conversation was interrupted by a dust-covered old Buick coming down the lane. The two stepped outside, and Garin made sure the door closed firmly behind him.

"It's Mr. Moeller," Garin said with relief. It was getting so he immediately believed any new developments automatically meant trouble.

His neighbor slowly stepped from the car and straightened slowly like a plant seeking the sun. He glanced at Lorenzo and Garin walking to his car then turned his attention to the crumpled windmill and shed.

"Snot on a doorknob," the old man said in surprise. "What happened here?"

"Ah, what do you mean?" stammered Garin.

"What do I mean? What do you think? I'm talking about this," Old Man Moeller replied as he swept his hand across the scene, taking in the splintered boards and twisted metal.

"Well, you see, ah, I'm not sure." Garin nervously licked his lips as he tried to think of a good excuse for the damage. He looked to Lorenzo.

"Not sure?" the old man asked in surprise.

"He means he doesn't know if it was a high wind or a tornado that skimmed by here," Lorenzo interjected. "Remember that thunderstorm with the high winds about two weeks ago? That's when it happened."

"I got a few limbs knocked down, but nothin' like this."

"Well, you know how those tornadoes are," said Garin. "They can touch down for a few hundred feet and then go a couple miles before they drop again, if they ever do."

The old man scratched at a three-day growth of white stubble on his chin. "Oh yeah, I almost forgot why I came. Remember we were talking about that hunk of quartz my grandfather found?"

Garin had been trying to nonchalantly inspect the surrounding skyline for any sign of a flying wyvern, but his neighbor's question jerked his attention back to the conversation.

"Ah, quartz? Oh, the rock your grandfather gave to some grotto."

"Same one. Funniest thing, some stranger came by soon after you left and was asking about rocks. He got real excited when I mentioned the quartz crystal."

"Oh? That's weird."

"I thought so too. He even wanted to know if anyone else had been asking about it." Old Man Moeller was watching the two men closely.

"He didn't happen to be dressed like a biker, in leather and stuff?" asked Garin.

"A motorcycle rider, not quite," he snorted. "This guy was dressed in his Sunday best, or something you'd wear to a funeral. He could have stepped out of some mafia movie--was wearing a black suit and tie and real dark sunglasses. His hair looked like it had a quart of ten-thirty in it, all greased back. Kinda looked like the devil, himself, in a business suit. Gave me the spooks."

"Did you mention your conversation with Garin?" Lorenzo wanted to know.

The farmer lifted an eyebrow and squinted at Lorenzo. "You know, that's another funny thing. Told him I hadn't seen anyone for a couple days. Don't make a habit of lying to visitors, but it seemed the thing to do at the time."

He turned and walked back to his car, speaking over his shoulder. "Well, just thought you might wanta know. Pretty strange business, but none of it my concern."

Old Man Moeller stopped at his car and carefully went to one knee to retrieve something from the ground. He held it up to Garin and Lorenzo once he straightened. It was yellow and blue and the size of a saucer.

"Why, look at this," the old farmer said as he slid into his car, "looks just like a dragon scale."

Garin watched the cloud of dust fade long after the car disappeared. He turned to Lorenzo. "Tell me I'm not going crazy."

"You're not going crazy."

"Did you hear what he said?"

"Yeah, said it looked like a dragon's scale."

"That's crazy. Why would Old Man Moeller say that?"

"Because it was a dragon scale," Lorenzo answered as he walked onto the porch.

"Yeah, but..." Garin wasn't going to get anything more from Lorenzo, who had already disappeared through the kitchen screen door.

~ * ~

"Is this your camper?" Garin asked from a small couch.

He was next to Searene. The two apprentices were sitting further back and Vlad and Rorianne were in a small kitchen booth.

"No, borrowed it from a friend," Lorenzo answered.

Garin shook his head and smiled. "Does he know what nefarious activities we're up to?"

"Sure does."

"Yeah, right. You told him you needed it so you could steal a magical gem from the Dickeyville Grotto."

"Yup. Remember what I told you about strange experiences? He's had them too."

"Who's he?"

"Your uncle."

"My uncle? You mean Al?" he asked incredulously. "Get out of here."

"The one and only."

"Come on. Uncle Al doesn't do anything other than fish, watch TV and go to work. Bowling is probably too much excitement for him."

"Someday I'll have to tell you about how boring your Uncle Al is."

Garin didn't want to ask any more questions. The world was already crazy enough. He felt as if he had suddenly been told he was adopted or hooked a small mermaid from the farm pond. He didn't think he could ever be sure of anything again.

It was hard for Elfred and Drestin to feel they were nearing the end of another part of their quest while traveling in such luxury. They were stretched out on two heavily padded swivel chairs. To them, a quest meant hardship and hard work. This was too easy.

"Would you like another ale?" asked Elfred, holding out a bottle of Dubuque Star.

Drestin eyed it with uncertainty. "Do you think we should? It tastes weak, but it is still intoxicating."

"We are still hours from the theft. Do not worry. Great gods of Anvorial, look outside."

Drestin leaned over and peered out a window. The camper was on a long, narrow bridge crossing the Mississippi River from Iowa into Illinois. They were leaving Dubuque and would soon be in East Dubuque.

Elfred looked at the line of flowing headlights and again wondered if there really wasn't magic in this world.

The main street of East Dubuque is made up almost entirely of bars, some offering strip shows and the rest featuring live music. It was ten p.m. and the sidewalks were already rowdy and packed with inebriated partiers wandering from bar to bar. Others bunched in groups of three or four to lean against their cars and watch the girls walk by. The sidewalks were littered with cigarette butts.

"It looks like a fair," said Drestin as he looked out of the window.

Lorenzo gave up trying to find a parking space on the main drag and parked several blocks away near a massive bridge footing. They stopped to buy a half dozen chili dogs and ate them while they wound their way down the sidewalk.

Rorianne strode easily through the crowd, unintimidated by the noise and people. She paused in front of each door to look within. Several catcalls drifted out from a stripper bar. Searene was slightly nervous and made sure she

148

wasn't cut off from the others. Drestin and Elfred were voted down when they wanted to enter a tavern with dancers. The rest picked one featuring a blues band, and they walked through the noise and smoke to a back table.

"I still miss my sword," Rorianne grumbled as she took a sip from her beer. "I do not like taverns nor the breed of men who inhabit them. Their minds are riddled by too much ale, and they have no respect for a lady."

Garin had been about to finish the last of the beer in his glass and refill it from the pitcher, but decided to nurse what he had a bit longer. Her comments didn't stop Lorenzo or the two apprentices, but Garin noticed Vlad had put his own glass back on the table.

They didn't talk while the band played. Even in the farthest corner, the amplified instruments overwhelmed their words. Garin didn't mind. He had no idea what the otherworlders thought of the music, but he enjoyed the maniacal rifts the lead guitarist would occasionally slide into.

They leaned over the table and began talking after the band went on break. Lorenzo and Garin tried answering the many questions the others had about everything from the electric guitars to the writing on T-shirts. Garin was beginning to relax when Lorenzo leaned over and whispered, "Check out the last guy at the bar."

Dressed in a black suit and tie, the man would have faded into the dark if it weren't for his white shirt and equally pale face. He was also wearing sunglasses.

"Looks like one of the Blues Brothers. He must be with the band."

"No, he came in while the music was still playing."

The stranger turned to face their table as if he heard their whisperings. Garin felt as if he were being closely studied even though it was impossible to see the man's eyes. He also felt a sudden chill, though the bar was hot and stuffy. The man stood from his stool and began crossing the floor toward the group.

"Shit," mumbled Garin.

"See, I wish I had brought my sword," complained Rorianne.

"I could fuck around, act mysterious and utter vague threats," the man said with a voice echoing from an empty tomb, "but I won't. I don't go in for melodrama. Go back to where you came from, or I will see you all die a very slow and painful death. You will writher on the floor as you choke on your own black blood. The Jewel of Myrlyn is already claimed."

He grinned the smile of a skull. One of Garin's legs began to shake, and he felt as if he couldn't breathe. Pure evil radiated from the man. Elfred and Drestin also appeared paralyzed by the stranger's sudden appearance. Searene stared with open-mouthed amazement.

"He is telling the truth," Vlad whispered to Lorenzo. "Could you have wizards here after all?

The man turned to leave but was jerked back. Two glasses toppled and spilled beer across the table. Lorenzo had grabbed the stranger by the collar.

"Not so fast, Dr. Doom, you've got some explaining to do."

Lorenzo stepped to the side and dumped the man into his chair. The stranger appeared too shocked to protest. He tried standing and was slammed back into the chair.

"You dare touch..."

"Put a sock in it." Lorenzo's voice had taken on an unexpected tone of command. "I don't care who you are or how funny you dress, I don't like your attitude. You're going to tell us who sent you, or I'm going to take you out back and beat the shit out of you."

Rorianne had slipped a knife out from somewhere and held it under the table between the man's legs. "I agree with my companion. You will speak now or you will not care what happens later when you are taken to that alley."

Garin looked over at Vlad. He was sitting back in his chair and smiling, letting the two handle the situation. Elfred and Drestin appeared stunned by the latest occurrences.

"You will regret you ever dared lay hands upon me," the man hissed between clenched teeth.

"I already do, you feel oilier than shit. Now cut the crap and talk," Lorenzo countered.

"I will say nothing, you dog."

Lorenzo sighed. "I knew you were going to make this difficult,"

Rorianne continued holding the blade against the stranger as Lorenzo hauled him to his feet. Garin nervously looked around. No one seemed to be aware of the mini-drama unfolding in the shadowed corner.

"Make a wall," Vlad ordered and the group stood to block their prisoner from view.

Lorenzo maintained his grip and Rorianne pricked the man when it looked as if he were about to struggle. A small, dark spot formed on the white shirt. He gasped and clutched at his stomach. They herded him out the back door into a well-lit alley full of parked cars. They marched in silence until they returned to the motor home. Lorenzo continued walking the stranger to the river's edge.

"Talk."

"I will see you all..."

Rorianne pricked him again.

"Did you know they once had scuba divers working on the foundation of this bridge? It was so murky they could only see a couple feet in front of their masks."

It's a fine time for Lorenzo to begin a lecture, Garin thought, but refrained from interrupting.

"Every now and then one of the divers would shoot to the surface and refuse to go back down. It seems they'd turn around and be looking into the face of a giant catfish, its mouth as big as a wash tub. Sometimes they never find the bodies of drowned fishermen and figure those giant catfish get them. I've heard the only way to catch one of the monsters is by baiting a meat hook with a live cocker spaniel. I've always wondered what would happen if you'd gut a man and toss him in."

The faraway sound of laughing voices could be faintly heard, almost drowned out by the sound of water lapping on the banks. It was dark under the bridge, and a half moon cast only faint, rippling reflections across the water. The lights of several barges could be seen across the river. Garin wished he could see the man's face better.

"You don't scare me," the stranger said. It was a brave reply, but it betrayed him with a slight quivering in the voice.

"I will do the gutting," Rorianne volunteered, making it sound like something she would relish rather than the act being a chore.

Lorenzo jerked the man's hand behind his back. Garin thought he was going to break the man's arm and was about to protest then saw that his friend was worrying a ring off their prisoner's finger.

"Now that's the oldest trick in the book," he said, holding a ring up to the faint moonlight. "What is it, viper venom, a plant toxin, goo off some South American toad?"

"What have you got?" asked Rorianne.

"I saw him monkeying with his ring. It appears it can project a small needle and I'm betting it's not coated with sugar frosting.

The man seemed to lose some of his cockiness with the loss of the ring. Rorianne lifted her blade to catch the tip of it in a nostril.

"Let me flay his nose so he will look like a pig," she asked in a cold, firm voice. Garin wasn't sure she didn't mean it.

"Sure, go ahead."

She pressed a little harder and the man whimpered.

"Wait," Garin interrupted. "You can't cut a man's nose off."

"Why not?" Rorianne asked as if puzzled. "It is soft tissue and my blade is whetted."

Garin watched the man's Adam's apple move as he swallowed. He was holding his head back as far as he could to escape the blade.

"You just can't." Try as he might, that was the best argument Garin could come up with. He looked at the others. "You're not going to stand by and let her cut his nose off, are you?"

Elfred scratched his head. "I believe so."

"I am not going to try stopping her," said Drestin. "You know how she hates to be crossed."

"I think we should start with his ears," opinioned Vlad.

Garin looked frantically to Searene. She acted as someone caught in the middle of a family fight. "Maybe they should only cut the very tip off."

"You're out voted," observed Lorenzo. "Sorry."

Even in the dim light, Garin could see Rorianne's widening grin. She tensed as if preparing for the slice.

"No, wait, please. I will tell you."

"Damn, I was almost hoping he would not talk," cursed Rorianne, who pulled the knife away and wiped the point on the stranger's shirt.

"All right, who sent you?" Lorenzo asked again.

"The Dark One."

"Who?"

"The Dark One. I've tried for years to contact him. I've read everything I could about him, but..."

"Who is 'him?'"

"Why, Satan, of course," their prisoner replied as if it were the stupidest question he'd ever heard. "I've tried Jamaican and Haitian black magic, read old books on European witches and cults. I even managed to find the Book of Eibon and the Pnakotiv fragments, but none of them worked. Then I found the monstrous and forbidden Necronomicon by the mad Arab Abdul Alhazred. Last month I was attempting a rite and He answered me. His voice came from the air and He promised me riches and eternal life if I became his servant."

Vlad frowned and looked to Rorianne. "It looks like the King of Lancene and his magicians have found other ways to reach into this world than through just the gate."

The man, no longer appearing as threatening as when they first met, looked from face to face in puzzlement.

"King of Lancene, magicians, gates? What are you talking about? I work for Satan."

"You've been duped. That voice came from a mortal just like us, albeit a rather sicker individual, at least compared to me and my friends. I'm not so sure about you."

"Not Satan?"

"Sorry, Charlie," Lorenzo sighed. "What did he tell you to do?"

"I, ah, he wanted me to stop you. He said I should kill you if you would not desist."

"Is he lying?" Lorenzo asked Vlad.

"No, there is no doubt. My ability has also seemed to increase just as Elfred's magic. He speaks what he believes to be the truth."

Lorenzo contemplated the wanna-be Satanist then turned to the others. "Should we make him Purina Catfish Chow or let him go?"

"Let him go," Garin quickly said before other opinions could be voiced. "We must be on with the quest."

Rorianne grimaced and waved as if she were tired of the subject. "Let the fool loose if he pledges to no longer meddle with that he does not understand."

The stranger was eagerly nodding his head in compliance.

Lorenzo leaned closer, his nose almost touching the other's. "Don't you ever worry about your immortal soul?"

The man's eyes widened.

"You're fucking around with some heavy shit. Get off this Satan kick. Take up golf, collecting stamps, or even performing New Age music--anything, but stay away from riding goats naked, bad mouthing the Tri-lateral Commission and kissing Satan's naked butt. Hear?"

The man vigorously nodded his head in agreement. Lorenzo released his grip and the man took off running back toward the lights.

"I probably should have duct taped him to the bottom of the bridge," Lorenzo said then turned and slapped Garin on the back. "You were brilliant--had me almost believing you were worried we'd really snip his snout. There's nothing like the bad cop, good cop routine to loosen a tongue."

"What do you mean?" Rorianne asked in a perplexed voice. "If he had waited more than two more seconds to speak, I would have cut off his nose."

Lorenzo glanced at the princess then back to Garin and shrugged. "Whatta woman."

Chapter Eleven

Though it was still fairly early in the night, Lorenzo gave in to Rorianne's impatience and steered the van toward Dickeyville.

"You're sure you don't want to see Princess Fantasia do her dance routine with a fifteen foot python?" Lorenzo asked her as they left East Dubuque.

Her cold stare was enough of an answer.

"How did you know that guy wouldn't have you writhing on the floor choking on your own black blood? He scared me shitless," Garin asked, leaning forward from the seat behind Lorenzo.

"I make a point never to be intimidated by someone who dresses straight off a Wal Mart rack and wears imitation Rayban sunglasses. I've seen these wannabe Satanists before. Sure, they're brave when they have a knife to a chicken's throat, but grab them by the collar and shake them a little and they always fold."

"Satanists? In Bear River?"

"No, it was while I was doing a stint in Miami as a private investigator. With the influx of Caribbeans, there was a lot of voodoo and stuff going on. A farmer hired me to see what was happening to all his fainting pygmy goats. At first I thought it was a group of Haitians. I wasted three weeks infiltrating their ranks. I'd worked my way into their priesthood by the time I discovered the real culprits. Of course I already was an initiate--that had been my cover for a couple months in Cuba back in ninety-five.

"It turned out to be some wacko suburbanites sacrificing the goats on weekends. There is nothing stranger to see than some pudgy insurance agent in a purple cowl pouring goat blood on his neighbor's naked wife next to the barbecue grill. They should have stuck to bowling."

It didn't take long to cross into Wisconsin and reach Dickeyville. The small grotto was on a main thoroughfare next to the Holy Ghost Catholic Church. They slowly drove by the structures coated with everything from shells, stalactites, melted glass, broken plates, fossils, tourist knickknacks, and marbles. They turned to circle the block. Lorenzo pulled into the parking lot of a small softball diamond and flipped off the camper's lights.

"We can cut through the back to reach the grotto," Lorenzo said as he sorted through a cloth bag and pulled out a mallet and several chisels.

"I can carry the hammer," volunteered Rorianne.

"How many of us are going? Wouldn't it be safer for just Lorenzo and me?" asked Garin.

"I will be the one to take the Jewel of Myrlyn. It is in the Chronicles," Rorianne spoke very resolutely.

Vlad joined in, "I will also go as the last heir of the Rohnelds and as the one who can recognize the Jewel of Myrlyn."

Garin groaned and felt only a little better when the two apprentices, both with silly smiles on their faces from the beer they were drinking, graciously offered to stay in the motorhome. Lorenzo was digging deeply into a bag and began pulling out clothing. He stood and held one of the outfits in front of Rorianne. It was a nun's habit.

"I think this should fit."

She looked down at the garb in puzzlement.

"It's what the women devotees of this religion wear," he explained as he bent to pull out the rest of the clothes.

"Lorenzo, these are for monks," Garin protested. "There aren't any monks around here. We'll stick out more in those than if we were dressed like that Satanist."

"There is a monastery on the outskirts of Dubuque," he corrected his young friend.

"What would they be doing out at this time of night?"

"Tell me, Garin, what do monks do at night?" Lorenzo asked in a distracted voice, squinting in the dim light while trying to read the size of a robe. "What they do for leisure entertainment when they get wild hairs up their butts? Bowl, water ski, stock car racing? I think not. Have you ever seen a monk umping a Little League game or roller blading? No. To most people, the night life of a monk is as little fathomed as what cows do after dark."

"Maybe they sit around in fishnet stockings while eating pizza and watching X-rated cable," Garin said in a voice laden with exasperation.

"The cows?"

"No, the monks."

"Maybe," Lorenzo answered while holding a robe up in front of Garin. "I think this might be a little tight around the shoulders."

"But I suppose you know because you once were disguised as a friar while doing undercover work for the CIA in the Vatican."

"Yes, I know, but it was as a Sardinian Coptic ascetic in Istanbul, and I'm still not at liberty to say for whom."

"Ok, what do they do at night?"

"The cows?"

"No, the monks."

"Can't say."

"Why?"

"It's a secret."

"Ok, then what do cows do at night?"

"Can't say."

"Cows have secrets?"

"No, but you wouldn't want to know."

Garin sighed and took another tack. "Why do we need these outfits if we're sneaking in through the back?"

"They keep security lights on all night."

"I'm beginning to feel sick."

"Just nerves. Now let's dress and be off. The game's afoot. And remember to turn off your cell phone."

"This is crazy," Garin grumbled to no one in particular as they climbed the park hill to the back of the grotto. They paused briefly to let an auto pass, then made a wild dash to press themselves against the outer wall of the main shrine. It half circled the grotto like a horseshoe.

"There are several shrines and gardens here," Lorenzo whispered to the group. "We're behind the wall encompassing the main one housing the grotto of the Blessed Virgin. Over there is the fountain and the patriotic shrine, that's the sacramental shrine of the Holy Eucharist, over there is the Sacred Heart shrine, around back of the church is the Christ the King shrine, and there are the Stations of the Cross. We'll check out the main one first. Follow me."

"This is crazy," muttered Garin again as they trooped single file to the front of the grotto. "Now he thinks he's a tour guide."

They stopped in front of the small building that had a glass partition across the entrance. Inside was a small statue of Mary surrounded by a dizzying array of rocks and glass shards coating the walls. Garin looked hopefully at several large quartz crystals, but Vlad's gaze quickly passed over them.

"What is the purpose of this shrine?" Rorianne wanted to know.

"To glorify God," Lorenzo answered, "and to offer a place of beauty to meditate and contemplate God."

"You glorify your god with discarded pottery and broken glass?"

"Beauty and the desire to create art take many strange forms," admitted Lorenzo. "A priest built this between 1925 and 1930. It's dedicated to love of God and love of country."

"Look, here's a starfish, and over there is a lump of coal," Garin pointed out.

"We'll circle and see if the stone is on the inside of the walls or the outside of this shrine."

Lorenzo next led them through a garden and to several other shrines. Garin poured over the varied shards of porcelain, recognizing the remains of saucers, cups and small cream pitchers. He ran his finger over hunks of amber glass and pieces of onyx and amethyst. Vlad shook his head at each one.

The last shrine seemed to be in honor of Columbus. His statue perched about twelve feet above their heads and overlooked a fountain. Vlad gasped and pointed to the arch over the statue's head. His gaze was glued to a shard of green crystal about the size of Garin's forearm.

Garin shook his head. "You know, this would never make a good movie. In all the ones I've seen, the jewel is usually the eye of some heathen idol in the middle of a jungle guarded by a bunch of spear-wielding natives. How am I ever going to tell my grandchildren that my biggest adventure involved stealing a green piece of quartz from above a Christopher Columbus statue in Dickeyville, Wisconsin, after hitting the bars in East Dubuque? It lacks a certain intrigue and romance."

"Are you sure it is the jewel?" the princess asked, ignoring Garin's rambling.

"You would have no doubt if you could see it as I do. It is what we search for," said Vlad.

Rorianne softly sobbed and leaned her head against the stone wall. The others waited silently until she pulled herself together and rummaged through her habit for the hammer and chisel.

"Here," said Lorenzo, shinning a small flashlight onto the object of the quest.

Garin caught his breath. The stone did look like a large, green quartz crystal, except it seemed to suck in the faint beam of light and after condensing it into a tiny, pulsating star, hurl it back to where Garin thought he could feel its cold light chilling his face.

"It is the one. I...I..." Rorianne began to affirm the discovery, then stopped when she couldn't find her voice to say more.

The others held their breaths as Rorianne began carefully climbing the wall. She reached the statue of Christopher Columbus and took time to find a secure perch. Placing the chisel to the surrounding mortar, she tapped the hammer gently against the head of the chisel. The faint sound of a faraway bell rang from the hammer and chisel, the stone, the wall and even from within each of the quest members--then the stone dropped from its resting place and Rorianne grabbed for it in surprise. She clasped it tightly to her breast and whispered a prayer.

They began their walk back to the motor home in silence.

"I can't believe how well everything went," Garin finally said to Lorenzo. "Especially after what else has happened."

"I think you may have spoken to soon."

Lorenzo's comment made Garin miss a step as he nervously looked about for some sign of trouble. The streets and ballpark were empty. He started to relax until he looked to where the motor home was parked. Flickering beams of light shot into the sky to reflect off the clouds like anti-aircraft search beams, waving about like the groping tentacles of a monstrous octopus.

"Holy shit. What the hell is going on?"

The group picked up their hems and began running. The lights were now changing colors, from deep, ocean blues to dazzling yellows and reds. They stopped outside the door in a semicircle.

Vlad hesitated then turned the handle. The door flew open and the four stumbled back before the blinding light now bursting from the entrance.

As quickly as it had erupted, the light vanished and everyone was left blinking away tears. Garin squinted to see the two apprentices stumbling from the vehicle, both with sheepish looks on their faces.

"Holy shit." Garin knew it was getting repetitious, but it was the only thing he could think to say.

"Ah, you are probably wondering what that was all about," Elfred asked in a slightly intoxicated slur.

"No," Lorenzo answered and hurriedly began herding everyone back into the vehicle.

Garin had to be pushed before he could make his feet work. He climbed the step, paused to peer into the dark interior of the RV then let himself be reluctantly pulled in. Lorenzo quickly shucked his robe and slid behind the wheel. He didn't wait for the group to be seated, but slammed his foot down on the accelerator and sent the motor home squealing onto the street.

"Sorry," he said as several of the group picked themselves from the floor, "but I thought it would be wise to be as far from here as possible when the cops arrive to investigate the grand opening of a new car dealership."

"I want to know what happened," Garin demanded of Elfred. The apprentice magician looked embarrassed.

"I, ah, was showing Searene a simple spell to make a small light, but suddenly it grew in size. I forgot how your world has been affecting my magic."

"I would think by now, apprentice, that you would be more wary of using your powers for trivials," Vlad rebuked his younger quest mate.

Breaking the uneasy mood, Lorenzo turned onto a main thoroughfare and cheerfully exclaimed, "We did it. Let's hit the road. I could use a soft bed and a few hours of Zs."

The return trip was uneventful, and Garin found himself drifting in and out of sleep. He was once awakened by a cycle of intense snoring from Elfred and Drestin. Rorianne remained awake, her knees drawn to her chin and the stone clutched tightly in her arms. Vlad sat near her and stared pensively out the window.

Searene cuddled against Garin, and he placed an arm around her. The dim moonlight shining through the window was just enough for him to examine her sleeping face. He tried reading the lines and features. What kind of person was she? Sleeping, she looked very vulnerable.

Searene opened her eyes and smiled at Garin.

"Do you still fear to be part of the quest?"

He shifted in his seat and answered, "No. I must be crazy, but if the rest of you are willing to risk your lives for this jewel, I guess I can."

"We risk our lives not for the jewel but for the people it would hurt. If you come, you will be the bravest of the quest."

"Me? How do you figure?"

"It is not your world that is in peril, it is ours. You be out of danger here in your own world where magic has no hold. The others and I face this evil because we must or perish. You do it for friendship."

"What about Lorenzo?"

She smiled again. "Your Lorenzo goes because he is an adventurer and the lure of such a quest is like milk to a babe. You go, though you would rather shun such adventures. That takes more bravery."

"You could always stay in this world."

"No, I have been chosen. Men surmise that women want only to raise children and have a hearth to tend. There be some truth to that, as it is also with men. The two apprentices secretly yearn for a quiet domicile and babes about their feet, but they also want respect. They imperil their lives and that future for the regard of their friends and their own self-esteem."

"Even though I am just a woman," she continued in a jesting tone that Garin also recognized as determined candor, "I also want respect, more so after having been a kitchen wench and drudge for a dim-witted smuggler. This quest redeems me, no matter what ill consequences may befall me. And afterwards, if I survive, I can then hope for the things you men expect me to crave."

"I, ah..."

"You do not have to respond," Searene laughed as she roughed Garin's hair. "I can speak of my honor without it threatening your manhood."

"I don't feel threatened," he answered, half in a sleepy confusion.

"Good. That is what I like of you, Garin. You will make someone a good husband as well as a fine hero."

He knew she was teasing him, but Garin didn't care. The closeness of her body and the continuing cadence of the van on the highway were making his eyelids heavy. He didn't want to admit her words gave him a warm feeling of satisfaction that fended off most of the worry nagging at the back of his mind. He shifted again in his seat to find a more comfortable position and drifted into a light sleep.

They stumbled like zombies from the motor home when they reached the farm, Elfred and Drestin already complaining of headaches.

"I'll sleep in the RV as kind of a first line defense," Lorenzo said. "Ralp can stay with me as a guard dog."

Garin didn't pay attention to the sleeping arrangements. He forced one foot in front of the other until he was up the stairs and lying face down on his bed. He felt the mattress sag under the weight of another body as he fell asleep, too tired to even say goodnight to Searene.

~ * ~

Ralp had torn a hole through the screen window and was sitting on Elfred's chest. The apprentice shoved him off and wearily sat up in bed. Drestin was still out cold to the world. Elfred forced himself to the bathroom, then into his apprentice garb and new footwear. He looked down at the high-top basketball shoes Garin had given him and wiggled his toes. They looked funny but felt more comfortable than his blockish boots.

Elfred was almost afraid to open the barn door, fearful Shadow's wound was worse than it had appeared yesterday. The dragon weakly lifted its head and looked back with slightly glazed eyes. Its scales were a dull black. Even the apprentice magician could recognize the effect of poison. He had feared telling Drestin of the possibility. Elfred had heard tales of Lancenian dragons having their talons dipped in venom. There were supposedly no known cures and even magic usually failed in aiding the victims.

He thought of Vlad's rebuke last night, but looking at the dragon stiffened his resolve. Elfred couldn't let Drestin see Shadow in this shape. The apprentice stood with his legs spread and head thrown back, straining to recall the renewal incantation. Usually a common spell used only for slight ailments, he was hoping this world would again magnify his power. Shadow watched on as the young sorcerer waved his fingers through the air as if weaving his chant into an invisible tapestry.

A glow began shimmering around the giant steed, first like fireflies shimmering at night over dew-wet grass. The visible manifestation of the incantation intensified swifter than Elfred anticipated until he could no longer look at the dragon. He dropped his arms. A cold hand squeezed his chest as he questioned the safety and logic behind his brash decision. An afterimage of the dragon glowed purple against the inside of his eyelids. Elfred finally gained the courage to peek then opened his eyes wide in astonishment.

Shadow was standing, his wings partially unfolded as if he wished to be flying at that very moment. He was glowing though no direct sunlight was falling on his scales. The dragon lowered his head to nudge Elfred.

"You have done well," Vlad's voice startled the apprentice. Elfred almost tripped when spinning around in guilty surprise.

"I, ah, I am sorry, I..."

"Speak no more. I saw the dragon earlier this morning and knew it was mortally ill. You saved Shadow's life, as well as our quest. Not only can we return through the gate, but the dragon is now strong enough to elude pursuit. The princess is up and she demands we leave soon. She bid me to command you to cast a healing spell for the combat injuries, knowing this world could strengthen your spells. I had not yet told her of the dragon's dire infirmity, and now I will not be forced to. Come, let us eat a morning meal. We have a long day ahead of us."

~ * ~

Garin sat alone in his room. He could hear the noisy preparations going on downstairs. On his desk was a model of the space shuttle Challenger. A decal was peeling off the left wing and it was coated in dust. He opened and shut the cargo bay doors and remembered carefully gluing the model together those many years ago. He had wanted to be an astronaut.

That was a far cry from the public relations job he now held, Garin mused, writing boring press releases on new products, stock information for investors, year-end reports and articles for a monthly newsletter. It now looked like he was going to get the adventure he'd dreamed of as a kid, only instead of from the cockpit of a rocket, it was to be on the back of a dragon.

Garin shook his head. He was supposed to be packing for the trip, not mooning around in his bedroom. They'd told him to pack light so he was only including a jacket, several shirts and jeans and a few changes of underwear and socks. An old pair of square-toed cowboy boots still fit. He threw them in the backpack then changed his mind, slipping on the boots and putting his loafers in the pack. He took one last look at his room and headed downstairs.

Rorianne was impatient, hustling about the house trying to get her fellow questers to hurry. She and Vlad were back in their original traveling garb, as well as wearing their swords. The apprentices were also back into their home world clothes, though Garin smiled when he noticed Elfred was still wearing his high tops.

"Are you sure the dragon is prepared for flight?" she asked Drestin for the third time.

"Yes, Shadow is harnessed and the gear is already stowed. We have only Garin's provisions to pack. We can all thank Elfred for his quick thinking and magical healing spell. Otherwise Shadow would not fly today."

The princess glared at Garin and he hastened out the door with the dragon apprentice. He watched Drestin carefully tie the pack over the dragon's left haunch.

Garin found he wasn't nervous. It was still too unreal for a reaction to set in. Lorenzo was sleeping under a nearby tree, dressed in jeans and a colorful tie-dyed Grateful Dead T-shirt sporting dancing skeletons in jester garb. He had told Garin earlier that he'd learned to take naps and eat whenever he could on any kind of trip.

"You never know when you'll next have the chance for either," he advised his younger friend. "Learned that hang gliding over an Iranian nuclear power station while taking infrared photos for the Israeli secret service back in ninety-nine. Crash landed in the mountains and had to hide with the Kurds for over a month before I was smuggled home on a Liberian freighter."

Two days ago Garin would have chalked it up to the idle ramblings of a lunatic. Now he wasn't so sure.

"Let us mount," ordered Rorianne. She was standing with arms clasping elbows, tension written on every part of her body.

The dragon kneeled. Drestin showed Garin how to use Shadow's knee as a step before grabbing onto the harness and pulling himself the rest of the way to his seat. He perched there nervously as the others followed suit. It would be crowded, but the dragon apprentice had assured him Shadow could handle the load. He gazed about the farmstead as the others climbed on, and for the first time realized he might never see the place again. That thought had never bothered him until now.

Garin didn't hear any commands. The dragon abruptly hunkered even lower then leapt into the air. Garin almost lost his grip. Even Vlad appeared surprised by the powerful liftoff.

Garin had flown numerous times in commercial jets and believed he was prepared for the flight. But a pressurized cabin is completely different from riding the back of a dragon. The wind whipped his hair and he could feel the temperature drop as they quickly gained altitude. Soon the surrounding fields took on the aspect of a riotous green quilt, and the surrounding farmhouses looked like pieces on a Monopoly board. He was startled to see a small figure standing in the yard at Old Man Moeller's place--waving!

Elfred sat directly behind Vlad and gave him directions by pointing his finger. The dragon turned and twisted several times as if chasing an invisible bird. Then instantaneously the sun shifted in the sky and the ground below rippled into a map of rugged hills and timber. They were through the gate.

Garin had only a few seconds to savor his amazement before Shadow jerked to the side and climbed almost straight up like a stunt plane. The sky around them was teaming with other dragons bent on attacking the newcomer. His stomach churned as their mount dodged and swerved crazily through the Rovers swarming about like mad bees. For a brief instant Garin locked eyes with a grizzled warrior as they shot under his dragon's wing. It was over in just a few heartbeats. Once free of the encircling ambush, Shadow easily outraced the pursuers until they were just a cluster of dots behind them.

"The magic, it must still be stronger from Garin's world," gasped Vlad to the others. "I have never been on such a ride."

Minutes later the Lancenians were completely lost to sight. The time of day was different, and the sun was directly above them. Vlad tried slowing the dragon to get his bearings, but Shadow couldn't stop and they continued the mad flight across the sky. Each beat of his wings sent them catapulting forward.

The dragon apprentice watched in disbelief as the magic churned in chaotic swirls about the wings. It no longer resembled the faint, shimmering Northern Lights he'd seen when they began the quest, but a nightmarish infernal of serpentine flames twisting and lashing about the whole dragon.

"We must land," cried Elfred. "The magic is out of control. I can see it surging about us. We must land now."

Saying and doing were two different things. Shadow was berserk, driven mad by the power storming through his body. The humans could only hang on tightly as they raced on and on. Shadow soared higher than Vlad had ever ridden a dragon, higher than he thought possible, far above the clouds.

Garin's legs kept going to sleep, and he constantly shifted in his seat. He looked at the sun and guessed several hours had passed. It appeared the dragon was beginning to tire. Vlad was coaxing Shadow to halt his mad rush. They descended through the clouds and could once again see the land beneath them.

Vlad calmed the dragon to where the beast stopped beating his wings. They'd glide downwards until Shadow would instinctively correct his flight. The tiniest flicker of the wings would send them surging upwards. Twice they came close to landing on a grassy plain, only to see the ground hurl away from them seconds before touch down. Using his wings was as much of a reflex for Shadow as blinking.

They were lucky to be on an exceptionally intelligent dragon. Shadow seemed to realize he must keep his wings perfectly frozen. He fought to hold them steady, and on the fifth attempt he slammed into the earth and skidded a dozen yards before coming to rest in a large flowering bush. The crushed blooms filled the air with a sweet fragrance.

Garin unfastened the clasps on his belt with trembling fingers and slid thankfully to the ground. Vlad wasted no time in leading the dragon under a massive, sprawling tree. Shadow had to hunch down to get beneath the bottom branches that were themselves the size of regular tree trunks.

Rorianne paced anxiously as Drestin strapped Shadow's wings and covered them with the canvas used to disguise the dragon from the rascally traders. "What happened? Will he be able to fly again, and if so, when?"

Vlad and Drestin worried about the animal, checking it for injuries and rapping Shadow behind the ear for his heroic behavior.

"No wonder there is no magic in Garin's world," Elfred said. "It would soon destroy anyone with magical abilities. Shadow's flying powers are amplified to the point he was about to burn up in a deluge of energy. I can only guess it will slowly dissipate now that we are home."

"And how long will that take?"

"I have no idea."

"Damn!" Rorianne cursed. "We are so close to ending this quest."

"How do we end it?" Garin asked. "I know the stone is to be destroyed, but how? And where?"

The question didn't have a soothing effect on the princess. She glared at Garin as if he were the cause of the problem.

"The prophecy says it must be destroyed by the fires of the pillars that hold up the sky," Vlad answered when it became apparent Rorianne did not want to discuss it.

"What's that?"

Rorianne still didn't answer. He could tell she hadn't yet solved that part of the Chronicles.

"I know," Drestin said matter-of-factly from where he was sitting near the dragon.

"Oh? Pray tell us this, oh wise apprentice. Was this something you learned while cleaning dragon manure from the stables?"

Rorianne paused when she saw the effect of her caustic response. Drestin's face fell, and it was obvious he was hurt by her retort. She rubbed her forehead and looked to Vlad who returned her glance with a frown.

"I am sorry, Drestin," she sighed and walked over to sit beside him. "This quest is beginning to tire me with its many hindrances. Tell me what you think this means?"

Drestin looked up at the others then to the princess. "The pillars that hold up the sky--they must be the mountains of stone columns Shadow and I fled to when we drew off the dragons. They are the ones on the map not far from the gate. The gem must be destroyed by its lightning."

The princess leaned her head back and took a deep breath then slowly breathed out. She smiled and placed a hand on the apprentice's shoulder.

"I should have realized that when we flew over those mountains. I have been so fearful of failing, or that one of you would become the leader, that I have stumbled in trying to unravel the remaining mystery. You are right, of course."

She stood and walked to the dragon, rapping it gently. "And we shall return to those mountains once Shadow has recovered."

Rorianne had so drawn the attention of the others that none noticed the arrival of a flight of dragons until the shadows flashed through their midst. Both Vlad and Rorianne spun and drew their swords.

"What is this?" cried the Bulgavian king. "No Rover could have caught us after that race."

Rorianne lowered her sword and smiled as she watched the half dozen dragons land in a circle around them. "It is not the Lancenians. These are members of the Thurbian army, my brother's soldiers."

There were four soldiers to the dragon and most of them dismounted to warily enclose the group.

"Throw down your weapons," ordered an old sergeant who remained mounted. "You have trespassed onto Thurbian soil and are under arrest."

"Since when are visitors to this country automatically criminals?" asked Rorianne. She realized none of these border guards recognized her in the caravan garb.

"Since ordered by King Grantor," he snapped back. "There will be no more questions. Throw down your arms or you will be cut down and buried on the spot you stand."

Vlad edged forward and stood elbow to elbow with the princess. "Your warmth in welcoming visitors to Thurbia leaves something to be desired, little man. Why do you not get off your dragon and come to the front so we may teach you manners."

The sergeant wasn't expecting such a response from the small group. He looked surprised, then angrily ordered his men to move on the strangers.

"Stop," Rorianne demanded. "Do you know who you are speaking to? I am..."

Her words were drowned out by the sudden roar of a monster wind that thundered outwards from the questers and slammed into the men, sending them rolling and tumbling backwards. The dragons ducked their heads and clawed madly at the ground, but even the giant beasts were slowly pushed backwards. One-by-one they turned and leaped into the air, to be carried away like leaves in a spring storm. Rorianne turned to search for Elfred. He stood with upraised arms and wearing a look of stunned amazement. The winds immediately ceased when the apprentice magician dropped his hands.

"I, ah, I only meant to frighten them," he spoke with a stammer.

"That you did," Vlad observed as he watched the soldiers slowly climbing to their feet and looking nervously around for their mounts.

The sergeant had tumbled from his dragon and was flat on his belly and holding onto a small bush. Vlad pulled him to his feet and pushed him toward Rorianne. The Thurbian didn't look like he was prepared to fight.

"Do not hurt the man," Rorianne ordered. "He was only following the orders of my brother."

The sergeant did a double take when he heard her words. He started gasping like a carp pulled to shore and fell to one knee.

"Forgive me, Princess. I did not recognize you. I am sorry if I offended you, but we were only following King Grantor's decree. No strangers are to be allowed across the border now that we are at war with Lancene."

"Lancene? War? How can this be?" The princess sheathed her sword and stepped forward to grab the sergeant by his tunic. "How is my brother? Are they to Castle Raven? When did this come about?"

"Three thousand Lancenians are camped not far from the castle, and King Vasper appears ready to begin the siege any day. He has built wooden towers with wheels that he means to use in sending his warriors over our walls."

"This is ridiculous. Our forces would never allow warriors to approach so close."

"Princess, there are only the royal guards and several companies of reserves to defend the castle."

"What? What do you mean? Where are the rest?"

The border guard was becoming a bit dazed at being jerked around by Rorianne. Vlad laid a hand on her arm and she reluctantly released the man.

"They are off fighting in Trinton."

"Trinton? What are you talking about? Trinton. You are lying." Drestin pushed his way through the others to stand before the sergeant, who looked as if he was preparing himself for another shaking.

"No. King Grantor declared war on Trinton after signing a treaty with Lancene. We were to split the kingdom. But instead of joining in the invasion, King Vasper warned the Trintons. They ambushed our troops and those not killed were taken prisoners. And now the Lancenians camp at our door."

"The fool, the stupid fool. What made him think he could trust Vasper?"

The rest of the Thurbian soldiers were cautiously approaching. They had overheard enough to realize the identity of their strangely dressed princess. Their dragons had returned and were circling overhead.

"Quick, we must reach the castle," she commanded. "Call down your mounts. We will leave immediately."

She turned to Drestin and Searene. "You will stay here with Shadow until he has recovered then follow us to Castle Raven."

The Thurbian dragons were landing and the men quickly mounting. She motioned for the other members of the quest to join her on the largest beast. Lorenzo paused to whisper for several seconds with Drestin and Searene before slipping away.

Garin followed wordlessly, too bewildered by what was happening to say anything. It wasn't until their new dragon had leaped into the air that he realized Lorenzo was missing. Maybe he was on one of the other mounts. He didn't believe now was the time to bother Rorianne with the disappearance.

Chapter Twelve

The guards kept their dragons skimming the forest and closely skirting the hilltops. They were maintaining a sharp watch for enemy dragons while trying to stay low and out of easy sight. In an hour the formation of dragons dropped to skim above the churning waters of a fast flowing river. The dragons followed the river's turns and twists until suddenly they were above a broad, deep valley and the river plunged seven or eight hundred feet like a mist-shrouded waterfall.

To the left, huddled almost against the valley wall, Garin could see Castle Raven. To the right was a large encampment of men. Numerous pennants flew over a city of tents. Five towers of rough-hewn planks stood at least fifty feet high.

The Trintons urged their mounts to fly faster as a group of Lancenian dragons took off from the encampment to intercept the newcomers. There was no doubt they could reach the castle in time, but Garin worried when he saw the castle walls bristled with large crossbows. Instead of arrows, the weapons were loaded with large spears. He guessed they were this world's counterpart to anti-aircraft weapons. The wicked, barbed heads looked capable of tearing an ugly hole in dragon wings. He hoped the gunners could recognize friend from foe. They did--the six Trinton dragons passed safely over the wall and landed in a large courtyard while their pursuers circled out of range of the bows.

Rorianne leaped to the ground as soon as her mount touched down, not waiting for the dragon to kneel for the usual off-loading. She pushed her way through a circle of surprised soldiers who stepped quickly out of her way after the sergeant yelled her identity. The princess swiftly climbed a flight of massive stone steps and disappeared into an arched doorway.

Vlad, Elfred and Garin stood uneasily by the dragons as a circle of curious soldiers gathered, peppering the border guards with questions. The mob quieted slightly when they heard there was a master mage among the group, though they looked puzzled when they saw only the garb of a magician's apprentice. Several stared in puzzlement at the high tops.

A guard, dressed brightly in a red cape, yellow silk tunic, and black pants, came running down the steps from which Rorianne had disappeared on only moments before.

"His Majesty King Grantor demands your presence," he related between gasps for air.

The impatient guard turned without waiting to see if they would follow and briskly set off back up the steps. Garin would have tried keeping up with the man, but Vlad purposely fell into a languid, unruffled stroll the others were forced to follow. At the door, the guard turned and urged them to make haste in a sharp voice.

"We are not servants," Vlad said simply, but either his tone of voice or cool stare was enough to restrain the soldier. Though it obviously took great effort, the guard moved at a slower pace.

The entrance led into a long hall. To one side were tall, extremely narrow windows. On the opposite wall were a long line of statues, dented shields, crossed swords, mounted torches, and suits of armor.

"Quite impressive, yes?" whispered Elfred.

Garin looked about and nodded politely, though to him, the decor looked like something from a nightmarish yard sale at a trailer court. He wanted to tap one of the torch holders to see if it was plastic.

"Ah." Vlad had broken his cool deportment for just a second to admire a piece of art.

Garin turned his head in the direction Vlad was looking. It was of a reclining female nude painted on black velvet.

"It is contemporary art," Vlad whispered almost huffily after observing Garin's raised eyebrows. "I am thinking of acquiring such works for my own castle."

"Ah, of course, an exquisite piece," Garin agreed in a solemn voice. "I have a wonderful tapestry in the same modernistic school. It would look great in your throne room. It's of a bunch of dogs smoking cigars and playing pool..."

Their discourse came to an end as their guide stopped in front of a massive pair of oak doors. These opened smoothly and the three were almost pushed into a large audience chamber. On the far end of the room were two thrones, the larger one much more ornate and positioned higher. A long strip of dark green and purple carpet started at the trio's feet and led to the thrones. It was bordered by more royal guards of the same flamboyant dress.

"Approach," cried a guard.

Vlad, Elfred, and Garin began the long walk.

Garin sniffed. The others didn't seem to notice the strong scent of incense, perfume, and body odor.

If it hadn't been for the introductory wild dragon ride, this surreal trek might have severely strained Garin's ongoing acclimation. It is one thing to acknowledge a completely new reality on an intellectual level, such as a world of magic and dragons, and another thing to accept it on a more primitive, gut level. The dragon flight had more than taken care of the gut-level acceptance.

Still, Garin's sanity felt shaken when he saw from the corner of his vision a two-headed dwarf amongst the audience, staring at him with four ruby-red eyes.

They stopped at the end of the rug and craned their necks to look up at Princess Rorianne and her brother, King Grantor. The young king had his sister's blonde hair and many other similar features, though his were now twisted into a scowl. Deep lines in his face said that the dour expression was permanent. Grantor kept his lame hand hidden inside a velvet sleeve.

Several advisors standing to the side were also scowling and one hissed, "Kneel before His Majesty."

Elfred, used to the ways of royalty, dropped to one knee. Garin looked at Vlad, who stood staring intently at both sitting figures, then reluctantly dropped to his own knee.

"I said to kneel, knave."

Vlad returned the man's glare then reverted his gaze back to the king. Both stared silently at each other as several guards nervously shifted their weight.

"Silence, Frensten, I cannot expect a fellow monarch to bow before an equal. Welcome, King Vladimir Dragol."

The identity of the visitor drew involuntary gasps from everyone within hearing. The soft rustling of fabric broke the silence as the men-at-arms tensed and grabbed their hilts. The king smiled at the reaction of his audience. Garin didn't like the insincere smile any better than the scowl.

"Your majesty, I am prepared to offer the aid of Bulgavia in the defense of your kingdom. Let me send a message and I can have 4,000 Dragoons here in two days."

"I thank you for your help, King Dragol, but I am afraid the Lancenians plan to attack by morning light. My sister has told me she welcomes your own sword in defense of Castle Raven. She says you are a valiant warrior. I have heard the kings of Bulgavia are awesome figures in battle. Maybe the sight of you among my men will strike fear into the hearts of King Vasper's soldiers."

"I will do anything I can to protect the Princess Rorianne," Vlad answered, now gazing at the woman. Rorianne smiled back. A scowl returned to Grantor's face.

"You must be tired after such a harrowing adventure of which my sister has briefly spoken. I will have you shown quarters where you may rest and eat. I know my sister longs to get out of those dreadful traveling clothes."

King Grantor leaned over the arm of his chair and whispered into the ear of an advisor then stood stiffly and withdrew through an exit hidden in the drapes behind the thrones. He was followed closely by his sister. Vlad seemed surprised by the abrupt end to the audience and stood for several seconds looking at the empty seats. Guards encircled the three and escorted them back across the vast chamber.

Garin took the opportunity to look about the throne room. The room's decor was more of the same as the hallway, walls covered with swords and shields, corners filled with statues of naked men and women and daylight streaming in through tall, narrow windows. Large arches climbed from the floor near the walls and soared to the center of the distant ceiling.

The audience was full of faces, some smiling, but most appearing puzzled by the trio. He again saw the two-headed dwarf and smiled weakly. The dwarf grinned back broadly from both heads and gave a friendly wave.

They were led to a side passage and followed a route that took them continually down countless flights of stairs and through a number of pathways dimly lit by torches.

"I take it that we're not getting the penthouse suite," Garin muttered as he ran his hands along the damp stones of the wall. He wrinkled his nose at the sour odor carried upwards by a sluggish draft of air.

"This King Grantor has an odd sense of hospitality," Elfred agreed.

Vlad paused when they began down a narrow tunnel of steps, casually kicked the lead two soldiers down the stairs and turned with drawn sword to the four very surprised soldiers above them.

Garin stumbled into Elfred while trying frantically to get out of the way of Vlad's blade.

~ * ~

"I still do not believe you brought him here, sniffing at your door like a dog searching for a bitch in heat," growled Grantor as he paced in Rorianne's chambers.

"Grantor, you go too far. I will not listen to such filth. King Dragol has acted with nothing but honor toward me. It is you who must do the explaining. What is this of you attacking Trinton? They have been our allies for centuries. It is only because we have stood together that we have both survived. Did you go mad to throw in with Vasper? You know of the Chronicles of Myrlyn. The King of Lancene is totally evil."

"You speak drivel. Those old tales are the mutterings of ignorant peasants. There is no jewel, and you have been on a fool's errand."

Rorianne stood watching her brother in silence. The narrow vein of weakness and petty pride that flowed through the crippled king had grown during her absence. She said nothing of the green crystal hidden in the pack on her bed.

"You must forget about this Dragol. His bloodline is famous for beguiling females. It was all a charade designed to worm his way into our court so he can add Thurbia to his spoils."

"He promised to fight with us when Vasper attacks," she reminded her brother.

"You believe him? Bah, he will be running like a jackal once the battle begins."

He waved for silence when she started to protest. "I have no time for this bickering. Defenses have to be readied."

"Those I travel with--you will not harm them," Rorianne said with a firmness of voice her brother could never master. He flinched as if under a physical weight when she slowly spoke the words.

"They will be properly cared for, I promise you that," he said as he quickly went through the door.

An aide waiting outside stood silently as the king spoke. "Well, did Frensten carry out my orders?"

"Yes, he has sent them to the dungeon."

~ * ~

Garin and Elfred backed down the stairs as Vlad battled the soldiers above them. The narrow stairwell allowed only one soldier to face the Bulgavian king at a time.

"Have I overlooked something? What did I miss? What the hell is going on?" asked Garin.

"It could be that King Vladimir wanted quarters with a better view," guessed Elfred.

"Shit, is this how you complain about room service?"

The two young men pressed themselves against the wall as the body of a guard rolled by. His yellow blouse now blotched with red.

"You know kings; they can be very finicky at times." Elfred added.

"Remind me not to piss him off."

"To your rear, the others are returning," Vlad warned as he dipped passed an opponent's guard and nicked him in the thigh.

Garin turned to see the two guards the king had kicked down the steps. Their swords were unsheathed and both looked angry and determined.

"What's he telling us for?"

"I think Vlad means for us to dispatch them."

"How?"

"I believe I will be forced to use magic."

"Are you crazy? You'll kill us all in this narrow place. Don't you carry a knife?"

"I do, would you like it?"

Garin reexamined the length of the approaching blades. "Okay, but be careful."

Elfred raised his arms, the cuffs of his gray cowl falling to his elbows. Garin crouched and curled into a ball with his arms over his head. The apprentice magician began mumbling what his new friend took to be an arcane, mystical spell. The lead guard paused at the sight of Elfred's maneuverings, but the other pushed him forward and the soldier continued hesitantly.

The first sign of what the spell embodied was a cool feeling on Garin's back. He pulled away and saw the stones were beginning to profusely sweat. A trickle developed then a small stream. The water was flowing down the walls and stairs. Garin scooted back four steps to be above the stream. This time both guards stopped. The lead soldier panicked when a deluge erupted from the ceiling and he shoved his way past his fellow guard to flee downwards. The other soldier quickly followed.

Elfred dropped his hands and looked about expectantly. He frowned when the water continued flowing, even picking up in volume. Garin didn't like the looks of it. Another body almost knocked Elfred off his feet. The corpse rolled on to be carried away by the small creek that was rapidly turning into a river. The remaining guard stared at Vlad's bloodstained blade and decided caution was the better part of valor. He turned and fled.

Water was gushing beneath Garin's feet. He climbed to where Vlad stood and observed the springs were sprouting higher and higher in the stairwell. Vlad leaned against the wall to catch his breath then pulled away and looked at his wet shoulder.

"Magician, what mischief have you now performed?"

"I, ah, it was just a simple water spell used to fill a cup or jug."

"The gods help us when you execute a major incantation. It is time to end it."

Elfred was forced several more steps upwards before answering. "I do not know if I am able. It should have ceased when I dropped my hands."

All three were now retreating to higher ground.

Garin was having a relapse. He felt as if he were in the grip of a lingering dream. Flying dragons, sword fights, magical spells--it was still too much to grasp. He watched with the detachment of a remote observer as the passage below began filling.

"They have closed the way above us," Elfred observed.

Garin looked up to see a stout door blocking the exit. He gazed back at the rapidly rising water level and abruptly lost his disconnection.

"We'll drown. We have to get out of here," Garin yelled as he leaped up the steps and threw himself against the door, managing only to bruise his shoulder.

"What'll we do?"

"I have another idea," Elfred answered as he began raising his hands.

Vlad grabbed an arm and forced it down. "I do not know if that would be wise."

The king gazed into the water below and pondered their dilemma.

"Just why did you begin that fight?" Garin asked, his curiosity momentarily overcoming his fear.

"We were not being led to the type of quarters I preferred."

"What?"

"Our route was not to a guest chamber of my liking. We were being taken to the dungeon. King Grantor could only be planning treachery."

A horrible thought struck Garin. "The dungeon? Does that mean we've drowned a bunch of poor prisoners?"

"No, the guards must have closed a door further down to make this tunnel fill so quickly." Vlad climbed to the top of the stairs and rapped his knuckles against the thick iron bands holding the timbers together. "It is stout and well made, too formidable for my saber. Perhaps we will again need the aid of the magician."

Garin grabbed the arm that Vlad had just released. "Elfred, what are you going to do? Not that I don't trust you. But I just had the most awful vision of you using a drying spell and turning us into steamed broccoli."

"I am going to transport us outside the castle."

"Are you sure we won't wind up thirty feet above the ground or inside a tree?"

The apprentice magician sighed. "Usually a mage would take a dim perspective of someone questioning his competency, but under the circumstances, I will tell you that I will do the best I can."

Garin released the arm, though the answer wasn't as assuring as he'd hoped to hear. He couldn't afford to be choosy with water lapping around his boots. Elfred raised his hands and began another mumbled incantation. Garin shut his eyes and held his breath. He didn't know what to expect, but he was hoping for something at least painless.

He opened his eyes when the echoing of dripping water was replaced with the touch of a gentle breeze in his hair. Garin looked about in surprise at the smooth transition to the outdoors then let out a shriek. He was teetering on the tip of a ledge and looking down at the valley floor almost a thousand feet below. He windmilled his arms and backpedaled to safer ground, there to collapse to his knees where he tightly gripped a small cedar tree until his shaking stopped.

Rorianne's castle was far across the box canyon. The keep sat atop a rugged outcropping of rock, its foundation stones flowing down into the myriad gullies and crevices like melted wax. He forced himself to crawl back to the edge and scan the distant valley floor for traces of his friends, fearing they might have materialized further out and fell to their deaths. There were no signs of bodies, only the Lancene army--a nest of busy ants scurrying among tiny tents and pennants.

The waterfall marked where the river entered the canyon. It was hidden by a massive cloud of boiling fog with a brilliant rainbow shimmering in the spray. Garin knew what looked like toothpicks dropping over the falls were the trunks of immense trees. The river emerged from the haze not far from the castle and snaked its way past King Vasper's army to disappear around a bend. Behind the fortress, far enough away that it could not be used from which to fire weapons past the castle walls, rose an unassailable wall of bare stone that marked the end of the canyon.

Garin turned and saw more cliffs rising thirty or forty feet above his head. Not knowing what he would do when he reached the top, the newest of the questers began carefully picking his way up a narrow fissure.

~ * ~

Vlad found himself a dozen yards from the edge of the forest ringing most of the valley. At his back was the castle. King Vasper's army was spread before him not more than a quarter of a mile away. Like Garin, he immediately dropped to his knees. Vlad decided he was yet undetected and set off crawling in the high grass to the sheltering woods.

Like most forests under royal protection, its trees were very old. Ancient oaks twisted into fantastic shapes. Vlad believed he could see leering faces and contorted bodies in the gnarled branches. An immense, fallen cottonwood blocked an elk trail and the young king could barely see over it. Thick clusters of ferns and woodland flowers bordered the downed trunk as neatly as if they'd been purposely planted. He left the path and circled the obstacle, stopping at the roots and peering into the rotted heart of the giant. A sign the termites were not yet finished with their house/meal was the fresh sawdust spilling to the ground like a drifting sand dune.

Vlad drifted silently through the thin undergrowth as he'd been taught in the Dragoons and by the royal master of the hunt. The skills of both disciplines complimented each other. He knew how to remain undetected from both man and beast. Several times he watched from hiding as secretive deer or trampling Lancenians passed. The enemy soldiers were not the elite Rovers, but unskilled peasants drafted into service. Much like the pawns in a chess game, they were spent cheaply and often used to take the brunt of enemy charges until the more valuable skills of the professional troops were called upon.

He made his way slowly along the forest fringe until he finally was even with the Lancenian camp. There was much more traffic through this part of the woods as scouts continually combed the forest for spies or Thurbian units planning hit and run skirmishes. Vlad eyed a flock of tethered dragons behind a picket of vigilant soldiers and ached to get his hands on one. He knew it would be suicide to try such a thing in daylight.

He leisurely scanned the army camp and made note of the numerous siege weapons, among them several mangonels. Mounted on four wheels, the weapon used two massive coils of rope twisted tight by a winch. A shaft rose from between the ropes, or skein, with a bucket at its end. Before firing, the shaft was pulled back by another winch, further straining the ropes. Bulgavian soldiers called it a "nag" because the rear kicked like a horse when the shaft was released to fling its ammunition like a giant mousetrap.

There were piles of timbers and rope that Vlad knew were the parts to even larger weapons. Too heavy too move, these would be constructed on the spot when the forces moved closer to the castle. Called trebuchets, their shafts were made from the trunks of entire trees. Instead of a bucket at the end, it used large slings to hurl projectiles. These could be boulders or even diseased corpses. Plagues were better weapons than stones.

Circling these siege weapons were ballistas or giant crossbows. They were to defend against aerial attacks. The massive bow was bent by a windlass.

Then there was the circle of gray tents flying no banners. They stood by themselves away from the rest of the camp. No one dared attack them. These belonged to the wizards. Magic was mostly a defensive weapon. Conjurers accompanied an army mainly as safeguard that the other side wouldn't actively use sorcery. As nuclear weapons in Garin's world forced countries to honor a policy of MAD (Mutually Assured Destruction), neither side here wanted to unleash the annihilative forces an increasing spiral of sorcery could bring about.

That didn't mean divining or even a playful tweak at the weather never occurred--but it wasn't a major factor in warfare. Individual wizards did occasionally battle, their duals frowned upon by all the occult guilds. It was only when some tremendously powerful wizard occasionally appeared in history that the balance was tipped. Then the bullying conjurer might sweep aside his fellow magicians without fear of reprisal until the survivors grudgingly put away their differences to fight the common enemy.

Such master wizards were rare, Vlad thought gratefully. But where skill was lacking, a tool of immense power like that of Myrlyn's Stone could wreak chaos and mass destruction. All bets were off if such a weapon should fall into the hands of King Vasper and his evil minions. No army or group of magicians would be able to stand in his way.

Vlad retreated to the base of the valley wall and used the trees growing from fractures in the rock as the rungs of a ladder. He stopped when he found a small ledge and settled in to wait for nightfall. The young king was almost asleep when the sound of thunder shook the ground and almost threw him from his perch.

~ * ~

Elfred froze when he found himself standing in the midst of the Lancenian forces. No one seemed to notice his sudden appearance. A young and dirty page ran past him carrying a bucket of water for his master's morning toilet. Elfred was facing the wizards' tents and held his breath when an old mage stepped out to urinate on a thistle plant and take the water from the servant. He cuffed the boy along side the head before stepping back into his canvas billet.

Half of Elfred's amazement was natural. Finding oneself in the midst of an enemy encampment is reason enough for bewilderment, but the apprentice knew his magical appearance was an impossibility. The camp was no doubt protected against such infiltration by dozens of spells weaving in and out along the camp boundary like the reeds of a basket. Any one of the numerous barrier incantations spoken by the master magicians should have been enough to prevent the appearance of a novice like himself. At the very least, an alarm should have sounded at his arrival. And there were such spells in place. With his heightened sensitivity, Elfred could feel the thick flow of the wizardry about him.

Yet here he stood, like a scarecrow in the middle of a cornfield. Elfred tried devising an excuse or story for his presence, but his mind was a complete blank. The dumbfounded apprentice magician could only think to pull his up hood and hide his face.

He watched the young servant rubbing where the wizard had landed his blow. The groundless punishment meted out by the magician rankled Elfred. He had watched Geldlelf disperse such random acts of violence on Drestin, and the memories still brought his blood to a boil.

The offending sorcerer again exited his tent and emptied the bucket on the same thistle plant. He paused before lifting the door flap to reenter the tent when he spotted the lone figure dressed in the garb of an apprentice.

"What are you doing standing about like some lazy soldier? Does not your master have something for you to do?"

"Ah..."

"Speak up, you indolent lout, or I will give you something to be dumb about. What is your name, or did your whore of a mother forget to give you one before she tossed you into a pile of pig shit?"

Elfred had forgotten that most apprentices were treated as if they were boot camp recruits.

"Ah..."

The crotchety wizard didn't wait for Elfred to stutter a lame excuse but flicked his right hand and spit out a brief curse. The apprentice was surprised to see the incantation forming. It appeared as a blue vapor with sparks of orange. The spell quickly grew and Elfred intuitively knew it would soon bolt across the open space to seethe about him like a horde of maddened bees. He didn't know how he was suddenly aware of such things, but Elfred was sure the enchantment was meant to cause numerous and very painful boils and blisters. The arrogance of the wizard caused Elfred to clench his jaw and before he realized what he was doing, he flicked his own wrist and quickly uttered an obscure spell he had once read. He was surprised he even remembered the bewitchment.

A red sphere of vaporous light rolled from his fingers and shot across the meadow to smother the other's curse then flowed about the surprised wizard. It dissolved the magician's black robe and left him standing in the field naked, his bony and grub-white body not looking very imposing. He squawked like a plucked chicken and raised his hands to smash the foolishly brash apprentice.

Elfred snapped off another spell. The old wizard staggered, fell to his knees and began vomiting dead fish and toads. A shudder would seize his spindly body each time he lifted his head to pronounce a curse and more rotting fish would be disgorged. By now other magicians were coming out to investigate the sounds of voluminous retching. Pointing an accusing finger, the puking sorcerer managed to choke out a warning.

A quick-thinking sage recognized that the apprentice was not one of their own and lifted his hands. Bright bolts of energy erupted from his fingertips and streaked towards the stranger. Elfred was feeling cocky and he made a slight, almost careless wave with one hand that split the cold fire so it flowed harmlessly about him. The ease of the defense spurred the rest of the mages to hurriedly unleash their own curses.

Elfred yawned and leaned against empty air as if there was an invisible wall beside him. He nonchalantly nodded his head and a violent wind slammed into the wizards, blowing the words to the incantations from their mouths. Pegs popped and the tents hopped and skipped away like shirts blowing off a clothesline in a summer squall. A particularly gruff looking magician slapped his hands together and the winds immediately died. Elfred realized he was probably facing the King of Lancene's personal sorcerer.

The two looked at each other for several seconds.

"Who are you, my brave little apprentice?" Though the mage stood at least sixty feet away with his hands behind his back, his words came to Elfred as if they were spoken right next to him. "I would have thought that word of such a talented novice would have reached my ears. Why have you come among us to cause this trouble? The young are often foolhardy, so I will ignore this breach of courtesy if you stop this nonsense and place yourself in my custody. I can use a gifted apprentice like yourself. Submit to me and I will teach you knowledge to go along with that talent."

The magician was smiling sincerely, unaware that Elfred could see the powerful spell gathering behind the sweetly lying mage. The head wizard had no intention of letting such rogue powers survive to grow and become a challenge to his own authority.

"I appreciate your offer," said Elfred. "It would be an honor to work with one as great and famous as yourself."

The magician smiled wider, little aware that though Elfred's hands were motionless, his toes were wildly wiggling. The apprentice had never heard of spells being cast by one's feet, but it appeared to be working. A glowing stream of green light flowed toward the master magician like a small river of melted candle wax. The wizard appeared unaware of the probe as it tapped into his own spell and began siphoning off power. The luminous mist behind the Lancenian flickered dimmer and brighter as it struggled to build strength.

The mage's smile faltered for a second as he realized his incantation was not gaining in power. His fingers worked busily behind his back, and Elfred watched the glow flickering more wildly. The rest of the mages stood uneasily about, knowing their leader was up to something by the feel of energy in the air. A sweat was breaking out on the wizard's forehead. He now appeared as just a silhouette to the apprentice as the spell churned fiercely behind him. Immense power was being generated, and Elfred was awed by the wizard's strength. He could see it flowing through his own spell and watched from the corners of his eyes as it gathered and swelled the midsection of his magical conduit. The bulge grew until it looked like an egg swallowed by a snake.

Growing impatient, the tiring Lancenian thrust his hands out and uttered a blasphemous curse that made even the other deviant mages cringe. Nothing happened and the wizard paled when he realized what degree of power was needed to cancel such an incantation.

Elfred wasn't smiling. Keeping the immense energy bottled up was beginning to test even his newly acquired powers. It surged and swelled, struggling to burst from its confinement. Another mage lifted his hands to challenge, the apprentice and the distraction was all it took.

~ * ~

Rorianne rushed to her window when she heard the thundering roar. She stumbled as the floor rolled beneath her feet and grit rained from the ceiling. Outside, an immense, jet-black cloud boiled into a monstrous pillar, casting its shadow across the enemy camp and even shading the castle. She stared in disbelief as it reached a great height then spread outwards taking the shape of a giant umbrella.

~ * ~

King Vladimir cautiously wove his way through the trees. He stopped occasionally to watch clumsy Lancenian soldiers crash through the underbrush. They were also headed in the direction of the earth-shaking explosion. Once again Vlad marveled at the ineptitude of the men and wondered why the infamous Rovers weren't deployed. They probably considered the boring guard duty too demeaning, Vlad decided.

The leaves far above his head were rustling as if from a rain, but the grit and small pebbles falling around him told of a different kind of storm. He reached the edge of the woods and stared dumbstruck at the giant column of dirt and smoke reaching above the scattered clouds. Vlad immediately realized it rose from where the wizards had been quartered. Further down the valley was the rest of the encampment, all the tents flattened or blown away. Many of the siege weapons lay on their sides. Soldiers and horses scrambled about in panic. If Thurbia had even a token army left, Vlad thought bitterly, they could easily defeat their enemy at this moment.

For the first time he noted there were no dragons to be seen, not even corpses. Vlad again examined the scene before him and decided most of the force must have been directed straight up, or the concussion would have killed everyone in the valley and flattened the trees he was now standing beneath. The dragons must have instinctively taken to the air when the earth first shuddered and were caught in the following high winds.

He returned his gaze to the giant mushroom cloud that had now grown to where it was blocking the sun. He recognized some of the debris in the churning, dark pillar--flapping tents and the broken bodies of dragons. Unlike other magical explosions he had witnessed, this blast had sucked air inwards and up, hurling the torn earth and rubble miles into the sky. His attention was jerked away by the sound of snapping limbs. He turned to see the shattered body of a large red and green dragon lying among broken branches, its wings twisted like crumpled paper. Up and down the valley he could hear other large objects smashing through the trees. A boulder plowed into earth not far from where he stood and sent up a giant geyser of dirt.

Vlad began quickly back tracking to the shelter of the cliff.

~ * ~

Some apprentice has pissed off the big boys, Garin thought as he watched a small mini-drama unfold beneath his eyes. He was lying belly down on a smooth, weathered ledge warmed by the sun. He felt like a large, lazy lizard--or maybe like a small boy lying on a bed and gazing at toy soldiers dispersed across his floor. The tiny, gray-garbed figure down in the valley faced a semicircle of black-robed wizards. He squinted again to see if his eyes were playing tricks. Wasn't the kneeling figure naked? He wondered what kind of strange and bizarre rituals were under way.

Not much was happening below and Garin found himself almost drifting to sleep. He rubbed his eyes and in that brief instance the world burst apart. The rock beneath him jumped and heaved. A gargantuan black serpent thrust its head from the earth and began climbing to the heavens. Seconds later a tidal wave of sound and fury smashed against the walls of the valley. Garin was bounced and rolled backwards into a grove of small cedars. He no sooner came to rest, partially wedged between two trees, when the wind shifted one hundred eighty degrees and began screaming and clutching at him from the opposite direction. He frantically grabbed at branches and fought to keep from being dragged back to the ledge and hurled over the side.

Garin was completely exhausted when the maniacal wind died. His shoulders ached and several scrapes stung from his skidding across the rock. He rolled over and looked in amazement at the mushroom cloud still rising into the air. It looked exactly like the films he'd seen of nuclear explosions, only there had been no initial blinding light. He hoped this meant there was also no radiation, then hurried to find shelter when the debris began falling.

~ * ~

"Now is the time you must act," Rorianne fiercely urged her brother. "Look at our enemy. King Vasper's forces are in disarray. Whatever the cause of this mishap, we must take advantage of it."

"We do not have the strength. My cowardly generals led my best soldiers into a Trinton ambush. Our only chance of survival is to hope King Vasper changes his mind because of this and calls off the attack."

Rorianne fought back a bitter denunciation dealing with the fate of their army. She also stopped short of accusing her brother of being a coward. For the first time she found herself wondering if her brother's skepticism about Myrlyn's prophecy wasn't just a sham. Did Grantor deny the quest because he did not have the courage to face the foretold deaths?

"At least let King Vladimir send for help among his own people. Even the Rovers fear the Bulgavian Dragoons."

"Hah, you still whine about your Dragol hero," Grantor snarled. "Well, your precious King Vladimir and two other friends have fled the castle, leaving you and the rest of us to our fates. They value their own craven skins above yours."

"You lie," was all Rorianne could answer. She retreated to the window and watched the outlines of the strange cloud blur as it slowly dissipated.

~ * ~

Hunger drove Garin to search for food. He wasn't about to descend into the valley with all the crazy happenings going on below. A wagon trail led him through a land not as green and lush as the valley. Still, there were farm fields and he even once spied a brown and white milk cow. It was smaller and leaner than the cattle he was used to, but it was still too big for someone armed with only a Swiss Army knife.

The trail led to what once had been a homestead on the banks of a small creek. He walked slowly among the burned ruins of a house and several small barns. Only the stone foundations and charred wood remained. He guessed it to be the work of the famed Lancenian Rovers and wished he'd thought to have at least brought along his father's shotgun.

Garin resisted looking too closely at the ruins of the house. Several vague, blackened shapes suggested things he didn't want to contemplate. The same went for a scrap of blue cloth he spotted among the bushes by the creek. He was about to continue his trek when a faint cry caught his attention. He cocked his head. There it was again. It came from the bushes.

Garin forced to himself to investigate the noise, even after approaching close enough to see the bare feet of a woman sticking out from a blue skirt. She lay face down under a bush and the buzzing flies scattered in annoyance at his arrival. Garin reached down and pulled the infant from under one outstretched arm, being careful not to look into the face of the corpse. He ran quickly to the creek and released his breath just as he began to feel dizzy.

The baby looked to be about six or seven months old. Garin wasn't experienced at judging a baby's age, but it was big enough to crawl. Being picked up caused the infant to crank up the volume from whimpers to full-fledged screaming. It didn't take a Dr. Spock to see the baby was thirsty and hungry. Garin looked helplessly about. He wetted a corner of his shirt in the creek and squeezed water into the child's mouth.

That sufficed until the baby began protesting the lack of substance to the liquid. Garin held the infant as best he could while it screamed and squirmed. He looked at its red and twisted little face and wondered what abuse he could be further subjected to that could top this. His thoughts of self-pity were interrupted by another protesting voice. Garin looked up into the face of the cow he had spied earlier. It stood examining him with large, brown, accusing eyes. He hadn't been off the farm long enough that he didn't recognize a cow needing to be milked.

"Come here, bossy. Are we glad to see you."

It took several minutes for him to find a cup in the remains of the house and wash it in the creek. The cow followed impatiently as the baby continued its wailing. The Hemphills hadn't had a dairy operation--just a beef herd, corn, and soybeans. But Garin's dad had kept a dairy cow for family use and he vaguely remembered helping milk it as a kid. The skill did not return easily. Bossy shuffled nervously as unfamiliar hands tried finding the right stroke to drain the swollen udder.

A few drops dribbled out and minutes later he had the milk flowing in rhythmic skirts. He drank a quick cup of the warm liquid then tried feeding the baby. It was unused to anything but its mother's breasts and protested all the while Garin fought to feed it drop-by-drop.

The next chore, Garin realized, was to bathe it. The baby smelled terrible and squirmed uncomfortably in his arms. It was dressed in a soiled gown and a rag diaper. He pulled off both and began beating them on rocks in the creek. The baby squealed even louder during its turn in the cold stream. It was then he discovered the infant was a boy. Garin wrapped him in his own shirt while the baby's clothes dried. Fed and bathed, the infant drifted to sleep in Garin's arms. He laid the baby in the grass when he spotted a lone chicken searching among the ruins.

The rooster was suspicious of the strange human, but wanting to be fed its accustomed grain, won out over caution. Garin cleaned it by the creek so he could continuously wash his hands while completing the distasteful task. He remembered his mother scalding the chickens in boiling water to make the plucking easier. He seared the feathers off in the fire before placing the chicken on a spit over the coals. The baby woke again and he fed it more milk from the cow, which was keeping close to its new master.

Though the chicken was tough and charred, Garin ate it all before washing again in the creek. He sat and looked from the cow to the baby. Elfred and Drestin had described a quest as an exciting adventure. Somehow he hadn't imagined that included babysitting and tending a cow. The baby grinned at Garin and tried pulling off his nose. He had to admit the kid was cute with his large dark eyes and curly brown hair.

His only hope was to discover a surviving farmstead where he could find a home for the orphan. There was no way he could return to the turmoil in the valley until the kid was safe. He sighed, stood, and looked over his shoulder to check if the cow would follow before continuing his walk.

The baby seemed to grow in weight. Garin shifted it from arm to arm and finally seated the boy on his shoulders with the chubby legs on both sides of his neck. He held the ankles firmly and tried ignoring the pounding and pulling of hair. He also attempted to overlook the drooling--though he was unable to ignore the baby wetting.

That created a problem since the rag diaper and gown weren't yet dry. He wound up carrying the baby naked and hoped the kid could hold off from further releases until the diaper dried. He didn't and Garin held him at arm's length while the baby squirted. The kid grinned and laughed as if it was great sport.

Garin was taken by surprise when two Lancenian soldiers appeared over the rise of the next hill. He dropped into the tall grass bordering the trail and crawled to where he could spy upon them from behind a fallen tree. They hadn't spotted Garin, but they did see the cow and let out explosive whoops and yells. Their mounts were two old nags that refused to be hurried, no matter how the soldiers kicked and cursed.

Garin guessed they weren't viewing the cow as a renewable food resource, but as an immediate beef dinner. Adrift in the strange world, he had found the cow's presence strangely comforting. He clenched his teeth when he thought of them killing the gentle creature. A dozen rescue plans flashed through his mind, but they were all flawed in that the soldiers carried swords and he was armed with only a baby.

The soldiers were obviously not the cream of King Vasper's troops. Both were slovenly from head to foot with oily hair, wrinkled uniforms, scuffed boots, and missing most of their teeth. They dismounted and attempted to circle the cow with swords drawn. Bossy didn't like the looks of them any more than Garin. She bolted from the trail and began wading through the tall grass toward Garin's hiding place. He had been worried about the baby crying and hadn't considered the cow giving him away.

Garin looked frantically around and spotted a branch about the size of a walking stick. He grabbed it and prepared to put up a hopeless fight.

He could hear the cow and men coming closer, but didn't dare raise his head to look. It was a nightmare. He could feel the gagging in the bottom of his throat that often preceded vomiting.

Inches from his nose were several small aphids crawling on a weed. The clarity in the tiny details of the bugs and fuzzy stem was almost hallucinatory. Garin wished the tiny scene was all there was to the world. Bossy rounded the log and bellowed apprehensively. He looked up to see her worried brown eyes.

"Come on, yah. We are not about to hurt yah. No, girl, we want to be yah friends, do not we, Creb?"

"Not me, I wanna eat 'er."

Garin listened as the crunch of weeds grew louder and knew he couldn't wait any longer. The lead soldier didn't have time for much except an astonished gasp before the club took him square across the forehead. His eyes rolled up and he dropped with a thud. Garin could hardly believe he did it.

The other soldier froze in his steps and gawked stupidly at the apparition. He was tall and underfed. Garin raised his club and gave what he hoped was an intimidating grimace. He didn't feel threatening, but the remaining adversary must have thought so. The soldier spun and ran for his horse, almost falling off the other side in his haste to mount. Garin stared in amazement as the lout screamed and kicked the nag. Garin believed he could have walked backwards and still caught up with the sluggish horse. He watched them until they disappeared over the hill.

The baby stayed safely asleep. Garin walked to the remaining horse and began going through the small pack. He found several items of clothes that could do as diapers, though he would have preferred to wash them first.

A dark bruise forming on the Lancenian's forehead told Garin his defeated opponent was still alive. He felt much better knowing the man wasn't dead. The soldier was too pathetic looking to merit ill feelings. Garin kneeled and was examining the bruise when the soldier moaned. The Lancenian blinked with unfocused eyes before fixing in on the face looming above him then whimpered and flung his arms over his face.

"I'm not going to hurt you if you behave," Garin said as he took the man's sword and stood. "Don't try anything and you can leave in one piece."

The soldier peeked from under an arm. "Please, yer lordship. Yah would not wanna hurt a defenseless man who has five hungry babes at home."

"Get up if you can. You took quite a wallop."

"That is all right, yer lordship. I have a thick noggin, I do, or so my Gessie says."

Garin was awed. The man had taken a blow that would have killed most people, yet the soldier appeared hardly worse for the thump.

"I'm going to confiscate some of your clothes and horse, but I'll let you go with your life. Leave right now. Don't try to sneak back, or the next time I'll be forced to do a better job."

The man looked puzzled at the thought of anyone wanting his rags. "Yer lordship, I am indebted for your mercy, but I am a poor man who has only that horse to farm with come the war being over. Please let me keep the old girl, she is not worthy of a fine Thurbian gentleman like yah."

"I'm not a Thurbian and you can stop calling me 'Lordship.' Fine, keep the nag," Garin surrendered, not liking the part of a victor demanding spoils. "Take the horse and get back to your war."

"Thank you, Yer.."

"Garin."

"...Yer Garin."

"No, just Garin."

The Lancenian looked uncomfortable with the informal title.

"I'm not a lord or anything," he continued. "Just get on your nag and go."

"Ah, my...ah, Garin, sire, could I have my clothing?"

"No."

"No?"

"No."

"I do not think yah have seen the tunics and trousers closely, sire. They are of the poorest linen."

The conversation was interrupted by a wailing from behind the log. Keeping an eye on the prisoner, Garin picked up the baby and patted him on the back.

The soldier gawked at the tot.

"He's an orphan, thanks to you and the rest of your brave warriors."

"Ah, but that would not be me or me mates' doings. That butchery is the work of the Rovers. They are the only ones who enjoy such killing of women and children. Like me said, me have babes of me own back home."

"Now you see why I am confiscating your clothes. They're for the baby."

"He is no relation to yah?"

"No, I told you I'm not a Thurbian. I found him at a farm under his mother's body."

"I believe yah. I have never seen a Thurb dressed as yah, nor anyone else, come to that. And you have an odd pick in weapons," he said, eying the stick and thoughtfully rubbing his goose egg.

"Don't get any ideas or you'll get another whack for your troubles."

"Peace," the soldier replied as he held up his hands. "I have no cause to wish yah harm. Just let me go and yah have seen the last of me."

Garin waved his stick. "Then go, and take the nag with you."

The soldier hesitated. "Have yah been feeding the wee one from the cow?"

"Does it look like I can nurse him?"

"You must be careful. A babe used to a mother's tit can get colicky from cow milk. And he now be big enough for some solids."

"I'll remember that."

The soldier rubbed his bruise one more time and sighed.

"Here, let me help yah swaddle the child. He will catch the coughs if yah do not bundle him up."

The Lancenian kneeled at his pack, pulled out an off-white tunic and brushed it flat on the ground. He lifted his arms for the child. Garin still didn't trust the man but admitted he needed all the help he could get.

The soldier did possess some child-rearing skills. He laid the baby on the shirt and with the expertise of a professional gift wrapper, pulled, folded and tied the tunic until the kid was neatly bundled.

"Me name is Hermie," he volunteered while examining his work.

Garin found it strange making introductions with a man he'd brained only a few minutes before.

"What is the babe's name?"

"He hasn't said."

"I doubt there will be anyone who can tell yah. It is up to yah to give it a new name."

"Me?" Garin looked down at the baby in surprise. "Whoever I find to take the kid can name him."

"He is yours. The folks around here are a strange brood. They worry about changelings, and do not believe in taking a foundling. Yah will have no luck in that."

"Me? The baby? What would I do with a baby?"

"What will the babe do without yah?"

"Here, take him. You said you have a bunch. One more shouldn't hurt."

"I would if I was home. The sergeant would not understand me having the babe as spoils. Me misses would love the little one. But I canna return until this damned war is over or the King would take me from me home as a deserter."

"You might live longer as a deserter," Garin said. "I have a feeling things aren't going to go well with your army now that the king of Bulgavia is here, not to mention a powerful wizard from Trinton. You saw what happened to your own wizards, didn't you?"

"King Dragol is here?" Hermie paled at the name. "Aye, I do not wish to tangle with the Dragoons. They say they are more mad than our Rovers. Me and me buddy were up here scrounging for food when the evil fell upon the king's wizards. We heard about it. I do not think I would like to meet this mage, either."

The soldier nervously ran his fingers through his greasy hair.

"I have no love for fightin', but me whole family would suffer if I should take tail. King Vasper treats deserters and their families very harshly."

"If your king survives this battle."

Hermie looked around as if to make sure there were no eavesdroppers. "Aye, he wouldn't be missed by many of his own soldiers. At least those who are not Rovers."

"Then again, you wouldn't be a deserter."

"How is that?"

"You're my prisoner. I've decided not to release you. You'll remain my captive and take care of the baby."

A smile crossed Hermie's face. "Right yah are. Poor me, taken prisoner. It is bad luck, but I canna be blamed. Me own buddy will bear witness that we were overpowered and me probably killed. I bet you he reports it was half a battalion that attacked us."

"Get your things together and we'll get moving," Garin said as he took the infant.

He now faced a new quandary. He hadn't gotten rid of the kid, yet he needed to find others of the quest. That meant heading back to danger.

"You will want this." Hermie was offering him his sword, hilt first.

Garin gingerly took the blade. It was a crude sword, far heavier than the rapier he'd used during a semester college course in fencing--a class he'd almost flunked and of which he could remember little.

Hermie pulled another shirt from his bag and quickly devised a sling for the baby to hang from the simple saddle. Taking the reins of the horse, he pulled it around and looked to Garin for guidance.

"I guess we should head back to where I landed, though I'm not that fond of getting too close to the battle."

"Where yah landed?"

"It's a long story."

"Good, it will make the walking more agreeable."

Garin took a deep breath. "It started when I woke up with one hell of a hangover. Some salesperson was trying to sell me windows when a wyvern flew by my window..."

The small caravan presented an odd picture--an infant hanging from the side of a swayed-back horse, a bruised peasant conscript and a stranger in off-world blue jeans and cowboy boots--followed closely by a milk cow.

~ * ~

Most of the tents were back up. Soldiers scurried about making repairs to the siege weapons while King Vasper persisted in storming among the men, angrily shouting orders between heated curses. The monarch stopped to face a contingent of soldiers escorting a battered and dazed wizard. He was the master magician who had attacked Elfred.

"Sire, this appears to be the only sorcerer to have survived the attack."

The mage needed aid in walking and the men appeared to disdain the contact. Common soldiers held little liking for magicians and their dirty ways of fighting. They preferred to face familiar, cold steel.

King Vasper examined his remaining wizard with a critical eye.

"It seems, Mage Koranth, that you and your flunkies were not the caliber of magicians you led me to believe. How could one lone wizard defeat you so easily and almost wipe out my army?"

"He was no simple wizard," the shaken sorcerer replied. "I barely managed to escape with my life. He wielded a power I would not have believed possible. It was if Myrlyn had returned from the dead."

It was King Vasper's turn to appear startled.

"Myrlyn, you say?"

He turned to look at the distant fortress and cursed under his breath.

"The stone, that whimpering girl of a king must have the stone. Why did I not think of that?"

None among the retinue appeared eager to answer the king's question.

"Tell me, Koranth, could you have faced Myrlyn's Stone?"

Eager to rationalize the recent fiasco, the wizard quickly agreed that not only was it possible, it was most probably the case. Turning to the castle and stretching out his arms, the mage closed his eyes and disjointedly waved his fingers in the air like the antennas of some weird insect.

"I detect a strange power in the Thurbian castle. But it sits alone, not in the possession of a mage who can wield it. Nor do I detect any magicians in the court of more than mundane talents."

Turning back to the king, the wizard said, "Most likely the apprentice who attempted to employ the jewel was destroyed in the holocaust. It would take the mastery and knowledge of a mage of my skill to safely exploit its full powers."

King Vasper grunted his skepticism of the wizard's ability or his reasoning then turned to an aide. "Quick, bring me a messenger. I believe it is time to offer terms to King Grantor."

~ * ~

Elfred had only a split second to cast a spell. The simple ward was meant only as protection from minor blows or slashes, but he found himself encased in a sphere stronger than dragon scales. He floated with hands and feet stretched out against the magical shell. No light pierced the coal darkness and his breathing was the only sound to reach his ears. There was no feeling of motion. The apprentice could have been buried miles deep in hardened lava. The blackness puzzled him since the enchantment usually created an invisible barrier.

The magical shell was insulation against the outside forces. It also horded Elfred's own body heat and the air slowly grew hot and stale, yet he wavered in canceling the incantation. What waited for him outside? He was coming close to lifting the spell when there appeared to be a slight lightening of his gloomy enclosure. He squinted and blinked, not sure if he was imagining the shift.

The bubble was gradually changing to a dark gray and Elfred could just make out the silhouettes of his arms and hands. Occasionally, the transformation reverted for seconds to pitch darkness, only to emerge from the blackness to greater light. Elfred leaned forward and pressed his nose against the bubble. What he first took to be a swarm of insects he could now see was a cloud of dust and grit. The light grew and the debris thinned.

Elfred was abruptly cast into bright sunlight. He blinked as he attempted to adjust his eyes to the return of daylight then froze when he saw the sun was between his feet. He was also severely distressed to see the rich, dark greens of fields and woods looming far above his head. Thousands of tons of dirt and rock had been pulverized and vomited far into the sky, with Elfred's tiny bubble of magic riding within the heart of the flow. It was now flung clear and began its drop.

There was no feeling of up and down and Elfred could only tell the sphere was tumbling because the earth and sky continued trading places-- though the visuals were enough to send his stomach in similar spinnings. Features on the earth quickly grew larger and Elfred braced for the impact. The sphere slammed into the earth and created a mini-explosion, kicking up more dirt and sending Elfred bouncing back into the sky. The magical force field continued protecting him from outside inertia.

The bubble bounced several more times before rolling into the midst of a startled gathering of soldiers. Several fell backwards as they scrambled to remove themselves from the path of the cartwheeling figure. Elfred came to a halt in the middle of a cooking fire. To the astonished soldiers, it appeared as if the apprentice magician was standing on his hands in the middle of their coals.

The dramatic entrance created several problems. The already spooked soldiers appeared extremely annoyed that their haunch of venison was smashed into the fire. It appeared to Elfred as if the soldiers hung upside down from a cavernous ceiling. They silently gibbered and shook their fists as Elfred wondered how to remove the spell without falling headfirst into the coals.

A young soldier caught Elfred's eye. He stood silently back from the rest and was intensely examining the stranger.

"Can you push me out of the fire?" Elfred yelled, his voice sounding strange and muffled in the protective sphere.

The young warrior heard nothing, but saw that the apprentice was trying to speak. He pushed two soldiers out of his way and kneeled to look directly into Elfred's face. He watched as the stranger again appeared to speak then tentatively reached out to find his hand stopped an arm's length from the Elfred's chest. While the rest of the soldiers watched in perplexed silence, the young swordsman ran both hands up the sides of the invisible obstacle. He hunched his shoulders, leaned forward and pushed against the barrier. Elfred watched the sky revolve to its rightful position and eagerly muttered the counter spell that would free him from the hot and stuffy bubble.

The apprentice dropped to his knees with the return of gravity and gasped with pleasure as a breeze blew over clothes now soaked in sweat.

A scowling swordsman stepped forward to prod the stranger to his feet with his blade. He was stopped by the younger soldier who reached out a helping hand.

"Are you all right, magician? You appear taxed. Would you like some water or wine?"

Elfred smiled his gratitude and took the offered hand as he climbed shakily to his feet.

"Thank you. Yes, I could use some water. I feel as is I have been wrung dry."

The warrior gave no verbal command, yet one of the others in the small troop quickly retrieved a skin of water and handed it to him.

"You are somehow connected with the great discharge," the man said to Elfred as he motioned to the sky.

It was not a question but a statement. The apprentice looked over his shoulder to see for the first time what his magic had invoked. The dark column hung eerily in the sky. The comment sent a low murmuring through the rest of the soldiers and they eyed their guest with new respect.

The apprentice looked about and saw that he was no longer on the valley floor. He turned back to his questioner and realized the band wore the uniforms of Thurbians.

"Yes, and I can duplicate the feat if provoked."

The soldier smiled. "I have no doubt of that, mage. You have amply provided proof of your powers. But you will find no provocation here. You are among friends. An enemy of King Vasper is welcomed among us."

"Even a Trintonian?" Elfred said with more ill will than he meant to show.

The young warrior didn't lose the smile, though it took on a bittersweet edge. "Especially one from Trinton, to whom we have much to explain. I am Prince Sephin, cousin to King Grantor and Princess Rorianne, though I find pride in only claiming lineage with Princess Rorianne. The cowardly attack on Trinton was reluctantly carried out by our army. Grantor will find no further allegiance from the surviving troops."

Elfred studied the prince. He had the open, strong face of Rorianne. Sephin was close to the apprentice's height, though of a broader build like Vlad. He seemed sincere. The apprentice wished the princess was present to verify the prince's statements.

"You remind me of Rorianne," Elfred blurted out his thoughts.

The prince's eyebrows lifted in surprise. "Are you of royal blood? You must know the princess very well to address her so informally to her own cousin, mage."

The small-village apprentice would have found himself stuttering and awed before anyone of such elevated station only days ago, but he now found these royal inborn pretensions of superiority very irritating.

"I do. Rorianne and I are both on a quest together."

The prince's eyebrows stretched even higher. "The quest for Myrlyn's Stone? You believe in this chase after rainbows? King Grantor has said his sister is possessed of delusions and the legend nothing more than stories for children."

Elfred drew a breath to tell the prince just how much of a children's tale the jewel was then clamped his mouth shut. There was no sense in giving away Rorianne's secret to someone he wasn't yet sure of.

"It is more than delusions on the part of your princess cousin. If Grantor would have paid heed to its warnings, he would not have Vasper camped on his front door."

Sephin silently studied his guest for a great length of time, almost to the point of rudeness, before slowly pulling away his gaze as if it were an act of great difficulty. He rubbed his face and looked back at Elfred with tired eyes.

"I believe you, wizard. I would be a fool to doubt your word, just because it seems incredible, after witnessing what I have today. At the moment I am not in a position to offer you much assistance with this quest, though I will do what I can. I would also like to believe that as a questmate of the princess, you would lend us aid."

Elfred looked around at the assembly. "Just what are you doing here?"

"As amusing as it might seem, this is the headquarters of the Free Thurbian Army. Most are of my company of Foresters, riders specially trained to fight in rugged highlands and woods. Our horses are bred for sure-footedness and strength. Cavalry trained for such terrain is unusual and that is why we were able to escape the Trinton ambush. The rest of my men are combing the countryside for other Thurbs who managed to escape and return home. I hope to draw at least three hundred men under my banner by tonight. We will be only a few against the thousands of Lancenians, but we know the land and they do not.

"There is death for those who do not know the land...and the sky," the prince said mysteriously as he looked at the gathering clouds. "Only yesterday we lured a detachment of Rovers into the woods and killed over a dozen."

The other soldiers remained busy while the two spoke. They had rescued the venison from the coals. The aroma was making Elfred's mouth water. Sephin noticed his guest's hunger or the aroma had a similar effect on the prince. He ordered a soldier to bring them servings and motioned the apprentice to sit on one of a dozen stumps ringing the fire.

"I am sorry I have neglected to ask your name," said the prince as he claimed a nearby log.

"It is Elfred, Your Majesty."

"Hah, you are a strange one. Your tone of voice says you think little of royal titles, yet I believe they are as commonly used in Trinton as Thurbia."

"Traveling widens one's outlook," Elfred answered cryptically.

"I hope your travels do not take you before my cousin. King Grantor is not known for holding an informal court. He frowns on presumptuous commoners."

"Are you saying I am presumptuous?" Elfred bridled.

"Whoa, Magician Elfred," laughed Sephin. "I was only giving fair warning, though after witnessing your clash with the Lancenian sages, maybe it is I who should tread more carefully."

Elfred had to smile back. "I have no right yet to claim the title of magician, sire, being still an apprentice."

"I would wager there will be few guildmeisters brave enough to reject your entry after word spreads of what has transpired today. But I am being a rude host, plaguing you with conversation while your food cools. We can continue after we have eaten."

Chapter Thirteen

Vlad had silently raided the cache of a small detachment of Lancenians posted as forward guards in the woods. He slipped through their haphazard line and made off with a sack of dried fruit and salted beef, then returned to his refuge, a small cave just above the tree tops.

The sun had already set behind the towering cliffs on the opposite side of the valley. Only the top half of the bluffs high above his head were still in direct sunshine. He sat on the ledge eating from the stolen supplies and admired the way the rosy light played off the wall of limestone.

A lone soldier with a white flag had left the Lancenian camp and was making his way by horse to Rorianne's castle. Vlad worried at a chunk of jerky as he idly watched the messenger approach the base of the keep's hill.

Vlad was tired of skulking about and decided he would soon take some kind of action, though he had yet to figure out what that would be.

~ * ~

Rorianne knew a messenger had arrived from King Vasper. The servants were a buzz as rumors grew and multiplied faster than stable flies. She paced back and forth across the tiled floor of her room, wondering what kind of mischief her brother was now plotting. Grantor's guards had turned her away at the court chamber doors when she tried entering the hall. The princess found herself chewing on a strand of hair, a nervous habit she had as a child. Thinking of those days brought her up short.

She stuck her head out the door and peered up and down the hall. It was empty except for the row of her ancestors staring blankly from their portraits. Rorianne eased the door shut behind her and ran to a narrow marble staircase, pausing again to make sure no one was about. She held her hand over a small, unglazed olive oil lamp to protect the flame. A winding route took her down the stairs and through a maze of seldom-used corridors.

Though she hadn't traversed this section of the castle for years, the princess wove her way straight to the large, empty room. It was once a chamber for ladies-in-waiting where they could sew or gossip between chores for the royal family. It hadn't been used in Rorianne's memory. She made her way to an oak bookcase and brushed away a dusty spider's web. Running her hand under a lower shelf, she found a small indentation. The princess pushed the hidden lever as she applied pressure to the panel with her left shoulder. The secret door opened as smoothly as if it were used every day.

The passageway seemed smaller than that from her childhood memory. Rorianne smiled as she remembered excitedly exploring the tunnels after being shown them by her grandfather's cousin. The old man made her promise not to tell anyone, not even her brother. She now wondered if he had seen what Grantor would become.

Rorianne stopped in a small alcove halfway to the council chambers. Several portals allowed narrow rays of light to stream into the room and fall upon pieces of furniture the young princess had once lugged from all over the keep. A tiny table covered in dust was still laid out in chipped china for one lone rag doll sitting on an equally diminutive chair. She couldn't help giving her childhood playmate a pat on the head before continuing her trek.

Rorianne at last came to the passageway in the council chambers. It was a small tunnel running directly over the doorway behind the throne. She wormed her way into it and crawled for twenty feet before stopping. Small fissures between the stones allowed her to peer into the vast hall. Her brother's voice could be heard shouting petulantly at the messenger.

"What madness is this? I tell you that legend is just that, an old tale meant to put babes to sleep. There is no quest and there is no jewel. It is just part of my sister's mad desire to behave like a man instead taking on the duties of a royal dame."

"King Vasper does not believe so," a lower-pitched voice answered, "and he is never wrong. His Highness believes the attack upon his wizards was brought about by this jewel. He warns that it did not harm his troops, and he will sack the castle and have your head on a pike if it is not turned over to him immediately."

It was a sign of Grantor's cowardice that he didn't have the messenger knocked to his knees at such impudent speech, thought Rorianne. Such imports were usually delivered with more tact, which meant even the messenger knew the Thurbian monarch was too cowed by Vasper's close presence to punish him.

"And if we have such a tool of power, how does your king know we will not destroy him and his army as was done to his wizards."

The messenger smiled. "King Vasper has said that such a power can only be used safely by a sorcerer of the highest level, something your lordship has failed to retain, filling this court with only cheap charlatans and toadies."

Grantor winced at the accusation, knowing his own counselors had warned him about hiring only second-rate mages. His miserliness had also caused him to allow his moat to fill in, which would have deterred the mobile siege towers from making contact with his castle ramparts.

"And you say King Vasper will halt his campaign if I give him the jewel?"

"He promises to withdraw his forces at once if he receives Myrlyn's Stone by tomorrow noon."

Rubbing his forehead, Grantor chewed his lip and nervously tapped the leg of his throne with his twisted foot.

The messenger smiled at such an unroyal demeanor. Yes, his king would pull his forces away, the messenger smirked, so they would not be in harm's way when he leveled this spineless cripple's keep with the Stone of Myrlyn.

"If such a jewel exists, it must be in my sister's possession," replied Grantor. "Guards, go immediately to Princess Rorianne's room and search for any unusual gems."

Rorianne was backing out of the small tunnel in a near panic. She painfully knocked her knee against a corner stone while exiting into the main passageway, causing her to limp as she began frantically retracing her route. The lamp flame went out, and the princess was forced to navigate through the darkness by memory and out-stretched hands. Twice she was forced to turn around after taking a wrong passage before she finally pushed her way out the bookcase.

Not caring if she was observed by servants, she flew down the hallways, gasping for deep breathes as she climbed the last flight of stairs. Rorianne flung her door open to find her room still undisturbed. She ran to her bed and dragged out the soiled and worn traveling pack. It appeared unmolested and she pressed her forehead against the coarse canvas in relief.

The running of many boots on stone floor echoed faintly up the steps as Rorianne returned to the staircase. The guards were not yet visible and it was hard to tell how far off they were. She ran to the nearest door and tugged on the latch. It was locked. She repeated this three times with similar failures. The dozen men appeared at the top of the steps before the princess could try another door or flee down the corridor. She froze, clutching her pack to her chest and staring into the swirling grain of the dark wood of the door.

Rorianne remained immobile for several moments, stunned by disbelief when the guards ran past her without a word. Maybe they hadn't seen her in the shadow of the recessed doorway or mistook her for another member of the household, but they were gone and only the echoing sounds of their footsteps marked their passage.

She shook herself from the daze and plunged back into her flight. Later, after what seemed like an eternity, Rorianne sank gratefully to the floor, her bruised knee still throbbing. She was sitting next to the small table and chairs of her childhood playroom. The hidden passageway was the only haven she believed safe from her brother's patrols. She leaned her head back against the wall and hugged the doll to her chest while wishing she had thought to bring her sword.

~ * ~

"He is either lying or is the buffoon I first took him for," King Vasper stormed to his aides after the messenger was sent away. "How do you let a woman escape in one's own castle?"

"The stone is still in the keep," volunteered Mage Koranth. "If she has it, she has not left the walls of the castle."

King Vasper frowned and clenched his fists in frustration. "Then tomorrow I will send you to the castle to find the jewel. You will also return with the woman. My Rovers will teach her what happens to those who attempt to thwart my will."

"Your majesty, a Hitite priest has arrived and asks permission to set up his tent," an aide bravely broke into his king's reverie.

As disgruntled as Vasper felt, he took time to calm himself before contemplating the newest trial. Hitie was a local god of death and destruction, allied with a similar deity in Lancene called Bannatt. Though Hitie had a small following in Thurbia, his brother death god was more successful under the patronage of the Lancenian government, namely King Vasper. He bartered his financial support in exchange for certain favors the priests of the death cult were only too happy to supply.

"Are you sure he is what he claims and not a spy?"

"Sire, who would dare masquerade as a death god priest?"

The man was right, Vasper thought. The priests zealously guarded their malicious reputation and no one, king or slave, dared offend them. To go falsely garbed as such would be to invite a relentless pursuit that could only end in a most horrible death.

"He has probably come to watch his god at work. Find him a space to pitch his tent away from the troops."

~ * ~

"Halt where you are," came an order from someone hidden above their heads.

209

Garin stopped and tried locating the source of the voice in the thick oak canopy. They were following a narrow deer trail through a forest that bordered the valley rim.

"Drop your sword, Lancenian scum, or I will set an arrow between your beady eyes."

Garin sighed. "There's no call for rudeness, especially when I'm not Lancenian scum. I am a personal friend of Princess Rorianne and this Lancenian scum is my prisoner. We are also traveling with an infant, so unless you want to start changing shitty diapers, I suggest you don't mess with my beady eyes."

A soldier stepped out of the brush behind them as another appeared to their right. The still hidden voice said, "How does a foreigner know Princess Rorianne?"

"I am a questmate."

He didn't know how the soldiers would take that after his visit with King Grantor, but it had to be better than being Lancenian scum.

"Questmate? Do you know the wizard who also claims such status?"

"Why, yes I do. Do you know where he is?"

"What is his name and appearance?"

"Elfred. He is about my height with black hair and dressed in the gray of an apprentice magician, though he might be wearing high tops."

"High tops?"

"Ah, magical footwear."

A rustling of leaves forewarned Garin of the soldier's appearance as he dropped to the ground in front of them. Like the others, he was dressed in a dark green tunic that went almost to the knees, tights and what looked like mountain boots of the same color. He examined the small troupe in wonder, taking in the cow that followed closely behind.

"You do not appear to be too imposing," the soldier admitted ruefully, "but you could be spies. We will let Prince Sephin decide. Give me your sword and follow us."

They walked behind the stout ponies of the Trintonian soldiers for over an hour, occasionally crossing small glades or stands of dwarf cedars, but always returning to the thick woodlands. Their destination was a small clearing along the canyon rim. The tents and ponies were hidden among the trees, though the men sat on rocks and logs in the open where they could keep watch on the action below.

Garin gave a whoop when he spotted Elfred. He was flooded with a sense of relief at the sight of a familiar face. Maybe he was still in trouble, but at least he was with a friend. The two hugged and pounded each other on the back. He was surprised to find his eyes misting. Garin had worried that the apprentice had fallen victim to the prophecy.

"How are you? Have you seen Vlad? Where did you land?" both asked at the same time.

"Me? I landed right down there," Elfred laughed and pointed to the deep crater now visible on the valley floor.

"Holy shit, that was you? I saw you down there before the explosion. The wind almost sucked me over the ledge. I should have guessed that was you. My god, that's a big hole. Wait until it rains, the pit will turn into a lake."

Elfred considered the crater and shook his head. "They better name it Lake Elfred."

A lone soldier walked up to the pair. "Prince Sephin will see you now."

Elfred accompanied Garin as he followed the trooper to the small band's leader. Garin immediately detected a resemblance to Rorianne. Sephin appeared surprised when Garin extended his hand but quickly recovered and returned the greeting. He then stood back and examined his guest's strange garb of cowboy boots, blue jeans and T-shirt.

"Elfred has told me he is a member of Rorianne's quest. Looking at you makes me believe Myrlyn's Gate has already been crossed."

Sephin was astute, the apprentice had to admit. He obviously knew the main details of the legend and guessed from Garin's strange attire that he was from another world.

"We will sit and let our new companion rest from his travels. And while we relax, maybe the two of you would share your recent adventures."

Elfred sighed. He wasn't sure if he should divulge details about the magical stone, but it would be difficult explaining why members of the quest would leave Garin's world empty handed. Sephin was shrewd and probably already guessed that Myrlyn's Stone was somewhere near.

"Ah, Your Majesty, or whatever," Garin said. "I came with two companions--I guess you could make that three. Are they being taken care of? The Lancenian soldier is my prisoner, and I feel responsible for him. He could have escaped any time he wanted but stayed to help me with an infant. The baby might also need changed or fed by now."

Elfred raised his eyebrows in puzzlement.

"I'll tell you about it later," Garin said when he noticed his friend's look.

Though Garin had seen only soldiers upon entering the camp, an old woman was summoned by the prince and told to see after the child. He commanded a soldier to make sure the cow was kept safe and did not find its way into someone's stew pot. Sephin looked back to Elfred after the others departed. The apprentice took that as a cue.

"It began, Prince Sephin, when a friend and I were in the Boar's Breath Inn..."

~ * ~

Now that he had time to rest and think, Garin's thoughts turned to Searene. Her safety has been in the back of his mind all day. Were she and Drestin all right? Was Shadow able to fly yet? He hoped the dragon was still grounded so they would not arrive at the castle to find the same unfriendly greeting waiting for other members of the quest. Sephin told him that no dragons had been spotted recently landing at the keep but did mention the coming and going of a messenger from King Vasper's camp to the castle. Garin hoped that didn't mean ill for Rorianne.

"What did you think of Sephin?" asked Elfred, surprising Garin because he believed his friend already asleep.

"Oh, I don't know. He seems nice enough. Reminds me of some people at the place I work. They're basically okay as long as nothing gets in the way of their advancement. I'm betting the prince is aiming for the throne, which would be an improvement over the current monarch. I just wonder how that would set with Rorianne. When push comes to shove, what would happen to his contender's quest mates? I don't think he'd harm us, but you can bet we'd probably get to know the dungeons of Castle Raven real well."

"My thoughts never traveled such paths. I hope it does not come to that."

"No kidding, I have enough to worry about without getting involved in a palace coup."

"Yes. The completion of the quest."

"I wasn't thinking of that," Garin admitted. "What am I going to do with a baby?"

~ * ~

Vlad was lying in knee-high grass not far from two guards. He stopped his approach when he saw they were Rovers and not regular troops. Though the Rovers had reputations of being ruthless warriors, it appeared they weren't that disciplined when it came to boring missions like guard duty. Bulgavian Dragoons idly talking and joking on the picket line would have been quickly and severely punished. Vlad weighed his options and crawled stealthily forward, making a circle to stop behind the two men.

He held another debate in his head. He could continue and not risk an attack on the guards. But if an alarm were set later in camp, his escape route would be obstructed by two alerted Rovers. Vlad decided to remove the peril now.

It wasn't his preferred way to fight, and he had grimaced as a youth when Dragoon instructors taught the prince how to silently and quickly take out enemy sentries. Vlad didn't believe he could have done it if they had been two ordinary soldiers, but listening to the Rovers' abominable conversation on recent activities gave resolve to the hand holding the dagger. He wiped the bloody blade on the pant leg of one of the dead men and continued his reconnaissance.

The king didn't know what he hoped to accomplish. He had grown very impatient in his hiding place. Well rested after having napped through most of the day, he finally decided to survey the enemy lines. Passing picket after picket had proven so easy that he proceeded much deeper into the enemy camp than he intended.

Vlad worked his way to a tent on the outer perimeter of the camp. He wished he hadn't now that he recognized it as a tent belonging to a death god priest. As King of Bulgavia, he was the titular head of such a temple in his own country. The Draculs had always been on good terms with the various death cults, flooding their alters with the blood of countless sacrifices. Vlad's mother had made sure her son remained free of the cult's influences.

"It is not often that a king bows so low before a mere priest," a soft voice spoke behind him.

Though startled almost to the point of what felt like a minor heart attack, Vlad fought to remain motionless as he slowly released his breath. How could anyone have crept upon him so quietly? He tried imagining the exact location of the voice and ran through the body moves needed to quickly turn and hurl his knife.

"Don't even think about it," the priest ordered. "You're fast, but not that fast."

The voice was maddeningly familiar.

"And besides, the princess would hardly approve of us fighting."

Vlad recovered more quickly from the second shock and rolled over to peer at the scarlet robed priest looming over him.

"Lorenzo! How can this be? What are you doing in the vestures of a Hitish priest? Are you insane?"

"I'm afraid I've never sought a professional opinion on that matter. Would you like to come to my tent where we can speak in a more private manner?"

"Do you know you have sealed your death by dressing so?"

"Only if they find out. Really, these priests of Hitie are rather a comical lot. I thoroughly interrogated the former owner of this tent and found their creed to be very simplistic; a surprising blend of Masonic rituals and ceremonies taken almost directly from a cult I once bumped into--followers of Dorga, the fish-headed god of death. I also spoke briefly with a Bannatt priest of King Vasper's and easily beguiled the simpleton."

"What of the Hitite priest?"

"Hum, that is a different matter. I am afraid he had an accident. I had to bury him under a large manure pile at an abandoned farm. Let's talk inside the tent while we have time. They change sentries every so often, so if you've offed any of the guards, the whole camp may soon be up in arms."

Vlad allowed himself to be pulled into the tent. Though black on the outside, the tent's interior and carpeting were scarlet red. A smoking lamp was made of red stained glass. Vlad didn't like the smell of the oil or fat the lamp was burning. He nervously looked around at the hair wards, bone talismans, feathered charms, and several disgusting fetishes made of easily distinguishable human parts.

There were other strange wood, stone and, metal items--barbaric tools of torture that made Vlad shudder even though he'd seen similar devices in his own dungeon. He reached out to touch a coil of what looked like copper wiring.

"I believe that is to be placed in a fire and then wrapped around some poor soul," Lorenzo said after noticing the direction of Vlad's gaze. "Cute trinkets, huh? The guy had a weird sense of decor. But enough about my tent, what have you been up to?"

Vlad described the meeting with King Grantor and the resulting escape.

"I guess Elfred must have emerged among the Lancenian wizards and tried to astound them with a spell, which I would rate a successful first impression," Lorenzo said.

"You believe Elfred caused that eruption?"

"It looks like it. I know Vasper's man doesn't have the jewel--yet. I hear the king has demanded he receive it by noon. It looks like Grantor has agreed to give it up and open his gates, though the princess is said to be hiding somewhere in the castle with the jewel."

"We must stop him." The thought of Vasper coming in contact with Rorianne made Vlad sick. He knew she would fight to the death to protect the stone and carry out the quest.

Lorenzo gazed into the lamp in deep concentration. Looking at Lorenzo's taunt face lit by the eerie red lamplight, Vlad could almost believe he was facing a real Hitite priest.

"I'll take care of Vasper's remaining wizard," Lorenzo volunteered. "It will take a full-scale demolition of the castle to ferret Rorianne from her hiding spot with him out of the picture. I doubt Grantor is willing to let more than a handful of armed Lancenians in at one time, which means Vasper will have to attack.

"That gives us a little more time, but not much. His siege weapons are about on par with what Europeans used during the Middle Ages, quite inferior to those employed by the Romans over a thousand years earlier. But those siege towers should work. I expect an all-out attack to last not more than a day before Lancenians go pouring over the ramparts."

"What can I do?"

"How good are you at climbing in the dark?"

"Why?"

Lorenzo began absent-mindedly playing with a leather cord decorated with sharp, jagged beads. Vlad winced when he realized the dark stains spotting the cord were blood. It was a ritual garrote used in nighttime strangulations of innocent victims, usually friends or relatives of people the priesthood was trying to intimidate.

"Why?" Vlad repeated his question.

"Huh? Oh, sorry. My thoughts were drifting. I did pick up some gossip on my rather hurried trip here. A cousin of Rorianne has gathered a small force and is waging guerrilla warfare against the Lancenians. So far they've been pretty ineffectual, but they do halfway control the highlands now that Vasper has consolidated most of his forces here for the siege.

"I'm pretty sure Garin isn't in the valley, and who knows what happened to Elfred--but if the two are up above, Prince Sephin might have them. We're going to need to gather all our players if this quest comes to a climax soon, which the signs seem to indicate."

"You want me to scale the cliff in the dark and find a small band of hidden, ill-tempered Thurbians who might, or might not, know where Elfred and Garin are?"

"Hey, this is a quest," Lorenzo said with a smile. "If we didn't depend on happenstance, coincidences, the kindness of strangers, and wild luck, where would we be? Besides, I overheard several Lancene scouts saying they'd spotted a band of Thurbs directly above us in an oak grove. If you start the climb near the boulder that looks like a turtle, you should emerge from the canyon very close to their camp."

"And what of Drestin and Searene?"

"I have a feeling they'll be showing up very soon."

Vlad snorted and shook his head. "We should have a plan. It always seems to work out in the ballads, but this is real life. And I keep remembering that heroes don't always survive their ballad, especially in our dark quest."

Lorenzo frowned at the last comment then said, "I wouldn't worry about it. All we need to do is collect the members of the quest together with the jewel, find our way to the mountains mentioned in the chronicles, and wait around until the stone gets blasted by a bolt of lightning. What could be simpler than that?"

"I have a feeling you are not speaking of everything you know."

"If you want to pass out of this camp unnoticed," Lorenzo said as he crawled to the tent door and unknotted a few cords holding the flap closed, "you better leave now. I'll meet you at the base of the cliff tomorrow just before noon."

"How do you plan to contact Rorianne?"

"I may have to go in and get her."

"Is it so simple?"

"Piece of cake. Here, you might want this," said Lorenzo as he held out a very small crossbow and arrows, the projectiles only a fourth the size of a normal arrow. "I found it among our kindly priest's remains. I believe the head is coated with a nasty toxin. Now get going."

~ * ~

Elfred paced along the edge of cliff, looking from the moon and stars above his head to the tiny flickerings of torches below. He was worried about Vlad, wondering if the king had been projected into a dangerous situation due to his inept escape spell at the castle. True, even the most experienced mages would have a difficult time with the power surges he was experiencing from his visit to Garin's world, but the worry and guilt continued to gnaw at him.

There was a difficult incantation that only the most experienced adepts could carry out successfully. It allowed a wizard to snatch a person from within the walls of the strongest fortress or off the back of the fastest dragon. Finding the intended subject was the most difficult part of the spell.

He or she had to first cast a fifth sense, an invisible antenna that could detect the auras of energy projected by all living things. The chance of finding the subject increases if the spell caster is well acquainted with the person, or if the quarry is actively seeking to be found.

Elfred's general studies had brought the spell to his attention but only as an example of one type of magic. Apprentices weren't expected to recognize or even be aware of most of the subtle powers involved in such an incantation, let alone employ it. But the longer Elfred thought back to that lesson, the more obvious the spell's nuances became until it burned on the inside of his eyelids like a diagram scribed in fire.

Elfred closed his eyes and began following the twisted maze of the spell, reciting its formula as if it were written on a mass of tree roots--following a phrase until it came to a dead end then retreating to follow the next utterance to its end.

He became a fish, slipping into a gleaming delta of words and power, twisting and turning through the river of molten gold until he suddenly emerged into a cool ocean of darkness. Elfred concentrated on an image of Vlad and began a slow circling, the arc growing larger and larger until he could sense a far off light.

Unaccustomed to the spell, the apprentice could only tell that the aura was powerful and continually shifting into strange shapes and colors like a glowing oil slick. It grew in brightness as he approached but offered no additional clues to its identity.

Elfred was tiring. A wizard had to work quickly or face the danger of becoming trapped when the spell collapsed. Even his amplified power couldn't maintain the spell much longer. He made a quick decision and extended his field to encompass the energy mass then fell back to the familiar level of his own world.

Overwhelmed by fatigue, Elfred swayed dangerously near the drop off. His heart was pounding in his ears and he found himself gulping for air. He fought to remain standing and forced his feet to turn him to face the scuffling of feet.

A welcome died on his lips. Standing before him was not King Vladimir Dragol but a two-headed, red-eyed dwarf. The creature was not happy to find itself mysteriously snatched from its room and deposited in a darkened field. It decided to vent its rage on the probable culprit, Elfred, and leaped with fingers eager to tighten themselves around the apprentice's throat.

"What's going on?" A sleepy Garin was approaching with a Thurbian guard at his side.

Elfred used the distraction to dart under the dwarf's outstretched arms and run to his friend. Even that small effort almost sent the apprentice collapsing to the ground. Garin grabbed Elfred by the arm and began rapidly backpedaling when the guard lifted his torch to reveal the gleaming red eyes.

"Holy shit!"

The guard echoed Garin's sentiments with a similar exclamation and drew his sword.

"I, ah, was attempting, to rescue Vlad when the dwarf appeared," Elfred managed to say between gasps of air.

"Great, two heads pissed off are better than one. Can't you do something? Maybe send him back where he came from?"

"Give me time to catch my breath and I will," promised Elfred, though the magician didn't feel as confident as he hoped he sounded.

The dwarf wasn't waiting around to be punished by further magical tricks. He drew his sword and prepared to confront his tormentors. The guard also bared his blade.

"Ah, hold on a second," Garin interrupted the imminent battle. He remembered the unexpected return greeting of the dwarf and hated to see him hurt over a misunderstanding.

The dwarf and guard stopped in surprise as an unarmed Garin walked between the two.

"I, ah, think we can settle this without fighting. What we have here is just a simple misunderstanding."

"Stand back, such devilish imps fathom no such haggling," warned the guard.

Garin again smiled weakly at the dwarf as he had in the castle, trying to decide to which head he should direct his plea.

"I'm sorry about your abrupt appearance here, but it was a mistake. My friend, the wizard, would be glad to send you back."

The head on the right glanced at its twin, muttered a few foreign words and turned back to Elfred. In unison, the heads croaked an unintelligible string of words. Elfred nodded as if he understood and began his chant. The two heads turned to grin at Garin as they flickered then disappeared.

"Whoa," Garin gasped. "That was close."

He glanced over and in the moonlight could see the guard and Elfred were grinning.

"What's so funny?" he asked. "He looked like a pretty tough nut to crack. If it hadn't been for my diplomacy, we could've all been killed."

"More like as if it hadn't been for your cute smile," laughed Elfred weakly.

"What are you talking about?"

"This he was a she and the dwarf took a fondness to you back in the castle. She said you bear a coy smile and should look her up after your quest is completed."

~ * ~

Garin tried his best to describe the incident to Sephin without the guard and Elfred breaking into ribald laughter. Even the prince had a hard time holding back a smirk.

The prince waved his hand and fought back the laughter, suggesting the two return to their tent and adding that in the future, the apprentice might want to practice his art further from camp.

"God, I hate waking up like that," Garin complained as they crawled back into their sleeping mats. He figured the best defense was an offense and the complaint might prevent his friend from again mentioning the dwarf.

"I am sorry, though I thought it worth the risk to save Vlad,"

Garin couldn't help but feel sorry for the fledgling magician. A despondent tone had returned to Elfred's voice.

"I'm sure Vlad is all right. He can take care of himself. Let's get some rest. I have a feeling tomorrow is going to be a big day."

The wail of a hungry infant could be heard throughout the camp just as Garin was about to drift back to sleep. The baby didn't fuss again, and he tried telling himself the silence was because the old lady was feeding him. Only a minute ago Garin had been so tired he didn't think he could keep his eyes open with toothpicks. Now he lay in the dark, straining to the catch the faintest cry. He moaned, kicked off the blanket, and pulled on his boots.

A guard led Garin to the nursemaid's tent. It was identical to the canvas shelter he and Elfred were using, though this one had a milk cow staked next to it. The cow mooed a greeting and Garin scratched it behind an ear. The old lady didn't seem to mind his late-night visit , and she lit a small lamp so he could look at the sleeping baby.

"I never did find out the babe's name," she said.

"Charles," Garin replied without thinking. He was just as surprised with the answer as the woman.

"Charles? That is a strange name."

"It was my father's"

He was too tired ponder his unplanned christening of the child. Garin bid the woman good night and returned to his tent. Even Elfred's snoring failed to keep him awake a minute longer. Unfortunately, the slumber lasted only a couple hours before he was shaken from his sleep.

"Garin, Garin, wake up."

"Huh? Get out of here, it's still dark," he answered groggily.

"Wake up, it is I, Vlad."

"Vlad?"

The name sank slowly into Garin's semi conscious mind, finally creating a ripple that ponderously expanded to the point where the higher functioning sections of his brain could no longer ignore it.

"Vlad? Yeah, whadayah want...VLAD!! Vlad, what are you doing here?"

Garin pushed himself to his elbows and squinted at the faint silhouette framed by the open tent flap.

"Sh-h-h-h. We do not want to wake up the whole camp. Are these people friendly?"

"So far. God, Vlad, it's great to see you. Elfred has been having a fit worrying about you."

"Good. It will teach the apprentice to put more thought into his spells."

Vlad squeezed into the tent and the two recounted the most recent happenings.

"The wizard must be very exhausted to not wake up," observed Vlad.

Garin looked down at his new friend and questmate. "I think that most recent spell really wiped him out."

"That could signify a waning of his off-world powers. I wonder if that means our dragon is back into flying shape."

That set Garin to worrying again about Searene. "I hope they don't show up at the castle with that asshole Grantor running things. It's hard to believe he's related to Rorianne."

Vlad agreed, the face of the princess coming unbidden to his mind. He shook off the image. Even by the dim moonlight filtering through the open tent flap he could see that Garin was almost as weary as the apprentice sleeping next to him.

"We will speak more at daylight. Go back to sleep and I will scout the area and return when you wake."

"Is that safe? One of the guards might stick an arrow in you."

"Hah, I have not seen a soldier in either camp that can come close in skill to the most ancient and crippled Dragoon. The daunted Rovers are nothing more than overgrown bullies, too spoiled to carry out basic military duties. These Thurbs are easier to slink among unseen than that infant."

"And it is a snake that slinks, is it not?" A sword had appeared from nowhere to now delicately press against Vlad's neck. The voice belonged to Sephin. "But what could one expect from a Dragol?"

Garin was amazed at Vlad's aplomb. He hadn't flinched at the unexpected appearance of the blade poised near his jugular. The king of Bulgavia coolly turned to face the prince, who now kneeled where he could be seen at the tent's entrance.

"Please, Prince. Vlad meant no insult. They are the heated words of a warrior under stress. He is your cousin's questmate, and mine. We cannot fight among ourselves when we have a greater foe to face tomorrow."

Both Sephin and Vlad turned to look at Garin.

"Shit, now I'm even starting to sound like you guys. Come on, Prince, Vlad's not a bad guy, honestly."

"A cursed Dragol 'not a bad person.' That is bread for thought, bread that is hard to chew without choking. You killed our late king and maimed his son so that he is the misshapen soul that now rules our unhappy kingdom."

"I weary of such talk. I did not kill your king. It happened during the reign of my father while I was a child."

"We have been taught that the Dragols are one, unchanging through the centuries. Evil creatures that have sold their souls for immortality."

"Only fools would believe such."

Sephin tensed and the blade pressed a breath deeper into Vlad's neck, causing a single drop of blood to well from beneath the point, black in the dim light. Vlad's face remained stone, and the prince quickly pulled back the blade.

"I must admit surprise at finding His Royal Highness, King Vladimir Dragol, Supreme Ruler of Sylvquin, Lord of the Western Mountains, Protector of Anjeiv, Master of the Red Plains, and Emperor of the Bulgavian Empire, being called Vlad by a commoner. But then, it appears even my usually pompous cousin is addressed as such."

The Thurb prince stared at his prisoner for several moments. Garin wanted so say something that would convince the prince to pull the blade away, but no words came and he could only helplessly watch the small drop of blood slowly roll down Vlad's throat.

The point retreated several more inches then dropped to pierce the cloth floor of the tent.

"A knight rested at our hold several years ago. He spoke of a quest and a brief stay at Castle Ghasda, a guest of King Dragol. Many of the keep thought the rigors of the knight's venture had addled his brain. He spoke of the king as a mild-mannered young man, friendly and generous."

Sephin shifted his weight as if the crouch was beginning to cramp his legs.

"My cousin is usually a good judge of character. If she and these two think well of you, I will give you the benefit of a doubt. But know this. You will be the last of your infamous line if I find you are planning treachery. For now I will spare your life."

King Vladimir Dragol allowed himself the faintest of a smile. "And I yours."

"Mine?" scoffed Sephin.

Vlad slowly pulled an edge of Garin's blanket off his other hand, revealing the miniature crossbow given to him by Lorenzo.

"I have been told the bolt is poisoned. I would not have left this world by myself."

Sephin might have paled, but Garin couldn't tell in the dim light. He did detect the faint hint of a quiver in the prince's voice.

"And yet you did not speak of your counter. How did you know that one droplet of blood would slake my thirst? We could have both died."

"Do you forget the Dragol art of truth witching? It also gives one a good notion of another's feelings and merit. Though you may suffer not knowing what nature of man you face, I am luckier. Your emanations are those of an honorable man who would hesitate to spill the blood of an unarmed prisoner."

"Only hesitate?"

Vlad smiled but remained silent.

"I see now why you have won the confidence of these two and my cousin, King Dragol," laughed Sephin. "Come, I will find you quarters suitable to your station."

"These will do fine, Prince Sephin. I am sure my questmate will not object to making room and lending a bit of his cover."

"As you will, but I would appreciate you remaining in this tent until daybreak when I can explain to my men why a Bulgavian Dragoon is among us. I fear the sight of you would cause a tumult that would again disrupt my sleep."

"As you wish."

"And to assure the safety of such an honored guest, I will set several guards at your tent."

"You are too kind."

Sephin dropped the tent flap, and the soft tread of his footsteps quickly faded. Garin released a deep breath.

"You guys are nuts. I about crapped my pants when he had that sword to your neck."

"In such quarters I can only be thankful that you did not," Vlad observed dryly as he kicked off his boots and wormed his way between Garin and the tent wall. "Since the choice is no longer mine, I believe I will rest until morning."

Vlad was soon asleep and Garin lay listening to the soft breathing of his tent mates. The anxious meeting of the two blue-bloods had jerked him from his stupor. He rubbed his eyes and sighed while wondering what he had done to deserve this. Garin wasn't aware that he was again growing drowsy before falling asleep minutes later.

Chapter Fourteen

"What do you mean, my mage is dead?" thundered Vasper as he strode from his tent into the cool, damp air. An overcast sky hid the sun, the angry, swollen masses of clouds looking as if they were scraping the land above the ridge. More immediate clouds of fog gusted from the king's mouth in the chilled air, and the bottom half of his boots were darkened from the thick dew carpeting the meadow.

"Was he killed by magic? Has the other wizard returned? He told me no one of power remained in the keep."

The bearer of the bad news trembled under the king's rage. "He, he was strangled with a priest's garrote."

"What? Impossible. A priest, even one of a death god, could not kill a magician of Koranth's rank. Why have you not brought the priest before me? Are my own men too craven to fulfill their duty to their king?"

Vasper was furious. Priest or no priest, he would have the man gutted and strangled by his own intestines. He doubted the temple would protest since the priest had interfered with the inner workings of his court, a political move not usually sanctioned by its elders.

"Your Lordship, the priest is gone."

"Who allowed this?"

"No one, Your Majesty. The tent and the priest disappeared during the night."

"Are you telling me that a priest carrying a tent managed to slip by my guards without anyone noticing?"

The soldier was sweating profusely.

"Two Rovers must have tried to stop him. We found them dead with their throats slashed, though no one heard them cry out."

King Vasper was so aggravated he couldn't find his voice to order the man's death. He angrily waved him away and the soldier scuttled quickly for safety.

~ * ~

The sounds of shouting and men hurriedly packing gear and tearing down the tents woke Elfred. He rubbed his eyes and almost elbowed Garin because his partner was hogging the cramped space, crowding him against the side of the tent. Then he saw that a third figure was sharing their quarters, making a large lump under the blanket.

"Hello, who is our guest?" the apprentice magician asked as he shook Garin awake.

The lump sat up and the blanket fell away, revealing the mussed black hair and puffy eyes of King Vladimir Dragol.

"Vlad! How in hades did you get here?"

"It was not easy, nor as simple a trip here, as that of a certain two-headed dwarf."

Elfred's wide smile took on a sheepish cast. "I was trying to find you."

Vlad laughed. "Yes, Garin told me you cast a net for me, but brought up stranger fish."

A Thurb soldier stuck his head in the door. "You must rise. Prince Sephin is breaking camp. King Vasper is preparing to attack Castle Raven."

Garin was shaken awake by his friends and the three crawled from the tent. They had barely stood when two soldiers began pulling up their tent stakes. They made their way through a light drizzle to where Sephin was delegating duties to his men. His tired, young face was creased with worry.

"What is happening?" Vlad asked.

"I had thought we had more time, but it appears King Vasper is impatient and readying for an attack. He is moving up his assault platforms."

"He must have found his last wizard dead and decided on a personal search of the castle," said Vlad.

Sephin looked questioningly at his royal guest and Vlad related his conversation with Lorenzo.

"Curse the Lancenian. I had hoped Vasper would wait a few more days so the rains could really begin. The River Russ can surge from its banks in a matter of hours, flooding most of the valley. That is why the bottom land is kept in pasture and not grain."

Sephin and the others walked to the edge of the cliff where he could see the Lancenian soldiers. They and their siege equipment were moving through a light fog that turned the men into ghost images.

"With King Vasper not aware of our river's treacherous nature, my few men could have waited at the escape routes to capture the survivors. The winds and lightning will soon become so fierce even dragons would have done him little good. I must not delay the attack. He and his army will be safe once they breach the castle."

Vlad scrutinized the battlefield laid out like some children's game below them. "What do you plan?"

"I must burn those scaffolds. With them gone, King Vasper can fling his pebbles for days before breaching the walls of the castle."

Vlad shook his head. "It would be suicide. Vasper will have his Rovers guarding the weapons."

"This is not your war. I do not expect you to understand. Even though I would rebel against King Grantor, I am still a Thurbian. I must do what I can or die trying. It is the only honorable thing to do."

Trying not to bristle at the unspoken insult, Vlad replied softly, "Honor is not something beyond my understanding, but it does dead men little good."

A dozen men rode up, one holding the reins of a large white stallion. They looked in surprise at the black-garbed Dragoon. The prince mounted the horse and looked down at the three.

"You may accompany us if you wish. Though every sword raised against King Vasper is welcomed, this is not your battle and there will be no onus if you stay behind."

"I will join you, for I too have reason not to see the walls of Castle Raven fall," Vlad answered.

Prince Sephin turned his gaze to the other two.

Garin felt like he was going to throw up. His parent's farm suddenly seemed like paradise. Even changing dirty diapers took on a new attraction. How had he gotten into this?

"Ah, yeah, I'll, ah, come."

Sephin smiled and looked to Elfred.

"I warn you, I am not well practiced at riding a horse."

"We will find you a steady mount," the prince assured him and motioned for a soldier to bring to bring more horses. "The remainder of my party will circle the valley to meet us at another camp."

Sephin accorded his volunteers the honor of letting them ride beside him. Soon they were surrounded by a large host of riders who began falling into place behind their leader.

Garin watched from the corner of his eyes as one soldier after another leaned from his saddle to pass on the identity of the mysterious person dressed in the black leather garb of a Bulgavian Dragoon. The reactions were almost comical in their similarity. Eyes would widen and mouths would shape words of disbelief. When they finally accepted the idea that the dreaded Kind Vladimir Dragol of Bulgavia was riding on the right hand of their prince, they'd tighten their shoulders in apprehension and look nervously about them.

This would also pass. The soldiers knew they were on a suicide mission to vainly fling themselves against the invincible Rovers. The inevitability of their fate hung over them like the dark, oily smoke of a bone fire. But as word of the King of Bulgavia's presence passed among them, fear turned to amazement then hope. King Vasper and his Rovers were only recent tortures designed to plague small countries and defenseless farmers and merchants. The Dragols were legend, woven into a thousand stories and tales. Petty kings came and went, but there had always been King Vladimir Dragol. Though hatred remained, the dread was lifting. No one had ever defeated a king of Bulgavia, and one was riding at the front of the company as if he were a friend of Prince Sephin.

Garin was handed something and he looked down to see the old sword given to him by Hermie. He slid in under his belt so both hands were free.

"We must make haste, the route we take to the valley floor is steep and treacherous, but our mounts are trained upon such terrain."

Of the three, only Vlad seemed at ease in a saddle. Garin owned a pony as a child and rode it about his parent's 300-acre farm, but that had been years ago. Elfred had even less experience.

The small army followed the rim of the canyon for half an hour before coming to a bite in the ledge. It was the entry to a frighteningly narrow ledge. Garin stared at the route in disbelief, but was too shocked to do anything when Sephin turned his horse to the trail and Garin's mount followed.

A half dozen men with bows stationed themselves on the ledge in case Vasper sent dragons to attack the vulnerable troupe.

Garin was riding an old mare that calmly began the descent, seemingly oblivious to the thousand foot drop only inches from her hooves. He could hear the protests of other horses behind him that were not taking the itinerary as well, along with the nervous urgings of their riders.

There was only one way to make the harrowing descent, Garin decided, and that was with closed eyes. His knuckles turned white as he tightly gripped the reins. Several times he was forced to look about when the horse stumbled on the loose rubble of the path. He quickly clamped his eyes shut again to ward off a wave of dizziness.

Garin was sure he'd aged years when they finally reached the bottom and the soldiers began reassembling. They were in a small grove of cottonwood trees, halfway between the castle and the slowly moving Lancenian army. Between them and the castle was the River Russ. Figuring he owed the mare big time for the safe trip, Garin let the horse mill along the foot of the cliff to graze on the tall grass. That's how he unexpectedly came upon the broken bodies of a rider and his mount. He hadn't heard them fall and looked quickly away.

It took almost an hour for the remainder of the troupe to finish the climb down the cliff. Thunder began booming over their heads. Garin noticed Vlad peering anxiously down the valley and asked what was bothering him.

"I told Lorenzo I would meet him somewhere before noon, but I worry Sephin would believe I was shirking the attack if I left for the rendezvous."

"I wouldn't be concerned," Garin tried to allay his questmate's fear. "Lorenzo always seems to be on top of things. I'm surprised he isn't here to meet us."

He walked his horse to where Elfred was sitting under a tree and found him just as agitated.

"Last night's melee has left me feeble. I have tried marshaling just a small amount of energy, but I cannot grasp it. I am powerless when I am needed the most."

"It will come back. You said it was a very complex incantation that would drain even a master mage."

"But I fear that my abilities will only return to where they were before visiting your world. Once again I will be just an unremarkable magician's apprentice."

"From what I heard, you were doing fine before you ever crossed Myrlyn's Gate. You'll do just as well once you are back to normal. Remember, you were chosen for the quest because of who you are."

Their talk seemed to buoy the apprentice, and Garin moved on to where he could peer across the fog-shrouded valley. He realized that comforting his friends had seemed to soothe his own nervousness. The clouds were growing darker. He hoped Sephin knew plenty of escape routes if his predicted flooding occurred.

With the last rider down the cliff, the prince maneuvered to the edge of the woods. Garin climbed back upon his horse and rode to Sephin's side. A passing rider gave him two hide bags full of pitch to tie to his saddle. He guessed them to contain at least three gallons of the liquidly tar. It was to be used in setting the wood ramparts ablaze.

"We must continue moving swiftly once we are in the open and sighted by King Vasper's scouts. They will attempt to move back a wall of lancers to bar our advance from the side, which we must avoid. Trying to break through lancers would weaken us severely, especially when we still have the Rovers to face. We can only be thankful King Vasper did not believe this undertaking worrisome enough to bring more of his army."

"Why are the Rovers not riding their dragons?" Garin asked. "I thought they always fought from the air."

"Dragons are used for attacks on small contingents far from fortifications or to transport men. Large dragons bred specially for such missions can carry almost a dozen soldiers," Sephin answered patiently, even though some of his officers appeared unhappy with his taking the time to explain such basic facts to the strangers. "But their wings make them too vulnerable to come in close contact with the crossbows of a castle. Normal ground fighting is usually reserved for lesser-trained troops, with special forces such as the Rovers saved for more vital assignments--like that of guarding the siege weapons. Even then, I hear the Rovers chafe under such mundane tasks."

"They will chafe under my sword," an impatient captain muttered, and Sephin smiled at the answering confirmations among the rest of his men.

"I believe Elfred's meeting with Vasper's magicians resulted in the destruction of the dragons," Vlad volunteered.

Knowing his men were growing increasingly impatient, Prince Sephin held up his hand, and a nearby soldier raised a banner. A swell of silence flowed across the company at the sight of the signal. The men around them tensed and repositioned themselves in their saddles. Torches were lit. Sephin waited several more moments, glanced quickly about him, then dropped his hand and kicked his horse. The banner tilted forward and the horsemen moved ahead like one large beast. The horses quickly picked up speed, and Garin found himself racing out of the trees and across the grassland.

He could only locate the river by the thick band of fog hanging above it. The land fell until they crossed a sandy flood plain littered with rotting driftwood. He was almost thrown when the mare leaped a log that abruptly appeared out of the fog. He fought to slip his right foot back in the stirrup as the pommel of his blade punched him painfully in the side. The sound of three hundred charging horses matched the rumbling of the thunder high above them.

Garin had a hard time imagining the shallow, wide band of water as a menace. They easily crossed it, sending up plumes of spray and froth. Just as abruptly they hit the opposite bank. It was steeper and he clung to the horse's mane to keep from rolling backwards off the saddle.

The forward Lancenian forces were just now discovering the sudden appearance of an enemy on their flank. Sephin was overjoyed to have advanced this far before being observed. As the prince predicted, a chorus of trumpets ordered a rush of leading foot soldiers back toward the attackers. It was too late for Vasper's force. Even Garin could tell they would reach the quickly forming formation of Rovers before the point soldiers could wheel around to cut off their charge with a wall of long, wicked lances. King Vasper's forces were prepared for a suicide charge from the castle and were caught off guard by the surprise assault from the side. They had never considered the remnant of the Thurbian army skulking above them as a real threat. Archers further to the back vainly loosed a swarm of arrows that fell far short of the Foresters .

Garin fumbled for his sword and managed to free it without disemboweling himself. The first wave of riders slammed into the tightly packed mass of Rovers who were virtually defenseless against cavalry without their dragons or a wall of long lances. Many were trampled under the iron hooves of the small war chargers, others cut down by Thurbian sabers. The attack slowed as the enemy began to claim victims among the riders and horses. These bodies had to be jumped or dodged. Soon the Thurbians were almost at a standstill as they had to hack their way through the regrouping Rovers. They furiously swung their swords as the Lancenians tried dragging the riders from their saddles or cutting the legs of the horses out from under the Foresters.

It was Garin's own inexperience that saved him. As a trained warrior, he would have slowed to slash at his enemies. But it was all Garin could do to hold onto his horse, and the old mare continued her wild charge through the melee. He abruptly found himself past the chaos and still madly plunging deeper into the enemy formation. Ahead were the wheeled ramparts being pulled slowly forward by a long file of bound slaves. A mass cheer burst from the prisoners when they saw Garin approaching. They dropped the immense ropes and grabbed the guards carrying whips and clubs. He heard the screams of overseers not swift enough to run beyond the lengths of the shackles.

The horse began to slow. She was breathing heavily with great snorts, shaking her head to fling off a film of sweat. Garin turned to see the rest of the Foresters still fighting their way through the Rovers. The cries of the slaves drew his attention. They held up their arms and begged to be cut free. Garin kicked the exhausted mare and galloped to the first line of men. He hacked the bonds of several slaves before handing them the sword to continue the liberation.

He could see a wave of enemy horsemen rushing from the rear of the column. They were kept in reserve since the cavalry was useless in a charge on stonewalls. Garin pulled his horse's head around and sent her running towards the first tower. His legs collapsed after sliding off the horse. He had to grip the saddle for a dozen heartbeats before trusting his trembling legs enough to stand unaided. He threw the skin bags of pitch over his shoulder like saddlebags and half ran, half stumbled to the base of the tower.

Two soldiers with drawn swords came jogging around the immense wheels and stopped in surprise upon seeing their visitor. Garin's first impulse was to drop the bags and run. Then half a dozen slaves arrived to throw themselves upon the Lancenians. He tried ignoring the screams while scaling the structure. He remembered that many of the soldiers were poor conscripts wanting nothing more than to return home to tend their fields. He cursed King Vasper as he pulled himself up the roughly hacked beams.

Garin paused to catch his breath and turned to see the first of the Thurbs reaching the towers. He pulled the stops from the bags and let the pitch flow down to where the axle met the wheel, figuring an immobile tower was as good as no tower. A passing Forester heard Garin's call and stopped to hurl his torch into the oil. Nothing happened. It almost went out before Garin scrambled down to pull it from the thick, black puddle. He ran the flame up and down a tar-drenched beam of pine.

The fire slowly worked its way up the spar and only after the tower was safely blazing did Garin gaze about the battlefield. He proudly observed that his was the first wooden rampart to be set ablaze. It hadn't gone unnoticed. Sephin pulled his horse to a stop and hailed Garin to acknowledge the feat. He waved back, feeling foolishly pleased at the recognition.

"Remount, Sir Garin. We best retreat before we are overwhelmed. Our goal has been accomplished," the prince shouted.

The mare was still standing where he left her. It took all of his remaining energy to climb back in the saddle. He let the horse have her head, totally wrung out now that his adrenalin rush was over. The horse needed no commands to follow the survivors of the raid. They now fled a fresh and vengeful advancing Lancenian cavalry.

~ * ~

King Vasper wasn't happy. He had brought only a fraction of his militia to Thurbia, but still, that should have been more than enough men to crush a minor kingdom that had just suffered a major military defeat. He had left a massive force of dragons at home to guard an area where legend placed Myrlyn's Gate, but it would take two days to call them to Thurbia. And now a puny enemy force had severely damaged his main siege equipment.

Cutting trees and building new towers could take weeks. Catapults could shatter the timbered walls of minor keeps, but the stone missiles would take longer against a fortress like Castle Raven. His only hope was that the fool Thurb king opened the gates as he had promised.

Maybe the most damaging occurrence was the decimation of a company of Rovers, witnessed by the rest of his troops and the castle populace. Terror was often a greater weapon than swords. Whole armies had fled without a fight before the dreaded, invincible Lancenian Rovers.

The king of Lancene knew the reputation of his Rovers was undeserved. They were deadly swordsmen, but still basically thugs--too undisciplined for maneuvers that called for extended teamwork. He unleashed them only when walls toppled or the enemy was on the run. Then the Rovers would live up to their legendary cruelness. He believed such slaughter was now needed. No witnesses to this recent humiliation could be left to spread the word when the Thurb castle was finally cracked like the shell of an obstinate stewing turtle. It would also mean hunting down the escaped slaves and cutting out their tongues.

King Vasper watched as his cavalry slowed its pursuit and halted. The fleeing Thurbs were across the dry moat, up the gentle incline and beneath the walls of the castle--now under the protection of the archers manning the castle ramparts. He ordered the horns to sound recall and climbed back on his own horse. He had questions to ask of his surviving soldiers.

The wounded Rover wasn't happy to see his king. Vasper was noted for his lack of sympathy for those who failed him.

"I do not know, Your Majesty. Two sound like your description of Prince Sephin and the apprentice sorcerer, but the others I have never seen. I did behold a horseman wearing the black leather of a Dragoon and fighting like a demon.

"A Bulgavian slave on a tower screamed that it was King Dragol," scoffed the Rover, who stopped in mid-laugh when a searing pain clawed at his stomach. He drew a shallow breath and continued. "The Dragoon was young with long black hair. I could not tell anymore than that."

A physician came running at the king's beckoning.

"Will this man recover fully from his wounds?"

The doctor looked down at the anxious, pale face of the soldier. "Your Highness, it is hard to tell. He could..."

"I do not want any of your hemming and hawing. Will this man be able to return to his unit?"

"He will most likely recover from the wound, but he will never be able to reassume the duties of a Rover."

The king looked over his shoulder at several accompanying guards. "I do not need to coddle a bunch of crippled cowards."

He walked away to the sounds of pleading that ended abruptly.

"Start questioning anyone who witnessed the attack from close quarters. I want to know who the Dragoon is."

The thought that Bulgavia was allying with the Thurbian prince, no matter how improbable, was disconcerting. Vasper had been led to believe the new king was spineless and shied from battle. But he wasn't about to rule anything out while the quest for Myrlyn's Stone was in process. Such prophecies often scare up big fish.

~ * ~

Rorianne was sore and hungry. The stone floor of her childhood playroom was not a bed. She stretched and climbed to her feet. The morning light was a welcomed sight. She pressed her face to cracks and was startled to see the landscape had changed dramatically since the previous evening. The wooden siege towers were burning and the Lancenian army was approaching the castle in a slow, orderly march.

There was now a more ominous, dark wall of clouds slowly rolling into the valley. She smiled at the churning clouds as if they were blue sky. The stormier clouds pressed their paler cousins like wolves snapping at the heels of sheep.

A bit of motion caught her attention and she stretched on her toes trying to see what activity was going on beneath her. The angle was too sharp to see much except that there was a group of horseman directly beneath her. They wore the dark green of Thurb Foresters. Rorianne caught her breath. She saw a flash of black. Though it was impossible to identify anyone from her position, she felt sure it was Vlad.

The passages seemed smaller and dirtier as Rorianne strained to remember the route to a small balcony. The outlook couldn't be viewed from above and appeared from the ground as part of the support structure for an observation turret. It had once offered an unfettered view of a world forbidden to an orphan princess.

Rorianne squeezed through the small portal and was forced to remain kneeling. There was only two feet of clearance between the floor of the turret above her head and the stone guardrail circling the secret perch. The view was just as extraordinary as she remembered. She could now see the milling horsemen below her. They were Foresters and she heard her cousin shouting angrily at the gatekeeper to lower the drawbridge.

"I am terribly sorry, m'lord, but the King has ordered that you not be allowed entrance. He says you have offended King Vasper and must leave or the Lancenian king will think you were under his Majesty's orders."

"Go? Are you crazy, man? Where are we to go? Since when are Thurbian troops not given shelter by their own king?"

"I am terribly sorry, Prince Sephin," the guard sincerely repeated. "We have been ordered to soon open these doors, and your soldiers are to be annihilated if they attempt to enter."

"Why, in Gredghan's name, are you opening the gates if not to give us entrance?"

"King Grantor plans to let King Vasper enter as a show of good faith so he will end the war."

"Is Grantor mad? There is no good will with Vasper. He will enter and laugh at the stupidity of Thurbs while he roasts you over a celebration fire."

"I believe you, Prince, but I must obey orders. If I were you, I would attempt to return to the woods before the Lancenians advance further."

Rorianne gripped the weathered banister and listened in disbelief. Her brother was turning away his own troops and opening the castle to a treacherous enemy! It would only be a matter of time before Vasper followed the jewel's powerful emanation to herself.

Then, in the nervous swirl of the horses below, she saw three familiar figures.

"Vlad, Elfred, Garin!"

They immediately looked up at the cry of their names.

Without thinking, she threw the crystal over the stone guardrail and watched it tumble to hit the ground near her questmates. She wasn't worried about the jewel breaking. After all, would not it take the lightning of the strange mountain to do that? Elfred leaped from his horse to retrieve the jewel before it was trampled into the mud.

Rorianne could hardly believe what she'd done, but the impulse had been overpowering.

"You must flee with it," she cried. "Do not let it fall into the hands of King Vasper."

"Rorianne," Vlad yelled back. "You can leave with us."

"There is no time, go."

"Is it the jewel?" Sephin demanded as he guided his horse towards them through his men.

"Yes," Elfred answered simply.

The prince barked sharply at several of his men. "Quick, take this man from here. Whatever happens, do not let him or what he carries fall into the hands of the Lancenians. Hurry."

Elfred had little time to protest. He looked to Vlad for help.

"Go, apprentice. We must keep the jewel safe. Do not fail Rorianne."

"You should join them. You are a member of the quest," the prince said.

"Not while there is another member of the quest left behind."

Sephin smiled. "I might wonder if there is more to that, but time is not a luxury I now have to hear of such."

"What are you planning to do?"

"I have only one choice. That is to prevent the Lancenians from entering the castle gates. We will fight from without the walls if we are not allowed behind them. This is not your quarrel. Once again, I offer you a chance to follow after the magician."

The horses were becoming skittish, sensing the fear of their riders as the Lancenian Army relentlessly approached.

Vlad was forced to pull his reins back sharply to quiet his mount. "As I said last night, you are not the only one with honor. I promised Princess Rorianne my sword in defense of the castle. I will keep that vow."

"Then we shall face King Vasper together," the prince answered. He stood in his stirrups and yelled to his men. "The King of Bulgavia rides beside me against the Lancenians. Let no man say this Vladimir Dragol is without honor."

The prince swung his horse about and the men fanned out behind him to make a small, sorry wall of tired horses and battered men against the oncoming enemy.

~ * ~

Four horsemen broke away from the Foresters and began galloping parallel to the castle walls. Too far away to have seen the jewel drop, King Vasper watched the four running with little interest. Soon there would be few places any survivors of the Thurbian army could hide. Vasper did smile when he saw the gates open and that the small force of Foresters were not allowed to enter. They would soon be forced to join the other four or be crushed then he would control Castle Raven.

The Lancenian army moved relentlessly forward. King Vasper didn't want another surprise, and he kept his men in a tight formation that would be impervious to any attack the Thurbs could muster. The castle walls grew and for the first time he could make out the individual Foresters. It was then he heard the faint cry of the prince's praise for Vlad echo off the massive castle walls, and King Vasper knew for sure that he faced a Dragol.

His soldiers continued their steady march. The Lancenian monarch nervously glanced to the sky and the wooded borders at the foot of the canyon walls. What could the Foresters and the King of Bulgavia be up to? It was suicide for the small group to fight his army and no Dragol was ever suicidal. Crazy in battle, yes. It was said they would often go into a berserker rage, unheedful of wounds or weariness. But that was in regular battle, not some hopeless gesture that only stupid romantics like Prince Sephin would make. The Dragols were always vicious, cruel pragmatists--the type of ruler he could understand--until now.

Vasper ordered the horns to sound and the moving tide of men slowed to halt. The Lancenian soldiers looked at the small force before them then at each other in puzzlement. Why were they stopping?

King Vasper frantically tried detecting some flaw in his plan. It was very simple. He would pause outside the range of arrows and send in a detachment to search out treachery. A larger force would enter once the gate was cleared, and King Vasper could add one more small kingdom to his own. But why was the Dragol here? Why alone? What was he up to? Was he also after the jewel? Where was the trap?

Vasper signaled for the troops to rest, but remain alert. He would only continue the attack after he'd sent scouts to fan through the surrounding trees searching for hidden forces. Vasper wanted to know what kind of snare the king of Bulgavia was setting. Soldiers worked quickly to set up a tent for their king as a light rain began.

~ * ~

Elfred paused and turned to gaze back at both armies before disappearing into the trees. He looked to the sky and felt the power of Myrlyn's Stone throbbing in his hands. For anyone but a skilled wizard to use the jewel was suicide, according to Rorianne's interpretation of the chronicles.

The apprentice ordered the Foresters up into the trees. They refused to abandon him. Elfred began a chant and the emerald light of the crystal pierced the mage's flesh to detail the bones in his hands. A rumbling from above answered the beginning of his incantation that tortured the ears of the Foresters. The winds picked up and the horses whinnied nervously. Elfred paused in his chant and again ordered them to seek higher ground, speaking in the Voice of Command that few could speak or refuse. This time they obeyed.

~ * ~

The Thurbs, both those inside and outside the castle, observed in amazement as the Lancenians halted their approach. Sephin and Vlad watched with suspicion as their enemy encamped right on their doorstep. The Foresters were becoming drenched while sitting silently on their horses. The rains had abruptly increased and the valley was now almost as dark as if it were night instead of mid-morning. Water ran down Vlad's saber and dripped to the ground. His leathers were growing heavy.

"We may have the rain needed to overflow your river," noted Vlad.

"I have never seen it come in this quickly, but I fear the rains have still not appeared in time. I am perplexed by King Vasper's halt, but I fear it will not be long before they again attack."

Garin nervously reined his horse around and pulled up along side Vlad. The Bulgavian king looked deep in dark thought as he stared wordlessly across the glistening grassland at similarly mounted figures gazing back. Vlad was reflecting on his upcoming death. Would word of his last and only battle leave the valley to erase some of the bitter legacy of the Dragols? Would Bulgavia revert to its bloody past? He had installed good men in the court and army, but his tutors taught him a history that revealed many well-intentioned men turning into villainous kings. What kind of leader would Sephin have made? Had Vasper always been so vile?

One thought he kept to the back of his mind--how did Rorianne now view her hated questmate? He wanted to turn and see if the princess was still watching from her eyrie. Vlad almost laughed at his own vainness which would have shattered the image of the brooding, mad Bulgavian king. He hoped the Rovers were now gazing at the black horseman and knew fear. For some, Vlad vowed, it would be their last dread. He would not go easy, and for once a Dragol would die for a righteous cause.

Garin forced himself not to speak. He could tell Vlad was psyching up for battle, something he himself wasn't able to do. Instead, Garin badly wanted to talk, to do something to take his mind off the upcoming slaughter. The rain was picking up, causing him to blink and wipe away the water continually dripping into his eyes.

The sky and landscape were a bleak, metallic gray. It was hard to believe that only yesterday the valley had appeared a sunny Eden. He could see the small, pale faces of the Lancenians in the front ranks through the sheets of rain. They were peasants like Hermie--the expendables, cannon fodder. Further back stood lancers and behind them, archers. He hoped Elfred escaped and would complete the quest. For a moment Garin wondered if it really mattered. A century from now some ring, jewel, or other object of power would probably have to be saved or recovered, he cynically decided. More would die fighting what they believed was the quest to end all quests. Do these prophecies always demand that someone is die in faraway lands? Was this all a vicious cycle for some crazy god's amusement? These lines of thought were deepening his sullen mood.

The lament of some great mother beast for her dead offspring echoed eerily off the sides of the canyon walls, only slightly muffled by the pounding rain. He could see a dozen Lancenian trumpeters with heads turned up and long, slim brass horns pointing skyward. A ripple moved through the enemy formation as if it were a dog shaking the water from its fur.

One of Garin's last thoughts before the opposing mass of men began moving forward was how wet clothes made him itch. The Foresters stirred about him, and he instinctively knew that Sephin would soon order his own charge. They would rush forward through a hail of arrows to chop down the inept conscripts before they, themselves, died on the long lances further back. Maybe some would break through to slaughter a few archers.

It all seemed so pointless and not at all romantic like the fantasy books he'd read as a teenager. Where were John Carter of Mars or Elrick of Melborne when you needed them? At that moment Garin realized he was to be one of the sacrificial pawns in the prophecy. He only hoped he was to be the only one, though it looked like Vlad would be joining him. It was strange to realize that he almost felt more saddened at the thought of his new friend's death than of his own.

Garin was first to see the immense dragons slamming into the ground. They were coming in for fast, rough landings to his far left. There appeared to be hundreds of them dropping through the blinding rain. Black clad figures dressed as Vlad swarmed off the massive mounts that made Shadow look like a pup. Among them appeared a smaller dragon. To Garin's amazement he realized it was Shadow.

Garin's despondency vanished as if only moments before he had not been contemplating his own death. This sudden reprieve produced a strong resolve. Lorenzo was right. He would never again let himself feel at the mercy of the prophecy. He would create his own fate.

The Lancenians were now aware of the surprise appearance of an enemy force on their flank.

Sephin raised his arm to command his own horns to announce the charge when he was startled by a hand grabbing his wrist. It was Garin.

"Please don't. Those in front are just poor peasants who are being forced to fight. It would be slaughter."

If Sephin was surprised at such strange sentiments, he was even more bewildered when the dark king of Bulgavia spoke in agreement.

"They are nothing. Follow me in ranks of four and we can smash through to Vasper who thinks he is safely hidden."

Vlad didn't wait for the prince to concur. He urged his horse into the rain. It took Prince Sephin several moments for Vlad's words to sink in, then he called out to his trumpeters and they blew a seldom-used command. Some of the newer Foresters didn't recognize the signal and they shouted excitedly to those about them. Sephin wasn't waiting to see if his men were falling into the new formation. He impulsively urged his own mount after Vlad, and the men were forced to follow as best they could.

Garin was having the same problem again--holding onto his new sword while trying to remain seated. The front line of foot soldiers was already disintegrating in confusion from the surprise appearance of a side attack. They quickly scattered before the Foresters. Even the veteran archers and lancers were rattled by the materialization of the dreaded Bulgavian Dragoons. The bowmen had flung only a few arrows before the slim column of hill ponies punched through the second ranks.

Though Sephin and Vlad were amazed by the unexpected aid, Vasper wasn't. The king of Bulgavia's lunatic behavior had to be a ruse, he had earlier reasoned, and was expecting some surprise maneuver. He quickly drew his forces into a defensive circle. The veteran troops the king used as reinforcements presented a formidable wall of lances and shields from which another formation of archers stood safely behind.

Sephin realized the futileness of the attack. He wasn't prepared to have his men die uselessly now that the castle was no longer in immediate danger. The Foresters pulled back just as the Dragoons were also retreating to a distance safe from the Lancenian archers. The prince eyed the newcomers and was surprised to find he wasn't feeling threatened by the terrible Bulgavian soldiers. His apprehensions about Vladimir Dragol had vanished when the king unexpectedly argued against the slaughter of the peasant soldiers.

The Foresters milled in confusion until Sephin called them to his banner and word spread that the Bulgavians were not a second invasion force. The men remained tense. To their minds, the Dragoons and Rovers were cut of the same sinister cloth, and the Bulgavians' sudden appearance, no matter how timely, was intimidating.

Garin was having trouble telling what was happening. The Dragoons had quickly fallen back and regrouped into a wedge-shaped formation, looking as if they were ready for another assault. It was impossible to tell through the downpour just how many Bulgavians were now massed on the soggy plains. Vlad had disappeared into the black smudge of his men.

The last of Vasper's conscripts could be seen evaporating into the trees to join the earlier freed slaves.

Forgotten and belonging to neither group, Garin felt the lonely observer. He glanced at the Lancenian army. The men remained poised with their backs to the river. How long would the standoff last until someone decided to continue the conflict? Though the Lancenians had been caught off guard, they now appeared prepared for further battle. They still had the advantage of more men and a fresh cavalry.

A Forester broke from formation and galloped to Garin's side.

"The Prince would like you to speak with you," the soldier said.

The ground beneath the grass had quickly turned to mud, and Garin could tell his mount found the terrain difficult to traverse. Sephin managed a crooked smile as Garin approached and leaned over to grasp his arm.

"I thank you and King Dragol for riding with us. It is an act I will not forget," the Thurbian prince said. "But for now, I would ask you to speak with the king and warn him that the river will soon be leaving its banks. This will occur very swiftly and I urge him to have his men ready to mount their dragons."

The prince paused to mop the water dripping down his forehead and into his eyes.

"I am about to lead my men to another passage from the valley before we are trapped. Please explain to King Dragol that we are not fleeing battle."

"I doubt Vlad would think of you as a coward," Garin answered dryly. "Not after what's just happened."

A worried Forester interrupted to urge the prince to start the withdrawal.

"We will camp above in the maple forest to the east of the castle. That is where the others wait for us," Sephin quickly continued. "Tell King Dragol that his forces are welcome to join us. You may return, if you wish, and accompany us."

Garin took it as a dismissal when the prince turned away to begin issuing orders. He gently kicked his own mount and headed it towards the Bulgavians.

The first thing he noted was that many of the Dragoons were in their early twenties, even the soldiers who were obviously officers. He wondered if the older officers of Vlad's father's reign had all been purged. His approach was observed and several soldiers broke away to intercept him.

He stopped when two of them lifted their long lances.

"I must see Vlad, it's urgent."

"You mean King Vladimir Dragol?" the youngest soldier snarled.

Feeling shaky and weak after what he believed was to have been a suicidal last stand, besides being thoroughly soaked, Garin was in no mood for name games.

"Listen shithead, I'm your king's questmate and I'll call him what I damn well please. I'm sure he'll let me know if he doesn't like it. Now one of you get your ass back there and tell him that Garin's got an important message from Prince Sephin."

For a second he believed the lancer was going to run him through. The soldier wore a dangerous expression as he raised his weapon a foot higher to aim it directly at Garin's chest. Another soldier gave a short laugh and pushed the lance down.

"That will not be necessary," he said. "I will take you to the King. I have heard much about you from a young lady."

The words puzzled Garin until he realized the only person the soldier could be speaking of was Searene. He was surprised to find himself feeling slightly jealous at the thought of the Dragoon having spoken with her.

The soldier took the reins of the mare and walked back to the Bulgavian formation. The others parted to let the party squeeze through until they reached a small open area where Vlad was deep in conversation with several officers.

"Garin," Vlad said as he looked up. "Your friend, Lorenzo, never ceases to surprise me. My men tell me that yesterday Drestin and Searene arrived to tell of the invasion and our peril. Lorenzo told them to fly to Bulgavia with the message rather than follow us to Castle Raven. My men flew all night to reach us."

"That's great, but listen. Sephin says the river's about to blow and he's getting his men out of here. He suggests you get your troops ready to fly because when the water comes up, it comes up fast," Garin anxiously relayed the warning.

Vlad frowned. "I hope that fool Grantor knows enough to close his gates and not offer the Lancenians a shelter."

"The castle gate closed soon after we landed," one of the Dragoons volunteered.

"Even a dunce such as Grantor must be wise enough to take advantage of the rains," Vlad observed. "Have the men prepare to remount. We will want to move quickly so the Lancenians do not attack as we break formation."

Garin peered over the heads of the Dragoons through the sheets of rain and could see the Foresters beginning their own withdrawal.

"Sephin said you can meet them near the woods to the east of the castle. I'm going to join them. I'll see you there."

"You may ride with us. You did not appear to be enjoying our descent."

"It's tempting," Garin admitted then looked down at his mount. "But I'm not going to leave the horse here after what we've gone through. At least I won't have to be looking down on this ride. Do you want me to take your horse?"

Vlad hesitated, looking around at his men and over to the horse he'd been given by the Foresters.

"Bring me the mount," he told one of the soldiers. Looking back to Garin, he said, "I will travel with you and Prince Sephin. I will need his help to free Rorianne if we are to complete the quest."

"Your Highness, it is too dangerous...," an officer began protesting his king's decision. Vlad cut him off with a wave of the hand.

"I have not been the child king for sometime," he reminded the soldier. "I still must finish this quest before I return to Bulgavia."

"But..."

"Enough. There is no time for argument. My questmate and I are traveling with the Thurbians. You are still in charge here. Have the men back on the dragons and to the top of the cliffs before King Vasper becomes suspicious."

Vlad walked quickly to his horse. The troops parted for them as they rushed to catch up with Sephin. Behind them the rear ranks of the Bulgavian troops began mounting the dragons, leaving for last the front few rows facing the Lancenians as a screen.

Prince Sephin had posted three Foresters in the rear to keep watch in case Garin decided to rejoin them. They appeared surprised to see Vlad but did not comment on the extra guest. They had seen the Bulgavian King fiercely fighting side-by-side with their prince. Sephin also showed surprise when the pair joined him at the front of the company.

"Have you decided to renounce your crown and become a Forester?" he joked. "We always have room for a strong sword arm."

"To be one of your Foresters would be an honor, Prince Sephin, but I'm not sure my countrymen would understand. I am asking that I be allowed to ride with you until I am reunited with Princess Rorianne and the quest is completed."

"You mean we have a princess to rescue?" asked Sephin. Though tired and bruised, the prince was in high spirits. He was smiling broadly as he spoke with Vlad.

Vlad answered, "I hope to have your cooperation, or at least approval."

"I will help you all I that can, if only because I do not want to see your troops shedding Thurbian blood. I have my own goals and our efforts could be mutually helpful."

"Could that possibly be seeing King Grantor taken from his throne?"

"That is one objective."

"There are others?"

Sephin tried smiling slyly at the Bulgavian king. "I believe I detect an interest in my cousin that goes beyond that of a quest. It would be advantageous to have my cousin become the queen of Bulgavia rather than the ruler of Thurbia."

Vlad ruefully shook his head, though not to deny the insinuation. "I am afraid your cousin does not look favorably upon me. She would just as soon marry the King of Lancene as a Dragol."

"Do not be so sure. My cousin is no fool, though often bull-headed. You and Princess Rorianne would make a magnificent twosome."

It was Vlad's turn to smile. "And to have a cousin in the royal court of Bulgavia would not be a bad political move."

"That has possibly entered my mind."

Garin watched over his shoulder as they drew further from the Bulgavians and Lancenians, both groups fading into indistinct ghost armies. He thought he could see the vague shapes of dragons taking to the air.

Garin was surprised to find the climb out of the valley was worse than the descent. The narrow trails were now dangerously slick, but this time the occasional sounds of falling rocks couldn't force Garin to open his eyes. He flinched every time he felt the horse stumble or slip.

The Bulgavians were already making camp when the Foresters arrived at the woods. A small group of Thurbians looked very relieved to see their prince arrive, not knowing whether to believe the Bulgavians who spoke of being allies.

Garin stepped off his horse to be almost bowled over by a young woman. He caught his balance by grabbing the saddle and looked down into the rain-drenched, beaming face of Searene.

"I was so worried about you when I heard there was to be a battle," she said, giving him a second strong squeeze.

"Searene, what are you doing here?"

"We accompanied the Bulgavians. Do you think I would have let them leave me behind now that I am on a quest? Only we were forced to remain up here, away from the fighting."

Garin looked for Drestin as they led the horse to the shelter of the trees. He didn't see the dragon apprentice, but he did spot Hermie and the Thurbian nursemaid approaching. She carried a small, wrapped bundle.

"Hermie," Garin said in surprise.

"Me lordship, I am comforted to see you alive. We watched until the rain was too much."

"The babe is doing fine. He will make you a fine son," said the woman as she peeled back a corner of the oilcloth covering the infant. Garin looked into the small, round face and once again wondered at his impulsive act in naming the child Charles after his father.

"You are quick, Garin, to become a father in so short of time," Searene impishly commented.

He ignored her jesting and took the baby, only to place it in the girl's arms. "And you shall be a mother even sooner."

An expression of surprise crossed her face before it was replaced with a look that Garin couldn't read. The old woman winked at Hermie. It was only when the group continued walking that Garin realized a possible connotation behind his answering gibe.

They traveled deeper into the woods and passed a line of green tents and tethered dragons. Across a small gully, now swollen from the heavy showers, was the Forester camp. Two large trees had been downed, and their trunks lay across the stream. He steadied Searene as she crossed the makeshift bridge with the infant.

They led him to a large canvas canopy stretched between a number of trees and acting as a meeting hall. Sections sagged under the relentless downpour. He watched as a gush of water spilled to the ground after a Thurbian soldier propped a stick under one of the bulges. Crude tables and chairs were at the center where Sephin and Vlad were already seated with several Bulgavian and Forester officers. They looked up as Garin and his band approached. The officers frowned when they saw Hermie's tattered uniform.

"Have you been treated well, my Lancenian prisoner?" Sephin asked.

"Well enough, sire. But I am told many of me fellow countrymen escaped to the cliffs at the beginning of the battle, and I pray they are treated as kindly."

"We do not torture or murder our prisoners, though surviving Rovers will have to answer to Thurbian justice for the atrocities they have performed. We no doubt will release the others if they promise to leave our lands and not return."

"You can be assured that me and me mates will scurry away as fast as possible."

A Forester interrupted to report on the most recent observations of the valley. He stood at attention and stiffly described the swollen waterfall raging so that its thunder could be heard from his lookout. Though it was difficult to peer through the gray wall of rain, the soldier said it appeared the floor of the valley was completely submerged. It was impossible to tell the fate of the Lancenians.

Vlad called a Dragoon standing guard near the end of the shelter and ordered a reconnaissance flight be made.

Sephin stopped the soldier before he left. "Tell your man to be careful. The rain and winds make flying extra treacherous."

"How long will the rains last?" Vlad asked the prince.

"Usually this weather lasts only three to four days, and the valley fills to the foot of the castle. I can only hope Magician Elfred escaped to high ground. I am having my men scout the rim of the valley, but it is difficult in this weather. I would curse the rain if it had not so easily defeated King Vasper. We have the apprentice to partially thank for that, having destroyed the Lancenian flock of dragons."

Vlad stood and looked at the others.

"I, for one, am uncomfortable in this wet garb. I suggest we change and rest before meeting again."

It was easy to see that all those present, Thurbians and Bulgavians alike, agreed with his words. The king and prince clasped hands before separating.

"Garin, you may come with me. I am told Drestin impatiently waits for word of you and Elfred. You may share his tent, and I will find dry clothes for you to wear."

Garin said his goodbyes to the prince and turned to Hermie and the nurse. "Thanks for taking care of the kid. I'll come to see him later."

"No, you do not," Searene cut in. "I will look after the child since he is an orphan like myself."

Garin didn't know what to say. He looked at the smiling nurse.

"The babe is sweet, but I must get back to taking care of my larger boys. The little lass can care for Charles."

Hearing the name made Garin again wonder at the wisdom of his act. The name was foreign and would make the boy stand out after he was finally found a good home. He hoped Searene didn't become too attached to the baby. How could she raise a child by herself? He shook his head and followed the Bulgavians back to their camp. Searene marched along side of him while cooing to the baby.

"Garin," Drestin's voice shouted.

His questmate grabbed him and dragged him into a small tent. Searene followed closely behind.

"I'll get everything wet," he laughed as the dragon apprentice clapped him on the back and pushed him to a sitting position.

"Here is dry clothing, now tell me what has happened. Where is Elfred?"

Though Garin had spent a night with Searene, he felt uncomfortable undressing in front of her with Drestin present. His friend noticed the hesitation and sniggered.

"Turn your head, you hussy. Our friend would like some privacy."

Searene grinned and made a great display of shifting her position to face the front of the tent.

Garin began slipping out of the wet clothes as he started his tale. He was stopped several times by both Searene and Drestin, who asked for more details at certain parts of the story, especially when he told of Elfred fleeing with the gem. He continued with the recital after donning the garb of a Dragoon. He felt funny in the black blouse and pants. He didn't put on the jacket or footwear, preferring his own cowboy boots and finding the tent too warm for a coat.

He laid his own wet clothing to the side of the tent, which immediately boiled to life, making Garin almost fall over backwards in hasty retreat. A small, scaled head appeared. It was Ralp, irritated at being disturbed from his slumber. He quit his grumbling when he spotted Garin. The wyvern sprung across the tent and almost knocked Garin down for a second time. It squealed in glee and beat his wings against Garin in its delight.

The greeting continued for several seconds before the miniature dragon turned to scan the tent for the other questmate and master. Not spying Elfred, it jumped to the floor and pushed itself under the door flap.

"Ralp has been this way since Elfred left him with us. He drove the whole Bulgavian castle mad with his keening and screeching. He was so happy to be flying back here with Shadow."

The dragon's name made Garin feel guilty. He hadn't thought of the gallant beast since he had arrived.

"How is Shadow? Did the magic wear off?"

"It did not completely wear off until we reached Ghasda in Bulgavia," Drestin replied. "We were prepared to wait out the magic, but Lorenzo told us he did not think you and the others would be safe at Castle Raven. He urged us to seek help at Vlad's keep. I was worried that the brief rest was not adequate for the dragon, but Lorenzo is a wise man and his disquiet was enough for us to take the risk.

"Vlad's officers already knew the Lancenians had invaded Thurbia but could not launch an attack without their king's permission. I wondered if they even believed our story, but it was the excuse they were looking for to thwart King Vasper's latest plans of expansion. Vlad's generals had been wanting to attack the Lancenians for some time, but Vlad was against going to war."

Garin felt better in dry clothes, but he was still bone weary. He found it hard to think while so exhausted. Searene noticed his fatigue and laid the sleeping baby on a fur cover before brushing the hair from his eyes to look into his face.

"You are weary, Garin. You should rest."

"I'll sleep when I'm dead," he tried sounding flippant. "Let's get this quest thing over before it kills me. We've got to find Elfred and the stone, free Rorianne from the castle, and somehow get to those mountains to nuke the gem."

Garin ran his fingers through his wet hair and looked at his friends. "But for now I need something to eat or my stomach is going to eat itself."

Drestin grinned and crawled to the flap. He paused to slide into a cape of oiled canvas. "I will get you some soup and bread. It should not take long."

Drestin was barely out of the tent before Searene launched herself at Garin, sending him tumbling onto the pile of blankets and rugs.

"I yearned for you while we were parted," the young woman said as she pretended to be forcibly holding him down with her weight. "Did you miss me?"

The truth was that he did miss her. Throughout the whole recent ordeal, Searene had remained in the back of his thoughts, popping up whenever a rare minute of calm materialized. Garin pulled her close and marveled how she fit perfectly in his arms. Her hair smelled of flowers.

"Did you miss me?" she repeated as she pushed herself back up.

Searene had changed during the last few days, if that was possible in such a short time. Garin studied her face. She looked older. Not stressed or spent, but more mature. Maybe it was because she had lost what his mother would have called baby fat. Her cheekbones seemed more pronounced. Whatever it was, he decided, it suited her well. She looked radiant in the dim light of the tent.

"Have you gone deaf, Garin? Must I cuff you to bring forth speech?"

"Ouch, what are you doing?"

Searene was rapping her knuckles across the top of his head. He grabbed her wrists and rolled her off. She put up a brief struggle before Garin kneeled astride her.

"You are a beast. Must I yell for help?"

"Yes."

"Well, I shall."

"Yes, not for you to yell for help, but, yes, I missed you."

She smiled wickedly. "Yes? Then maybe I will not call for help. It is too bad Drestin will be returning soon or it would be you crying for succor."

Chapter Fifteen

Rorianne peered through the small opening in the castle wall. It offered only a vision of endless rain shrouding the entire valley. Occasionally a blinding flash of lightning burst brilliantly through the gloom and its thunder came rolling down the valley seconds later. She had no idea what had occurred after Vlad led the charge against King Vasper's forces. The princess rubbed her aching eyes, though she had allowed no tears to come to them. She cursed again the stupidity of her dealings with her own brother and the king of Bulgavia.

She rolled to her knees and began crawling back to the main passage. An unlucky guard was about to receive a knot on the head and the loss of his sword, Rorianne decided, then she would claim her throne. Her brother had more than proven himself unworthy to rule Thurbia.

She reached the main part of the hidden passage and climbed to her feet. A slight rustling ahead made her stop. She held her breath and listened intently. She was retracing her route in the dark solely by touch. It could have been a rat. The thought of running into a pack of them made her skin crawl.

"Out, out of my way, rats. Be gone."

"I hope there aren't any rats in here. Don't you keep a better castle than that?"

Rorianne immediately recognized the voice materializing out of the gloom. Its familiarity brought a wave of relief. She had not admitted to herself how alone she felt.

"Lorenzo! Lorenzo, is that you?"

"At your service, Princess. I knew I'd find your secret perch if I kept taking lefts and heading up."

"I can't believe you found me. Who told you of these passages?" She advanced slowly until her outstretched hand brushed against Lorenzo's chest then took one more step and buried her face in her questmate's wet tunic. "I am so glad to find you. I think Vlad and Garin are dead. It is my fault. My cursed brother..."

"Hold on, hold on," Lorenzo tried quieting her. He rested his chin on the top of her head and placed his arms around her in a protective circle. "Vlad and Garin are not dead, they are..."

"Vlad is alive?" she raised her head to verify the truth, but darkness cloaked Lorenzo's expression.

"Bulgavian Dragoons are here. They camp above with your cousin, Sephin and his Foresters. Vlad and Garin are with them, as well as Drestin and Searene."

Rorianne drew herself up and gently pushed away from her questmate.

"You must tell me how this came about--and," she said as an afterthought, "how you found me when none of the inhabitants of this castle have done so."

"This fortress, though larger, appears the duplicate of a ruin in my world near the city of Kaiserslautern, Germany. I pitched tent there years ago while riding an old Harley across Europe. The castle was built centuries ago by members of a secret trade union with connections to the Masonic Lodge. I've found they used about six basic layouts for their citadels, and your castle fits the one near Kaiserslautern. It also had hidden passages--"

"Garin is right," Rorianne said with a laugh as she interrupted Lorenzo. "You do sound like a tutor. You can tell me all of this when we have escaped. If you have found a way into the castle, that means you can lead me out of these walls."

"Are you afraid of heights and can you swim?" he asked the princess as they began retracing their trek.

"Why do you ask?"

"I'm afraid there are no secret passages into the castle. I had to fall back on some rock scaling experience in Arizona. It will be the old rope routine to a rather unstable row boat."

Rorianne was about to snap that she feared nothing but instead sighed and said, "I do not delight in such sport, but I will gladly do it to reunite us for the quest."

That thought led to another. "But we must find Elfred. He escaped with Myrlyn's Stone. I hope he has not fallen into the hands of King Vasper."

"Vasper is busy with other things right now," Lorenzo assured her. "Most of his troops are treading water and heading south. He and a few other drowned rats are clutching cliffs or sitting in trees. As for Elfred, he's babysitting a small experiment I've devised."

"You have seen him? The jewel is safe?"

"About as safe as anything in this crazy world."

They arrived at the hidden entrance, and Lorenzo held the doorway open for Rorianne. She gasped when she turned and saw him stepping into the light.

"You are in the garb of a death priest. How did you acquire this robe? It is death for anyone but a priest to wear this."

"That's a long story I'll gladly tell you as we're rowing away from here. Just throw this over your head and we'll be on our way."

Rorianne held the black, crudely woven sack in her hands. She recognized it as a shroud the priests of Hitite use in transporting difficult prisoners. Kings and beggars alike turned away when they saw a priest leading a draped captive. To consider the fate of the poor wretch would send shudders through the hardiest warrior.

Her fingers tremble uncontrollably, so deeply did the fear of the vile covering find root in Rorianne's soul. It was a testament to her courage that she finally lifted it above her head and let the sack fall to her knees. He gave her a cord to hold as if it were tied to her wrist hidden beneath the fabric.

"I've cut a tiny peek hole" Lorenzo assured her, "but act as if you are blind."

He led her from the dusty room and through several narrow hallways until they reached a main corridor. Three soldiers came marching briskly around a corner as if on official business. Their steps faltered upon spying the death priest and his pitiable victim. One looked questioningly at his cohorts before stopping and nervously saying, "Most Reverend, the King has ordered us to search every corner of the castle for his sister. May I see the identity of your prisoner?"

To the soldiers, the scarlet robed priest seemed to grow in height and the shadow within the cowl darkened.

"Tell your fool King Grantor that a Hitite priest shows his god offerings to no man or woman, unless they also wish to present their souls to the Destroyer."

The men shuddered and involuntarily moved back.

"And tell your fool king that if he remains on the throne for more than twenty days, I shall come to claim his soul."

The guards cast their eyes to the floor and hurriedly sidestepped the two.

"That should make your brother think about early retirement," chuckled Lorenzo when they were again alone.

This dread continued for the rest of their stroll through Castle Raven. Serving wenches, children, court advisers, minor wizards, and royal guards all became blind when the pair appeared. Conversations stopped and faces nervously turned away from the apparitions.

Their trek again took them to seldom-used passageways to halls wide enough for just one person and very cramped, twisting stairways. Lorenzo lifted and dragged open a massive wooden door. A gray light flooded the dim hallway. Rorianne removed the hood and a sudden burst of lightning and wind-driven rain made her blink. She followed Lorenzo silently along the stretch of the fortress wall until he stopped near a small turret. A three-pronged hook was wedged securely where the wall joined the small tower.

The shifting winds pushed and pulled at Rorianne as she looked far below to the speck of a boat jerking wildly at its mooring.

"Can you make it?" Lorenzo asked with apprehension.

She looked up from the forbidding scene below and said with surprising calm, "I would scale such heights and brave those rough waters a hundred times rather than wear that shroud again."

Rorianne surprised Lorenzo again when she sat on the waist-high wall, swung her legs over the edge, rolled to her stomach and disappeared over the ledge. He leaned out to watch the princess work her way down the swaying, knotted rope. She dwindled steadily until reaching the boat. Holding the bottom of the hemp line like an anchor, she waved for him to follow. Lorenzo snorted once and threw his own legs over the edge.

~ * ~

Elfred anxiously waited under a massive slab of stone that rose at an angle from the ground like a sinking ship, one of many strange formations dotting the edge of the canyon rim. He was above the castle on the opposite side of the valley from where the Bulgavians and Thurbians armies camped. He watched with interest as the lightning exploded almost at his feet, bursting in violent fits of energy below him. The valley appeared as a magic cauldron of swirling vapors and fire.

Not far from him in the rain was a pile of strange provisions Lorenzo had left behind. Though it made no sense, Elfred followed orders when Lorenzo told him to place the magic stone within a metal coffer then leave it unprotected atop another nearby outcropping. Elfred could not tell what kind of magic Lorenzo was attempting.

The holy hell had been scared out of Elfred when the death priest waylaid him just as he reached the top of the cliff. To wear such garb was pure insanity, but the apprentice found he was not shocked at Lorenzo's blasphemous behavior. He was relieved to hear that Drestin and Searene had arrived with reinforcements.

A faint blur suddenly materializing in the rain erupted into a small white and brown whirlwind of wings, tail, legs, and bright jewel eyes. Elfred was bowled over by the wyvern's enthusiastic greeting.

"Ralp, you little demon, how did you find me?" Elfred cried joyfully as he wrapped the tiny dragon on the head. "I am glad to see you. Where are the rest?"

Ralp slowly settled down and looked up from his master's lap as if to say, "Am I going to have to put a leash on you? Where have you been?"

"You slipped away from camp, yes? Missed me, did you not?" asked Elfred.

The wyvern had regained its usual jaded air and yawned as if now bored after being reunited with his master.

An idea leisurely formed in Elfred's head. He fumbled through his pockets until he found a piece of foolscap and a small stick of charcoal. After writing a short note and directions to his hiding spot, the magician apprentice carefully folded it before placing it in one of his small pouches.

"Take this to Vlad and Drestin, do you understand? Take it to Vlad and Drestin."

Ralp was in no hurry to leave Elfred or fly back through the nasty weather. It took several minutes of coaxing to get the wyvern to make the return flight. Watching the small dragon disappear into the rain, made Elfred feel alone again.

~ * ~

"No time for that now," Drestin cried to the two as he flung open the tent flap. "Ralp has just brought back a message from Elfred. He's just on the other side of the valley. Vlad is flying Shadow across and said his questmates were welcomed to come."

Garin and Searene quickly threw on the leather jackets and black oilskin capes. They bent their heads against the wind and rain as they made their way to where the dragons were tethered. Shadow spotted the trio and made a chortling sound that even Garin could tell was a happy greeting. He threw his arms around the dragon's neck and rapped Shadow on the head.

Vlad was already mounted and waved them to hurry. Garin felt clumsy compared to the others as he made his way slowly to the top. Drestin pulled him up the last couple feet. He connected his harness none too soon. Vlad ordered the wyvern to take flight and Shadow launched himself into the cheerless gloom to follow his smaller cousin. They quickly gained altitude to avoid the bolts of lightning that remained below the ridge.

Garin had no idea how the wyvern or dragon could navigate through the murk and was surprised how little time it took for them to cross the valley to where Elfred was holed up. Shadow had barely folded his wings when Elfred's greeting met them. The four quickly dismounted and ran to join their friend under the rock. There ensued a round of back clapping and garbled conversation as they all tried to ask or answer questions at the same time. They were just settling down when two more stepped from the endless downpour-- Lorenzo and Rorianne. No one was surprised more than Vlad as the two newcomers made their way through the group with hugs and handgrips. Rorianne threw herself into the king of Bulgavia's arms.

Vlad was so shocked that he let her pull away before he could think to return the hug and kiss, though a departing glance left no doubt that the princess of Thurbia now looked upon him with favor.

"You're probably all wondering why I asked you here today," Lorenzo said to the rest with a straight face. Garin took it as a wisecrack and grimaced as his friend continued.

"I'm glad to see we didn't have to wait for Vlad and the rest to get here. That means we can get on with the quest."

"We must rest and pack properly to make the Pillars of the Sky," Vlad cautioned. "You cannot mean that we would leave now in this condition?"

"Where is the Stone of Myrlyn?" Rorianne asked and looked to Elfred.

"It's there in that chest."

She squinted then opened her eyes wide in surprise when she spotted the object of their quest on the outcropping.

"Why do you not carry it? Why is it so far from where you stay?"

"That is a good question, is it not?" The hoarse voice belonged to none of seven questors.

King Vasper stepped into sight with a half dozen archers pointing their weapons at the questmates. The Lancenians looked bruised and half drowned but still deadly with their bows.

"What luck that one of my men spied the young magician huddled under this rock. Thank you for all gathering in one spot where you will be much easier to administer to, as well as presenting me with the stone. Come out where we can keep a better eye on you."

The seven slowly walked out into the rain, Rorianne nearly collapsing against Vlad with the sudden turnabout of events. Garin tripped and almost fell over the ledge when he stumbled on some of Lorenzo's provisions. He looked down to see an odd assortment of metal cups, tools and even a broken sword tied to a half-buried stake with what looked like copper wiring.

"Keep watch on them," Vasper ordered as he walked backwards to the box containing Myrlyn's Stone as if afraid to turn his face from the group.

An archer jerked when Lorenzo stumbled and sent the bundle of junk noisily rolling over the edge of the cliff. Vasper reached the jutting rock and lifted the metal box. He raised the lid and the jewel's glow reflected off his face. In the metal gray curtains of cloud and rain, the eerie green light made his face look as if it were floating free in the haze.

Lorenzo grabbed Rorianne when she tensed, as if she were about to charge the king of Lancene. He also said a few words to keep Vlad from pulling his sword.

"We cannot just let him have the stone," Vlad growled under his breath. "We are now dead. He cannot afford to let us live for fear the prophecy may still be fulfilled. It is better to die under arrows than in his squalid dungeons."

"Just keep the bastard talking," Lorenzo hissed back. "And when I say drop, don't ask questions, just do it."

Garin was puzzled by Lorenzo's actions. He knew his friend must have some plan in mind, but it eluded him.

"What's with the junk?" he whispered.

"Think Benjamin Franklin," was all Lorenzo answered.

King Vasper seemed mesmerized by the glowing stone. He cradled the chest in his arms as if it were a babe. He looked up to offer another taunt when the air cracked to the bomb burst of another bolt of lightning in the valley below. This one was so close that it momentarily blinded everyone. The resulting thunder shook the rock under their feet. Lorenzo yelled and the still blinded archers waved their bows wildly in front of them. Several arrows whizzed by the captives as they fell to the ground. A second, smaller bolt of light burst over the ledge and raced towards King Vasper. He opened his mouth, but no one was ever to know what he had planned to scream.

The electrical current following the copper wire surged into the box. Vasper threw his head back and convulsed in violent spasms. Emerald rays from the box began fluctuating in the same unrhythmic pulse. Green light burst from his eyes, nose, and mouth. His skin took on a luminosity as if he were being hollowed out like a jack-o'-lantern.

"Hurry, under the rock," Lorenzo yelled.

His voice seemed muffled and distant to ears deafened by the close lightning strike. Searene was frantically crawling to Elfred's shelter and paused only to grab Garin's arm. He was still dazed by the noise and light. Vlad reached the rock and shoved Rorianne under the ledge then turned to watch the end of King Vasper and the Jewel of Myrlyn, their fates now intertwined.

Lorenzo bumped into him and pressed his mouth to the dragon lord's ear. "Don't watch. Cover your eyes."

Vlad couldn't tear his eyes away from the gruesome sight of rolling balls of green fire now seeming to strip the meat from the king of Lancene's bones. Lorenzo elbowed Vlad sharply in the side and he grimaced in pain. The following violent expenditure of energy burned through Vlad's closed eyelids so fiercely that he threw his arms up to cover his face.

No one had to order the others not to look. They pressed themselves into the mud and waited for the end--and were surprised when it finally came and they found themselves still living. One-by-one the numbed survivors crawled out from the rock. They looked about in confusion. The silence was like a roar. There was no wind and the rain had stopped. Garin slapped his hands to make sure he wasn't deaf. The others sluggishly turned to the noise.

"What the hell happened?" Garin finally managed to ask.

Lorenzo was just getting to his feet. He coughed once and said, "I think the quest is over."

"How could this be true? We have not gone to the mountains told of in the chronicles," Rorianne protested. She pushed herself away from Vlad and took several faltering steps in the direction where King Vasper had last stood. Only a shallow, blackened depression now marked the spot.

"Lorenzo, what have you done?" Even Garin was aghast at the sudden, anticlimactic end. "You can't have destroyed the stone. What about the prophecy?"

"What did I tell you about prophecies?" Lorenzo answered with a smile. He leaned against the rock and looked at the others. "I decided we could avoid the nastier part of the chronicle if we ended the quest early--catch the gods off balance, so to speak, and end Drestin and Elfred's worry about an early death. Since it was obviously lightning that could destroy the stone, why not make use of what was at hand? I hadn't planned such a front row seat for the show, though cooking that bastard was frosting on the cake."

"That junk," Garin interrupted. "You used it to attract the lightning. Where did you get the wire?"

"You may thank those perverted priests of Hitie for that. It seems they store at most castles spools of copper wire for some bizarre forms of entertainment."

"It is over?" Rorianne asked, still in a daze. "The quest is over? And we all live?"

Vlad looked with worry into her pale, drawn face. "Yes, it seems we have all survived the quest." He seemed as shocked as the others. Taking a deep breath, Vlad added, "Though there may still be more of a journey ahead for us."

"Us?" the princess asked and her eyes refocused. She gazed up at Vlad and for once did not push away.

Drestin looked at Elfred. "We did it. It is over and we are still living. We are going to be heroes, live heroes."

"I knew it all the time," Elfred countered.

Drestin punched his friend in the arm. "Then why did not you tell me?"

The seven members of the quest looked at the others about them, caught between the joy of the quest's end and the knowledge that the small group would now disband. The realization made Garin hold on just a little tighter to Searene.

"Lorenzo, I want Searene to return with me."

She smiled and appeared less surprised than Garin at his words.

"No trouble. I still know a few people in the Company. I'll call in a few favors and they can jerk the strings of some feds in charge of the witness protection program. We'll have Searene fixed up as a Bosnian refugee, no trouble."

"Do not forget Charles," she reminded the two.

"Yes, there's the baby." Garin added.

Lorenzo smiled and shook his head. "Well, buddy boy, it's amazing what a difference in life a few days can make, isn't it?"

Chapter Sixteen

Vlad awoke and luxuriated in the feeling of a warm, dry and soft bed. He stretched and rolled over to stare at his new bride of four months. She was already awake and examining her husband.

"Vlad, I have something to tell you."

"I know," he smiled.

She propped herself up on an elbow and playfully smacked him with her other hand.

"You know? How could you? What was I going to speak?"

"You are going to tell me you are with child."

"How do you know?"

"A king of Dragol knows many things. You will have a son."

She smacked him again.

"You are mocking me. You cannot know that."

"I know it as I know what his name will be."

Rorianne rolled onto her back and groaned, "His Royal Highness, King Vladimir Dragol XIII, Supreme Ruler of Sylvquin, Lord of the Western Mountains, Protector of Anjeiv, Master of the Red Plains and Emperor of the Bulgavian Empire."

Vlad shook his head. "No, I think we should name him Lorenzo."

~ * ~

The old wizard sadly watched his former apprentice packing. Elfred placed the last item in the bag and turned to Manfred.

"I owe you much, Sorcerer Manfred. I do not think I would be alive today if it were not for your eccentric training."

"Nonsense, I only turned you in the right directions and you found your own ways."

Elfred crossed the room and placed his hands upon the old man's thin shoulders.

"All those nonsensical chores you sent me out on, they really had meaning. The walks and the experiments. You knew I was to be on that quest, did you not? All that time you knew it was to be me."

"I had my premonitions. I knew you would need more than the dim-witted apprenticeships offered most magicians today. The world is a lot different from some musty room full of dead books. It is not always the spell you use, but how you use the spell. You did well."

Manfred stepped back to get a better look at the recently initiated magician in his new conjuror robe.

"And now you are going to serve the court of the Dragols. That is a great climb for a Trinton lad."

"Drestin will be with me. He is to study under the royal dragon master, not some small-time swindler like Keldlief."

Manfred smiled again. "I fear for two young men in a great city like Ghasda."

"You old sneak. You know fully well that we have asked for the hands of Annabeth and Freta. Garin and I will return next season and have the greatest wedding feast this village has ever seen."

~ * ~

Everything appeared ready for their flight to Bulgavia. He tugged once more on the harness and felt a cool wetness on his neck. Shadow was nuzzling him.

The dragon master reached out to rap the beast on the head. He had been overjoyed when Vlad told him to keep the dragon. Now that the story of their adventure was out and how the two former apprentices were under the patronage of a Dragol, Destin doubted even the king of Trinton would ask for his return.

He turned when he heard a half cough. A wizened farmer stood framed in the doorway with his rumpled hat in hand.

"Excuse me Dragonmaster, me name is Preolen and I have come to thank yah."

"Thank me?"

"For saving me dragon. Without him I could not run me farm."

Destin stared at the old man but could not place his face.

"Your fool master said he had tuberculosis and wanted to put him down. But you were right, he did have lung flukes and the ragwort tea and sulfur fixed him right up. I also ran a few ducks over the pasture, like you said, to get rid of the snails carrying the flukes."

Now Destin realized who he was speaking with--the owner of one of the dragons used in his exam. He hadn't made it back in time to meet with his judges, so he never did hear how correct his diagnoses were. He was made a dragonmaster after word of his quest feats reached the ears of the guild masters.

"I am glad I could help you," Destin replied, feeling foolishly proud of the correct diagnosis. He wondered if Keldlief heard the results before he was taken away by the king's men.

~ * ~

Garin sat on a hill overlooking a creek as crooked as the old oak he leaned against. Below were a dozen head of cattle belonging to a nearby farmer who rented Garin's pasture. Among them was one smaller cow that matched no breeds other area farmers could recognize. They had asked him where he'd bought the strange animal, but Garin would shrug his shoulders and answer that it was from a faraway land.

He turned to watch Searene pointing out the wild flowers to Charlie. She picked a purple coneflower and tickled the boy under his chin. Garin smiled, thankful at last for the peace following their quest. The farm no longer seemed the prison he'd thought of it as only a few months before. He had decided to live in his childhood home and commute to nearby Dubuque.

"What a peaceful scene," Lorenzo's voice interrupted the contemplation.

Garin turned to see his friend emerging from the trees. He waved to Lorenzo and motioned for him to sit next to him under the tree.

"How's life treating you?" Lorenzo asked.

"Great, and yourself?"

"Not bad. Liquidated a few gems I appropriated from the priest of Hitie, and my share is enough for an extended vacation."

"Your share?"

"Yeah, I put half of it in your bank account."

"Lorenzo, you didn't..."

"Forget it. Consider it a wedding present. You'll need some cash until you find a new job."

Garin examined his friend. "You're up to something. What?"

"Well, there is a reason I came looking for you."

"Whatever crazy scheme you've cooked up now, I don't want any part of it. I've given up on quests and adventures."

"Walk down to the creek with me," Lorenzo said and started off without waiting to see if his friend would follow.

Garin climbed to his feet. He caught up with Lorenzo and began questioning him.

"It seems the Bennett brothers had a few sheep killed last night," Lorenzo answered.

"Coyotes? What's the big deal? It's probably stray dogs. They usually turn out to be the culprits."

"It wasn't coyotes or dogs."

"What, then?"

They stopped and Lorenzo pointed to a set of tracks in the mud running along the opposite bank. Garin drew in a breath. The prints were short, yet deep, wide boot tracks.

Garin looked at them in puzzlement. "Who is it?"

"I'll make a wild guess and say those tracks belong to a troll, maybe a love-sick troll at that."

Garin eyes widened and he looked to Lorenzo. "You're kidding, right? This is your idea of a sick joke."

Lorenzo just smiled.

"What are we going to do?"

"Oh, we'll think of something," Lorenzo said as he slapped Garin on the shoulder and led him back to his new family. "Kind of reminds me of the time we had to recapture some genetic experiments that went awry in Siberia. They were crosses between baboons, humans and grizzly bears. A few escaped over the Straits to Alaska and we spent three weeks chasing them over the tundra. We were just about to give up when..."

Also by Dan Ehl
Available at Rogue Phoenix Press

Jak Barley-Private Inquisitor
and the Temple of Dorga, Fish-Headed God of Death

As a private inquisitor, Jak Barley's job is fairly mundane-finding errant debtors and missing property, or proving the unfaithfulness of roving spouses. It's not a vocation that makes many friends.

Though a frequent patron of dark, wretched bars seldom visited by the more fastidious citizens of Duburoake, he still can be squeamish about some things--such as ghosts and rabid magicians.

Barley's latest cases are just that more upsetting, dragging him into contact with sinister specters, malicious mages, irate harpies, creepy death deities and royal plots.

It will take all of his backstreets cunning to stay alive, as well as the help of alchemist Olmsted Aunderthorn, his half brother, who uses the latest metaphysical laboratory techniques in solving crimes.

Jak Barley-Private Inquisitor
and the Case of the Seven Dwarves

Private Inquisitor Jak Barley wonders if his drinking cohorts at the King's Wart Inn are playing an elaborate prank on him. What else is he to think when seven dwarves want his help against a wicked witch they blame for poisoning an innocent young maiden staying with them named Frost Ivory?

But it is anything but a joke when Jak finds himself the target of deadly Reverian Assassins and malevolent Viper Mages - and again facing the dark and sinister forces of Dorga, the Fish-Headed God of Death. Along the way he tangles with voracious Blackwatch Goblins, vampires, angry piss dragons, and the most dangerous of all: a beautiful young witch's daughter.